SARAH MORGAN

USA TODAY bestselling author
Sarah Morgan

USA TODAY bestselling author Sarah Morgan
writes hot, happy contemporary romance,
and her trademark humor and sensuality have
gained her fans across the globe. Described as "a
magician with words" by *RT Book Reviews*, she has
been nominated three years in succession for
a prestigious RITA® Award from the Romance
Writers of America and won the award twice—
in 2012 for her book *Doukakis's Apprentice* and
in 2013 for *A Night of No Return*. She also won
the *RT Book Reviews* Reviewers' Choice Award
in 2012 and has made numerous appearances
in their Top Pick slot. Sarah lives near London
with her husband and children, and when she
isn't reading or writing she loves being outdoors,
preferably on vacation so she can forget the
house needs tidying. You can visit Sarah online
at sarahmorgan.com, on Facebook at
facebook.com/authorsarahmorgan and on
Twitter, @SarahMorgan_.

USA TODAY Bestselling Author

Sarah Morgan

MORE THAN SHE BARGAINED FOR

ISBN-13: 978-0-373-60985-7

More Than She Bargained For

Copyright © 2014 by Harlequin Books S.A.

The publisher acknowledges the copyright holder of the individual works as follows:

The Prince's Waitress Wife
Copyright © 2008 by Harlequin Books S.A.

Special thanks and acknowledgment are given to Sarah Morgan for her contribution to this work.

Powerful Greek, Unworldly Wife
Copyright © 2009 by Sarah Morgan

HARLEQUIN®
www.Harlequin.com

Printed in U.S.A.

CONTENTS

THE PRINCE'S
WAITRESS WIFE

Chapter 1

'Keep your eyes down, serve the food and then leave. No lingering in the President's Suite. No gazing, no engaging the prince in conversation, and no flirting. *Especially* no flirting—Prince Casper has a shocking reputation when it comes to women. Holly, are you listening to me?'

Holly surfaced from a whirlpool of misery long enough to nod. 'Yes,' she croaked. 'I'm listening, Sylvia.'

'Then what did I just say?'

Holly's brain was foggy from lack of sleep and a constant roundabout of harsh self-analysis. 'You said—you told me—' Her voice tailed off. 'I don't know. I'm sorry.'

Sylvia's mouth tightened with disapproval. 'What

is the matter with you? Usually you're extremely efficient and reliable, that's why I picked you for this job!'

Efficient and reliable.

Holly flinched at the description.

Another two flaws to add to the growing list of reasons why Eddie had dumped her.

Apparently oblivious to the effect her words were having, Sylvia ploughed on. 'I shouldn't have to remind you that today is the most important day of my career—catering for royalty at Twickenham Stadium. This is the Six Nations championship! The most important and exciting rugby tournament of the year! The eyes of the world are upon us! If we get this right, we're made. And more work for me means more work for you. *But I need you to concentrate!*'

A tall, slim waitress with a defiant expression on her face stalked over to them, carrying a tray of empty champagne glasses. 'Give her a break, will you? Her fiancé broke off their engagement last night. It's a miracle she's here at all. In her position, I wouldn't even have dragged myself out of bed.'

'He broke off the engagement?' Sylvia glanced from one girl to the other. 'Holly, is Nicky telling the truth? Why did he do that?'

Because she was efficient and reliable. Because her hair was the colour of a sunset rather than a sunflower. Because she was prudish and inhibited. Because her bottom was too big…

Contemplating the length of the list, Holly was swamped by a wave of despair. 'Eddie's been promoted to Marketing Director. I don't fit his new image.' So far she hadn't actually cried and she was quite proud of that—proud and a little puzzled. *Why hadn't she cried?* She *loved* Eddie. They'd planned a future together. 'He's expected to entertain clients and journalists and, well, he's driving a Porsche now, and he needs a woman to match.' With a wobbly smile and a shrug, she tried to make light of it. 'I'm more of a small family-hatchback.'

'You are much too good for him, that's what you are.' Nicky scowled and the glasses on the tray jangled dangerously. 'He's a b—'

'Nicky!' Sylvia gave a shocked gasp, interrupting Nicky's insult. 'Please remember that you are the face of my company!'

'In that case you'd better pay for botox before I develop permanent frown-lines from serving a bunch of total losers every day.' Nicky's eyes flashed. 'Holly's ex and his trophy-blonde slut are knocking back the champagne like Eddie is Marketing Director of some Fortune 100 company, not the local branch of Pet Palace.'

'She's with him?' Holly felt the colour drain from her face. 'Then I can't go up there. Their hospitality box is really close to the President's Suite. It would just be too embarrassing for everyone. All his colleagues staring at me—*her* staring at me—what am I going to do?'

'Replace him with someone else. The great thing about really unsuitable men is that they're not in short supply.' Nicky thrust the tray into the hands of her apoplectic boss and slipped her arm through Holly's. 'Breathe deeply. In and out—that's it—good. Now, here's what you're going to do. You're going to sashay into that royal box and kiss that sexy, wicked prince. If you're going to fall for an unsuitable man, at least make sure he's a rich, powerful one. The king of them all. Or, in this case, the prince. Apparently he's a world-class kisser. Go for it. Tangling tongues at Twickenham. *That* would shock Eddie.'

'It would shock the prince, too.' Giggling despite her misery, Holly withdrew her arm from her friend's. 'I think one major rejection is enough for one week, thanks. If I'm not thin and blonde enough for the Managing Director of Pet Palace, I'm hardly going to be thin and blonde enough to attract a playboy prince. It's not one of your better ideas.'

'What's wrong with it? Straight from one palace to another.' Nicky gave a saucy wink. 'Undo a few buttons, go into the President's Suite and flirt. It's what I'd do.'

'Fortunately she isn't you!' Sylvia's cheeks flushed with outrage as she glared at Nicky. 'And she'll keep her buttons fastened! Quite apart from the fact I don't pay you girls to flirt, Prince Casper's romantic exploits are getting out of hand, and I've had strict instructions from the Palace—no pretty waitresses. No one likely to distract him. *Especially* no blondes. That's why I picked you in the first place, Holly. Red hair and freckles—you're perfect.'

Holly flinched. Perfect? *Perfect for melting into the background.*

She lifted a hand and touched her unruly red hair, dragged into submission with the liberal use of pins. Then she thought of what lay ahead and her battered confidence took another dive. The thought of walking into the President's Suite made her shrink. 'Sylvia—I really don't want to do this. Not today. I just don't feel—I'm having—' What—a bad hair day? A fat day? Frankly it was a battle to decide which of her many deficiencies was the most pronounced. 'They're all going to be thin, blonde, rich and confident.' *All the things she wasn't.* Her hands shaking, Holly removed the tray of empty glasses from her boss's hands. 'I'll take these back to the kitchens. Nicky can serve the royal party. I don't think I can stand them looking at me as if I'm—'

As if I'm nothing.

'If you're doing your job correctly, they shouldn't be looking at you at all.' Unknowingly echoing Holly's own thoughts, Sylvia removed the tray from her hands so violently that the glasses jangled again. Then she thrust the tray back at Nicky. '*You* take these glasses back to the kitchens. Holly, if you want to keep this job, you'll get up to the President's Suite right now. And no funny business. You wouldn't want to attract his attention anyway—a man in his position is only going to be interested in one thing with a girl like you.' Spotting another of the waitresses craning her neck to get a better view of the rugby players warming up on the pitch, Sylvia gave a horrified gasp. 'No, no. You're here to work, not gape at men's legs—' Abandoning Holly and Nicky, she hurried over to the other girl.

'Of course we're here to gape at men's legs,' Nicky drawled. 'Why does she think we took the job in the first place? I don't know the first thing about scrums and line-outs, but I do know the men are gorgeous. I mean, there are men and there are men. And these are *men*, if you know what I mean.'

Not listening, Holly stared into space, her confidence at an all-time low. 'The wonder is not that Eddie dumped me,' she muttered, 'But that he got involved with me in the first place.'

'Don't talk like that. Don't let him do this to you,' Nicky scolded. 'Please tell me you didn't spend the night crying over him.'

'Funnily enough, I didn't. I've even been wondering about that.' Holly frowned. 'Perhaps I'm too devastated to cry.'

'Did you eat chocolate?'

'Of course. Well—chocolate biscuits. Do they count?'

'Depends on how many. You need a lot of biscuits to get the same chocolate hit.'

'I ate two.'

'Two biscuits?'

Holly blushed. 'Two packets.' She muttered the words under her breath and then gave a guilty moan. 'And I *hated* myself even more afterwards. But at the time I was miserable and *starving*! Eddie took me out to dinner to break off the engagement—I suppose he thought I might not scream at him in a public place. I knew something was wrong when he ordered a starter. He never orders a starter.'

'Well, isn't that typical?' Nicky's mouth tightened in disapproval. 'The night he breaks up with you, he finally allows you to eat.'

'The starter was for him, not me.' Holly shook her head absently. 'I can't eat in front of Eddie anyway. The way he watches me always makes me feel like a pig. He told me it was over in between the grilled fish and dessert. Then he dropped me home, and I kept waiting, but I just couldn't cry.'

'I'm not surprised. You were probably too hungry to summon the energy to cry,' Nicky said dryly. 'But eating chocolate biscuits is good news.'

'Tell that to my skirt. Why does Sylvia insist on this style?' Gloomily, Holly smoothed the tight black skirt over her hips. 'I feel as though I'm wearing a corset, and it's *so* short.'

'You look sexy as sin, as always. And eating chocolate is the first phase in the healing process, so you've passed that stage, which is a good sign. The next stage is to sell his ring.'

'I was going to return it.'

'Return it? Are you mad?' The empty glasses rattled again as Nicky's hands tightened on the tray. 'Sell it. And buy a pair of gorgeous shoes with the proceeds. Then you'll spend the rest of your life walking on his memory. And, next time, settle for sex without emotion.'

Holly smiled awkwardly, too self-conscious to confess that she hadn't actually had sex with Eddie.

And that, of course, had been her major drawback as far as he was concerned. He'd accused her of being inhibited.

She bit back a hysterical laugh.

A small family-hatchback with central locking.

Would she be less inhibited if her bottom were smaller?

Possibly, but she wasn't likely to find out. She was always promising herself that she'd diet, but going without food just made her crabby.

Which was why her clothes always felt too tight.

At this rate she was going to die a virgin.

Depressed by that thought, Holly glanced in the direction of the President's Suite. 'I really don't think I can face this.'

'It's worth it just to get a look at the wicked prince in the flesh.'

'He hasn't always been wicked. He was in love once,' Holly murmured, momentarily distracted from her own problems. 'With that Italian supermodel. I remember reading about them. They were the golden couple. Then she died along with his brother in that avalanche eight years ago. Horribly sad. Apparently he and his brother were really close. He lost the two people he loved most in the world. A family torn apart. I'm not surprised he's gone a bit wild. He must have been devastated. He probably just needs someone to love him.'

Nicky grinned. 'So go up there and love him. And don't forget my favourite saying.'

'What's that?'

'If you can't stand the heat…'

'Get out of the kitchen?' Holly completed the proverb but Nicky gave a saucy wink.

'Remove a layer of clothing.'

Casper strolled down the steps into the royal box, his handsome face expressionless as he stared across the impressive stadium. Eighty-two thousand people were gradually pouring into the stands in preparation for the breathlessly awaited match that was part of the prestigious Six Nations championship.

It was a bitterly cold February day, and his entourage was all muttering and complaining about freezing English weather.

Casper didn't notice.

He was used to being cold.

He'd been cold for eight long years.

Emilio, his Head of Security, leaned forward and offered him a phone. 'Savannah for you, Your Highness.'

Without turning, Casper gave an almost imperceptible shake of his head and Emilio hesitated before switching off the phone.

'Another female heart broken.' The blonde shivering next to him gave a disbelieving laugh. 'You're cold as ice, Cas. Rich and handsome, admittedly, but very inaccessible emotionally. Why are you ending it? She's crazy about you.'

'That's why I'm ending it.' His voice hard, Casper watched the players warming up on the pitch, ignoring the woman gazing longingly at his profile.

'If you're ditching the most beautiful woman in the world, what hope is there for the rest of us?'

No hope.

No hope for them. No hope for him. The whole thing was a game, Casper thought blankly. A game he was sick of playing.

Sport was one of the few things that offered distraction. But, before the rugby started, he had to sit through the hospitality.

Two long hours of hopeful women and polite conversation.

Two long hours of feeling nothing.

His face appeared on the giant screens placed at either end of the pitch, and he watched himself with detached curiosity, surprised by how calm he looked. There was a loud female cheer from those already gathered in the stands, and Casper delivered the expected smile of acknowledgement, wondering idly whether any of them would like to come and distract him for a few hours.

Anyone would do. He really didn't care.

As long as she didn't expect anything from him.

He glanced behind him towards the glass windows of the President's Suite where lunch would be served. An exceptionally pretty waitress was checking the table, her mouth moving as she recited her checklist to herself.

Casper studied her in silence, his eyes narrowing slightly as she paused in her work and lifted a hand to her mouth. He saw the rise and fall of her chest as she took a deep breath—watched as she tilted her head backwards and stared up at the ceiling. It was strange body language for someone about to serve lunch.

And then he realised that she was trying not to cry.

Over the years he'd taught himself to recognise the signs of female distress so that he could time his exit accordingly.

With cold detachment he watched her struggle to hold back the oncoming tide of tears.

She was a fool, he thought grimly, *to let herself feel that deeply about anything.*

And then he gave a smile of self-mockery. Hadn't he done the same at her age—in his early twenties, when life had seemed like an endless opportunity, hadn't he naively allowed his emotions freedom?

And then he'd learned a lesson that had proved more useful than all the hours spent studying constitutional law or international history.

He'd learned that emotions were man's biggest weakness, and that they could destroy as effectively as the assassin's bullet.

And so he'd ruthlessly buried all trace of his, protecting that unwanted human vulnerability under hard layers of bitter life experience. He'd buried his emotions so deep he could no longer find them.

And that was the way he wanted it.

Without looking directly at anyone, Holly carefully placed the champagne-and-raspberry torte in front of the prince. Silver cutlery and crystal glass glinted against the finest linen, but she barely noticed. She'd served the entire meal in a daze, her mind on Eddie, who was currently entertaining her replacement in the premium box along the richly carpeted corridor.

Holly hadn't seen her, but she was sure she was pretty. Blonde, obviously. And not the sort of person whose best friend in a crisis was a packet of chocolate biscuits.

Did she have a degree? Was she clever?

Holly's vision suddenly blurred with tears, and she blinked frantically, moving slowly around the table, barely aware of the conversation going on around her. Oh dear God, she was going to lose it. Here, in the President's Suite, with the prince and his guests as witnesses. It was going to be the most humiliating moment of her life.

Trying to pull herself together, Holly concentrated on the dessert in her hand, but she was teetering on the brink. Nicky was right. She should have stayed in bed and hidden under the duvet until she'd recovered enough to get her emotions back under control. But she needed this job too badly to allow herself the luxury of wallowing.

A burst of laughter from the royal party somehow intensified her feelings of isolation and misery, and she placed the last dessert on the table and backed away, horrified to find that one of the tears had spilled over onto her cheek.

The release of that one tear made all the others rush forward, and suddenly her throat was full and her eyes were stinging.

Oh, please, no. Not here.

Instinct told her to turn around, but protocol forbade her from turning her back on the prince, so she stood helplessly, staring at the dusky pink carpet with its subtly intertwined pattern of roses and rugby balls, comforting herself with the fact that they wouldn't notice her.

People never noticed her, did they? She was the invisible woman. She was the hand that poured the champagne, or the eyes that spotted an empty plate. She was a tidy room or an extra chair. But she wasn't a *person*.

'Here.' A strong, masculine hand passed her a tissue. 'Blow.'

With a gasp of embarrassment, Holly dragged her horrified gaze from those lean bronzed fingers and collided with eyes as dark and brooding as the night sky in the depths of winter.

And something strange happened.

Time froze.

The tears didn't spill and her heart didn't beat.

It was as if her brain and body separated. For a single instant, she forgot that she was about to make a giant fool of herself. She forgot about Eddie and his trophy blonde. She even forgot the royal party.

The only thing in her world was this man.

And then her knees weakened and her mouth dried because he was *insanely* handsome, his lean aristocratic face a breathtaking composition of bold masculine lines and perfect symmetry.

His dark gaze shifted to her mouth, and the impact

of that one searing glance scorched her body like the hottest flame. She felt her lips tingle and her heart thumped against her chest.

And that warning beat was the wake-up call she needed.

Oh, God. 'Your Highness.' Was she supposed to curtsy? She'd been so transfixed by how impossibly good-looking he was, she'd forgotten protocol. What was she supposed to do?

The unfairness of it was like a slap across the face. The one time she absolutely did *not* want to be noticed, she'd been noticed.

By Prince Casper of Santallia.

Her horrified gaze slid back to the tissue in his hand. And he *knew* she was upset. There was no hiding.

'Breathe,' he instructed in a soft voice. 'Slowly.'

Only then did she realise that he'd positioned himself right in front of her. His shoulders were wide and powerful, effectively blocking her from view, so that the rest of his party wouldn't see that she was crying.

The problem was, she could no longer remember *why* she'd felt like crying. One sizzling glance from those lazy dark eyes and her mind had been wiped.

Shrinking with embarrassment, but at the same time relieved to have a moment to compose herself, Holly took the tissue and blew her nose. Despair mixed with fatalistic acceptance as she realised that she'd just given herself a whole new problem.

He was going to complain. And who could blame him? She should have smiled more. She should have paid attention when the bored-looking blonde seated to his right had asked her whether the goat's cheese was organic.

He was going to have her fired.

'Thank you, Your Highness,' she mumbled, pushing the tissue into her pocket. 'I'll be fine. Just don't give me sympathy.'

'There's absolutely no chance of that. Sympathy isn't my thing.' His gorgeous eyes shimmered with sardonic humour. 'Unless it's sympathy sex.'

Too busy holding back tears to be shocked, Holly took another deep breath, but her white shirt couldn't stand the pressure and two of her buttons popped open. With a whimper of disbelief, she froze. As if she hadn't already embarrassed herself enough in front of royalty, she was about to spill out of her lacy bra. Now what? Did she draw attention to herself and do up the buttons, or did she just hope he hadn't noticed…?

'I'm going to have to complain about you.' His tone was gently apologetic and she felt her knees weaken.

'Yes, Your Highness.'

'A sexy waitress in sheer black stockings and lacy underwear is extremely distracting.' His bold, confident gaze dropped to her full cleavage and lingered. 'You make it impossible for me to concentrate on the boring blonde next to me.'

Braced for an entirely different accusation, Holly gave a choked laugh. 'You're joking?'

'I never joke about fantasies,' he drawled. 'Especially sexual ones.'

He thought the blonde was boring?

'You're having sexual fantasies?'

'Do you blame me?' The frank appraisal in his eyes was so at odds with her own plummeting opinion of herself, that for a moment Holly just stared up at him. Then she realised that he *had* to be making fun of her because she knew she wasn't remotely sexy.

'It isn't fair to tease me, Your Highness.'

'You only have to call me Your Highness the first time. After that, it's "sir".' Amused dark eyes slid from her breasts to her mouth. 'And I rather think you're the one teasing *me*.' He was looking at her with the type of unapologetic masculine appreciation that men reserved for exceptionally beautiful women.

And that wasn't her. She knew it wasn't. 'You haven't eaten your dessert, sir.'

He gave a slow, dangerous smile. 'I think I'm looking at it.'

Oh God, he was actually flirting with her.

Holly's legs started to shake because he was so, so attractive, and the way he was looking at her made her feel like a supermodel. Her shrivelled self-esteem bloomed like a parched flower given new life by a shower of rain. This stunningly attractive, handsome guy—this gorgeous, mega-wealthy prince who could have had any woman in the world—found her so attractive that he wanted to flirt with her.

'Cas.' A spoiled female voice came from behind them. 'Come and sit down.'

But he didn't turn.

The fact that he didn't appear willing or able to drag his gaze from her raised Holly's confidence another few notches. She felt her colour mount under his intense, speculative gaze, and suddenly there was a dangerous shift in the atmosphere. Trying to work out how she'd progressed from tears to tension in such a short space of time, Holly swallowed.

It was *him*, she thought helplessly.

He was just gorgeous.

And way out of her league.

Flirting was one thing, but he had guests hanging on his every word—glamorous women vying for his attention.

Suddenly remembering where she was and who he was, Holly gave him an embarrassed glance. 'They're waiting for you, sir.'

The smooth lift of one eyebrow suggested that he didn't understand why that was a problem, and Holly gave a weak smile. He was the ruling prince. People stood in line. They waited for his whim and his pleasure.

But surely his pleasure was one of those super-groomed, elegant women glaring impatiently at his broad back?

Her cheeks burning, she cleared her throat. 'They'll be wondering what you're doing.'

'And that matters because…?'

Envious of his indifference, she laughed. 'Well—

because generally people care what other people think.'

'Do they?'

She gave an awkward laugh. 'Yes.'

'Do *you* care what other people think?'

'I'm a waitress,' Holly said dryly. 'I have to care. If I don't care, I don't get tips—and then I don't eat.'

The prince lifted one broad shoulder in a careless shrug. 'Fine. So let's get rid of them. What they don't see, they can't judge.' Supremely confident, he cast a single glance towards one of the well-built guys standing by the door and that silent command was apparently sufficient to ensure that he was given instant privacy.

His security team sprang into action, and within minutes the rest of his party was leaving the room, knowing looks from the men and sulky glances from the women.

Ridiculously impressed by this discreet display of authority, Holly wondered how it would feel to be so powerful that you could clear a room with nothing more than a look. *And how must it feel to be so secure about yourself that you didn't care what other people thought about your actions?*

Only when the door of the President's Suite closed behind them did she suddenly realise that she was now alone with the prince.

She gave a choked laugh of disbelief.

He'd just dismissed the most glamorous, gorgeous women she'd ever seen in favour of—*her*?

The Prince turned back to her, his eyes glittering dark and dangerous. 'So.' His voice was soft. 'Now we're alone. How do you suggest we pass the time?'

Chapter 2

Holly's stomach curled with wicked excitement and desperate nerves. 'Thank you for rescuing me from an embarrassing moment,' she mumbled breathlessly, desperately racking her brains for something witty to say and failing. She had no idea how to entertain a prince. 'I can't imagine what you must think of me.'

'I don't understand your obsession with everyone else's opinion,' he drawled. 'And at the moment I'm not capable of thinking. I'm a normal healthy guy, and every one of my brain cells is currently focused on your gorgeous body.'

Holly made a sound somewhere between a gasp and a laugh. Disbelieving, self-conscious, but hopelessly flattered, she stroked her hands over her skirt, looked at him and then looked towards the door. '*Those* women are beautiful.'

'Those women spend eight hours a day perfecting their appearance. That's not beauty—it's obsession.' Supremely sure of himself, he took possession of her hand, locking her fingers into his.

Holly's stomach curled with excitement. 'We're not supposed to be doing this. They gave me this job because they thought I wasn't your type.'

'*Major* error on their part.'

'They told me you preferred blondes.'

'I think I've just had a major shift towards redheads.' With a wicked smile, he lifted his other hand and carelessly fingered a strand of her hair. 'Your hair is the colour of a Middle Eastern bazaar—cinnamon and gold. Tell me why you were crying.'

Caught in a spin of electrifying, exhilarating excitement, Holly's brain was in a whirl. For a moment she'd actually forgotten about Eddie. If she told him that her boyfriend had dumped her, would it make her seem less attractive?

'I was—'

'On second thoughts, don't tell me.' Interrupting her, he lifted her hand, checking for a ring. 'Single?'

Detecting something in his tone but too dazed to identify what, Holly nodded. 'Oh yes, completely single,' she murmured hastily, and then immediately wanted to snatch the words back, because she should have played it cool.

But she didn't feel cool. She felt—*relieved that she'd left the engagement ring at home.*

And he was smiling, clearly aware of the effect he was having on her.

Before she could stop him, he pulled the clip out of her hair and slid his fingers through her tumbling, wayward curls. 'That's better.' Very much the one in control, he closed his fingers around her wrists and hooked her arms round his neck. Then he slid his hands down her back and cupped her bottom.

'Oh.' Appalled that he seemed to be focusing on all her worst features, Holly gave a whimper of embarrassment and fought the impulse to wriggle away from him. But it was too late to take avoiding action. The confident exploration of his hands had ensured he was already well acquainted with the contours of her bottom.

'*Dio*, you have the most fantastic body,' he groaned, moulding her against the hard muscle of his thighs as if she were made of cling film.

He thought she was fantastic?

Brought into close contact with the physical evidence of his arousal, Holly barely had time to register the exhilarating fact that he really did find her attractive before his mouth came down on hers in a hungry, demanding kiss.

It was like being in the path of a lightning strike. Her body jerked with shock. Her head spun, her knees were shaking, and her attempt to catch her breath simply encouraged a still more intimate exploration of her mouth. Never in her life had a simple kiss made her feel like this. Her fingers dug into his shoulders for support and she gasped as she felt his hands slide *under* her skirt. She felt the warmth of his hands against her bare flesh above her stockings, and then he was backing her against the table, the slick, erotic invasion of his tongue in her mouth sending flames leaping around her body and a burning concentration of heat low in her pelvis.

He was kissing her as though this was their last moments on Earth—*as if he couldn't help himself*— and Holly was swept away on the pure adrenaline rush that came with suddenly being made to feel irresistible.

Dimly she thought, *This is fast, too fast.* But, even as part of her analysed her actions with a touch of shocked disapproval, another part of her was responding with wild abandon, her normal insecurities and inhibitions dissolved in a rush of raw sexual chemistry.

Control slipped slowly from her grasp.

When Eddie had kissed her she'd often found her mind wandering—on occasions she'd guiltily caught herself planning meals and making mental shopping lists—but with the prince the only coherent thought in her head was *Please don't let him stop.*

But she *had* to stop, didn't she?

She didn't do things like this.

What if someone walked in?

Struggling to regain some control, Holly gave a low moan and dragged her mouth from his, intending to take a step back and think through her actions. But her good intentions vanished as she gazed up at his lean, bronzed features, her resolve evaporating as she took in the thick, dark eyelashes guarding his impossibly sexy eyes. *Oh, dear God*—how could any woman say no to a man like this? And, if sheer masculine impact wasn't enough, the way he was looking at her was the most outrageous compliment she'd ever received.

'You're staring at me,' she breathed, and he gave a lopsided smile.

'If you don't want men to stare, stay indoors.'

Holly giggled, as much from nerves as humour. 'I am indoors.'

'True.' The prince lifted one broad shoulder in an unmistakeably Latin gesture. 'In which case, I can't see a solution. You'll just have to put up with me staring, *tesoro.*'

'You speak Italian?'

'I speak whichever language is going to get me the result I want,' he purred, and she gave a choked laugh because he was so outrageously confident and he made her feel beautiful.

Basking in warmth of his bold appreciation, she suddenly felt womanly and infinitely desirable. Blinded by the sheer male beauty of his features, and by the fact that this incredible man was looking at *her*, her crushed heart suddenly lifted as though it had been given wings, and her confidence fluttered back to life.

All right, so she wasn't Eddie's type.

But this man—*this incomparably handsome playboy prince who had his pick of the most beautiful women in the world*—found her irresistible.

'You're staring at me too,' he pointed out, his gaze amused as he slid his fingers into her hair with slow deliberation. 'Perhaps it would be better if we both just close our eyes so that we don't get distracted from what we're doing.'

'What *are* we doing?' Weak with desire, Holly could barely form the words, and his smile widened as he gently cupped her face and lowered his mouth slowly towards hers.

'I think it's called living for the moment. And kissing you is the most fantastic moment I've had in a long time,' he said huskily, his mouth a breath away from hers.

She waited in an agony of anticipation, but he didn't seem in a rush to kiss her again, and Holly parted her lips in expectation, hoping that he'd take the hint.

Why on earth had she stopped him?

With a faint whimper of desperation, she looked into his eyes, saw the laughter there and realised that he was teasing her.

'That isn't very kind, Your Highness.' But she found that she was laughing too and her body was on fire.

'I'm not kind.' He murmured the words against her mouth. 'I'm definitely not kind.'

'I couldn't care less—please...' She was breathless and trembling with anticipation. 'Kiss me again.'

Flashing her a megawatt smile of male satisfaction, the prince finally lowered his head and claimed her mouth with his. He kissed her with consummate skill, his touch confident and possessive as he drew every last drop of response from her parted lips.

Her senses were swamped, her pulse accelerating out of control. Holly was aware of nothing except the overwhelming needs of her own body. Her arms tightened around his neck and she felt the sudden change in him. His kiss changed from playful to purposeful, and she realised with a lurch of exhilarating terror that this wasn't a mild flirtation or a game of 'boy kisses girl'. Prince Casper was a sexually experienced man who knew what he wanted and had the confidence to take it.

'Maybe we should slow this down,' she gasped, sinking her fingers into the hard muscle of his shoulders to give extra support to her shaking knees.

'Slow works for me,' he murmured, sliding his hands over the curve of her bottom. 'I'm more than happy to savour every moment of your utterly delectable body, and the game hasn't started yet. Why rush?'

'I didn't exactly mean—oh—' her head fell back as his mouth trailed a hot, sensuous path down her throat 'I can't concentrate on anything when you do that—'

'Concentrate on *me*,' he advised, and then he lifted his head and his stunning dark eyes narrowed. 'You're shivering. Are you nervous?'

Terrified. Desperate. Weak with longing.

'I—I haven't actually done this before.' Her whispered confession caused him to still.

'Exactly what,' he said carefully, 'Haven't you done before?' He released his hold on her bottom and slid his fingers under her chin, forcing her to look at him, his sharply intelligent eyes suddenly searching.

Holly swallowed.

Oh God, he was going to walk away from her. If she told him the truth, this experienced, sophisticated, gorgeous man would let her go and she'd spend the rest of her life regretting it.

Was she really going to let that happen?

No longer questioning herself, she slid her arms back round his neck. She didn't know what was going on here, she had no idea why she was feeling this way, but she knew she didn't want it to stop. 'I meant that I've never done anything like this in such a public place.'

He lifted an eyebrow. 'We're alone.'

'But anyone could walk in.' She wished he'd kiss her again. Would he think she was forward if *she* kissed him? 'What would happen then?'

'They'd be arrested,' he said dryly, 'And carted off to jail.'

'Oh—' Reminded of exactly with whom she was dealing, Holly felt suddenly intimidated. Please, *please,* let him kiss her again. When he'd kissed her she'd forgotten he was a prince. She'd forgotten *everything*. Feeling as though she were standing on the edge of a life-changing moment, Holly gazed up at him and he gave a low laugh.

'You talk too much, do you know that? So—now what? Yes, or no?' He smoothed a rebellious strand of hair away from her flushed cheeks in a slow, sensual movement, and that meaningful touch was enough to raise her temperature several degrees.

He was giving her the choice.

He was telling her that, if he kissed her again, he was going all the way.

'Yes,' she whispered, knowing that there would be a price to pay, but more than willing to pay it. 'Oh, yes.'

If she'd expected her shaky encouragement to be met with a kiss, she was disappointed.

'If you want to slow things down,' he murmured against her throat, 'I suppose I could always eat the dessert that's waiting for me on the table.'

Holly gave a faint whimper of frustration, and then he lifted his head and she saw the wicked gleam in his eyes. 'You're teasing me again.'

'You asked me to slow down, *tesoro*.'

She was finding it hard to breathe. 'I've definitely changed my mind about that.'

'Then why don't you tell me what you want?' He gave a sexy, knowing smile that sent her body into meltdown.

'I want you to kiss me again.' *And not to stop.*

'Do you?' His head lowered to hers, thick lashes partially shielding the mockery in his beautiful eyes. 'You're not supposed to give me orders.'

'Are you going to arrest me?'

'Now, there's a thought.' He breathed the words against her mouth. 'I could clap you in handcuffs and chain you to my bed until I'm bored.'

Her last coherent thought was *Please don't let*

him ever be bored, and then he lifted her, and the demands of his hands on her thighs made it impossible for her not to wrap her legs around his waist. There was the faint rattle of fine bone-china as he positioned her on the table, and only when she felt the roughness of his zip against the soft flesh of her inner thigh did she realise that he'd somehow manoeuvred her skirt up round her waist.

With a gasp of embarrassment, she grabbed at the skirt, but she felt the hard thrust of his body against hers.

'I *love* the stockings,' he groaned, his dark eyes ablaze with sexual heat as he scanned the lacy suspender-belt transecting her milky-white thighs.

Thighs that definitely weren't skinny.

The fragile shoots of her self-confidence withered and died under his blatant scrutiny, and Holly tugged ineffectually at the hem of her skirt, trying to cover herself. 'Sylvia insists on stockings,' she muttered, and then, 'Do you think you could stop looking at me?'

'No, I definitely couldn't,' he assured her, a laugh in his voice as he released his hold on her bottom, grasped her hands and anchored them firmly around his neck. 'Take a deep breath in for me.'

'Why?'

A wicked smile transformed his face from handsome to devastating. 'Because I want you to undo a few more buttons without me having to move my hands again. I'm never letting go of your bottom.'

Hyper-sensitive to that particular subject, Holly

tensed, only to relax again as she registered the un-mistakeable relish with which he was exploring her body. 'You *like* my bottom?'

'I just want to lose myself in you. What's your secret—exercise? Plastic surgery?' He gave another driven groan, captured her hips and drew her hard against his powerful erection. 'What did you *do* to it?'

'I ate too many biscuits,' Holly muttered truthfully, and he gave a laugh.

'I love your sense of humour. And from now on you can expect to receive a box of your favourite kind of biscuits on a daily basis.'

Slightly stunned that he actually seemed to *love* her worst feature, and trying not to be shocked by his unashamed sexuality, Holly was about to speak when his mouth collided with hers again and sparks exploded inside her head. It was like being the centre piece at a fireworks display, and she gave a disbelieving moan that turned to a gasp as her shirt fell open and her bra slid onto her lap.

'Are these also the result of the famous biscuit-diet?' An appreciative gleam in his eyes, he transferred his attention from her bottom to her breasts. '*Dio*, you're so fantastic I'm not even *thinking* about anything else while I'm with you.'

Something about that comment struck a slightly discordant note in her dazzled brain. Before she could dissect his words in more detail, he dragged his fingers across one nipple and shockwaves of pleasure sliced through her body. Then he lowered his dark head and flicked her nipple with his tongue.

Tortured by sensation, Holly's head fell back. Inhibitions blown to the wind by his expert touch, driven to the point of explosion by his vastly greater experience, she knew she was completely out of control and didn't even care. She felt like a novice rider clinging to the back of a thoroughbred stallion.

The burning ache in her pelvis grew to unbearable proportions, and she ground herself against him with a whimper of need. Desperate to relieve the almost intolerable heat that threatened to burn her up, she dug her nails into his shoulders.

'Please—oh—please.'

'My pleasure.' His eyes were two narrow slits of fire, his jaw hard, streaks of colour highlighting his cheekbones as he scanned her flushed cheeks and parted lips. Then he flattened her to the table and came down over her, the muscles in his shoulders bunched as he protected her from his weight.

Feeling as though she'd been dropped naked onto a bonfire, Holly gave a low moan that he smothered with a slow, purposefully erotic kiss.

'You are the most delicious thing that has ever been put on my table, my gorgeous waitress,' he murmured, his desperately clever fingers reaching lower. The intimacy of his touch brought another gasp to her lips and the gasp turned to a low moan as he explored her with effortless skill and merciless disregard for modesty.

'Are you protected?' His husky question didn't

begin to penetrate her dazed brain, and she made an unintelligible sound, her legs tightening around his back, her body arching off the table in an attempt to ease the fearsome ache he'd created.

His mouth came down on hers again and she felt his strong hands close around her hips. He shifted his position, tilted her slightly, and then surged into her with a decisive thrust that drew a disbelieving groan from him and a shocked gasp from Holly.

An explosion of unbelievable pleasure suddenly splintered into pain, and her sharp cry caused him to still instantly.

Pain and embarrassment mingled in equal measure and for a moment Holly dug her nails hard into his shoulders, afraid to move in case moving made it worse. And then suddenly the pain was gone and there was only pleasure—dark, forbidden pleasure that beckoned her forwards into a totally new world. She moved her hips restlessly, not sure what she wanted him to do, but needing him to do *something*.

There was the briefest hesitation on his part while he scanned her flushed cheeks, then he surged into her again, but this time more gently, his eyes holding hers the whole time as he introduced her to an intimacy that was new to her. And it was pleasure such as she'd never imagined. *Pleasure that blew her mind.*

She didn't know herself—her body at the mercy of sensual pleasure and the undeniable skill of an experienced male.

Controlled by his driving thrusts, she raced towards a peak and then was flung high into space, stars exploding in her head as he swallowed her cries of pleasure with his mouth, and reached his own peak with a triumphant groan.

Gradually Holly floated back down to earth, aware of the harshness of his breathing and the frantic beating of her own heart. He'd buried his face in her neck, and Holly focused on his glossy dark hair with glazed vision and numb disbelief.

Had that really just happened?

Swamped by an emotion that she couldn't define, she lifted her hand and tentatively touched him, checking that he was real.

She felt an immediate surge of tension through his powerful frame and heard his sharp intake of breath. Then he lifted his head, stared down into her eyes.

To Holly it was the single most intimate moment of her life, and when he opened his mouth to speak her heart softened.

'The match has started,' he drawled flatly. 'Thanks to you, I've missed kick-off.'

Keeping his back to the girl, Casper stared blankly through the glass of the President's Suite down into the stadium, struggling to regain some measure of control after what had undoubtedly been the most exciting sexual encounter of his life.

On the pitch below, England had possession of the ball, but for the first time in his life he wasn't in his seat, watching the game.

Which was something else that he didn't understand.

What the hell was going on?

Why wasn't he rushing to watch the game?

And since when had he been driven to have raw, uncontrolled sex on a table with an innocent woman?

Innocent.

Only now was he realising that all the signs had been there. And he'd missed them. *Or had he ignored them?*

Either way, he was fully aware of the irony of the situation.

He'd had relationships with some of the world's most beautiful, experienced and sophisticated women, but none of them had made him feel the way she had.

This was possibly the first time he'd enjoyed uncomplicated, motiveless sex. Sex driven by sheer, animal lust rather than human ambition.

Yes, the girl had known he was a prince.

But he was experienced enough to know that she'd wanted him as a man.

Hearing the faint brush of clothing against flesh, he knew she was dressing. For once he was grateful for the iron self-control and self-discipline that had been drilled into him in his few years in the army, because that was the only thing currently standing between restraint and a repeat performance.

It must have been novelty value, he reflected grimly, his shoulders tensing as he heard her slide her feet into her shoes. That was the only explanation for the explosive chemistry they shared.

Which left them where, precisely?

He turned to find her watching him, and the confusion in her beautiful green eyes turned to consternation as a discreet tap on the door indicated that his presence was required.

The girl threw an embarrassed glance towards the door and frantically smoothed her skirt over her thighs. It was obvious from the uneven line of buttons on her shirt that she'd dressed in a hurry, with hands that hadn't been quite steady. Her hair was still loose, spilling over her narrow shoulders like a fall of autumn leaves, a beacon of glorious colour that effectively announced their intimacy to everyone who saw her.

Focusing on her soft mouth, Casper felt a sudden urge to power her back against the table and lose himself in her incredible body one more time.

'They'll be waiting for you in the royal box.' Her husky voice cut through his disturbingly explicit thoughts, and she hesitated for a moment and then walked over to him.

'Y-your Highness—are you all right?'

Casper stared down into warm green eyes, saw concern there, and suddenly the urge not to let her go was almost painful. There was something hopeful and optimistic about her, and he sensed she hadn't yet discovered that life was a cold, hard place.

Her smile faltered as she studied the grim set of his features. 'I guess this is what you'd call a bit of an awkward moment. So—well—' she waved a hand '—I have to get back to work and you—well…' Her voice tailed off and her white teeth clamped her lower lip. Then she took a deep breath, closed the gap between them, stood on tiptoe and kissed him on the mouth. 'Thank you,' she whispered. 'Thank you for what you've given me.'

Caught by surprise, Casper stood frozen to the spot, enveloped by a warm, soft woman. She tasted of strawberries and summer and an immediate explosion of lust gripped his body.

So he wasn't dead, then, he thought absently, part of him removed from what was happening. *Some things he could still feel.*

And then he heard a massive cheer from the crowd behind him and knew instantly what had happened.

Not so innocent, he thought grimly. Not so innocent that she didn't know how to work the press to her advantage. She was kissing him in the window, in full view of the cameras covering the game and the crowd.

Cameras that were now focusing on them.

She might have been sexually inexperienced, but clearly that hadn't prevented her from having a plan.

Surprised that he was still capable of feeling disillusioned and furious with himself for making such an elemental mistake, Casper locked his fingers round her wrists and withdrew her arms from his neck.

'You can stop now. If you look behind me, I think you'll find that you've achieved your objective.'

Confusion flickered in her eyes and then her attention fixed on something behind him. 'Oh my God.' Her hand covered her mouth. 'H—how did you know?' Her voice was an appalled whisper and she glanced at him in desperate panic. 'They filmed me kissing you. And it's up on the giant screens.' Her voice rose, her cheeks were scarlet, and her reluctant glance towards the stadium ended in a moan of disbelief. 'They're playing it again and again. Oh God, I can't believe this—it looks as though I'm—and my hair is all over the place and my bottom looks *huge*, and—everyone is looking.'

His eyes on the pitch, Casper watched with cool detachment as his friend, the England captain, hit a post with a drop-goal attempt.

'More importantly, you just cost England three points.'

With cold detachment, he realised that he was now going to have to brief his security team to get her out of here, but before he could speak she gave him a reproachful look and sped to the door.

'Do *not* leave this room,' Casper thundered, but she ignored him, tugged open the door, slipped between two of his security guards and sprinted out of sight.

Unaccustomed to having his orders ignored, Casper stood in stunned silence for a few precious seconds and then delivered a single command to his Head of Security. 'Find her.'

'Can you give me her name, Your Highness?'

Casper stared through the door. 'No,' he said grimly. 'I can't.'

All he knew was that she clearly wasn't as innocent as he'd first thought.

Feeling nothing except a desperate desire to hide from the world, Holly sprinted out of the room, shrinking as she passed a television screen in time to overhear the commentator say, *'Looks like the opening score goes to Prince Casper.'*

Hurtling down the stairs, she ran straight into her boss, who was marching up the stairs towards the President's Suite like a general leading an invading army onto enemy territory.

'Sylvia.' Her breath coming in pants, Holly stared at the other woman in horrified silence, noticing the blaze of fury in her eyes and the tightness of her lips.

'How dare you?' Sylvia's voice shook with anger. 'How dare you humiliate me in this way? I picked you especially because I thought you were sensible and decent. And you have destroyed the reputation of my company!'

'No!' Horribly guilty, overwhelmed by panic and humiliation, Holly shook her head. 'They don't even know who I am, and—'

'The British tabloid press will have your name before you're out of the stadium,' Sylvia spat. 'The entire nation heard the commentator say "That's one girl who isn't lying back thinking of England". If you wanted sleazy notoriety, then you've got it.'

Holly flinched under the verbal blows, feeling as vulnerable as a little rowing boat caught in a heavy storm out at sea. *What had she done?* This wasn't a little transgression that would remain her private secret. This was—this was… 'Prince Casper has kissed lots of women,' she muttered. 'So it won't be much of a story—'

'You're a waitress!' Sylvia was shaking with anger. 'Of course it's a story!'

Holly stared at her in appalled silence, realising that she hadn't once given any thought to the consequences of what they were doing. She hadn't thought at all. It had been impulse, chemistry, intimacy; she bit back a hysterical laugh.

What was intimate about having your love life plastered on sixty-nine-metre screens for the amusement of a crowd of eighty-two thousand people?

She swallowed painfully. 'Sylvia, I—'

'You're fired for misconduct!'

Her world crumbling around her, Holly was about to plead her case when she caught sight of Eddie striding towards them, his face like a storm cloud.

Unable to take any more, Holly gasped another apology and fled towards the kitchens. Heart pounding, cheeks flaming, she grabbed her bag and her coat, changed into her trainers and made for the door.

Nicky intercepted her. 'Where are you going?'

'I don't know.' Feeling dazed, Holly looked at her helplessly. 'Home. Anywhere.'

'You can't go home. It's the first place they'll look.' Brisk and businesslike, Nicky handed her a hat and a set of keys. 'Stick the hat on and hide that gorgeous hair. Then go to my flat.'

'No one knows who I am.'

'By now they'll know more about you than you do. Go to my flat, draw the curtains and don't answer the door to anyone. Have you got the money for a cab?'

'I'll take the bus.' Too shocked to argue, Holly obediently scooped her hair into a bunch and tucked it under the hat.

'No way.' Nicky stuffed a note in her hand. 'Get a taxi—and hope the driver hasn't seen the pictures on the screen. Come to think of it, sit with a hanky over your nose. Pretend you have a cold or something. Go, go, *go*!'

Realising that she'd set into motion a series of events that she couldn't control, Holly started to walk towards the door when Nicky caught her arm.

'Just tell me one thing,' she whispered, a wicked gleam in her eyes. 'The rumours about the prince's talents—are they true?'

Holly blinked. 'I—'

'That good, huh?' Nicky gave a slow, knowing smile. 'I guess that answers my question. Way to go, baby.'

Ruthlessly focusing his mind on the game, Casper watched as the England winger swerved round his opponent and dived for the corner.

The bored blonde gasped in sympathy. 'Oh no, the poor guy's tripped. Right on the line. Why is everyone cheering? That's *so* mean.'

'He didn't trip, he scored a try,' Casper growled, simmering with masculine frustration at her inappropriate comment. 'And they're cheering because that try puts England level.'

'This game is a total mystery to me,' the girl muttered, her eyes wandering to a group of women at the back of the royal box. 'Nice shoes. I wonder where she got them? Are there any decent shops in this area?'

Casper blocked out her comments, watching as the England fly-half prepared to take the kick.

A hush fell over the stadium and Saskia glanced around her in bemusement. 'I don't understand any of this. Why is everyone so quiet? And why does that gorgeous guy keep staring at the ball and then the post? Can't he make up his mind whether to kick it or not?'

'He's about to take a very difficult conversion kick right from the touchline. He's concentrating.' Casper's gaze didn't shift from the pitch. 'And if you open your mouth again I'll have you removed.'

Saskia snapped her mouth shut, the ball snaked through the posts, the crowd roared its approval, and a satisfied Casper turned wearily to the fidgeting blonde next to him. 'All right. *Now* you can ask me whatever you want to know.'

She gave him a hopeful look. 'Is the game nearly over?'

Casper subdued a flash of irritation and resolved never again to invite anyone who didn't share his passion for rugby. 'It's half time.'

'So we have to sit through the whole thing again? Tell me again how you know the captain.'

'We were in the rugby team at school together.'

Clearly determined to engage him in conversation now that there was a pause in the game, Saskia sidled a little closer. 'It was very bad of you to kiss that waitress. You are a very naughty boy, Cas. She'll go to the newspapers, you know. That sort always do.'

Would she?

Casper stared blankly at the crowd, trying to blot out the scent of her hair and the taste of her mouth— the softness of her deliciously rounded bottom as she'd lifted herself against him.

For a brief moment in time, she'd made him forget. And that was more than anyone else had ever done.

'Why does your popularity never dip?' Clearly determined to ingratiate herself, Saskia kept trying. 'Whatever you do, however scandalous you are, the citizens of Santallia still love you.'

'They love him because he's turned Santallia from a sleepy, crumbling Mediterranean country into a hub of foreign investment and tourism. People are excited about what's happening.' It was one of Casper's friends, Marco, who spoke, a guy in his early thirties who had studied economics with him at university and now ran a successful business. 'Santallia is *the* place to be. The downhill-ski race has brought the tourists to the mountains in the winter, and the yacht race does the same for the coast in the summer. The new rugby stadium is sold out for the entire season, and everyone is talking about the Grand Prix. As a sporting venue, we're second to none.'

Hearing his successes listed should have lifted his mood, but Casper still felt nothing.

He made no effort to take part in the conversation going on around him and was relieved when the second half started because it offered him a brief distraction.

'What Santallia really wants from you is an heir, Cas.' Saskia delivered what she obviously thought was an innocent smile. 'You can't play the field for ever. Sooner or later you're going to have to break your supermodel habit and think about the future of your country. Oh no, fighting has broken out on the pitch. They're all sort of locked together.'

Leaving it to an exasperated Marco to enlighten her, Casper watched as the scrum half put the ball into the scrum. 'That was never straight,' he murmured, a frown on his face as he glanced at the referee, waiting for him to blow the whistle.

'Did you read that survey that put you top of the list of most eligible single men in the world? You can have any woman you want, Cas.' Oblivious to the impact of her presence on their enjoyment, Saskia continued to pepper the entire second half with her inane comments, all of which Casper ignored.

'A minute of play to go,' Marco murmured, and Casper watched as England kept the ball among the forwards until the final whistle shrilled.

The crowd erupted into ecstatic cheers at the decisive England victory, and he rose to his feet, abruptly terminating Saskia's attempts to converse with him.

Responsibility pressing in on him, he strolled over to his Head of Security. 'Anything?'

'No, sir,' Emilio admitted reluctantly. 'She's vanished.'

'You found out her name?'

'Holly, sir. Holly Phillips. She's a waitress with the contract catering company.'

'Address?'

'I already sent a team to her home, sir. She isn't there.'

'But I'm sure the photographers are,' Cas said grimly, and Emilio nodded.

'Two rows of them, waiting to interview her. Prince and waitress—it's going to be tomorrow's headlines. You want her to have protection?'

'A woman who chooses to kiss me in full view of television cameras and paparazzi doesn't need my protection.' Casper spoke in a flat, toneless voice. 'She knew exactly what she was doing. And now she's lying low because being unavailable will make it look as though she has something to hide. And having something to hide will make her story more valuable.'

She'd used him.

Casper gave a twisted smile. *And he'd used her, too, hadn't he?*

Emilio frowned. 'You think she did it to make money, sir?'

'Of course.' She'd actually had the temerity to thank him for what he'd given her! At the time he'd wondered what she meant, but now it was blindingly obvious.

He'd given her media opportunities in abundance.

He searched inside himself for a feeling of disgust or disillusionment. *Surely* he should feel something? Apparently she'd considered the loss of her virginity to be a reasonable price to pay for her moment of fame and fortune and that attitude deserved at least a feeling of mild disappointment on his part.

But disillusionment, disgust and disappointment all required expectations and, when it came to women, he had none.

Emilio was watching him. 'You don't want us to find her, Your Highness?'

Ruthlessly pushing aside thoughts of her soft mouth and delicious curves, Casper glanced back towards the pitch where the crowd was going wild. 'I think we can be sure that when she's ready she'll turn up. At this precise moment she's lying low, laughing to herself and counting her money.'

Chapter 3

'You have *got* to stop crying!' Exasperated and concerned, Nicky put her arms round Holly. 'And—well—it isn't that serious, really.'

'Nicky, *I'm pregnant!* And it's the prince's baby.' Holly turned reddened eyes in her direction. 'How much more serious can it get?'

Nicky winced. 'Isn't it too soon to do a test? It could be wrong.'

'It isn't too soon. It's been over two weeks!' Holly waved a hand towards the bathroom. 'And it isn't wrong. It's probably still on the floor where I dropped it if you want to check, but it doesn't exactly give you a million options. It's either pregnant or not pregnant. And I'm *definitely* pregnant! Oh God, I don't believe it. Once—*once*—I have sex and now I'm pregnant. Some people try for *years*.'

'Yes, well, the prince is obviously super-fertile as well as super-good looking.' Nicky gave a helpless shrug, searching for something to say. 'You always said you couldn't wait to have a baby.'

'But *with* someone! Not on my own. I never, ever, wanted to be a single mother. It was the one thing I promised myself was never going to happen. It *really* matters to me.' Holly pulled another tissue out of the box and blew her nose hard. 'When I dreamed about having a baby, I dreamed about giving it everything I never had.'

'By which I presume you mean a father. God, your dad *really* screwed you up.' With that less than comforting comment, Nicky sank back against the sofa and picked at her nail varnish. 'I mean, how could anyone have a kid like you, so kind and loving, and then basically just, well, walk out? And you were seven—old enough to know you'd been rejected. And not even coming to find you after your mum died. I mean, for goodness' sake!'

Not wanting to be reminded of her barren childhood, Holly burrowed deeper inside the sleeping bag. 'He didn't know she'd died.'

'If he'd stayed in touch he would have known.'

'Do you mind if we don't talk about this?' Her voice high-pitched, Holly rolled onto her back and stared up at the ceiling. 'I have to decide what to do. I've lost my job, and I can't go home because the press are like a pack of wolves outside my flat. And the whole world thinks I'm a giant slut.' Dying of embarrassment, her insides twisting with regret, she buried her face in the pillow.

And she *was* a slut, wasn't she?

She'd had sex with a total stranger.

And not just sex—recklessly abandoned, wild sex. Sex that had taken her breath away and wiped her mind of guilt, worry, *morals*.

Whenever Eddie had touched her, her first thought had always been *I mustn't get pregnant*. When the prince had touched her the only thought in her head had been more, *more…*

What had happened to her?

Yes, she'd been upset and insecure about herself after her break up with Eddie, but that didn't explain or excuse it.

And then she remembered the way the prince had planted himself protectively in front of her, shielding her from the rest of the group. What other man had ever shown that degree of sensitivity? He'd noticed she was upset, shielded her, and then…

Appalled with herself, she gave another moan of regret, and Nicky yanked the sleeping bag away from her.

'Stop torturing yourself. You're going to be a great mother.'

'How can I be a great mother? I'm going to have to give my baby to someone else to look after while I work! Which basically means that someone else will pick my baby up when it cries.'

'Well, if it's a real bawler that might be an advantage.'

Holly wiped the tears from her face with a mangled damp hanky. 'How can it be an advantage? I want to be there for my baby.'

'Well, perhaps you'll win the lottery.'

'I can't afford to play the lottery. I can't even afford to pay you rent.'

'I don't want rent, and you can sleep on my sofa as long as you need to.' Nicky shrugged. 'You can't exactly go home, can you? The entire British public are gagging for pictures of you. "Where's the waitress?" is today's headline. Yesterday it was "royal's rugby romp". Rumour has it that they're offering a reward to anyone who shops you. Everyone wants to know about that kiss.'

'For crying out loud.' Holly blew her nose hard. 'People in the world are starving and they want to write about the fact that I kissed a prince? Doesn't anyone have any sense of perspective?' *Thank goodness they didn't know the whole story.*

'Well, we all need a little light relief now and then, and people love it when royalty show they're human.' Nicky sprang to her feet. 'I'm hungry and there's no food in this flat.'

'I don't want anything,' Holly said miserably, too embarrassed to admit to her friend that the real reason she was so upset was because the prince hadn't made any attempt to get in touch.

Even though she knew it was ridiculous to expect him to contact her, a small part of her was still desperately hoping that he would. Yes, she was a waitress and he was a prince, but he'd liked her, hadn't he? He'd thrown all the other people out of the room so that he could be with *her*, and he'd said all those nice things about her, and then...

Holly's body burned in a rush of sexual excitement that shocked her. Surely after sex as mindblowing as that, he might have been tempted to track her down?

But how could he get in touch when the press was staking out her flat? She had a mental image of the prince hiding behind a bush, waiting for the opportunity to bang on her door. 'Do you think he's really annoyed about the headlines?'

'Don't tell me you're worrying about *him*!' Nicky had her hand in a packet of cereal. 'He just pulls up his bloody drawbridge, leaving the enemy on the outside!'

Holly bit her lip. She was the one who'd kissed him by the window. *She'd had no idea.* 'I feel guilty.'

'Oh, please! This is Prince Casper we're talking about. He doesn't care what the newspapers write about him. *You're* the one who's going to suffer. If you ask me, the least he could have done was give you some security or advice. But he's left you to take the flak!'

Holly's spirits sank further at that depressing analysis. 'He doesn't know where I am.'

'He's a prince,' Nicky said contemptuously, flopping back down on the sofa, her mouth full of cereal. 'He commands a whole army, complete with special forces. He could find you in an instant if he wanted to. MI5, FBI, I don't know—one of that lot. One word from him and there'd be a satellite trained on my flat.'

Shrinking at the thought, Holly slid back into the sleeping bag. 'Close the blinds.' *What had she done?*

'Well, you can go on hiding if that's what you want. Or you could give those sharks outside your flat an interview.'

'Are you mad?'

'No, I'm practical. Thanks to His Royal Highness, you have no job and you're trapped indoors. Sell your story to the highest bidder. "My lunchtime of love" or "sexy Santallian stud"?'

Appalled, Holly shook her head. 'Absolutely not. I couldn't do that.'

'You have a baby to support.'

'And I don't want my child looking back at the year he was conceived and seeing that his life started with me dishing the dirt on his dad in the papers! I just want the whole thing to go away.'

It was ironic, she thought numbly, that she'd fantasised about this exact moment ever since she was a teenager. She'd *longed* to be a mother. Longed to have a child of her own—to be able to create the sort of family she'd always wanted.

She'd even lain awake at night, imagining what it must be like to discover that you were pregnant and to share that excitement with a partner. She'd imagined his delight and his pride. She'd imagined him pulling her into a protective hug and fiercely declaring that he would never leave his family.

Not once, ever, had she imagined that she'd be in this position, doing it on her own.

One rash moment, one transgression—*just one*—and her life had been blown apart. Even though she was in a state of shock, the deeper implications weren't lost on her. Her hopes of eventually being able to melt back into her old life unobserved died. She knew that once someone spotted that she was pregnant it wouldn't take long for them to do the maths.

This was Prince Casper of Santallia's child.

Nicky stood up. 'I need to buy some food. Back in a minute.' The front door slammed behind her, and moments later Holly heard the doorbell. Assuming Nicky had forgotten something, she slid off the sofa and padded over to the door.

'So this is where you've been hiding!' Eddie stood in the doorway, holding a huge, ostentatious bunch of dark-red roses wrapped in cheap cellophane.

Holly simply stared, suddenly realising that she'd barely thought about him over the past two weeks.

'I didn't expect to see you here, Eddie.'

He gave a benign smile. 'I expect it seems like a dream.' Sure of himself, Eddie smiled down at her. 'Aren't you going to invite me in?'

'No. You broke off our engagement, Eddie. I was devastated.' Holly frowned to herself. Her devastation hadn't lasted long, though, had it? It had been supplanted by bigger issues—but should that have been possible? Did broken hearts really mend that quickly?

'I can't talk about this on the doorstep.' He pushed his way into the flat and thrust the flowers into her hands. Past their best, a few curling petals floated onto the floor. 'Here. These are for you. To show that I forgive you.'

'Forgive me?' Holly winced as a thorn buried itself into her hand. Gingerly she put the flowers down on the hall table and sucked the blood from her finger. 'What are you forgiving me for?'

'For kissing the prince.' Eddie's face turned the same shade as the roses. 'For making a fool of me in public.'

'Eddie—you were the one partying in that box with your new girlfriend.'

'She was no one special. We both need to stop hurting each other. I admit that I was furious when I saw you kissing the prince, then I realised that it must have been hard on you, watching me get that promotion and then losing me. But it seems to have loosened up something inside you. A whole new you emerged.' He grinned like a schoolboy who had just discovered girls. 'You've always been quite shy and a bit prim. And suddenly you were, well, wild. When I saw you kissing him, I couldn't help thinking it should have been me.'

Looking at him, Holly realised that not once during her entire passionate episode with the prince had she thought 'this should have been Eddie'.

'I know you only did it to bring me to my senses,'

Eddie said. 'And it worked. I see now that you are capable of passion. I just need to be more patient with you.'

The prince hadn't been patient, Holly thought absently. He'd been very *impatient*. Rough, demanding, forceful.

'I didn't kiss the prince to make you jealous.' She'd kissed him because she couldn't help herself.

'Never mind that now. Put my ring back on your finger, and we'll go out there and tell the press we'd had a row and you kissed the prince because you were pining for me.'

Life had a strange sense of humour, Holly reflected numbly. Eddie was offering to get back together. But she was already being propelled down a very different path.

'That isn't possible.'

'We're going to make a great couple.' He was smugly confident. 'We'll have the Porsche and the big house. You don't need to be a waitress any more.'

'I like being a waitress,' Holly said absently. 'I like meeting new people and talking to them. People tell you a lot over a cup of coffee.'

'But who wants to be weighed down with someone else's problems when you can stay at home and look after me?'

'It *can't* happen, Eddie—'

'I know it's like a fairy tale, but it *is* happening. By the way, the flowers cost a fortune, so you'd better put them in water. I need the bathroom.'

'Door on the right,' Holly said automatically, and

then gave a gasp. 'No, Eddie, you can't go in there.' Oh, dear God, she'd left everything on the floor—he'd see.

Wanting to drag him back but already too late, she stood there, paralysed into inactivity by the sheer horror of the moment. The inevitability was agonising. It was like witnessing a pile-up—watching, powerless, as a car accelerated towards the back of another.

For a moment there was no sound. No movement.

Then Eddie appeared in the door, his face white. 'Well.' His voice sounded tight and very unlike himself. 'That certainly explains why you don't want to get back together again.'

'Eddie—'

'You're holding out for a higher prize.' Looking slightly dazed, he stumbled into the living room of Nicky's flat. Then he looked at her, his mouth twisted with disgust. 'A year we were together! And we never—you made we wait.'

'Because it didn't feel right,' she muttered, mortified by how it must look, and anxious that she'd damaged his ego. That was the one part of this whole situation that she hadn't even been able to explain to herself. Why had she held Eddie at a distance for so long and yet ended up half-naked on the table with Prince Casper within thirty minutes of meeting him? 'Eddie, I really don't—'

'You really don't *what*?' He was shouting now, his features contorted with rage as he paced across Nicky's wooden floor. 'You really don't know why you slept with him? Well I'll tell you, shall I? *You slept with him because he's a bloody prince!*'

'No—'

'And you've really hit the jackpot, haven't you?' He gave a bitter laugh. 'No wonder you weren't excited about my Porsche. I suppose he drives a bloody Ferrari, does he?'

Holly blinked. 'I have no idea what he drives, Eddie, but—'

'But it's enough to know you're getting a prince and a palace!'

'That isn't true. I haven't even decided what to do yet.'

'You mean you haven't decided how to make the most money out of the opportunity.' Eddie strode towards the door of her flat, scooping up the flowers on the way. 'I'm taking these with me. You don't deserve them. And you don't deserve *me*. Good luck in your new life.'

Holly winced as the flowers bashed against the door frame and flinched as he slammed the door.

A horrible silence descended on the flat.

A few forlorn rose petals lingered on the floor like drops of blood, and her finger stung from the sharp thorn.

She felt numb with shock. Awful. And guilty, because it was true that she'd shared something with the prince that she hadn't shared with Eddie.

And she didn't understand that.

She didn't understand any of it.

Two weeks ago she would have relished the idea of getting back together with Eddie.

Now she was just relieved that he'd gone.

Sinking onto Nicky's sofa, she tried to think clearly and logically.

There was no need to panic.

No one would be able to guess she was pregnant for at least four months.

She had time to work out a plan.

Flanked by four bodyguards, gripping a newspaper like a weapon, Casper hammered on the door of the fourth-floor flat.

'You didn't have to come here in person, Your Highness.' Emilio glanced up and down the street. 'We could have had her brought to you.'

'I didn't want to wait that long,' Casper growled. In the past few hours he'd discovered that he was, after all, still capable of emotion. Boiling, seething anger. Anger towards her, but mostly at himself, for allowing himself to be put in this position. What had happened to his skills of risk assessment? Since when had the sight of a delicious female body caused him to abandon caution and reason? Women had been throwing themselves in his path since he'd started shaving, but never before had he acted with such lamentable lack of restraint.

She'd set a trap and he'd walked right into it.

'I *know* she's in there. Get this door open.'

Before his security team could act, the door opened and she stood there, looking at him.

Prepared to let loose the full force of his anger, Casper stilled, diverted from his mission by her captivating green eyes.

Holly.

He knew her name now.

She was dressed in an oversized, pale pink tee-shirt with a large embroidered polar bear on the front. Her hair tumbled loose over her shoulders and her feet were bare. It was obvious that she'd been in bed, and she looked at him with shining eyes, apparently thrilled to see him. 'Your Highness?'

She looked impossibly young, fresh and naïve and Casper wondered again what had possessed him to get involved with someone like her.

She had trouble written across her forehead.

And then she smiled, and for a few seconds he forgot everything except the warmth of that smile. The anger retreated inside him, and the only thing in his head was a clear memory of her long legs wrapped around his waist. Casper gritted his teeth, rejecting the surge of lust, furious with himself, and at the same time slightly perplexed because he'd never in his life felt sexual desire for a woman dressed in what looked like a child's tee-shirt.

This whole scenario was *not* turning out the way he'd expected.

How could he still feel raw lust for someone who'd capsized his life like a boat in a storm? And why was she staring at him as if they were acting out the final scenes of a romantic movie? After the stunt she'd pulled, he'd expected hard-nosed negotiation.

'I see you didn't bother dressing for my visit.' Ignoring the flash of hurt in her eyes, he strode into the tiny flat without invitation, leaving his security team to ensure their privacy.

'Well, obviously I had no idea that you'd be coming.' She tugged self-consciously at the hem of her tee-shirt. 'It's been well over two weeks.'

Casper assessed the apartment in a single glance, taking in the rumpled sleeping bag on the sofa. *So this was where she'd been hiding.* 'I have a degree in maths. I know exactly how long it's been.'

Her eyes widened in admiration. 'You're good at maths? I always envy people who are good with numbers. Maths was never really my thing.' Colour shaded her cheeks. 'But I always had pretty good marks in English. I think I'm more of a creative person.'

At a loss to understand how the conversation had turned to school reports, Casper refocused his mind, the gravity of the situation bearing down on him. 'Do you have any idea what you've done?'

Biting her lip, she looked away for a few seconds, then met his gaze again. 'You're talking about the fact I kissed you in front of the window, aren't you?' Her glance was apologetic. 'It's probably a waste of time saying this, but I really *am* sorry. I honestly had no idea how much trouble that would cause. You have to remember I'm not used to the press. I don't know how they operate.'

'But you're learning fast.' Her attempt at innocence simply fed his irritation. He would have had more respect for her if she'd simply admitted what she'd done.

But no confession was forthcoming. Instead she gave a tentative smile. 'Well, I've been amazed by how persistent they are, if that's what you're saying. That newspaper you're holding—' she glanced at it warily '—is there another story today? I don't know how you stand it. Do you eventually just get used to it?'

Her friendliness was as unexpected as it was inappropriate, and Casper wondered what on earth she thought she was doing. Did she really think she could act the way she had and still enjoy civilised conversation?

The newspaper still in his hand, he strolled to the window of the flat and looked down into the street. How long did they have? By rights the press should already have found them. 'I've had people looking for you.'

'Really?' Her face brightened slightly, as if he'd just delivered good news. 'I sort of assumed— Well, I thought you'd forgotten about me.'

'It would be hard to forget about you,' he bit out, 'Given that your name has been in the press every day for the past fortnight.'

'Oh.' There was a faint colour in her cheeks, and disappointment flickered in her eyes, as if she'd been hoping for a different reason. 'The publicity is awful, isn't it? That's why I'm not at my flat. I didn't *want* them to find me.'

'Of course you didn't. That would have ruined everything, wouldn't it?' He waited for her to crumble and confess, but instead she looked confused.

'You sound *really* angry. I don't really blame you, although to be honest I thought you'd be used to all the attention by now. D-do you want to sit down or something, sir?' Stammering nervously, she swept the sleeping bag from the sofa, along with a jumper, an empty box of tissues and a pair of sheer black stockings that could have come straight from the pages of an erotic magazine. Bending over revealed another few inches of her impossibly long legs, and Casper's body heated to a level entirely inconsistent with a cold February day in London.

'I don't want to sit down,' he said thickly, appalled to discover that despite her sins all he really wanted to do was spread her flat and re-enact their last encounter.

Her gaze clashed with his and everything she was holding tumbled onto the floor. 'C—can I get you a drink? Coffee? It's just instant—nothing fancy—' Her voice was husky and laced with overtones that suggested coffee was the last thing on her mind. Colour darkened her cheeks and she dragged her gaze from his, clearly attempting to deny the chemistry that had shifted the temperature of the room from Siberian to scorching.

'Nothing.'

'No. I don't suppose there's much here that would interest you.' She tugged at the tee-shirt again. 'Sorry—this whole situation is a bit surreal. To be honest, I can't believe you're here. I mean, you're a prince and I'm—'

'Pinching yourself?'

'It is weird,' she confided nervously. 'And a bit awkward, I suppose.'

'Awkward?' Shocked out of his contemplation of her mouth by her inappropriate choice of adjective, Casper turned on her. 'We've gone way beyond *awkward*.' His tone was savage, and he saw her take several steps backwards. 'What were you thinking? What was going on in that manipulative female brain of yours? Was it all about making a quick profit? Or did you have an even more ambitious objective?'

The sudden loss of colour from her face made the delicate freckles on her nose seem more pronounced. 'Sorry?'

Casper slammed the newspaper front-page up onto the coffee table. 'I hope you don't live to regret what you've done.'

He watched as she scanned the headline, her soft, pink lips moving silently as she read: *Prince's Baby Bliss*. Then her eyes flew to his in startled horror. 'Oh, no.'

'Is it true?' The expression on her face killed any hope that the press had been fabricating the story to increase their circulation figures. 'You're pregnant?'

'Oh my God—how can they have found out? How can they possibly know?'

'*Is it true?*' His thunderous demand made her flinch.

'Yes, it's true!' Covering her face with her hands,

she plopped onto the sofa. 'But this isn't how— I mean, I haven't even got my head round it myself.' Her hands dropped. 'How did they find out?'

'They rely on greedy people willing to sell sleaze.' The bite in his tone seemed to penetrate her shock, and she wrapped her arms around her waist in a gesture of self-protection.

'I take it from that remark that you think I told them. And I can see this looks bad, but—' She broke off, her voice hoarse. 'It wasn't me. Honestly. I haven't spoken to the press. Not once.'

'Then how do you explain the fact that the story is plastered over the front pages of every European newspaper? The palace press-office was inundated with calls yesterday from journalists wanting a comment on the happy news that I am at last to be a father.' He frowned slightly, disconcerted by her extreme pallor. 'You're very pale.'

'And that's surprising? Have you *read* that thing?' Her voice rose. 'It's all right for you. You're used to this. Your face is always on the front of newspapers, but this is all new to me, and I hate it! My life doesn't feel like my own any more. *Everyone* is talking about me.'

'That's the usual consequence of selling your story to a national newspaper.'

But she didn't appear to have heard him. Her eyes were fixed on the newspaper as though he'd introduced a deadly snake into her flat.

'It must have been Eddie,' she whispered, her lips

barely moving. 'He knew about the baby. He's the only one who could have done this.'

'You disgust me.' Casper didn't bother softening his tone, and shock flared in her green eyes.

'*I* disgust *you*?' She couldn't have looked more devastated if he'd told her that a much-loved pet had died. 'But you—I mean, we—'

'We had sex.' Casper delivered the words with icy cool, devoid of sympathy as yet another layer of colour fled from her cheeks. 'And you used that to your advantage.'

'Wait a minute—just slow down. How can any of this be to my advantage?' Gingerly she reached for the newspaper and scanned the story. Then she dropped it as though she'd been burned. 'This is *awful*. They know *everything*. Really private stuff, like my dad leaving home when I was seven and the fact I was taken into care, stuff I don't talk about.' Her voice broke. 'My whole life is laid out on the front page for everyone to read. And it's just *horrible*.' Her distress appeared to be genuine and Casper felt a flicker of exasperation.

'What exactly did you think would happen? That they'd only print nice stories about you? Nice stories don't sell newspapers.'

'*I didn't tell them!*' She rose to her feet, her tousled hair spilling over her shoulders. 'It *must* have been Eddie.'

'And what was his excuse? He didn't feel ready for fatherhood? Was he only too eager to shift the responsibility onto some other guy?'

Puzzled, she stared at him for a moment, and then her mouth fell open. 'This isn't Eddie's baby, if that's what you're implying!'

'Really?' Casper raised an eyebrow in sardonic appraisal. 'Then you have been busy. Exactly how many men were you sleeping with a few weeks ago? Or can't you remember?'

Hot colour poured into her cheeks, but this time it was anger, not embarrassment. 'You!' Her voice shook with emotion and her eyes were fierce. 'You're the only man I was sleeping with. The only man I've *ever* slept with. And you know it.'

Casper remembered that shockingly intense and intimate moment when he'd been *sure* she was a virgin. Then he reviewed the facts. 'At the time I really fell for that one. But virgins don't have hot, frantic sex with a guy within moments of meeting him, *tesoro*. Apart from that major miscalculation on your part, you were pretty convincing.'

She lifted her hands to her burning face. 'That was the first time I'd ever—'

'Fleeced a billionaire prince?' Helpfully, Casper finished her sentence, and her eyes widened.

'You think I set some sort of trap for you? You think I *faked* being a virgin? For heaven's sake— what sort of women do you mix with?'

Not wanting to dwell on that subject, Casper watched her with cool disdain. 'I know this isn't my baby,' he said flatly. 'It isn't possible.'

'You mean because it was just the once.' She sank back onto the sofa, stumbling over the words.

'I know it's unlikely, but that's what's happened. And you might be a prince, but that doesn't give you the right to speak to me as though I'm—' Unsure of herself, her eyes slid to the door, as if she were worried the security guards might arrest her for treason.

'What are you, Holly? What's the correct name for a woman who sleeps with a guy for money?'

Her body was trembling. 'I haven't asked you for money.'

'I'm sure what you earned from the newspapers will keep you and *Eddie* going for a while. What did you have planned—monthly bulletins to keep the income going? *Now* I understand why you thanked me.'

'Th—thanked you?'

'As you kissed me in the window.' His mouth curved into a cynical smile. 'You thanked me for what I'd given you.'

'But that was—' She broke off and gave a little shake of her head. 'I was feeling *really* low that day. The reason you walked over to me in the first place was because I was crying. And I thanked you because you made me feel good about myself. Nothing else. Up to that point in my life, I knew nothing about the way the media worked.'

'You expect me to believe that it's coincidence that you've been in hiding for over two weeks? You were holding out for the big one. The exclusive to end all exclusives.' He saw panic in her eyes and felt a flash of satisfaction. 'I don't think you have any idea what you've done.'

'What *I've* done? You were there, too! You were

part of this, and I think you're being *totally* unfair!'
Her hands were clasped by her sides, her fingers
opening and closing nervously. 'I'm having *your*
baby. Frankly, that in itself is enough to make me
feel a bit wobbly, without you standing there accusing me of being a—a—' She choked on the word.
'And, as if that isn't bad enough, you're telling me
you don't believe it's yours!'

'You want to know what I think?' His tone was
the same temperature as his heart—icy cold. 'I think
you were already pregnant when you turned on the
tears and had sex with me on my table. That's why
you were crying. I think you were panicking about
how you'd cope with a baby on a waitress's salary.
And you saw me as a lucrative solution. All you had
to do was pretend to be a virgin, and then I wouldn't
argue a paternity claim.'

'That's all rubbish! I had sex with you because—'
She broke off and gave a hysterical laugh. 'I don't
know why I had sex with you! Frankly the whole
episode was pretty shocking.'

Their eyes collided, and shared memories of that
moment passed between them like a shaft of electricity.

His eyes dropped to her wide, lush mouth and he
found himself remembering how she'd tasted and
felt. Even though he now realised that she couldn't
possibly have been a virgin, he still wanted her with
almost indecent desperation.

'*Stop* looking at me like that,' she whispered, and
Casper gave a twisted smile, acknowledging the

chemistry that held them both fast. Invisible chains, drawing them together like prisoners doomed to the same fate.

'You should be pleased I'm looking at you like that,' he drawled softly, 'Because good sex is probably the only thing we have going for us.'

Even as his mind was withdrawing, his hands wanted to reach out and haul her hard against him. He saw her eyes darken to deep emerald, saw her throat move as she murmured a denial.

'I honestly don't know what's going on here,' she muttered. 'But I think you'd better leave.'

Somehow her continuing claim at innocence made the whole episode all the more distasteful, and the face of another woman flashed into his brain—a woman so captivating that he'd been blind to everything except her extraordinary beauty. 'What sort of heartless bitch would lie about the identity of her baby's father?' Ruthlessly he pushed the memories down, his anger trebling. 'Don't you have a conscience?' His words sucked the last of the colour from her cheeks.

'Get out!' Her voice sounded strange. High pitched. Robotic. 'I don't care if you're a prince, just get out!' Her legs were shaking and her face was as white as an Arctic snowfield. 'I was *so* pleased to see you. That day when you comforted me when I was upset—I thought you were a really nice, decent person. A bit scary, perhaps, but basically nice. When I opened the door and saw you standing there I actually thought you'd come to see if I was OK—can you believe that? And now I feel like a complete fool. Because you weren't thinking about me. You were thinking about yourself. So just go! Go back to your palace, or your castle, or wherever it is you live.' The wave of her hand suggested she didn't care where he lived. 'And do whatever it is you want to do.'

'You've robbed me of that option.'

'Why? Even if the world does think I'm having your baby, *so what*? Don't tell me you're worried about your reputation. You're the playboy prince.' There was hurt in her voice, that same voice that only moments earlier had been soft and gentle. 'Since when has reputation mattered to you? When you have sex with a woman, everyone just smiles and says what a stud you are. I'm sure the fact that you've fathered a child will gain you some major testosterone points. Walk away, Your Highness. Isn't that what you usually do?'

'You just don't get it, do you?' His voice was thickened and raw. 'You have no idea what you've done.'

What exactly *had* she done?

Appalled, Holly stared at him.

The anger in his face was real enough. It was clear that he genuinely believed that he couldn't be the father of her baby. And her only proof was the fact that she'd been a virgin.

But he didn't believe her, did he?

And could she blame him for that? It was true that she hadn't behaved like a virgin. The entire encounter had been one long burst of explosive chemistry.

It had been the only time in her life that she'd been out of control.

And that chemistry was back in the room, racking up the tension between them to intolerable levels, the electricity sparking between them like a live cable. His gaze dropped to her lips and she saw in his eyes that his mind was in exactly the same place as hers.

It was like a chain reaction. His glance, her heartbeat, harsh breathing—*her or him?*—and tension— tension like she'd never experienced before.

Streaks of colour accentuated his aristocratic cheekbones and he stepped towards her at exactly the same moment she moved towards him. The attraction was so fierce and frantic that when she heard a ringing sound she actually wondered whether an alarm had gone off.

Then she realised that it was the phone.

Hauling his gaze from hers, Casper inhaled sharply. '*Don't* answer that.'

Still reeling from the explosion of sexual excitement, Holly doubted she'd be capable of answering it even if she'd wanted to. Her legs were trembling and the rhythm of her breathing was all wrong.

She watched dizzily as he crossed the room and lifted a bunch of papers from the printer.

Mouth grim, shoulders tense, he leafed through them and then lifted his gaze to hers. 'What were you doing? Profiling your target?'

Having completely forgotten that she'd actually printed out some of the sheets on him, including a particularly flattering picture, Holly suddenly wished she could sink through the floor. 'I—I was looking you up.' What else could she say? She could hardly deny it, given that he was holding the evidence of her transgression in his hands.

'Of course you were.' He gave a derisive smile. 'I'm sure you wanted to know just how well you'd done. So, now we've cleared that up, let's drop the pretence of innocence, shall we?'

'OK, so I'm human!' Her face scarlet, her knees trembling, Holly ran damp palms over her tee-shirt, wishing she could go and change into something else. He looked like something out of a glossy magazine, and she was dressed in her most comfortable tee-shirt that dated back at least six years. 'I admit that I wanted to find out stuff about you. You were my first lover.'

'So you're sticking to that story.' He dropped the papers back onto the desk and Holly lifted her chin.

'It's *not* a story. It's the truth.'

'I just hope you don't regret what you've done when you have two hundred camera lenses trained on your face and the world's press yelling questions at you.'

She shrank at the thought. 'That isn't going to happen.'

'Let me tell you something about the life you've chosen, Holly.' Tall and powerfully built, he looked as out of place in her flat as a thoroughbred racehorse in a donkey derby. From the stylish trousers and long cashmere coat, to the look of cool confidence on his impossibly handsome face, everything about him shrieked of enormous wealth and privilege. 'Everywhere you go there will be a photographer stalking you, and most of the time you won't even know they're there until you see the picture next day. Everyone is going to want a piece of you, and that means you can no longer have friends, because even friends have their price and you'll never know who you can trust.'

'I don't need to hear this—'

'Yes, you do. You won't be able to smile without someone demanding to know why you're happy and you won't be able to frown without someone saying that you're suffering from depression and about to be admitted to a clinic.' He hammered home the facts with lethal precision. 'You'll either be too thin or too fat—'

'Too fat, *obviously*.' Heart pounding, Holly sank down onto the sofa. 'Enough. You can stop now. I get the picture.'

'I'm describing your new life, Holly. The life you've chosen.'

There was a tense, electric silence and she licked her lips nervously. 'What are you saying?'

'You have made sure that the whole world believes that this is my baby. And, as a result, the whole world is now waiting for me to take appropriate action.'

Pacing back over to the window, he stared down into the street.

Holly had a sudden sick feeling in her stomach. 'A—appropriate action? What do you mean?'

There was a deathly silence and then he turned,

his eyes empty of emotion. 'You're going to marry me, Holly.' The savage bite in his tone was a perfect match for the chill in his eyes. 'And you may think that I've just made your wildest dreams come true, but I can assure you that you're about to embark on your worst nightmare.'

Chapter 4

'So when do you think he'll be back?' Holly paced across the priceless rug in the Georgian manor house. 'I mean, he's been gone for two weeks, Emilio! I haven't even had a chance to talk to him since that day at the flat.' *The day he'd announced that she was going to marry him.* 'Not that this house isn't fabulous and luxurious and all that—but he virtually kidnapped me!'

'On the contrary, His Highness was merely concerned for your safety,' Emilio said gently. 'The press had discovered where you were and the situation was about to turn extremely ugly. It was imperative that we extracted you from there as fast as possible.'

Remembering the crowd of reporters that had suddenly converged on Nicky's flat, and the slick security operation that had ensured their escape, Holly rubbed her fingers over her forehead. 'Yes, all right, I accept that, but that doesn't explain why he hasn't been in touch. When is he planning to come back? We need to *talk*.'

There was so much she needed to say to him.

When she'd opened the door to the flat and seen the prince standing there, her first reaction had been one of pure joy. For a crazy moment she'd actually thought that he was there because he'd spent the past two weeks thinking about her and decided that he needed to see her again. Her mind had raced forward, imagining all sorts of unrealistic scenarios that she was now too embarrassed to even recall. Her crazy, stupid brain had actually started to believe that extraordinary things *could* happen to someone ordinary like her.

And then he'd strode into her flat like a Roman conqueror neutralising the enemy.

Remembering everything he'd said to her, she felt a rush of misery.

He didn't believe it was his baby and the injustice of that still stung. True, she wasn't exactly proud of the way she'd behaved, but it seemed he'd conveniently forgotten his own role in the affair.

And as for his proposal of marriage—well, that unexpected twist had more than kept her mind occupied over the past two weeks.

Had he meant it? *Was he serious?* And, if he was serious, what was her response going to be?

It was the most difficult decision she'd ever had

to make, and the arguments for and against had gone round and round in her head like a fairground carousel. Marrying him meant being with a man who didn't know her or trust her, but *not* marrying him meant denying her baby a father.

And that was the one thing she'd promised herself would never happen to any child of hers.

Reminding herself of that fact, Holly straightened her shoulders and stared across the beautifully landscaped gardens that surrounded the manor.

Their baby was *not* going to grow up thinking that his father had abandoned him. She swallowed down the lump that sprang into her throat. *Their baby was not going to be the only child in school not making a Father's Day card.*

Which meant that her answer had to be yes, regardless of everything else.

What else mattered? Hopefully over time the prince would realise how wrong he had been about her, and once the baby was born it would be a simple matter to prove paternity. Perhaps, then, their relationship could develop.

Realising that Emilio was still watching her, she felt a squeeze of guilt. 'I'm sorry. I'm being really selfish. Is there any news about your little boy? Have you phoned the hospital this morning?'

Remembering just how taciturn and uncommunicative the prince's Head of Security had been when they'd first met, she was relieved that he'd responded to her attempts to be friendly.

'His temperature is down,' he told her. 'And he's

responding to the antibiotics, although they're still not sure what it was.'

'Your poor wife must be so tired. And little Tomasso must be missing you. I remember having chicken pox just after—' *Just after her father had left.* The feelings of abandonment were as fresh as ever and Holly walked across to him and touched his arm. 'Go home, Emilio,' she urged. 'Your wife would like the support and your little boy would dearly love to see his daddy.'

'That's out of the question, madam.'

'Why? I'm not going anywhere. I feel really guilty that you're stuck here with me. If it weren't for me, you'd be back home in Santallia.'

Emilio cleared his throat. 'If I may say so, your company has been a pleasure, madam. And you've been a great comfort since Tomasso was ill. I'll never forget your kindness that first night when he was first taken into hospital and you stayed up and kept me company.'

'I've never been thrashed so many times at poker in my life. It's a good job I don't have any money to lose,' Holly said lightly. 'The moment the prince turns up, you're going home.'

But what if he didn't turn up?

Perhaps he didn't want to marry her any more.

Perhaps he'd changed his mind.

Or perhaps he'd just imprisoned her here, away from the press, until the story died down? After all, he believed that she'd talked to the press. Was he keeping her here just to ensure her silence?

Her thoughts in turmoil, Holly spent the rest of the morning on the computer in the wood-panelled study that overlooked the ornamental lake. Resisting the temptation to do another trawl of the Internet for mentions of Prince Casper, she concentrated on what she was doing and then wandered down to the kitchen to eat lunch with the head chef and other members of the prince's household staff.

'Something smells delicious, Pietro.' Loving the cosy atmosphere of the kitchen, she warmed her hands on the Aga. Naturally chatty by nature, and delighted to find herself suddenly part of this close community, Holly had lost no time in getting to know everyone living and working in the historic manor house.

'It's a pleasure to cook for someone who enjoys her food, madam,' the chef said, smiling warmly as he gestured towards some pastries cooling on a wire rack. 'Try one and give me your verdict. You're eating for two, remember.'

'Well, I'd rather not be the size of two. I'm not sure I'm meant to be developing cravings this early, but already I don't think I can live without your *pollo alla limone*.' Holly still felt slightly self-conscious that everyone clearly felt so possessive about her baby. She bit into a pastry and moaned with genuine appreciation. 'Oh, please—this is *sublime*. Truly, Pietro. I've never tasted anything this good in my life before. What is it?'

Pietro blossomed. 'Goat's cheese, with a secret

combination of herbs—' He broke off as Emilio entered the room and Holly smiled.

'Emilio, thank goodness.' She took another nibble of pastry. 'You're just in time to stop me eating the lot by myself.'

'Miss Phillips.' The bodyguard's eyes were misted, and Holly dropped the pastry, alarmed to see this controlled man so close to the edge.

'What? What? Has something happened? Did the hospital ring?'

'How can I ever thank you? You are—' Emilio's voice was gruff and he cleared his throat. 'A very special person. My wife called—she just received a delivery of beautiful toys. How you managed to arrange that so quickly I have no idea. Tomasso is thrilled.'

'He liked his parcel?' Relieved that nothing awful had happened, Holly retrieved the pastry and threw Pietro an apologetic glance. 'Sorry. Slight overreaction there on my part. Just in case you can't tell, I briefly considered drama as a career. So he liked the toys? I couldn't decide between the fire engine and the police car.'

'So you bought both.' Emilio shook his head. 'It was unbelievably generous of you, madam.'

'It was the least I could do given I'm the reason you're not with him.' Holly frowned and glanced towards the window. 'What's that noise? Are we being invaded?'

Still clutching the spoon, Pietro peered over her shoulder. 'It's a helicopter, madam.' His cheerful smile faded and he straightened his chef's whites and looked nervously at Emilio. 'His Royal Highness has returned.'

Chilled by the wind, and battling with a simmering frustration that two weeks of self-imposed absence hadn't cured, Casper sprang from the helicopter and strode towards the house.

Although he'd managed to put several countries and a stretch of water between them, he'd failed to wipe Holly from his thoughts. Even the combined demands of complex state business and the successful conclusion to negotiations guaranteeing billions of dollars of foreign investment hadn't succeeded in pressing the Stop button on the non-stop erotic fantasy that had dominated his mind since that day at the rugby.

Even while part of him was angry with her for her ruthless manipulation, another part of his mind was thinking about her incredible legs. He knew she was a liar, but what really stayed in his head was her enticing smile and the taste of her mouth.

And that was fine. Because her manipulation had given him a solution to his problem.

As he approached the house, two uniformed soldiers that he didn't recognise opened the doors for him, backs ramrod straight, eyes forward.

Casper stopped. '*Where* is Emilio?'

One of them cleared his throat. 'I believe he is in the kitchen, Your Highness.'

'The *kitchen*?' Casper approached a nervous footman. 'Since when did my kitchen represent a major security risk?'

'I believe he is with Miss Phillips and the rest of the staff, sir.'

Having personally delivered the order that Emilio should watch her, Casper relaxed a fraction. Contemplating the difficult two weeks Holly must have had with his battle-hardened security chief, he almost smiled. Emilio had been known to drive soldiers to tears, but he felt no sympathy for her. After all, *she* was the one who had decided to name him as the father of her unborn baby. She deserved everything she had coming to her.

Striding towards the kitchen with that thought uppermost in his mind, he pushed open the door, astonished to hear the rare sound of Emilio's laughter, and even more surprised to see his usually reserved Head of Security straighten a clasp in Holly's vibrant curls in an unmistakeably affectionate manner.

Holly was smiling gratefully and Casper felt like an interloper, intruding on a private moment. Experiencing a wild surge of quite inexplicable anger, he stood in the doorway.

The rest of the staff were eating and chatting, and Emilio was the first to notice him. 'Your Highness.' Evidently shocked at seeing the prince in the kitchen, he stiffened respectfully. 'I was just about to come upstairs and meet you.'

'But you had other things to distract you,' Casper observed tightly, strolling into the kitchen and taking in the empty plates and the smell of baking in a single, sweeping glance.

Without waiting for him to issue the order, the various members of his household staff rose to their feet and hastily left the room.

Pietro hesitated and then he, too, melted away without being asked.

Only Emilio didn't move.

Casper slowly undid the buttons on his long coat. 'I'm sure you have many demands on your time, Emilio,' he said softly, but the bodyguard stood still.

'My priority is protecting Miss Phillips, sir.'

'That's true.' Casper removed his coat and dropped it over the back of the nearest chair. 'But not,' he said gently, 'from me.'

Emilio hesitated and glanced at Holly. 'You have the alarm I gave you, madam, should you need me for anything.'

There was no missing the affection in Holly's smile. 'I'll be fine, Emilio, but thank you.'

Watching this interchange with speechless incredulity, Casper was engulfed by a wave of anger so violent that it shook him.

Against his will he was transported back eight years, and suddenly he was seeing another woman smiling at another man.

Pain cut through the red mist of his anger, and he glanced down at his hand and realised that he was gripping the back of the chair so tightly his knuckles were white.

'Your Highness?' Holly's voice penetrated his brain. 'Are you all right?'

Locking down his thoughts with ruthless focus, Casper transferred his gaze to Holly, but the bitter taste of betrayal remained. 'Emilio is a married man. *Do you have no sense of decency?*'

'I— I'm sorry?'

'I've no doubt his wife and child will be sorry, too.'

Her expression changed from concern to anger. 'How dare you? How dare you turn everything beautiful into something sordid. Emilio and I are friends—nothing more.' She lifted a hand to her head. 'Oh God, I can't believe you'd even think— *what is the matter with you?* It's almost as if you believe the worst of people so that you can't be disappointed.'

Was that what he did? Stunned by that accusation, Casper felt as cold as marble. 'Despite a short acquaintance, Emilio would clearly die for you.'

'We've been living in each other's pockets for two weeks—what did you expect? On second thoughts, don't answer that.' She took a deep breath. 'Look, maybe you don't know me well enough to know *I* wouldn't do that, but you know Emilio. He was telling me that he's been with you for twenty years! How could you think that of someone so close to you?'

Because he knew only too well that it was the people closest to you who were capable of the greatest betrayal. And causing the greatest pain.

Casper released his grip on the chair and flexed his bloodless fingers.

'Whatever the nature of your relationship, Emilio is in charge of my security. He can't perform his duties effectively if he's flirting in the kitchen.'

'Nor can he perform his duties on an empty stomach. We were eating lunch, not flirting. Or aren't your staff allowed to eat lunch?'

'You're not a member of my staff.' Casper glanced round the homely kitchen. 'And there is a formal dining-room upstairs for your use.'

'It's as big as a barn, and I don't want to eat on my own. Where's the fun in that?' Her expression made it clear that she thought it should have been obvious that eating alone was a stupid idea. 'Sorry, but sitting alone at one end of a vast table is a bit sad. I prefer the company of real people, not paintings.'

'So you've been distracting Emilio.'

'Actually, yes. I've been trying to take his mind off his worries.' Her shoulders stiffened defensively. 'Did *you* know that his little boy has been taken into hospital? And he's been stuck here with me, fretting himself to death while—'

The anger drained from Casper. 'His son is ill?'

'Yes, and he—'

'What is wrong with the child?'

'Well, it started with a very high temperature. I don't think his wife was too worried at that point, so she gave him the usual stuff but nothing seemed to bring his temperature down. Then she was putting him to bed when—'

'*What is wrong with the child?*' Impatient for the facts, Casper sliced through her chatter, and she gave him a hurt look.

'I'm *trying* to tell you! You're the one who keeps interrupting.'

Attempting to control his temper, Casper inhaled deeply. 'Summarise.'

'I *was* summarising.' Affronted, she glared at him. 'So, his temperature went up and up and then he had a fit, which apparently can be normal for a toddler because they're hopeless at controlling their temperature, and so they took him in and did some tests and—'

'That isn't a summary, it's a three-act play!' Exasperated, Casper strode across to her and placed a finger over her mouth. 'Stop talking for one minute and answer my question in no more than three words—*what is wrong with Emilio's son?*'

Her lips were soft against his finger and he felt the warmth of her breath as she parted her lips to respond.

'Virus,' she muttered, and Casper withdrew his hand as if he'd been scalded, taken aback by the rush of sexual heat that engulfed him. The urge to take possession of her luscious mouth was so strong that he took a step backwards.

'And is his condition improving?'

'Yes, but—'

'That's all I need to know.' Needing space, Casper turned and strode purposefully towards the door, but she hurtled after him and caught his arm.

'No! No, it isn't all you need to know! "Virus" and "improving" doesn't give you a clue about what it's been like for poor Emilio! Those are just facts, but it's the feelings that matter.' She waved an arm. 'He was stuck here with me while they were doing all these tests, and he was worried sick and—' She broke off, clearly unsettled by his silence. 'Don't you *care*? You're *so* cold! Y-you just stand there looking at me, not saying anything. What do you think it's been like for Emilio being stuck here with me while his little boy is ill?'

Casper scanned her flushed cheeks and lifted an eyebrow in sardonic mockery. 'Noisy?'

Her hand fell from his arm. 'I'm only talking too much because you make me nervous.'

Only both of them knew that there was more than nerves shimmering between them.

It was there in her eyes—awareness, excitement, longing.

Distancing himself, Casper yanked open the door. 'Then I'll give you a moment to collect yourself.' He left the room, issued a set of instructions to a waiting security-guard, and then returned to the kitchen to find Holly pacing the room in agitation.

She threw him a reproachful look. 'All right, maybe I do talk a lot, but that's just the way I am, and nobody's perfect. And you're the one who left me here without even telling me when you'd be back!' Her chin lifted. 'Did you think I'd sit in silence for two weeks?'

Casper strode over to the large table and poured

himself a glass of water from the jug on the table. 'It was fairly obvious to me from our last meeting that you and silence have never been intimately acquainted.'

'Well, I don't expect you to understand, because you're obviously the strong silent type who uses words like each one costs a fortune, but I like people. I like talking to them.'

And they liked talking to her, if the buzz of conversation around the kitchen table had been anything to go by.

And she knew about Emilio's son.

Casper tried to remember a time when people had been that open with him, and realised that they never had been.

Even before tragedy had befallen the royal family of Santallia, he'd lived a life of privileged isolation. Because of his position, people were rarely open and honest.

And he'd learned the hard way that trust was one gift he couldn't afford to bestow.

Because of his error of judgement, his country had suffered.

And now he had the chance to make amends. *To give the people what they wanted.*

And as for the rest of it—physically the chemistry between them was explosive, and that was all he required.

He drank deeply and then put the glass down, his eyes locking with hers.

Immediately engulfed by a dangerous tension,

Casper tried to analyse what it was about her that he found so irresistibly sexy.

Not her dress sense, that was for sure. Her ancient jeans had a rip in the knees, her pale-pink jumper was obviously an old favourite, and the colour in her cheeks had more to do with the heat coming from the Aga than artful use of make-up.

Accustomed to women who groomed themselves to within an inch of their lives, he found her lack of artifice oddly refreshing.

Her beauty wasn't the result of expensive cosmetics or the hand of a skilled surgeon. Holly was vibrant, passionate and desperately sexy, and all he wanted to do was flatten her to the table and re-enact every sizzling moment of their first meeting.

Exasperated and baffled by the strength of that inappropriate urge, Casper dragged his eyes back to her face. 'Emilio failed to pass on the message that you were to buy a new wardrobe.'

'No. He told me.' She hooked her thumbs into the waistband of her jeans and the movement revealed a tantalising glimpse of smooth, flat stomach. 'I just didn't need anything. What do I need a new wardrobe for? I've spent the mornings helping Ivy and the afternoons helping Jim prune the trees in the orchard.'

'*Who* is Ivy?'

'Your housekeeper. She lost her husband eight months ago and she's been very down, but she has started joining us for lunch, and she's been talking about— Sorry.' She raised a hand in wary apology.

'I forgot you just want facts. OK, facts. I can do that. Ivy. Housekeeper. Depressed. Improving.' She ticked them off her fingers. 'How's that? You're smiling, so I must have done OK.'

Surprised to discover that he was indeed smiling, Casper shook his head slowly. 'Your gift for conversation has clearly given you a great deal of information about my staff.'

'It's important to understand people you work with.'

'When I left you here, my intention was not for you to work alongside the staff.'

'I had to do something with my day. You gave orders that I couldn't leave the premises. I was trapped here.'

'You were brought here for your own safety.'

'Was I?' Her brilliant green eyes glowed bright with scepticism. 'Or was I brought here for *your* safety, so that I couldn't talk to the press?'

'That particular boat has already sailed,' Casper said tightly, his temper flaring at her untimely reminder of just how effectively she'd manipulated the media. 'You're here for your protection.'

'Do you have any idea how weird that sounds?' Holly glanced pointedly at the rip in her jeans. 'I mean, one minute I'm a waitress who no one notices unless they want to complain about their food, and the next I'm someone who needs twenty-four-hour protection.'

'You're carrying the heir to the throne.'

'And that's all that matters?' She tilted her head to

one side, studying his expression. 'You'll put aside your personal feelings for me because of the baby?'

What personal feelings?

Emotion had no place in his life.

On one previous occasion he'd allowed himself to be ruled by emotion and the consequences had been devastating.

As far as he was concerned, his relationship with Holly was a business transaction, nothing more.

Casper stared into her anxious green eyes, wondering why she didn't look more triumphant.

She'd successfully secured a future for herself and her child.

Or was she suddenly realising just how high a price she'd paid for that particular social leap?

'I don't want to discuss this again.' Crushing any future urge on her part to dwell on the unfortunate circumstances of their wedding, Casper strolled forward, realising that he hadn't yet revealed the reason for his return.

'Y-you're a bit crabby. Perhaps you need to eat,' she said helpfully, scooping up a plate from the table. 'Try one of Pietro's pastries. It's a new recipe and they're really delicious.'

'I'm not hungry.' His intention had just been to deliver his orders and then spend the afternoon catching up on official papers. He hadn't expected to be drawn into a discussion.

Nor had he expected an ongoing battle with his libido.

'Just taste them.' Apparently unaware of his reluctance, she broke off a piece of the pastry and lifted it to his lips. 'They're fresh out of the oven. Try.'

Drowning in her subtle floral scent and her smile, Casper's senses reeled and he grasped for control. 'I have things to tell you.'

'Eat first.'

Casper ate the pastry and wished he hadn't, because as his lips touched her fingers again he was immediately plunged into an erotic, sensual world that featured Holly as the leading lady in a scene dominated by scented oils and silk sheets.

She withdrew her hand slowly, her eyes darkening as they both silently acknowledged the dangerous sexual charge that suffused every communication they shared.

'What is it you need to tell me, Your Highness?'

'Casper.'

For the space of a heartbeat, she looked at him and then she gave a twisted smile. 'I don't think so. I'm not comfortable enough with you. Maybe it's just because you've had a long journey, but you're very cold. Intimidating. I feel as though you're going to say "off with her head" any minute.'

'You can't call me Your Highness in the wedding ceremony.'

Shock flared in her eyes. 'I sort of assumed the wedding was off. You haven't *once* phoned me whilst you've been away.'

Casper thought of the number of times he'd reached for the phone before he'd realised what he was doing. 'I had nothing to say.'

Holly lifted her hands and made a sound that was somewhere between a sob and laughter. 'Well, if you had nothing to say to me in two weeks, it doesn't bode well for a lifetime together, does it? But I do have things I want to say to you.' She drew in a breath. 'Starting with your offer of marriage. I've given it a lot of thought.'

'That doesn't surprise me. I expect it's been two weeks of non-stop self-congratulation while you enjoy your new life and reflect on the future.' His cynical observation was met with appalled silence and she stared at him for a moment, her delicate features suddenly pinched and white.

Then the plate slipped from her hands and smashed on the kitchen floor, scattering china and pastry everywhere.

'How *dare* you say that? You have a real gift for saying really horrible things.' Her small hands curled into fists by her sides. *'Have you any idea how hard all of this is for me?* Well, let me tell you what my life has been like since you walked into it!

'First there is that huge picture of me on the screen so the whole world can see the size of my bottom, then the press crawl all over my life, exposing things about me that I haven't even told my closest friends and making me out to be some psycho nutcase. *Then* I discover I'm pregnant, and I was really happy about that until you showed up and told me that you didn't believe it was yours. So basically since I've met you I've been portrayed publicly as a fat, abandoned slut with no morals! How's my new life sounding so far,

Your Highness? Not good—so don't *talk* to me about how I must be congratulating myself because, believe me, my confidence is at an all-time low.' Her breathing rapid, she sucked in several breaths and Casper, who detested emotional scenes, erected barriers faster than a bank being robbed.

'I warned you that—'

'I haven't finished!' She glared at him. 'You think this is an easy decision for me, but it isn't! This is our baby's future we're talking about! And, whatever you may think, I didn't plan this. Which is why I've done nothing but agonise over what to do for the past two weeks. *Obviously* I don't want to be married to a man who can't stand the sight of me, but neither do I want my baby to be without a father. It's been a horrible, *horrible* choice, and frankly I wouldn't wish it on anyone! And if you need that summarised in two words I'd pick "scary" and "sacrifice".'

In the process of formulating an exit strategy, Casper looked at her with raw incredulity. *'Sacrifice?'*

'Yes. Because, although I'm sure having a father is right for our baby, I'm *not* sure that being married to you is right for me. And there's no need to use that tone. I don't care about the prince bit, nor do I care about your castle or your bank account.' Her voice was hoarse. 'But I won't have our child growing up thinking that his father abandoned him. And that's why I'll marry you. By the time he's old enough to understand what is going on, you will have realised how wrong you are about me and given me a big, fat apology. But don't think this is easy for me. I have no wish to marry a man who can't talk about his feelings and doesn't show affection.'

Casper responded to this last declaration with genuine astonishment. 'Affection?' How could she possibly think he'd feel affection for a woman who had good as slapped him with a paternity suit?

She rolled her eyes. 'You see? Even the word makes you nervous, and that says everything, doesn't it? You were quite happy to have hot sex with me, but anything else is completely alien to you.' She covered her face with her hands, and her voice choked. 'Oh, what am I doing? How can we even *think* about getting married when there's nothing between us?'

'We share a very powerful sexual chemistry, or we wouldn't be in this position right now,' Casper responded instantly, and her hands dropped and she gave a disbelieving laugh.

'Well, that's romantic. There's no mistaking your priorities. Summarised in three words, it would be sex, sex, sex.'

'Don't underestimate the importance of sex,' Casper breathed, watching as her lips parted slightly. 'If we're going to be sharing a bed night after night, it helps that I find you attractive.' Surprisingly, his statement appeared to finally silence her.

She stared at him, her eyes wide, her lips slightly parted. Then she rubbed her hands over her jeans in a self-conscious gesture. 'You find me—attractive? Really?'

'*Obviously* your dress sense needs considerable

work,' he said silkily. 'And generally speaking I'm not wild about jeans, although I have to confess that you manage to look good in them. Apart from that, and as long as you don't *ever* wear anything featuring a cartoon once you're officially sleeping in my bed, yes, I'll find you attractive.'

A laugh burst from her throat. 'I can't believe you're telling me how to dress—or that I'm listening.'

'I'm not telling you how to dress. I'm telling you how to keep me interested. It's up to you whether you follow the advice or not.'

'And that's supposed to be enough? A marriage based on sex?' She shook her head slowly. 'It doesn't make sense. I still don't understand why, if you genuinely don't believe this is your baby, you'd be willing to marry me. Instead of facts, why don't you give me feelings?'

He didn't have feelings.

He hadn't allowed himself feelings for eight years.

'Given all the research you did on the royal house of Santallia, I would think you'd be aware of the reasons. I'm the last of the line. I'm expected to produce an heir. To the outside world, it appears that I've done that.'

'You're giving me facts again,' she said softly. 'How do you *feel*, Your Highness?'

Ignoring her question, Casper paced over to the window, his tension levels soaring. 'The people of Santallia are currently in a state of celebration. The moment the story broke on the news, they were making plans for the royal wedding. There will be fireworks and state banquets. Apparently my popularity rating has soared. School children have already been queuing outside the palace with home-made cards and teddies for the baby—little girls with stars in their eyes.' He turned, looking for signs of remorse. 'Are you feeling guilty yet, Holly? Is your conscience pricking you?'

'Teddies?' Instead of retreating in the face of his harsh words, she appeared visibly moved by the picture he'd painted. Her hand slid to her stomach in an instinctively protective gesture, and he saw tears of emotion glisten in her eyes. 'They're that pleased? It *is* wonderful that everyone is longing for you to get married and have a baby. You must be very touched that they care so much.'

'It's because they care so much that we're standing here now.'

Her gaze held his. 'So, if they wanted you to have a baby so badly, and you're so keen to please them, why haven't you done it before? Why haven't you married and given them an heir?' She broke off abruptly and he knew from the guilty flush on her cheeks that her research had included details about his past relationships.

He could almost see her mind working, thinking that she knew what was going on in his.

Fortunately, she didn't have a clue.

No one did. He'd made sure of that.

The truth was safely buried where it could do no harm. *And it was going to stay buried.*

Observing his lack of response, she sighed. 'What's going on in your head? I don't understand you!'

'I don't require you to understand me,' Casper said in a cool tone. 'I just require you to play the part you auditioned for. From now on, you'll just do as you're told. You'll smile when I tell you to smile and you'll walk where I tell you to walk. In return, you'll have more money than you know how to spend, and a lifestyle that most of the world will envy.'

She opened her mouth and closed it again, her face a mask of indecision. 'I don't know. I really don't know.' She stooped and started picking up pieces of broken china, as if she needed to do something with her hands. 'I thought I'd made up my mind, but now I'm not sure. How can I accept your proposal when you *scare* me? You use three words, I use thirty. I've never met anyone so emotionally detached. I—I'm just not comfortable with you.' She put the china carefully on the table.

'*Comfortable?*'

She rubbed her fingers over her forehead, as if her brain was aching and she wanted to soothe it. 'We'll hardly be great parents if I'm bracing myself for conflict every time you enter a room. And then there's the fact that I don't exactly fit the profile of perfect princess.'

'The only thing that matters is that the world thinks you're carrying my child. As far as the people of Santallia are concerned, that makes you the perfect princess.'

'But not *your* perfect princess. You don't seem to care who you marry. Did you love her very much?' She blurted out the question as though she couldn't stop herself, and then gave an apologetic sigh. 'I'm sorry. Perhaps I shouldn't. But you lost your fiancée, Antonia, and it's stupid to pretend that I don't know about it, because everyone knew—'

No one knew.

'Enough!' Stunned that she would dare tread on such dangerous territory, Casper sent her a warning glance, and in that single unsettling moment he had the feeling that she was looking deep inside him.

'I *am* sorry,' she said quietly. 'Because I certainly don't want to hurt you. But I don't see how we're going to have any sort of marriage when you won't let another human being get close. You create this barrier around you. Frankly, how I ever felt relaxed enough with you to have sex, I have no idea. At the moment my insides feel as though I swallowed a knotted rope.' But even as she said the words the tension in the air crackled and snapped, and he saw her chest rise and fall as her breathing quickened.

The sexual chemistry was more powerful than both of them, and Casper wasn't even aware that he'd moved until his hands slid into her hair and he felt her lips parting in response to the explicit demands of his mouth.

Enforced abstinence and sexual denial had simply increased the feverish craving, and he hauled her hard against him, driven by a sensual urgency previously unknown to him.

Her lips were soft and sweet, and the scent and taste of her closed over him, drowning his senses until every rational thought was blown from his brain by a powerful rush of erotic pleasure.

She moaned with desperation, her arms winding round his neck, her body trembling against his as she arched in sensual invitation, her abandoned response a blatant invitation to further intimacy.

In the grip of an almost agonising arousal, Casper closed possessive hands over her hips and lifted her onto the kitchen table. She was pliant and shivering against him, the sensuous movements of her body shamelessly urging him on.

And then the gentle hiss of water boiling on the Aga penetrated the red fog in his mind and he froze, his seeking hands suddenly still as he realised what he was doing.

And where he was doing it.

Another time, another table.

Deploring the lack of control that gripped him whenever he was with this woman, he dragged his mouth from hers with a huge effort of will, and stared down into her dazed, shocked eyes. Her mouth was damp and swollen from his kiss, and she was shaking with the same wild excitement that was driving him.

His usual self-restraint severely challenged by her addictive sexuality, Casper released his grip on her hips and stepped backwards.

'Hopefully that should have satisfied any worries you might have about whether or not you'll be able to relax with me when the time comes.'

She slid off the table, her fingers fastened tightly round the edge for support. 'Your Highness.' Her voice was smoky with passion. 'Casper—'

'We're short on time.' Ruthlessly withdrawing from the softness he saw in her eyes, he glanced at his watch. 'I've flown in a team of people to help you prepare.'

'Prepare for what?' Her eyes dropped to his mouth, and it was obvious that she wasn't really listening to what he was saying—*that her body was still struggling with the electricity that sparked between them.*

'The wedding. We fly to Santallia tonight. We're getting married tomorrow.' He paused, allowing time for his words to sink in. 'And that's not a proposal, Holly. It's an order.'

Chapter 5

The roar of the crowd reached deafening proportions, and the long avenue leading from the cathedral to the palace was a sea of smiling faces and waving flags.

'I can't believe the number of people,' Holly said faintly as she settled herself in the golden carriage. The rings on the third finger of her left hand felt heavy and unfamiliar, and she glanced down in disbelief. 'And I can't believe we're married. You certainly don't hang around, do you? You could have given me a little more warning.'

'Why?'

Why? Only Casper could ask that question, she thought wryly. Fiddling nervously with the enormous diamond ring, she wondered whether there was something wrong with her. Here she was, living a life straight out of the pages of a child's fairy tale, and she would have swapped the lot for some kind words from the man next to her.

Her life was moving ahead too fast for comfort.

Having spent the previous afternoon with a top dress designer who had apparently cleared her schedule to accommodate the prince's request to dress his bride, she'd been transferred by helicopter to the royal flight and then arrived in the Mediterranean principality of Santallia as the sun was setting.

'I loved The Dowager Cottage, by the way.'

'It was built for my great-great grandmother so that she could escape occasionally from the formality of life in the palace. I'm pleased you were comfortable.'

Physically, yes, but mentally…

Unable to sleep, Holly had spent most of the night sitting on the balcony that looked over the sea, thinking about what was to come.

Thinking about Casper.

Hoping she was doing the right thing.

Exhausted from thinking and worrying, she'd eventually sprawled on the bed, only to be woken by an army of dress designers, hairdressers and make-up artists prepared to turn her from gauche waitress into princess. And then she'd been driven through this same cheering crowd to the cathedral that dominated the main square of Santallia Town.

She remembered very little of the actual service— very little except the memory of Casper standing powerful and confident by her side as they exchanged vows. And at that moment she'd been filled with a conviction that she was doing the right thing.

She was giving her baby a father. A stability that she'd never had. *Roots and a family.*

How could that be a mistake?

As the carriage began to move forward down the tree-lined avenue, she glanced at the prince, only to find him studying her intently.

Startlingly handsome in his military uniform, Casper lifted her hand to his lips in an old-fashioned gesture that was greeted with cheers of approval from the crowd. 'The dress is a great improvement on ripped jeans,' he drawled, and she glanced down at herself, fingering the embroidered silk with reverential fingers.

'It's impressive what a top designer can do when required, although I was terrified of tripping over on those steps.' She couldn't take her eyes from the cheering crowd. Everywhere she looked there were smiling faces and waving flags. 'They *really* love you.'

'They're here to see you, not me,' he said dryly, but she remembered what she'd read about him on the internet—about his devotion to his country—and knew it wasn't true.

Although he'd never expected to rule, Prince Casper had stepped into the role, burying his own personal grief in order to bring stability to a country in turmoil.

And they loved him for it.

'Do you ever wish you weren't the prince?' The question left her lips before she could stop it and he gave a faint smile.

'You have a real gift for voicing questions that other people keep as thoughts.' He relaxed in the seat, undaunted by the crowds of well-wishers. 'And the answer is no, I don't wish it. I love my country.'

He loved his country so much that he'd marry a woman he didn't love because the people expected it.

Holly glanced at the sun-baked pavements and then at the perfect blue sky. 'It's beautiful here,' she agreed. 'When I looked out of the window this morning, the first thing I saw was the sea. It felt like being on holiday.'

'You looked very pale during the service.' His eyes lingered on her face. 'You were on your feet for a long time. I was worried that you might keel over.'

'And presumably a prostrate bride wouldn't have done anything for your public image,' she said lightly. 'I was fine.'

'I'm reliably informed that the early weeks of pregnancy are often the most exhausting.'

He'd talked to someone about her pregnancy? Her heart lurched, and it suddenly occurred to her just how little she knew about his life here. Had he been talking to a woman? She was aware that his name had been linked with a number of European beauties. Was he...?

'No,' he drawled. 'I wasn't.'

Her eyes widened. 'I didn't say anything—'

'But you were thinking it,' he said dryly. 'And the

answer is no, my conversation wasn't with a lover. It was with a doctor.'

'Oh.' She blushed scarlet, mortified that her thoughts had been so transparent, but filled with unimaginable relief that he hadn't asked another woman. 'When did you speak to a doctor?'

'While you were at Foxcourt Manor, I interviewed a handful of the top European obstetricians. It's important that you feel comfortable with your doctor. After all, you're not good with detached and cold, are you?' He gave a faint smile as he alluded to their previous conversation, and Holly was so touched that for a moment she forgot the presence of the cheering, waving crowd.

'You did that for me?'

'I don't want you upset.'

'That was incredibly thoughtful.' She wanted to ask whether he'd really done it for her or the baby, but decided that it didn't matter. The fact that he'd noticed that much about her personality was encouraging.

'You're stunning,' he murmured, his gaze lingering on her glossy mouth and dropping to the demure neckline of her dress. 'The perfect bride. And you've coped with the crowd really well. I'm proud of you.'

'Really?' Deciding not to mention the fact that she found *him* far more intimidating than any crowd, Holly relaxed for the first time in what felt like an eternity. She felt drugged by happiness and weak with relief at the change in him.

He was unusually attentive and much more approachable.

Perhaps, she mused silently, he'd finally deduced that the baby must be his.

What other explanation was there for his sudden change of attitude?

'And now you need to fulfil your first duty as royal princess.' He smiled down at her. 'Smile and wave at the crowd. They're expecting it.'

Finding it hard to believe that anyone would care whether she waved at them or not, Holly tentatively raised her hand, and the immediate roar of approval from the crowd made her blink in amazement. 'But I'm just someone ordinary,' she muttered, and the prince's eyes gleamed with wry amusement.

'That's why they love you. You're living proof that fairy-tale endings can happen to ordinary people.'

The last of her insecurities faded and Holly gave a bubble of laughter, her mood lifting still further as she saw the smiles of genuine delight on the faces of the people pressing against the barriers.

Flanked by mounted guards, the carriage moved slowly down the tree-lined avenue, and ahead of her she was surprised to see Emilio's bulky frame.

'But you sent Emilio home.' Puzzled, she glanced at the prince. 'He came to say goodbye to me yesterday, and told me that you'd been brilliant.'

'He insisted on returning this morning.' Casper gave a faint smile. 'On such a huge public occasion he refused to entrust your security to anyone else.'

'Oh, that's so kind.' Incredibly touched, Holly

gave Emilio a wave. 'There do seem to be millions of people. What's this street like on a normal day?'

Casper settled back against the seat. 'The road leads directly to the palace. It's a favourite tourist route. Turn to the right at the bottom, and you reach the sea.'

Holly was still smiling at the crowd when she saw a toddler stumble and fall to the ground, his little body trapped against the metal barriers by the sheer pressure of the crowd. 'Oh no! Stop the coach!' Before Casper could respond, Holly opened the door of the carriage, hitched her white silk dress up round her middle and jumped down into the road.

Oblivious to the havoc she was creating in the security operation, she hurried across to the bawling toddler and the panicking mum. 'Is he all right? Oh my goodness—can everyone move back a bit, please?' Raising her voice and gesturing at the crowd, she breathed a sigh of relief as everyone shifted slightly and she saw the mother safely lift the sobbing child. 'Phew. It's a bit crowded, isn't it? Is he all right? There—don't cry, sweetheart. Have you got a smile for me?' She reached out to the child who immediately stopped crying and stared at her in wonder.

'It's your tiara, Your Royal Highness, it's all sparkly, and he loves everything sparkly.' The woman flushed scarlet. 'We all wanted to get a good view of you, madam.'

Holly noticed a trickle of blood on the child's forehead. 'He's cut his head on the barrier. Does someone have a plaster?'

'Holly.'

Hearing her name, she looked over her shoulder and saw Casper striding towards her, a strange expression on his face. 'Holly, you're giving the security team heart-failure.'

'I'm sorry about that, but do you have a handkerchief or something?' She glanced anxiously back at the toddler who now had his thumb in his mouth.

Casper hesitated and then produced a handkerchief from the pocket of his uniform.

Holly took it and leaned over the barrier to press it gently against the toddler's forehead. 'There. It doesn't look too bad when you look at it closely.' One of the security team produced a plaster and vaulted the barrier to deal with the child, and Holly suddenly realised that the crowd was cheering for Casper.

The prince delivered a charismatic smile and slipped his arm round his bride. 'Next time, don't leave the coach. It isn't safe.'

'It isn't safe for that toddler, either. People are crushing too close to the barriers. What was I supposed to do?' She knew it was foolish to read too much into his comment, but she couldn't help it. Would he warn her not to leave the coach if he didn't care about her?

The cheering intensified, and then there was a yell from the crowd that turned into a chant.

'Kiss her, Prince Casper! *Kiss, kiss, kiss...!*'

Holly blushed scarlet but Casper, clearly as experienced at seducing a crowd as he was women, pulled her gently into his arms and lowered his mouth to hers with his usual cool confidence. Stunned by the unexpected gentleness of that kiss, Holly melted against him, stars exploding in her head and her heart.

Would he kiss her like that if he didn't care?

Surely it was another sign that he finally believed that she must be telling the truth? *That he'd been wrong about her.*

The crowd gave a collective sigh of approval, and when Casper finally lifted his head there was another enormous roar of approval.

'Now you've charmed the crowd, we need to go back to the coach.' Amusement in his eyes, he tucked her hand into his arm. 'And you need to stop jumping out of carriages and behave with some decorum. Not only are you now a princess, but you're a pregnant princess.'

'I know, but—' She glanced towards the crowd. 'Some of these people have been standing outside all night, even the children—do we have to go in the carriage? Couldn't we just walk? We could chat to people along the way.'

Casper's dark brows locked in a disapproving frown. 'It would be a major security risk.'

'I *know* you don't care about that. When you're in public you always walk. I read that you have a constant argument with your bodyguards and the security services.' She bit her lip, suddenly wishing she hadn't reminded him of her internet moment, but he simply smiled and took her hand firmly in his.

'In this instance I was thinking of *your* safety. Don't you find the crowds daunting?'

'I think it's lovely that they've made the effort to come and see me get married,' Holly confessed. Spying two small girls holding a bunch of flowers that they obviously picked themselves, she pushed her elaborate bouquet towards an astonished Casper and hurried across. 'Are those for me? They're so pretty. Are they from your garden?' She talked to the girls, then to their mother, shook what felt like a million hands, and slowly and gradually made her way along the avenue towards the palace. But it took a long time because everyone had something to say to her and she had plenty to say in return.

Several people pushed teddies into her arms for the baby, and eventually she needed help to carry everything.

After an hour of chatting to a stunned and delighted crowd, Holly finally allowed herself to be urged back into the carriage.

'Clearly I misjudged you.' Casper settled himself beside her, indicating with his head that the procession should move on.

Holly's heart soared. 'Y-you did?'

'Yes. I thought you'd find the whole day impossibly daunting. But you're a natural.' He gave a wry smile. 'I've never seen anyone so skilled at talking about nothing with such enthusiasm and for such a long time.'

Holly digested this statement, decided that it was a compliment of sorts, and tried not to be disappointed that he'd been referring to the way she'd handled herself in public, rather than his opinion of her pregnancy.

Reminding herself that she had to be patient, she smiled. 'How can it be daunting when everyone is so nice?' Holly waved again and spied another group of children in the crowd. She opened her mouth to ask if they could stop, but Casper met her questioning glance with a slow shake of his head.

'No. Absolutely not. Delighted though I am that you've managed to please the crowd, we have about two hundred foreign dignitaries and heads of state currently waiting for us at the palace and we're already late. I'd rather not cause a diplomatic incident if we can avoid it.' But his tone was in direct contrast to the warmth in his eyes. 'You've done well, *tesoro.*'

His praise made her glow inside and out, and she felt so ridiculously happy that she couldn't stop smiling. All right, so they'd had a shaky start to their relationship, but one of the advantages of that was that it could only improve.

Feeling optimistic about the future, Holly smiled all the way through the formal banquet, all the way through the dancing and all the way up to the moment when she was finally escorted to the prince's private quarters in a wing of the palace suspended above the sea.

It was only as the door closed behind them, leaving the guests and the guards on the outside, that reality hit her.

They were alone.

And this was their wedding night.

Gripped by a sudden attack of nerves, Holly gave a faltering smile, instinctively breaking the throbbing, tense silence that had descended on them. 'So this is where you actually live. It's beautiful—so much light and space, and—'

'*Stop* talking.' Casper reached for her clenched hands, gently prised them apart and then slid them round his waist and backed her against the door with an unmistakeable sense of purpose.

Trapped between solid oak and six foot two of raw male virility, Holly found she could barely breathe, let alone talk. Dry mouthed, knees shaking, she was aware only of the simmering undercurrents of sexuality that emanated from his powerful frame as he took her face in strong, determined hands, his mouth on a direct collision course with hers.

Holly closed her eyes in willing surrender, senses singing, nerves on fire. When the kiss didn't come, she whimpered a faint protest. 'Casper?'

His mouth hovered a breath from hers. 'Open your eyes.'

Her eyes opened obediently and she stared up at him, her heart skipping several beats as she scanned the aristocratic lines of his masculine features. 'Please—kiss me.'

'I intend to do a great deal more than that, *angelo mio...*'

Held captive by his lazy, confident gaze her heart started to pound, and searing heat pooled low in her pelvis. She probably should have played it cool, but Holly was too aroused to remember the meaning of cool.

Her body was in the grip of a strong, explosive excitement that simply intensified as his mouth finally glided onto hers with effortless skill.

His tongue probed the interior of her mouth with erotic expertise, and Holly just melted, moaning low in her throat as his strong hands brought her writhing hips into contact with his potent masculine arousal.

'Not here.' His voice thickened, he pulled away from her and scooped her easily into his arms. 'This time, *tesoro*, we'll make it to the bed. And we're taking our time over it.' He strode through several rooms and then up a winding staircase that led to a bedroom in a turret.

Trembling, *mortified* by how much she wanted him, Holly clutched at his shoulders as he set her down on the floor, barely conscious of the beautiful circular room, the high arched windows or the vaulted ceiling. Her body was on fire with anticipation, and her entire focus was on the man now undressing her with deft, experienced fingers.

As tens of thousands of pounds worth of designer silk slithered unrestrained to the floor, her old insecurities resurfaced, and Holly was grateful for the relative protection of moonlight and underwear. But Casper showed merciless disregard for her inhibitions, peeling off her panties in a slick, decisive movement and tumbling her trembling, naked body onto the enormous four-poster bed.

'Don't move. I like looking at you.' Having positioned her to his satisfaction, Casper sprang to his feet and removed his own clothing with impatient fingers, his eyes scanning her squirming body and flushed cheeks as he undressed with unself-conscious grace and fluidity. 'You are *so* beautiful.'

As his carelessly discarded clothes hit the floor, Holly quickly discovered that there was more than enough light for her to make out bronzed skin and bold male arousal. Dizzy from that brief glimpse of raw masculinity, she drew in a sharp breath as he came down on top of her.

Shocked by the sudden contact with his lean, powerful frame, Holly's pulse rate shot into overdrive and she slid her hands over his shoulders, her back arching as his clever mouth fastened over her nipple, and he plundered her sensitive flesh with sure, skilled flicks of his tongue.

Lightning bursts of sensation exploded through her body, and as his seeking fingers traced a path to that place where the ache had become almost intolerable Holly shifted restlessly against the silk sheets, the wanton movement giving him the access he needed.

With slow, sensitive strokes, he explored the most intimate part of her until Holly was sobbing his name, begging him for more, in the grip of such a terrifying craving that she knew if he stopped now she'd die.

Casper shifted her hips and his own position, giving her just time to register the silken throb of his arousal before he plunged deep into her moist, aching interior, and her world exploded.

Rocketing from earth to ecstasy, Holly shot straight into a shattering climax, only dimly registering Casper's disbelieving curse and the sudden faltering of his rhythm as his own control was threatened by her body's violent response. Sobbing his name, Holly dug her fingers into the slick flesh of his shoulders, so out of her mind with excitement that she was incapable of doing anything except hold on as each driving thrust drove her back towards paradise.

Her body splintered into pieces again, and this time she felt him reach his own release, and she hugged him tightly, overwhelmed by what had to be the most incredible experience of her life.

'You're a miracle in bed,' Casper said huskily, rolling onto his back and taking her with him.

Stunned by the whole experience, and prepared to snuggle against his chest, Holly gave a whimper of shock as he closed his hands over her hips and lifted her so that she straddled him.

'Casper, we can't!'

But they did.

Again and again, until Holly couldn't think or move.

Finally she lay there, sated and exhausted, one arm draped over his powerful chest, her cheek against the warmth of his bronzed shoulder.

She could hear the sounds of the sea through one

of the open windows and she closed her eyes, feeling a rush of happiness.

She no longer had any doubts that she'd done the right thing.

They'd been married for less than a day and already his attitude to her was softening. Yes, he found it hard to talk about his emotions, but he didn't have trouble showing them, did he?

He'd been tender, passionate, demanding, skilled, thoughtful.

Just thinking about it made her body burn again, and she slid her fingers through the dark hairs that hazed his chest, fascinated by the contrast between his body and hers.

'I had no idea it was possible to feel like that.' She spoke softly and gently, and pressed an affectionate kiss against his warm flesh, hugging him tightly. 'You're fantastic—' She broke off as he withdrew from her and sprang from the bed.

Without uttering a single word in response to her unguarded declaration, he strode through a door and slammed it behind him.

Holly flinched at the finality of that sound, and her head filled with a totally unreasonable panic.

He'd left. He'd just walked out without saying anything. Desperate to stop him leaving, she kicked back the tangle of silken covers and sprinted towards the door.

And then she heard the sounds of a shower running and realised that the door led to a bathroom.

A tidal wave of relief surged over her and she

stopped. Her limbs suddenly drained of strength, she plopped back onto the bed.

He hadn't walked out.

He wasn't her father.

This was different.

Or was it?

Feeling unsettled, confused and desperately hurt, she lay on her back, staring up at the canopy of the four-poster bed.

Rejection wasn't new to her, was it?

So why did it hurt so badly?

Eventually the noise of the shower stopped and moments later Casper strolled back into the bedroom. He'd pulled on a black robe and his hair was still damp from the shower.

Without looking at her, he walked into what she presumed was a dressing room and emerged wearing a pair of trousers, a fresh shirt in his hand.

'Aren't you coming back to bed? Did I say something?' Feeling intensely vulnerable, Holly sat up in the bed and twisted the ends of her hair with nervous fingers. 'One minute we were lying there having a cuddle and the next you sprang out of bed and stalked off. I feel as though you're upset, but I don't know why.'

'Go to sleep.' He shrugged his shoulders into the shirt and fastened the buttons with strong, sure fingers. *Those same fingers that had driven her wild.*

'How can I possibly sleep? *Talk* to me!' Suddenly it felt wrong to be naked, and she reached for the silk nightdress that someone had laid next to her pillow and pulled it over her head. 'What's wrong? Is it the whole wedding thing?' She wanted to ask whether he was thinking about the fiancée he should have married, Antonia, but she didn't want to risk making the situation worse.

'Go back to bed, Holly.'

'How can I possibly do that? Don't shut me out, Casper.' Her voice cracked and she slid out of bed and walked over to him. 'I'm your *wife*.'

'Precisely.' He looked at her then, and his eyes were cold as ice. 'I have already fulfilled my side of the deal by marrying you.'

Holly froze with shock. 'Deal?'

'You wanted a father for your baby. I needed an heir.'

Her legs buckled and she sank down onto the edge of the bed. 'You make it sound as though I picked you at random.'

'Not at random. I think you targeted me very carefully.'

'You still believe this isn't your baby. Oh God. I really thought you'd changed your mind about that— you seemed different today—and when we—' She glanced at the rumpled sheets on the bed, her eyes glistening with tears. 'You made love to me and it felt—'

'We had sex, Holly.' His voice was devoid of emotion. 'Love didn't come into it, and it never will, make no mistake about that. Don't do that female thing of turning a physical act into something emotional.'

Her hopes exploded like a balloon landing on nails.

'It wasn't just the sex,' she whispered. 'You've been different today. Caring. Ever since the moment I arrived at the cathedral.' Her voice cracked. 'You've been smiling at me, you had your arm around me. *You kissed me.*'

'We're supposed to look as though we're in love.' Apparently unaffected by her mounting distress, he strode over to an antique table next to the window. 'Do you want a drink?'

'No. I don't want a drink!' Her heart was suddenly bumping hard and she felt physically sick. 'Are you saying that everything that happened today was for the benefit of the crowd?'

He poured himself a whisky but didn't touch it. Instead he stared out of the window, his knuckles white on the glass, his handsome face revealing nothing of his thoughts. No emotion. 'They wanted the fairy tale. We gave it to them. That's what we royals have to do. We give the people what they want. In this case, a love match, a wedding and an heir.'

She blinked rapidly, determined to hold back the tears. 'So why did you marry *me*?'

He lifted the glass to his lips. 'Why not?'

'Because you could have married someone you loved.'

He lowered the glass without drinking. 'I don't want love.'

Because he'd had it once and now it was gone?

Holly's throat closed. 'That's a terrible thing to

say and a terrible way to feel,' she whispered. 'I know you lost and I know you must have suffered, but—'

'You don't know anything.'

'Then tell me!' She was crying openly now, tears flooding her cheeks. 'I'm devastated that the whole of today was a sham. I know it's difficult for you to talk about Antonia, and frankly it isn't that easy to hear it, either. But I know we're not going to have any sort of marriage unless we're honest with each other.'

Please don't let him walk out on me. Please don't let that happen.

'Honest?' He slammed the glass down onto the table and turned to look at her. 'You lie about your baby, you lie all the way to the altar wearing your symbolic white dress, and then you suggest we're *honest*? It's a little late for that, don't you think?'

'It's your baby,' Holly said hoarsely. Her insides were twisted in pain as she felt her new life crumbling around her. 'And I don't know how you can believe otherwise.'

'Don't you? Then let me tell you.' He strolled towards her, his eyes glittering dark and deadly. 'It can't be my baby, Holly, because I can't have children. I don't know whose baby you're carrying, my sweet wife, but I know for sure it isn't mine. I'm infertile.'

Chapter 6

'No.' Holly sat down hard on the nearest chair, her heart pounding. 'That isn't possible,' she said hoarsely. 'I am living proof that it isn't possible. Why would you even think that?'

'Eight years ago I had an accident.'

The accident that had killed his brother and Antonia. 'I know about the accident.'

'You know only what I chose to reveal.' He paced across the room and stared out over the ocean. 'Everyone knew that Santallia lost the heir to the throne. Everyone knew my fiancée died. No one knew that the accident crushed my pelvis so badly that my chances of ever fathering a child were nil.'

Holly's mind was in turmoil. 'Casper—'

'We had a crisis on our hands.' He thrust his hands

into his pockets, the movement emphasising the hard masculine lines of his body. 'My brother was dead. I was suddenly the ruling prince and I was in intensive care, hitched up to a ventilator. When I recovered, everyone was celebrating. It was the wrong time to break the news to the people that their prince couldn't give them what they wanted.'

Holly sank her hands into her hair, struggling to take in what he was saying. 'Who told you?'

'The doctor who treated me.'

'Well, the doctor was wrong.' Her hands fell to her sides and she walked across to him, her tone urgent. 'Look at me, Casper. *Listen* to me. Whatever you may have been told—whatever you think—you are not infertile. I *am* having your baby.'

'Don't do this, Holly.' He drew away from her. 'I've accepted your child as mine, and that's all that matters. You've given me my heir. The public think you're a genius.' He stared into his drink. 'At some point, I'll have to tell the people the truth. Let them decide about the succession.'

As the implications of his words sank in, Holly shook her head, horrified by what that would mean. 'No. You mustn't do that.'

'Because your newfound popularity would take a nosedive?' He gave a cynical smile. 'You think Santallia might rather not know that its new innocent princess has rather more sexual experience than they'd like?'

'Casper, my sexual experience encompasses

you and only you.' Frustrated that she couldn't get through to him, Holly turned away and walked over to the window. Dawn was breaking and the rising sun sent pink shadows over the sea, but she saw nothing except her child's future crumbling before her. 'You should see a doctor again. You should have more tests. They made a mistake.'

'The subject is closed.'

'Fine. Don't have tests, then.' Anger and frustration rose out of her misery. 'But don't you *dare* announce to the world that this isn't your baby!' Her eyes suddenly fierce, she turned on him. 'I do *not* want our child having that sort of scar on his background. And once you've said something like that, you can never take it back.'

'They have a right to know about the baby's paternity.'

Holly straightened her shoulders. 'Once the baby is born, I'll prove our baby's paternity. Until then, you say nothing.'

'If you're so confident about paternity, then why wait? There are tests that can be done now. Or are you buying yourself more time?'

She lifted her hands to her cheeks, so stressed that she could hardly breathe. 'Tests now would put the baby at risk and I won't do that. But don't you dare tell anyone this isn't your baby. *Promise me, Casper.*'

'All right.'

Celebrating that minor victory, Holly sank onto the curved window seat and stared down at the sea lapping at the white sand below. 'Why didn't you tell me this when we were in London?'

'Because you didn't need to know.'

'How can you say that?'

'You wanted a father for your baby and I needed an heir. The details were irrelevant and they still are. You have a prince, a palace and a fortune. This drama is unnecessary.'

'I wanted our baby to know its father,' Holly whispered softly, her hand covering her abdomen in an instinctive gesture of protection. 'I thought marrying you *was* the right thing to do.'

'If it's any consolation, I wouldn't have let you make any other decision. And I don't want to talk about this again, Holly. You'll have everything you need and so will the baby.'

No. No, she wouldn't.

Holly closed her eyes, trying to ignore the raw wound caused by his admission that the whole day had been a lie.

She'd felt lonely before, but nothing had come close to the feeling of isolation that engulfed her following Casper's rejection.

She desperately wanted to talk to someone—to confide.

But there was no one.

She was alone.

Except that she wasn't really alone, was she? She had their baby to think about—to protect.

Once he or she was born, she'd be able to prove that Casper was the father. And until then she just had to try and keep their hopelessly unstable little family unit together.

That was all that mattered.

Starved of affection from Casper and desperately worried about the future, Holly threw herself into palace life and her royal duties.

She spent hours pouring over a map until she was familiar with every part of Santallia. Determined to develop the knowledge of a local, she persuaded Emilio to drive her round. The result was that she shocked and delighted the public by her frequent impromptu appearances. Oblivious to security or protocol, she talked to everyone, finding out what they liked and how they felt.

And one thing that always came across was how much they loved Casper.

'You're just what he needs,' one old lady said as Holly sat by her bed in the hospital, keeping her company for half an hour after an exhausting morning of official visits. 'After the accident we thought he wouldn't recover, you know.'

Holly reached forward to adjust the old lady's pillows. 'You mean because he was so badly injured?'

'No. Because he lost so much. But now he has you to love.'

But he didn't want love, did he?

Holly managed a smile. 'I need to go. Tonight it's dinner with a president and his wife, no less. Do you want more tea before I go?'

'I want you to tell me about the state visit. What will you be wearing?'

'Actually, I'm not sure.' Holly thought about her extensive wardrobe. No one could accuse Casper of being stingy, she thought ruefully. The trouble was, she now had such a variety of gorgeous designer clothes that choosing had become impossible, but even that wasn't a problem, because she now had someone to do it for her. When she'd first realised that a member of staff had been employed purely to keep her wardrobe in order and help her select outfits, she'd gaped at Casper.

'You mean it's someone's whole job just to tell me how to dress?'

He'd dismissed her amazement with a frown. 'How else will you know what to wear for the various occasions? Her job is to research every engagement in advance and make the appropriate choice of outfit. It will stop you making an embarrassing mistake.'

The news that he found her potentially embarrassing had done nothing for Holly's fragile confidence, and she'd humbly accepted the woman's help.

Thinking of it, Holly smiled at the old lady. 'I think I'm wearing a blue dress. With silver straps. A bit Hollywood, but apparently the president loves glamour.'

'You're so beautiful, he'll be charmed. And blue is a good colour for you. I've been admiring your bracelet—I had one almost exactly like that when I was your age.' The woman's eyes misted. 'My husband gave it to me because he said it was the same colour as my eyes. I lost it years ago. Not that it matters. The trouble with getting old is you don't have the same opportunities to dress up.'

'You don't need an occasion,' Holly said blithely, slipping the bracelet off and sliding it onto the old lady's bony wrist. 'There. It looks gorgeous.'

'You can't give me that.'

'Why not? It looks pretty on you. I must go or they'll start moaning at me. Try not to seduce any of the doctors.' Holly rose to her feet, silently acknowledging that part of her was reluctant to return to the palace. She loved visiting everyone and chatting. When she was out and about and talking to people, it was easier to pretend that she wasn't desperately lonely.

That her marriage wasn't empty.

Casper seemed to think that presents were a reasonable substitute for his company.

It had taken only a couple of days for her to discover that he set himself a punishing work schedule, spending much of the day involved in state business or royal engagements.

Since their wedding they'd spent virtually no daylight hours alone together. Every evening there seemed to be yet another formal banquet, foreign dignitaries to be entertained, another evening of smiles and polite conversation.

And the fact that he never saw her was presumably intentional, she thought miserably as she said her farewells to all the ladies on the ward and allowed Emilio to guide her back to the car.

Casper didn't want to spend time with her, did he?

All he wanted from the relationship was a hostess and someone with whom to enjoy a few exhausting hours of turbo-powered, high-octane sex every night.

He wasn't interested in anything else. Not conversation. Not even a hug. *Certainly* not a hug.

Holly slid into the back of the car, waving to the crowd who had gathered. *What would they say,* she wondered, *if they knew their handsome prince had never spent a whole night with her?*

He just took her to bed, had sex and then disappeared somewhere, as if he was afraid that lingering might encourage her to say something that he didn't want to hear.

Did he have another woman? Was that where he went when he left their bed?

To someone else?

Casper had a seemingly inexhaustible sex drive, and Holly was well aware that there had been another woman in his life when he'd first met her in England. One of the papers had mentioned some European princess, and another a supermodel.

Were they still on the scene?

Feeling mentally and physically exhausted, Holly rested her head on the back seat of the limousine and promptly fell asleep.

She woke at Emlio's gentle insistence, walked into her beautiful bedroom with the view to die for and flopped down on her huge, fabulous bed.

Just five minutes, she promised herself.

Five minutes, then she'd have a shower and get ready for the evening.

Simmering with impatience after a long and incredibly frustrating day of talks with the president and the foreign minister, Casper strode through to the private wing of the palace.

In his pocket was an extravagant diamond necklace, designed for him by the world's most exclusive jeweller who had assured him that any woman presented with such an exquisite piece would know she was loved.

Casper had frowned at that, because love played no part in the relationship he had with Holly. But she was doing an excellent job fulfilling her role as princess. She deserved to be appreciated.

And this was why she'd married him, wasn't it? *For the benefits that he could offer her.*

Contemplating her reaction to such a generous gift, a faint smile touched his mouth, and he mentally prepared himself for a stimulating evening.

Lost in a private fantasy which involved Holly, the diamonds and very little else, Casper strolled into his private sanctuary.

The first thing that hit him was the unusual silence.

Silence, he reflected with a degree of wry humour, had become something of a scarcity since he'd married Holly.

First there was the singing. She sang to herself as

they were getting ready for the evening. She sang in the shower, she sang as she dressed, she even sang as she did her make-up. And if she wasn't singing she was talking, apparently determined to fill every moment of the limited time they had alone together with details about her day. Who she'd spoken to, what they'd said in return—she was endlessly fascinated by every small detail about the people she'd met.

In fact silence was such an alien thing since Holly had entered his life, that he noticed the absence of sound like others would notice the presence of a large elephant in the room.

Slightly irritated that she obviously hadn't yet returned from her afternoon of visits, Casper removed his tie with a few deft flicks of his fingers while swiftly scanning his private mail.

Finding it strangely hard to concentrate without background noise, he had to force himself to focus while he scribbled instructions for his private secretary. Intending to take a quick shower while waiting for Holly to return, he took the stairs up to the bedroom suite.

Holly lay still on the bed, fully clothed, as if she'd fallen there and not moved since. Her glorious hair tumbled unrestricted around her narrow shoulders and her eyes were closed, her dark lashes serving to accentuate the extreme pallor of her cheeks.

In the process of unbuttoning his shirt, Casper stilled.

His first reaction was one of surprise, because she was blessed with boundless energy and enthusiasm and he'd never before seen her sleeping during the day.

His second reaction was concern.

Knowing that she was an extremely light sleeper, he waited for her to sense his presence and stir. Contemplating the feminine curve of her hip, he felt an immediate surge of arousal, and decided that the best course of action would be to join her on the bed and wake her personally.

Glancing at his watch, he calculated that if they limited the foreplay they would still make dinner with the president.

He dispensed with his shirt, his eyes fixed on the creamy skin visible at the neckline of her flowery dress. *Stunning*, he thought to himself, and settled himself on the edge of the bed, ready to dedicate the next half hour to making her *extremely* happy.

But she didn't stir.

Disconcerted by her lack of response, Casper reached out a hand and touched her throat, feeling a rush of relief as he felt warm flesh and a steady pulse under his fingertips.

What had he expected?

Unsettled by the sudden absence of logic that had driven him to take the pulse of a sleeping woman, he withdrew his hand and rose to his feet, struggling against an irrational desire to pick up the phone and demand the immediate presence of a skilled medical team.

She was just tired, he assured himself, casting another long look in her direction. Acting on impulse, he reached down and gently removed her shoes. Then he stared at her dress and tried to work out whether it was likely to impede her rest in any way. For the first time in his life, a decision eluded him. Did he remove it and risk waking her, or leave it and risk her being uncomfortable?

A stranger to prevarication, Casper stood in a turmoil of indecision, his hand hovering over her for several long minutes. In the end he compromised by pulling the silk cover over her body.

Then he backed away from the bed, relieved that at least there had been no one present to witness such embarrassing vacillation on his part.

He made thousands of decisions on a daily basis, some of them involving millions of pounds, some of them involving millions of people.

It was incomprehensible that he couldn't make one small decision that affected his wife's comfort.

Holly awoke to darkness. With a rush of inexplicable panic, she sat up and only then did she notice Casper seated by the window.

'What time is it?' Disorientated and fuzzy headed, she reached across to flick on the lamp by the bed. 'It must be really late. And I need to change for dinner.'

'It's one in the morning. You've missed dinner.'

The lamp sent a shaft of light across the room, and she saw that his white dress-shirt was unbuttoned at the throat and that his dinner jacket was slung carelessly over the back of the chair.

'I missed it?' Holly slid her hand through her

hair, trying to clear her head. 'How could I have missed it?'

'You were asleep.'

'Then you should have woken me.' Mortified, she pushed down the luxurious silk bed cover and realised that she was still wearing the clothes she'd had on when she'd done her day of royal visits. 'I only wanted a short nap.'

'Holly, you slept as though you were dead.' His dark eyes glittered in the subtle light. 'I decided that it was better to make your excuses to the president than produce a wife in a coma.'

Holly pulled a face. 'What must he have thought?'

'He thought you were pregnant,' Casper drawled, a faint smile touching his mouth. 'He and his wife have four children, and he spent the entire evening lecturing me on how a pregnant woman often feels most tired during the first few months and how rest is important.'

'God, how awful for you,' Holly mumbled, forcing herself to get out of bed even though every part of herself was dying to lie down and sleep for the rest of the night. 'I feel really bad, because I know how important this dinner was to you. Your private secretary told me that you wanted to talk about all that trade stuff and about carbon emissions or something. Some forestry scheme?'

A strange expression flickered across his face. 'You frequently talk to my private secretary?'

'Of course.' Holly tried unsuccessfully to suppress a yawn as she padded over to him in bare feet. 'Carlos and I often talk. How else am I going to know what the point of the evening is? I mean, you don't see these people because you like their company, do you?' Feeling decidedly wobbly, she sank down on the window seat next to him. 'I'm sorry I slept.'

'Don't be. Though I must admit you had me worried for a while. It wasn't until I was greeted with silence that I realised how accustomed I am to hearing you singing into a hairbrush.'

Holly turned scarlet at the thought that he'd witnessed that. 'You hear me singing?'

'The whole of the palace hears you singing.'

Horrified by that disclosure, Holly shrank back on the seat. 'I didn't know anyone could hear me,' she muttered. 'Singing always cheers me up.'

His eyes lingered thoughtfully on her face. 'Do you need cheering up?'

How was she supposed to answer that? Holly hesitated, knowing that if she told him that she felt lonely, *that she missed him*, he'd withdraw in the same way he always did when she made a move towards him. He'd remind her that his company wasn't part of their 'deal'.

'I just like singing,' she said lamely. 'But next time I'll make sure no one is listening.'

'That would be a pity, especially given that several of the staff have told me what a beautiful voice you have.' He reached into his pocket and withdrew a slim box. 'I bought you a present.'

'Oh.' She tried to look pleased. After all, he was trying, wasn't he? It wouldn't be fair to point out that her wardrobes were bulging with clothes and that she only had one pair of feet on which to wear shoes, and that what she *really* wanted was a few hours in his company when they weren't having sex. 'Thank you.'

'I hope you like it.' His confident smile suggested that he wasn't in any doubt about that, and Holly flipped open the lid of the dark-blue velvet box and was dazzled by the sparkle and gleam of diamonds.

'My goodness.'

'They're pink diamonds. I know you like pink. Apparently they're very rare.'

When had he even noticed that she liked pink?

He was such a contradiction, she thought numbly, lifting the necklace from the box and instantly falling in love with it. He spent hardly any time alone with her, but he seemed to be trying to please her.

And he'd noticed that she liked pink.

'It's beautiful,' she said honestly, fastening the necklace round her neck and walking across the room to admire herself in the mirror. 'Is it very valuable?'

'Would knowing how much it cost make it a more welcome gift?' There was an edge to his tone that she didn't understand.

'No, of course not.' She touched the sparkling diamonds nervously. 'I'm just wondering whether I dare wear it out of the bedroom.'

He relaxed slightly. 'It's yours to lose, keep or trade,' he drawled softly, and Holly frowned, puzzled by his comment but too tired to search for a hidden meaning.

'You do say the weirdest things.' Suppressing a yawn, she walked back to the window seat, feeling the weight of the diamonds against her throat. 'I've never worn diamonds before. And I never imagined wearing them in bed.'

'I intended them to go with your dress this evening.' His gaze was fixed on her face. 'You're extremely tired.'

'Long day.'

'Too long. The official visits have to stop, Holly.'

'What? *Why?*' Hurt and upset by the apparent criticism, Holly sat up straighter in her seat. 'What am I doing wrong? I've worked so hard.'

'Precisely. You're working too hard.'

For a moment Holly just gaped at him in disbelief. 'That's the most unfair criticism I've ever heard. How can I be working *too* hard?'

'If you're so exhausted you're falling asleep, then you're working too hard.'

'That's nothing to do with the official visits. I'm falling asleep because you keep me awake half the night!' She looked at him in exasperation, her temper mounting. 'Oh, that's it, isn't it? You don't like me working hard because you're afraid I'm going to be too tired to perform in the bedroom! Is that all you care about, Casper? Whether I have the energy for sex?'

'You're doing that uniquely female thing of twisting words for the purpose of starting a row.' Ice cool, he watched her with masculine detachment and Holly felt a flash of frustration.

'No, I'm not. I *hate* rows. I would never, ever choose to row with anyone. I *hate* conflict.' The ironic gleam in his eyes somehow served to make her even more infuriated. 'And you'd know I hate conflict if you'd bothered to spend a few hours alone in my company! But you don't, do you? Do you re-alise we've never even been on a proper date? You are so, so selfish! You just come to bed and do your whole virile, macho-stud thing, and then you swan off, leaving me.'

One dark brow lifted in cool appraisal. 'Leav-ing you?'

'Exhausted,' she muttered, and a sardonic smile touched his mouth.

'So I leave you to sleep. By my definition, that makes me unselfish, not selfish. And it brings me back to my earlier point, which is that you're work-ing too hard.'

'You always have to win, don't you?' Holly sank back down onto the window seat, the bout of anger having sapped the last of her energy. It just wasn't worth arguing with him.

'It isn't about winning. Believe it or not, I do have your welfare at heart. After I left you this afternoon, I asked a few questions. Questions I should have asked a long time ago it seems.' There was a frown in his eyes. 'It's no wonder you're so tired. Appar-ently you've been working flat out since the day after our wedding. You've been doing ten to fifteen vis-its a day! And you spend ages with everyone. From what I've been told, you don't even give yourself a lunch break.'

'Well, there's a lot to fit in.' Holly defended herself. 'Have you any idea how many requests the palace receives? People send letters, sometimes official and sometimes handwritten. Stacks and stacks of them. There have already been requests for me to go and visit schools and hospitals, open this or that, make an official visit, cut ribbons, smash bottles of champagne—I judged a dog show last week and I don't know *anything* about dogs. And then there are the individuals, people who are ill and can't get out—'

'Holly.' His tone was a mixture of amusement and disbelief. 'You're not supposed to say yes to all of them. The idea is that you pick and choose.'

'Well if I say yes to one and not another then I'm going to offend someone!' Holly glared at him and then subsided. 'And anyway, I'm enjoying myself. I like seeing people. For some reason that I absolutely don't understand, it cheers them up to see me. And I won't give it up!'

People liked her. People approved of her.

She felt as though she was making a difference, and it felt good.

'You're working yourself to the bone. From now on I'm giving instructions that you're to do no more than two engagements a day,' he instructed. 'On a maximum of five days a week.'

'No!' Horrified by that prospect, Holly pushed her hair out of her eyes. 'What am I going to do the rest of the time? You obviously don't want to see me during the hours of daylight, you're—you're like a vampire or something! You just turn up at night.'

Thick dark lashes concealed his expression. 'You have unlimited funds and virtually unlimited opportunities for entertainment.' His soft drawl connected straight with her nerve endings, and Holly felt everything weaken.

'Well there's no point in doing stuff if you don't have anyone to share it with. I'm lonely. And that's the other thing you don't seem to understand about me. I'm a people person. So don't tell me I have to stop doing my own engagements.'

'Holly, you're exhausted.'

'I'm pregnant,' she said flatly, pulling her legs under her and trying hard to hide another yawn. 'All the books say that in another couple of weeks I'll be bounding with energy.'

'And what are you going to do then?' His tone was dry. 'Work nights?'

Her eyes collided with his and Holly sucked in some air, horrified to discover that the mere mention of the word 'night' was sufficient to trigger a reaction in her body. Her nipples tightened, her pelvis ached and she suddenly felt as though she'd downed an entire bottle of champagne in one gulp.

Clearly tracking the direction of her thoughts, he gave a slow, confident smile and suddenly she wanted to thump him because he was unreasonably, unfairly gorgeous, and he knew it.

As his gaze welded to her mouth, Holly acknowledged the overwhelming surge of excitement with something close to despair. '*Don't* look at me like that. You're doing it again—all you think about is sex.'

'And what are you thinking about right now, *tesoro*? The share price?' His tone was mocking as he pulled her gently but firmly to her feet. 'A new handbag?'

A moan of disbelief escaped her parted lips as he brought his mouth down on hers and backed her purposefully towards the bed.

This was Casper at his most dominant and she really, *really* wanted to be able tell him that she was too tired, or just not interested.

'I can't believe you make me feel this way.' Her body exploded under the hard, virile pressure of his and she tumbled back onto the mattress, forced to admit that she was a lost cause when it came to resisting him.

She wanted him *so* much.

And if this was all their relationship was...

He came over her with the fluid assurance of a male who has never known rejection, arousal glittering in his beautiful eyes. 'Exactly how tired are you?'

Trying to look nonchalant, she shrugged. 'Why do you ask?'

He lowered his arrogant, dark head, his mouth curving into a sardonic smile as it hovered close to hers. 'Because I'm about to do my virile, macho-stud thing,' he mocked gently, and Holly felt her stomach flip with desperate excitement.

Weak with desire, *hating* herself for being so feeble where he was concerned, she gasped as his hand slid under the silk of her nightdress. 'Casper.'

His hand stilled and there was a wicked gleam in his eyes. 'Unless you're too tired?'

Driven by the desperate urgency of her body, Holly swallowed her pride. 'I'm not *that* tired…'

'You have time to shower while I make some calls.' Freshly shaved, his hair still damp, Casper straightened his silk tie and reached for his jacket. 'I'll join you for breakfast.'

Elated that he'd spent the entire night with her for the first time, and reluctant to risk disturbing the fragile shoots of their relationship, Holly decided not to confess that mornings weren't her best time and that she couldn't touch breakfast.

Waiting until he'd left the room, she slid cautiously out of bed, felt her stomach heave alarmingly and just made it to the bathroom in time.

'*Dio,* what is the matter?' Casper's voice came from right behind her. 'Are you ill? Is it something you ate?'

'Don't you knock? I thought I locked the door.' Mortified that he should witness her at her lowest, Holly leaned her head against the cool tiles, willing her stomach to settle. 'Please, Casper, show a little sensitivity and go away.'

'First you accuse me of not spending time with you, then you want me to go away.' Casper lifted his hands in a gesture of frustrated incredulity. 'Make up your mind!'

'Well, *obviously* I don't want you around while I'm being sick!'

'You're incredibly pale.' Looking enviably fit and impossibly handsome, he frowned down at her. 'I'm calling a doctor.'

'Casper.' She gritted her teeth, terrified that she'd be ill in front of him. 'It's fine. It happens all the time. It will fade in a minute.'

'*What* happens all the time?' His dark gaze was fixed on her face, the tension visible in his powerful shoulders. 'I've never seen you like this before.'

'That's because you're never here in the morning,' she muttered, wondering what cruel twist of fate had made him decide to pick this particular morning to linger in her company. 'You go to bed with me, but you choose to wake up somewhere else.' *With someone else.* The words were left unsaid, but a gleam of sardonic humour flickered in his very sexy dark eyes.

'You think I spend half the night making love with you and then move on to the next woman? A sort of sexual conveyor-belt, perhaps?'

'I honestly don't want to know where you go at three in the morning.' She gave a moan as another wave of nausea washed over her. 'Oh, go away, please. I don't even care at the moment—I can't *believe* you're seeing me like this. You're never going to find me sexy again.'

'There is not the slightest chance of that happening.' After a moment's hesitation he dropped to his haunches and stroked her hair away from her face with a surprisingly gentle hand. 'I am sorry you feel ill. Wash your face. It will make you feel better.' He stood up, dampened a towel and wiped it gently over her face.

'I already feel better. It passes.' She sat back on her heels and gave him a wobbly smile. 'I bet you're regretting all those times you could have stayed the whole night and had breakfast with me. I'm thrilling company in the morning, don't you think?'

With a wry smile, he lifted her easily to her feet. 'Does food help? If I suggested something to eat would you hit me?'

'I've never been an advocate of violence.' It felt weird, having a conversation with him that wasn't based on conflict. And frustrating that they were having it when she was still in her nightdress.

But at least she was wearing diamonds, she thought wryly.

Conscious of his sleek good looks and her own undressed state, Holly glanced towards the shower. 'I think I'd like a shower. Do I still have time?'

'Yes. But don't lock the door.' His tone was gruff. 'I don't want you collapsing.'

'I'm fine.' This new level of attentiveness was unsettling. There was a shift in their relationship that she didn't understand.

But she knew better than to read anything into it.

She showered quickly, selected a cream skirt from her wardrobe and added a tailored jacket that allowed a peep of her pretty camisole. She scooped her hair up and then had a moment of agonising indecision as she remembered that he seemed to prefer her hair down. Up or down? Removing the clips, her hair tumbled around her shoulders in a mass of soft curls.

Deciding that she should have left it up, she started to twist it again and then caught herself.

What was she doing? For crying out loud, she was going to eat breakfast with the man, that was all. It wasn't a formal dinner or a state occasion. Just breakfast.

Pathetic, she told her reflection. Absolutely pathetic.

It was just for the baby. For the baby's sake she wanted them to have a happy, successful marriage.

Afraid to examine that theory too closely in case it fell apart, she walked onto the terrace to join him for breakfast. Casper was talking on the phone, looking lean and sleek, his hips resting casually against the balustrade that circled the pretty balcony. Behind him stretched the ocean, the early-morning sunlight catching the surface in a thousand dazzling lights.

The billionaire prince, she thought weakly, envious of his confidence and the ease with which he handled his high profile existence. She'd watched him in action at state occasions and been impossibly awed by the deft way in which he handled every situation and solved every problem. She realised now that she'd had no idea of the weight of responsibility that rested on him, and yet he apparently coped easily, with no outward evidence of stress or self-doubt.

As he continued his conversation, his eyes slid to hers and held. Electricity jolted her and Holly's heart bumped hard against her ribs.

Wondering how he could have this effect on her when she'd just spent most of the night in bed with him, she plopped down onto the nearest chair.

She felt light-headed and dizzy and wasn't sure whether to blame pregnancy, lack of food or the shattering impact of the extremely sexy man who was currently watching her with disturbing intensity, apparently paying no attention whatsoever to the person on the other end of the phone.

Cheeks pink, trying to distract herself, Holly cautiously examined the food that had been laid out on the table.

Terminating the call, Casper dropped his phone into his pocket and strolled across to her. 'I've talked to the doctor.'

'You have?'

'He suggests that you eat dry toast now. And tomorrow you're to eat a dry biscuit before you move from the bed.'

'That sounds exciting. And guaranteed to put on extra pounds just when I don't need them.'

Casper gave a predatory smile. 'Since we've already established the positive impact of biscuits on a certain part of your anatomy, I think we can safely assume that I'm not going to find you sexually repulsive any time soon.'

'I didn't say you were.'

'But you were thinking it.' He sat down opposite

her and helped himself to fresh fruit. 'Eventually I'm hoping you'll realise that you have a fabulous body. Then we can make love with the lights on. Or even during daylight.'

She blushed, as self-conscious about his suggestion that they make love in daylight as she was flattered by his comments about her body. 'You're not around during the day.'

'The promise of you naked would be sufficient incentive to persuade me to ditch my responsibilities.'

'All you think about is sex. I don't know whether to be flattered or exasperated.'

'You should be flattered. I'm a man. I'm programmed to think about nothing but sex.' Apparently seeing nothing wrong in that admission, he reached across and lifted the coffee pot. 'More?'

Holly pulled a face and shook her head. 'I've gone off it. Don't ask me why. Something to do with being pregnant, I think.'

Without arguing, he poured her a fresh orange-juice instead. 'And now I want to know why you assumed I was spending part of the night with another woman.'

Her insides tumbled. 'Well—it just seemed like the obvious answer.'

'To what question?'

'To where you go at three in the morning. Up until today, you've never woken up next to me. We have sex. You leave. That's the routine.'

'That doesn't explain why you'd believe I was seeing another woman.'

'You're a man.' She mimicked his tone, hoping that her attempt at humour would conceal the fact that she was absolutely terrified of his answer. 'And that's what men are programmed to do.'

'I get up at three in the morning because I'm aware that you need some sleep,' he said softly. 'And if I'm in bed with you I don't seem to have any self-control.'

Stunned by that unexpected confession, Holly felt her insides flip. 'But by the time you leave the bed we've already—' Her cheeks heated. 'I mean surely even you couldn't?'

'I definitely could,' he assured her silkily. 'It seems where you're concerned, I have a limitless appetite. So you see, *tesoro*, you don't have to worry about the effects of daylight, biscuits, or anything else for that matter. I'm so addicted to your body I even find you sexy in a cartoon tee-shirt—not that I'd ever allow you to wear one of those again,' he went on, clearly concerned she might decide to put that claim to the test.

Basking in the novel experience of being considered irresistible, Holly sipped her orange juice. He didn't reveal anything about his own emotions and they didn't talk about their problems, but they seemed to have reached some sort of truce. 'So where *do* you go when you leave our bed?'

'I work. Usually in the study.'

Holly gave a disbelieving laugh because that altogether more simple explanation hadn't occurred to her. 'I just assumed— The thing is, I've been so worried.' Weak with relief, she confessed, 'I mean, I know you had loads of relationships before me.'

'I sense this is turning into one of those female questions where every answer is always going to be the wrong one,' he drawled and she bit her lip.

'But—were you with someone when we met at the rugby?'

'Technically, no.'

'What's that supposed to mean? I read about a supermodel—'

'You don't want to believe everything you read.'

'But —'

His tone was impatient. 'What can you possibly gain from this line of questioning?'

Reassurance? She gave a painful laugh as she realised the foolishness of that. Reassurance about what—that he loved her? He didn't. She knew he didn't. 'I was just—interested.'

'You were just being a woman. Forget it.' He rose to his feet. 'Remember that the past is always behind you. Are you ready?'

'For what?' She decided that this wasn't the right time to point out that the past wasn't behind him, even if he believed that it was. It was obvious to her that it was with him every agonising minute of the day. 'Where are we going?'

His gaze lingered on her face. 'To spend some time together. Isn't that what you wanted? You said that I don't spend any time with you during the day,' he reminded her softly. 'And that we've never actually been on a date. So we're going to rectify that.'

'We're going on a date?' Holly couldn't stop the smile. 'Where?'

'The most romantic city in the world. Rome.'

Chapter 7

'This is your idea of a date? When you said we were visiting romantic Rome, I imagined wandering hand in hand to the Spanish Steps and the Colosseum. Not sitting in a rugby stadium,' Holly muttered, taking her seat and waving enthusiastically to the very vocal crowd.

Casper gave her a rare smile. 'You wanted to be alone with me. We're alone.'

'This is your idea of alone?' Holly glanced at the security team surrounding them, and then at the enormous crowd who were cheering as the players jogged onto the pitch. 'Are you delusional?'

'Stadio Flaminio is a small stadium—intimate.'

Holly started to laugh. 'I suppose everything is relative. It's small compared with Twickenham. This time we're only in the company of thirty thousand people. But is this really your idea of romantic? A rugby match?'

'We met during a rugby match,' Casper reminded her, and their eyes clashed as both of them remembered the sheer breathless intensity of that meeting. 'I am mixing my two passions. Rugby and you.'

He didn't actually mean *her,* did he? He meant her body.

'I—I've never actually watched a game before,' Holly confessed shakily, dragging her eyes from his and wondering what it was about him that reduced her to jelly. 'I was always working. I don't even know the rules.'

'One team has to score more points than the other,' Casper said dryly, leaning forward as the game started, his gaze intent on the pitch.

'By all piling on top of each other?' Holly winced as she watched the players throw themselves into the game with no apparent care for their own safety. 'It's all very macho, isn't it? Lots of mud, blood and muscle.'

'They're following strict rules. Watch. You might find it exciting.'

And she did.

At first she sat in silence, determined not to ruin his enjoyment by asking inane questions, and equally determined to try and understand what he loved about the game. But, far from ignoring her, he seemed keen to involve her in everything that was going on.

There was a sudden roar from the crowd as a man powered down the field with the ball.

'He's fast,' Holly breathed, and Casper's shoulders tensed and then he punched the air.

'He's scored the opening try.'

'That's when he puts the ball down on the line—and that's five points, right?'

Casper was absorbed in the game, but not too absorbed to make the occasional observation for her benefit. Gradually he explained the rules, until the game no longer looked like a playground fight fuelled by testosterone, and instead became an extremely exciting sporting challenge.

Towards the second half of the match Holly discovered that she was leaning forward too, her eyes on the pitch, equally absorbed by what was happening. 'That was a brilliant run through the Italian defence.' Turning to find Casper watching her, she blushed. 'What? Did I say something stupid?'

'No.' His voice was husky and there was a strange light in his eyes. 'You are quite right. It *was* a brilliant run by England. You are enjoying yourself?'

'Very much.' She gave a tentative smile, and turned back to the pitch. 'That tackle was by the Italian hooker, is that right?' Suddenly aware that the sun was shining down on them, and she was far too hot, she released a few buttons on her jacket. 'I can't believe they named a rugby position after a prostitute.'

'They are called hookers because they use their feet to hook the ball in the scrum. They're a key…'

His voice tailed off in the middle of the sentence, and all his attention was suddenly focused on the delicate lace of her camisole. 'Sorry, what was the question?' He dragged his gaze up to hers, his eyes suddenly blank, and she gave a feminine smile.

'You were teaching me about rugby.'

'If you really want to learn,' he breathed, leaning closer to her, 'don't start undressing in the middle of my answer.'

'I was hot.'

He gave a wry smile. 'So am I.'

Delighted by the effect she was having on him, her eyes sparkled. 'Where were we? Oh yes—you were telling me about the hooker.'

He stroked a finger over her cheek. 'Unless you want to find yourself participating in an indecent act in a public place,' he purred, 'I suggest you stop teasing. And the hooker is a key position in attacking and defensive play.'

Suddenly she wished they were somewhere more private. 'So you played rugby at school and university, is that right?'. Swiftly she changed the subject. 'That's how you know the England captain?'

'He has been a close friend of mine for years.'

And watching rugby was probably one of the few occasions when he could switch off and forget he was a prince, Holly thought to herself as they both settled down to watch the game again.

The match ended with an England victory, and Casper and Holly joined the players at the post-match reception.

Casper was guest of honour and gave a short, humorous speech that had everyone laughing. Watching him mingle with the players and guests afterwards, Holly was fascinated by the change in him. As he smoothly and skilfully dealt with all the people who wanted to speak to him, there was no sign of the icily reserved man she'd been living with, and in his place was the confident, charismatic prince who had seduced her.

But this was his public persona, she reminded herself.

He switched on the charm and gave them what they expected.

But at what personal sacrifice?

He'd buried his own needs for those of other people.

And now he was laughing with the England captain, his old friend, and Holly pushed aside darker thoughts as he introduced her.

'You look different without the mud,' she confessed naïvely, and the man lifted her hand to his lips with laughter in his eyes.

'So you're the woman who distracted me at Twickenham. There I was, focusing on the ball, trying to block out the world around me, and suddenly Royal Boy here is kissing this stunning woman.'

Holly blushed. 'You've known each other a long time.'

'I know all his secrets, but I wouldn't dare tell.' The man grinned. 'He's bigger and tougher than me.'

Holly's eyes slid to Casper's broad shoulders and

she reflected on the fact that his physique was every bit as impressive as this man who was a sporting hero to millions. Her stomach squirmed with longing and she felt herself blushing as her eyes met his questioning gaze.

'I really enjoyed the game,' she said hastily. 'Thanks for taking me.'

The England captain punched Casper on the arm. 'I can understand why you married her. Any woman who thanks you for taking them to a game of rugby has got to be worth hanging onto.' He winked. 'And it helps that she looks gorgeous.'

'All right, enough.' Casper curved an arm around Holly's shoulders in an unmistakeably possessive gesture. 'Time for you to go and charm someone else.'

Finally they were escorted to the waiting limousine, and Holly slid inside. 'I really envy the fact that when you speak all the words come out in the right order.'

Casper's glance was amused. 'And that's surprising?'

'Well, I'm all right with words generally, but in a tricky situation they never come out the way I want them too. I always think of the right thing to say about four days after the opportunity to say it has passed. And I'm *hopeless* at standing up for myself because I hate conflict. The moment anyone glares at me I just want them to stop being angry, and the words tie themselves in knots in my mouth.'

'You stood up to me that day in your friend's flat.'

'That was an exception,' she muttered. 'You were saying awful things to me, none of them true. Generally if someone yells at me I turn into a mute.' The car sped through the centre of Rome, negotiating the clog of traffic and tourists.

'No matter how hard I try, I can't imagine you as a mute,' Casper said dryly, and Holly shrugged.

'I envy your confidence. I've never had much of that.' She studied his profile. 'You must miss the days when you could just go to rugby matches and spend time with your friends. Was it hard for you—becoming the ruling prince? I mean, it wasn't what you expected, was it?'

For a moment he didn't answer, then his mouth tightened slightly. 'The circumstances were hard.'

Had he just shut it away? she wondered. For eight years? If so, no wonder he seemed so cold and detached with her. He'd never given himself a chance to heal.

'Have you *ever* talked about it?' Concern for him made her bold. 'Sorry, but bottling it up for ever can't be a good thing.'

'Holly—'

'Sorry, sorry; OK, I won't ask again,' she said hastily. 'But do you think you could at least give me some detail about how your work evolved? It's just a bit embarrassing when people who have lived here all their lives say things to me and I have to look as though I know what they're talking about, while I really don't have a clue. Someone was praising you for your vision and courage—something to do with the way you transformed the way Santallia did things. I tried to look as though I knew what he was talking about, but obviously I didn't. I just thought it might help if you told me a bit about—things. I don't want to look thick.' Retreating slightly in her seat as she saw Casper lift long bronzed fingers to his forehead, she braced herself for the explosion of Mediterranean volatility that was inevitably going to follow a gesture of frank exasperation.

Surprisingly, when he looked at her there was laughter in his eyes. 'Has anyone ever told you you'd make an excellent torture weapon? You go on and on until a guy is ready to surrender.'

'It's just jolly hard to talk to people if you don't have all the information, and I don't happen to think silence is healthy,' Holly mumbled, and Casper gave a shake of his head.

'Fine. Tonight over dinner, I will outline the highlights of my life so far. And it's only fair to warn you that you'll be bored out of your mind.'

'We're having dinner? Don't tell me, there will be seven hundred other people there.'

'Just the two of us.'

'Just us?' A dark, dangerous thrill cramped her stomach. Perhaps finally, they'd have the opportunity to deepen their relationship. And she knew she wouldn't be bored hearing about his past. She was fast discovering that nothing about him bored her.

'Just us, Holly.' His voice was soft and his eyes lingered on her mouth. 'Late dinner. After our trip to the opera.'

'You're taking me to the opera? Seriously?'

'Given that you sing all the time, I thought you might enjoy it.'

In the darkened auditorium, Casper found himself focusing on Holly's face rather than the opera.

He could see the glisten of tears in her eyes as she responded to the emotional story being played out on the stage in front of them, and marvelled at how open she was with her feelings.

Since the curtain had risen, she'd appeared to have forgotten his existence, so lost was she in Mozart's score and the beauty of the singing.

Casper's eyes rested on the seductive curve of her shoulders, bared by the exquisite sequinned dress that appeared to be superglued to her exotic curves. Around the slender column of her neck were the pink diamonds, glittering against her smooth, pale skin.

From the tip of her simple satin shoes to the elegant coil of her newly straightened hair, she'd slipped into the role of princess with astonishing ease.

Their trip had somehow become public knowledge and, when their limousine had pulled up outside the opera house, a crowd had gathered hoping to see them.

But far from being daunted, or even disappointed that their 'private' evening had become public, she'd spent several minutes chatting, smiling and charming both the crowd and the photographers, until Casper had pointed out that they were going to miss the opera.

And when they'd walked into their box there had been no privacy because every head in the opera house had turned to gaze. Even now he was sure that half the audience were straining to catch a glimpse of his wife, rather than the soprano currently giving her all on the stage.

But Holly wasn't bothered.

He'd misjudged her, he admitted to himself, studying her profile in the darkness.

He'd thought that she would struggle with her new life.

But her only complaint was that he didn't spend enough time with her.

In the grip of a sudden surge of lust, Casper contemplated suggesting that they cut out during the interval, but he couldn't bring himself to do that because she was so obviously enjoying herself.

She was so enthusiastic about everything—meeting people, opera—even rugby.

Casper frowned slightly, admitting to himself that she'd surprised him. Over and over again. He'd expected her to struggle with the crowds and the attention but she'd responded like a professional. He'd thought she'd be tongue tied at official functions, but she was so warm and friendly that everyone was keen to engage her in conversation. He'd expected her to snap at him for dragging her to the rugby, but after the initial humour she'd shown as much interest and energy in that as she did with everything.

He remembered her comment about being lonely and his mind wandered back to the newspaper article that had revealed her pregnancy. At the time he'd been so angry, he hadn't paid attention.

But hadn't there been some revelation about her father?

'So this *palazzo* is owned by one of your friends?' Holly wandered onto the roof terrace, which felt like a slice of paradise in the centre of such a busy city. A profusion of exotic plants and flowers twisted around the ornate iron balustrade, and in the distance she could see the floodlit Colosseum. 'You certainly have influential friends.'

'It is more private than staying in a hotel, or as the guest of the President.'

For once they were guaranteed complete privacy, and that fact alone somehow increased the feeling of intimacy.

She'd wanted to be alone, but now that they were, she felt ridiculously self-conscious.

'I love the diamonds.' She touched her necklace and he smiled.

'They look good on you. I'm glad you didn't change.'

Aware that Casper had watched her more than the opera, Holly had opted to wear the same dress for dinner. The fact that he hadn't been able to take his eyes off her had been a heady experience.

'You like my dress?' Smoothing her hands over her hips in a typically feminine gesture, she glanced down at herself. 'It's not too clingy?'

'It's you I like,' he murmured, 'not the dress.' He

stroked a hand over her shoulder and Holly decided that she might wear the dress for ever.

'All right, now this feels like being on a date,' she said, laughing nervously as she took the glass of champagne he was offering her. 'The weather is gorgeous. It's really warm, considering it's only March.'

'You finally have me alone, and our topic of conversation is going to be the weather?' Casper trailed appreciative dark eyes down her body. 'Has today tired you out?'

'No.' Her nerves on fire, she walked to the edge of the balcony and stared at the ruins of the Colosseum, reminding herself to be careful what she said. 'It's been fun. Thank you.'

'It's probably less tiring than the visits you've been doing. You're in the early stages of pregnancy. Your doctor told me that it can be an exhausting time. Most women in your position would have been lying in the sun with a book.'

'If I wasn't married to you, I'd be waiting tables, pregnant or not,' Holly said dryly, glancing at her luxurious, privileged surroundings with something close to disbelief. 'Being married to you isn't exactly tiring. Someone else makes all the arrangements and tells me where I need to be and when. I even have someone who suggests what I wear. Someone does my hair and make-up. I just turn up and chat to people.'

'And chatting is your favourite occupation. Are you hungry?' Amusement shimmered in his eyes as he steered her towards the table. Silver glinted and candles flickered, and the air was filled with the scent of flowers. 'I must admit I hadn't expected you to cope so well with all the attention. When I first met you, you seemed very insecure. I hadn't factored in how warm and friendly you are. You have a real talent with people.'

'I do?' Warmed by his unexpectedly generous praise, Holly glowed, smiling her thanks at a member of staff who discreetly placed a napkin on her lap. 'That's a nice thing to say.'

'Why were you a waitress?'

'What's wrong with being a waitress?'

'Don't be defensive.' He waited while a team of staff served their food and then dismissed them with a discreet glance towards the door. 'There's nothing wrong with being a waitress, but you could have done a great deal more. You're obviously very bright— even if maths isn't "your thing".'

'I've never been very ambitious.' Holly sipped her drink, wondering if honesty would destroy the atmosphere. 'I know it isn't trendy or politically correct to admit to it, but all I really wanted was to have a baby. When other girls wanted to be doctors or lawyers, I just wanted to be a mum. Not just any mum, but a brilliant mum. And before you say anything, yes, I suppose a psychologist would have a field day with that and say I wanted to make up for my parents' deficient parenting—but actually I don't think that had anything to do with it. I think I just have a very strong maternal instinct.'

'You're right, it isn't politically correct to admit

that.' His eyes held hers. 'Most of the women I know think babies are something to be postponed until they've done all the other things in life.'

Not wanting to think about the women he knew, Holly looked away. 'I always saw children as a beginning, not as an end.' She glanced towards the open glass doors and saw several members of staff hovering. 'Do you think—could they just put the dishes on the table and leave us alone?'

She didn't even see him gesture and yet the staff melted away and the doors were closed, leaving them alone.

'I love it when you do that.' Holly grinned and picked up her fork. 'Do the whole powerful prince thing: "you are dismissed". Do you ever eat in restaurants?'

'Occasionally, but it usually causes too much of a security headache for all concerned. You enjoyed the opera, didn't you?'

'It was fantastic. The costumes, the music.' She sighed. 'Can we go again some time?'

'You've never been before? But you were living in London—a mecca for culture.'

'If you have money. And, even then, London can be a pretty lonely place,' Holly said lightly. 'Loads of people all going about their business, heads down, not looking left or right. I hated the anonymity of it—the fact that no one cared about anyone else. I always thought it would be great to live in a small village where everyone knows everyone, but I needed the work, and there's always work in a city.'

'You don't like being on your own, do you?'

Holly played with her fork. 'No. I suppose I was on my own a lot as a child and I hated it. After my dad left, my mum had to go out to work, and she couldn't afford childcare so she pretty much left me to my own devices. Then she died, and—' She poked at the food on her plate. 'Let's just say I don't associate being on my own with happy feelings. Screwed-up Holly.'

'You seem remarkably balanced to me, considering the state of the world around us.' He gave a faint smile. 'A little dreamy and naïve perhaps. Did you read fairy tales as a child?'

'What's that supposed to mean? I don't believe in fairies, if that's what you're asking me.'

'But you believe in love,' he drawled, curling his long fingers around the slender stem of his glass.

'Love isn't a fairy tale.'

'Isn't it?' The flickering candles illuminated the hard planes of his handsome face and the cynical glitter of his eyes.

'Do you realise how weird this is? I mean—you're the prince with the palace and you're telling me you don't believe in fairy tales. Bizarre.' Holly laughed. 'And, if you were already living out the fairy story, what did your nannies read you? Something about normal people?'

'I was swamped by literature drumming in the importance of responsibility and duty.'

Pondering that revealing statement, Holly studied him thoughtfully. 'So it was all about what your country needed. Not about you as a person. What was your childhood like? Did it feel weird being a prince?'

'I've never been anything else, so I have no idea. But my childhood was pretty normal.' He leaned forward and topped up her glass. 'I was educated at home, and then went to boarding school in England, university in the States and then returned here to work on the tourist development programme.'

'Everyone says you did a brilliant job. Do you miss it?'

'I still keep my eye on all the projects. I'm probably more involved than I should be.' He was unusually communicative, and if Holly was only too aware that they weren't talking about any of the difficult stuff, well, she decided it didn't matter. At least they were talking about *something*. And at least they were alone together instead of surrounded by a crowd of dignitaries.

'I wish we could do this more often,' she said impulsively and then blushed as he rose from the table, a purposeful gleam in his eyes.

'We will. And now that's enough talking.' He pulled her gently to her feet and she stood, heart thumping, and he slid his hands around her face and gave an unexpected smile.

'For the rest of the evening,' he murmured softly, 'It's actions, not words. How does this spectacular dress come off?'

'Zip at the back,' Holly murmured, offering no resistance as he lowered his head to hers.

As always the skilled touch of his mouth sent her head into a spin, and she gave a moan of pleasure as his arms slid round her and he pulled her hard against his powerful frame.

'I want you.' He murmured the words against her lips, his mouth hot and demanding. 'I want you naked, right now.'

Her tummy tumbling, Holly gasped as he lifted her easily and carried her through to the gorgeous bedroom. The French doors remained open and she could hear the faint rush of the sea as he laid her down on the four-poster bed.

Would he notice that her boobs had grown and that her stomach was now slightly rounded? Holly squirmed slightly against the sheets and he kissed her again, using his skill and experience to drive away her inhibitions.

When he slid a hand over her stomach she tensed, and when his mouth trailed down her body she moaned and arched against him, unable to resist what he did to her.

And he did it over and over again, until she finally floated back down to earth, stunned and disconnected and with no clue as to how much time had passed.

Casper shifted above her, fire and heat flickering in his molten dark eyes as his satisfied gaze swept her flushed cheeks. 'I've *never* wanted a woman as much as I want you.'

Heart thudding, Holly gazed up at him. 'I love you.' The confession was torn from her in that moment of vulnerability, and she wrapped her arms round him and buried her face in his neck, breathing in the scent of virile male. 'I love you, Cas. I love you.'

And it was true, she realised helplessly. She did love him.

He was complicated, and he'd hurt her, but somewhere along the way she'd stopped trying to make their relationship work for the sake of the baby, and had started to fall in love.

Or perhaps it had always been there. From that first moment they'd met at the rugby match. Certainly there'd been *something*. How else could you explain the fact that she'd shared an intimacy with him she'd never shared with any other man?

Shocked by her own revelation, it took her a moment to realise that Casper had made no response.

He hadn't spoken and he hadn't moved.

It was as if her words had turned him to stone.

And then he rolled out of the affectionate circle of her arms and onto his back.

The honesty of her confession somehow made his sudden withdrawal all the more shocking. Wracked by a sense of isolation and rejection, Holly instinctively snuggled against him, but his tension was unmistakeable.

'Don't ever say that to me, Holly. Don't ever confuse great sex with love.'

'I'm not confused. I know what I feel. And I don't expect you to say it back, but that doesn't mean I can't say it to you.' Tentatively, she slid her arm over the flat, muscular plains of his stomach. 'I love you. And you don't have to be afraid of that.'

He muttered something under his breath and then shook her off and sprang off of bed. '"I love you" has to be the most overused phrase in the English language. So overused that it's lost its meaning.'

Holly crumpled as she watched her gift devalued in a single stroke. 'It hasn't lost its meaning to me.'

'No?' His eyes hard, he thrust his arms into a robe. 'Usually when people say "I love you" they mean something else. They mean, "you're great in bed", or perhaps, "I love the fact that you're rich and you can show me a good time". For you it's probably, "I love the fact that you were prepared to take on my baby".'

Holly flinched as though he'd slapped her. 'How can you say that?' Her voice cracked. 'Even after this time we've spent together, you still don't know me, do you? I'm trying to do what's best for our child, and you're being needlessly cruel—'

'Honest.'

'I've never said those words to anyone in my life before, and you just threw them back in my face.' The breath trapped in her throat, she watched him. 'Just so that there is no misunderstanding, let me tell you what "I love you" means to me. It means that I care more about your happiness than my own. And I care *all the time*, not just when we're having great sex. "I love you" means ignoring the pain you inflict every time you accuse me of lying, because I *know* you've been hurt yourself even though you won't talk to me about it. It means being patient and trying to accept that you find it hard to share your thoughts and feelings with me. And it's because I love you that I'm still standing here, swallowing my pride and trying to make this work, even when you hurt me on purpose.'

There was a long, deathly silence and then he lifted his hands, pressed his fingers to his temples and inhaled deeply. 'If that's really what you feel, then I'm sorry,' he said hoarsely, and his voice was strangely thickened. 'I can't give you anything back. I don't have that capacity any more.'

Without waiting for her response, he strode out of the bedroom, leaving her alone.

Chapter 8

As the door slammed shut between them, Holly flopped back onto the pillows, emotionally shattered.

How had such a perfect evening ended so badly?

Why should her simple declaration of love have had such a dramatic effect on his mood?

She thought back to his dismissive comments about fairy stories, love and happy endings.

Yes, he'd lost his fiancée, but even extreme grief shouldn't lead to that degree of cynicism should it?

And what had he meant when he said he *couldn't* love?

Was he saying that he believed a person could only love once in their lives?

Was that what was going on in his head?

Or was he saying that he couldn't love *her*?

Frustrated and desperately upset, Holly slipped out of bed, slipped her arms into a silk robe and walked across the bedroom. She stood for a moment with her hand on the door, wanting to follow him and yet afraid of further rejection.

Her hand dropped to her side and she stared at the door, her head a whirlpool of indecision.

She wanted him to talk, and yet she was afraid of hearing what he had to say.

She didn't want to hear that loving and losing another woman had prevented him ever loving again.

Because that would mean that there was no hope for them.

And yet not talking about it wasn't going to change things, was it?

Hoping she was doing the right thing, Holly slowly opened the door, realising that she had no idea where he'd gone.

What if he'd left the *palazzo*?

And then she saw a chink of light under the door to the library that they'd been shown when they'd arrived earlier.

Taking a deep breath, she tapped lightly on the door and opened it.

Casper stood with his back to her, staring out of the window.

Holly closed the door carefully. 'Please don't walk away from me,' she said quietly. 'If we need to have a difficult conversation, then let's have it. But don't avoid it. We don't stand any chance if you don't talk to me.' She knew from the sudden tension in his shoulders that he'd heard her, but it seemed like ages before he responded.

'I can't give you what you want, Holly. Love wasn't part of our deal.'

'Stop talking about it as a deal!' She stared at his back helplessly. 'Could you *please* at least look at me? This is hard enough without being able to see your face.'

He turned and she froze in shock, because his handsome face looked as though it had been chiselled from white marble. His eyes were blank of expression and yet the depth of his pain was evident in the very stillness of his body.

'Talk to me, Cas.' Forgetting her own misery, she walked across to him. 'Why can't you love? Is it because you lost Antonia? Is that it? Is this still about your grief?' And then she saw something in his face—a hardness—and everything fell into place. His comments. His beliefs. His *cynicism*. Suddenly she just *knew*. 'Oh God—she did something dreadful to you, didn't she?'

'Holly—'

Ignoring his warning tone, she slid her hand into his larger one. 'All this time I've been assuming you were madly in love with her, and perhaps you were once.' Her eyes were on his rigid profile. 'But she let you down, didn't she? That's the reason you were so cynical about my motives. That's the reason you say you can't love. You don't *want* to let yourself love. Because you loved once before and she hurt you so badly. She did something, I know she did. *Tell* me about it.'

'Holly.' His voice thickened, and he turned on her. 'Just leave it.'

'No, I won't leave it.' She tightened her grip on his hand, refusing to let him withdraw. 'I want to know. I *deserve* to know.' Tears clogged her throat. *'What did she do?'*

A muscle worked in his lean jaw, and he stared at her, his eyes empty of emotion. 'She was sleeping with my brother.'

His revelation was so unexpected that Holly just stared at him. 'Oh, dear God.'

He gave a twisted smile and looked at her, his eyes strangely blank of emotion. 'Shall I tell you what Antonia meant when she said "I love you"? She meant that she loved the glitter and glamour of royal life. All the high-profile stuff. Only in those days I was working flat out in a commercial role. I didn't do many public engagements. I never expected to be the ruling prince. I didn't even want it. But Antonia did. For her, "I love you" meant "I love what you can do for my lifestyle", and once she found someone who could do more for her she transferred her "love" to them. The life my brother offered her was just too tempting.'

'I'm so sorry.'

'Don't be. I was naïve.' He removed his hand from hers. 'I was young enough and arrogant enough not to question her notion of love. I thought she cared about me and that what we shared was real.'

'The accident.'

Casper drew in a breath. 'We were on a skiing trip, Antonia and I. My brother joined us unexpectedly, and that was when I realised what was going on. Stupidly I confronted both of them, right there, at the top of the mountain where the helicopter had dropped us. My brother skied off and she followed.' He was silent for a moment. 'I went after them but I was quite a way behind. They caught the full force of the avalanche. There was nothing I could do. I was swept into a tree and knocked unconscious.'

'Did you tell anyone?' Her voice was soft. 'When you recovered, did you tell anyone the truth?'

'The country was in a state of crisis—defiling my brother's memory would have achieved nothing.'

'Forget about your country—what about *you*?'

'I couldn't forget about my country. I had a responsibility to the people.'

Holly swallowed down the lump in her throat. 'So you just buried it inside and carried on.'

'Of course.'

'And the only way to cope with so much emotion was to block it out.' Impulsively she slid her arms around his waist. 'Now I understand why you don't believe in love. But that wasn't love, Cas. She didn't love you.'

He closed his hands over her shoulders and gently but firmly prised her away from him. 'Close your book of fairy tales, Holly.' His voice was rough. 'The fact that you know the truth doesn't change anything.'

'It changes it for me.'

'Then you're deluding yourself.' His tone was harsh. 'Inside that dreamy head of yours, you're telling yourself that I'll fall in love with you. And that is never going to happen.'

She ignored the shaft of pain. 'Because you're afraid of being hurt again?'

'After the accident I switched off my emotions because that was the only way of getting through each day. I didn't want to feel. I couldn't afford to feel. How could I fulfil my responsibilities if I was wallowing in my personal grief?'

'So you shut it down, but that doesn't mean—'

'Don't do this!' With a soft curse, he lifted her face to his and forced her to meet his gaze. 'I'm not capable of feeling. And I'm not capable of love. I don't want love to be part of my life. We share great sex. Be grateful for that.'

That bleak confession made her heart stumble, and her voice was barely a whisper in the dimly lit room as she voiced the question that had been worrying her since the day she'd discovered she was pregnant. 'If you really can't love me, then I'll try and accept that. But I have to ask you one thing, Casper.' She was so terrified of the answer that she almost couldn't bear to ask the question. But she *had* to ask it. 'Do you think you can love our baby?'

His gaze held hers for a long moment and then his hands dropped to his side. 'I don't know,' he said hoarsely. 'I honestly don't know.'

Her hopes crashed into a million pieces.

'Don't say that to me, Cas.'

'You wanted the truth. I'm giving you the truth.'

And this time it was Holly who walked out of the room and closed the door between them.

'I'm worried about her, Your Highness. She isn't eating properly and she cancelled an engagement this afternoon.' Emilio's normally impassive features were creased with worry. 'That isn't like her. I thought you ought to know.'

Casper glanced up from the pile of official papers on his desk. 'I expect she's tired.' Holly had been asleep when he'd finally joined her in the bed the previous night. *Or had she been pretending?* He frowned, wondering why that thought hadn't occurred to him before. 'And pregnant women are often faddy in their eating.'

'The princess isn't faddy, sir.' Emilio acted as though his feet had been welded to the spot. 'She loves her food. Even hot-tempered Pietro didn't have a single tantrum when he was cooking for her. Since you came back from Rome two weeks ago, she has eaten next to nothing. And she's stopped singing.'

Casper slowly and carefully put down the draft proposal he was reading.

She'd also stopped smiling, talking and cuddling him.

Since that night in Rome, Holly had behaved with a polite formality that was totally at odds with her outgoing personality. She answered his questions, but she asked none of her own, and she was invariably in bed asleep by the time he joined her.

She was dragging herself around like a wounded animal trying to find a place to die, and Casper gritted his teeth.

He had no reason to feel guilty.

And it should be a matter of indifference to him that his Head of Security clearly suspected that he had something to do with Holly's current level of distress. 'You are responsible for her physical well-being, not her emotional health.' His tone cool, Casper closed the file on his desk. 'It isn't your concern.'

'The princess was extremely kind to me when Tomasso was ill.' Emilio stood there, looking as though a hurricane wouldn't dislodge him. 'I want to make sure nothing is wrong. Two days ago when she opened the new primary school she just picked at her food, and yesterday when lunch was sent up to the apartment it came back untouched. Shall I ask her staff to call the doctor?'

'She doesn't need the doctor.' Casper pushed back his chair violently and stood up. 'I'll talk to her.'

'I think she needs a doctor.' In response to the sardonic lift of Casper's eyebrows, Emilio coloured. 'It's just that, if there is something upsetting her, she might need to talk to someone.'

'*Talk* to someone?' Casper looked at him with naked incredulity. 'Emilio, since when did a hardened ex-special forces soldier advocate talking therapy?'

Emilio didn't back down. 'Holly likes to talk, Your Highness.'

'I had noticed.'

But he wasn't talking to her, was he? Casper lifted a hand and rubbed his fingers over his forehead. 'I'll talk to her, Emilio. Thank you for bringing it to my attention.'

Still Emilio didn't move. 'She might prefer to talk to someone outside. Someone who isn't close to her.'

'You think she won't want to talk to me?'

'You can be intimidating, sir. And you're very—blunt. Holly is very optimistic and romantic.'

Not any more. *He was fairly sure he'd killed both those traits.*

Reflecting on that fact, Casper sucked in a breath. 'I can't promise romantic, but I will make sure I'm approachable.'

'May I say one more thing, sir?'

'Can I stop you?'

Ignoring the irony in the prince's tone, Emilio ploughed on. 'I have been by your side since you were thirteen years old. Holly—Her Royal Highness,' he corrected himself hastily, 'isn't like any of the women you've been with before. She's genuine.'

Genuine? Casper shook his head, not sure whether to be relieved that she'd done such a good PR job on his staff, or exasperated that everyone just took her at face value. They saw nothing beyond the pretty smile and the chatty personality. Apparently it hadn't occurred to a single other person that this baby might not be his. That genuine, kind Holly Phillips might have another side to her.

That people and relationships were not always the way they appeared.

He wondered whether his loyal Head of Security had known Antonia had been sleeping with his brother.

'Thank you, Emilio. I'll deal with it.'

'Will you still be attending the fundraising dinner, sir?'

Casper frowned. 'Yes, of course.'

'The car will be ready at seven-thirty, sir.'

'One question, Emilio.' Casper lifted a hand and the bodyguard stopped. 'Which engagement did she cancel?'

Emilio met his gaze. 'The opening of a new family centre for children from split families, sir. It was an initiative designed to give lone parents support and children the opportunity to spend time with male role-models.' He hesitated and then bowed. 'I'll arrange the car for later.'

Casper stood still for a moment.

Then he cursed long and fluently, cast a frustrated glance at the volume of work on his desk, and turned his back on it and strode through the private apartments looking for Holly.

Holly lay on the bed with her head under the pillow.

She had to get up.

She had things to do. Responsibilities.

But her mind was so exhausted with thinking and worrying that she couldn't move.

'Holly.'

The sound of Casper's voice made her curl the pillow over her head. She didn't want him to see that she'd been crying. *She didn't want to see him at all.* 'Go away. I'm tired. I'm having a sleep.'

'We have to talk.'

She curled up like a foetus. 'I'm still trying to get over the last talk we had.'

She heard the strong tread of his footsteps, and then the pillow was firmly prised from the tight ball of her fists. 'You're going to suffocate yourself.'

Holly kept her face turned away from him. 'I think better under the pillow.'

The pillow landed on the floor with a soft thud, and then she felt his hands curve around her and he lifted her into a sitting position. 'I want to look at you when I talk to you.' His fingers lifted her chin and his eyes narrowed. '*Dio*, have you been crying?'

'No, my face always looks like a tomato.' Mortified, she jerked her chin away from his fingers. 'Just go away, Casper.'

But he didn't move.

'The staff tell me you're not eating. They're worried about you.'

'That's kind of them.' Holly rubbed her hands over her arms. 'But I don't fancy anything to eat.'

'You cancelled your engagement this afternoon.'

'I really am sorry about that.' She wished he wouldn't sit so close to her. *She couldn't concen-*

trate when he was this close. 'But the subject was a bit—painful. I just couldn't face it. I will go, I promise. The visit is going to be rearranged. Just not this week.' Why was it that she just wanted to fling her arms around his neck and sob?

Terrified that she'd give in to the impulse, she wriggled off the bed and walked over to the glass doors that were open onto the balcony.

A breeze played with the filmy curtains, and beyond the profusion of plants she could see sunlight glistening on the surface of a perfect blue sea.

Although it was only early April, it promised to be a warm day.

And she'd never felt more miserable in her life.

'Forget the visit.' Casper gave a soft curse and strode across to her, pulling her into his arms. 'Enough, Holly.' His voice was rough. 'This is about Rome, isn't it? We've been dancing round the issue for two weeks. Perhaps I was a little too blunt.'

'You were honest.' She stood rigid in his arms, trying to ignore the excitement that fluttered to life in her tummy.

She didn't want to respond.

'You're making yourself ill.'

'It's just hard, that's all.' Holly tried to pull away from him but he held her firmly. 'Normally when I have a problem I talk it through and that's how I deal with things.'

He cupped her face, his eyes holding hers. 'Then talk it through.'

'You make it sound so simple. But who am I supposed to talk to, Casper?' Her voice was a whisper. 'It's all private stuff, isn't it? I can just imagine what some of the more unscrupulous staff would do with a story like that.'

His eyes narrowed. 'You're learning about the media.'

'Yes, well, I've had some experience now.' She was desperately aware of him—of the hardness of his thighs pressing against hers, of the strength of his arms as he held her firmly.

'This is your chance to get your revenge.'

'You really ought to get to know me, instead of just turning me into some stereotypical gold digger. I don't want revenge, Casper. I don't want to hurt you. I just want you to love our baby.' And her. She wanted him to love her. 'And the fact that you can't…' The dilemma started to swirl in her head again. 'I don't know what to do.'

'You've lost weight.' His hands slid slowly down her arms and his mouth tightened. 'You can start by eating.'

'I'm not hungry.'

'Then you should be thinking about the baby.'

It was like pulling the pin out of a hand grenade.

Erupting with a violence that was new to her, Holly lifted a hand and slapped him hard. 'How *dare* you tell me I should be thinking about the baby? I think of nothing else!' Sobbing with fury and outrage, she backed away from him, his stunned expression blurring as tears pricked her eyes. 'From the moment I discovered I was pregnant the baby is the *only* thing I've been thinking of. When you turned up at the flat, that day you were *horrid* to me, I spent two weeks going round and round in circles trying to work out what to do for the best, but I decided that, as this is your baby, marrying you was the right thing to do. Even when you told me that you believe you're infertile I didn't panic, because I know it isn't true and sooner or later you're going to know that too. Then you told me that you couldn't ever love me and that *hurt*—' Her voice cracked. 'Yes, it hurt, but I made myself accept it because I kept reminding myself that it isn't me that matters. But when you said you didn't know if you could love our baby—'

'Holly.' His voice was tight. 'You have to calm down—'

'Don't tell me to calm down! Antonia did a dreadful thing to you. Really dreadful. But that isn't our baby's fault. And now I don't know what to do.' She paced the floor, so agitated that she couldn't keep still. 'What sort of a mother would I be if I stayed with a man who can't love his own child? I always thought that the only thing that mattered was to have a father. But is it worse to grow up with a father who doesn't love you? I don't know, and maybe I've done the wrong thing by marrying you, maybe I am a bad mother, but don't *ever* accuse me of not thinking about our baby!'

Casper muttered something in Italian and ran a hand over the back of his neck, tension visible in every angle of his powerful frame. 'I did *not* say that you were a bad mother.'

'But you implied it.'

'Enough!' It was a command, and Holly stilled, her legs trembling so much that she was almost relieved when he strode towards her and scooped her into his arms.

'I hate you,' she whispered, and then she burst into tears and buried her face in his shoulder.

'Dio, you have to stop this, you're making yourself ill. Ssh.' He laid her gently on the bed and then lay down next to her and pulled her into his arms, ignoring her attempts to resist. 'Calm down.' He stroked her hair away from her face but Holly couldn't stop crying.

'I'm sorry I hit you. I'm sorry.' Her breath was coming in jerks. 'I've never hit anyone in my life before. It's just that I so badly want you to love the baby. I *need* you to love it, Cas.' She covered her face with her hands. 'You don't know what it's like to have a father that doesn't care. It makes you feel worthless. If your own father doesn't love you, why should anyone else?'

He gave a soft curse, rolled her onto her back and lowered his body onto hers.

Then he gently removed her hands and wiped her face with the edge of the sheet.

'Hush.'

Still crying, she pushed at his powerful chest. 'Cas, don't—' But her protest was cut off by the demands of his mouth, and within seconds she could no longer remember why she hadn't wanted him to kiss her.

The explosion of sexual excitement anaesthetised the turmoil in her brain and she kissed him back, her body responding to his.

Only when she was soft and compliant did Casper finally lift his head.

'Don't use sex like this,' she moaned, and he gave a grim smile.

'I was trying to stop you crying. Now it is my turn to talk,' he said softly. 'And you're not going to interrupt.' He wiped her damp cheeks with a sweep of his thumb. 'I won't make you false promises of love. I can't do that, and it wouldn't be fair to you because I will not lie. But I do promise you this.' His dark eyes locked with hers, demanding her attention. 'I promise that I will be a good father to the baby. I promise that I will not walk off and leave the child, as your father did to you. I promise that I will do everything in my power to make sure that the child grows up feeling secure and valued. I accepted responsibility for the child and I intend to fulfil that responsibility to the best of my ability.'

Numb, sodden with misery, Holly stared up at him. It wasn't what she wanted, but it was a start. And, if he was prepared to do that for a child that he didn't believe was his, perhaps once he discovered that he was the baby's father then…

He'd coped with hurt by turning off his emotions. Maybe nothing could switch them back on again.

Her natural optimism flickered to life.

But she could hope.

* * *

'Your favourite lunch, Your Highness. *Pollo alla limone.*'

'Yum.' Holly put down the letter she was writing. 'Pietro, you have no idea how grateful I am that you decided to leave England and work here for a while. The whole of the palace must be rejoicing. Not that the other chefs weren't brilliant, of course,' she said hastily, and Pietro smiled as he placed a simple green salad next to the chicken.

'I'm not cooking for the rest of the palace, madam. Just for you. Those were the prince's orders.'

'Really? I didn't know that.' Thinking of all the other thoughtful gestures the prince had made since that terrible afternoon when she'd hit him, something softened inside her. 'He brought you all the way over here, for *me?*'

'His Royal Highness is most concerned about your comfort and happiness. But so are we all. You and the *bambino.* You say jump, we say "off which cliff?"' Pietro beamed as he lifted a jug. 'Sicilian lemonade?'

'Don't even bother asking. You know I'm addicted.' Smiling, Holly held out her glass to be filled. 'So, are you happy here?'

'*Si,* because to see you blooming with health gives me satisfaction. And when the baby comes no one will prepare his food except me! I have talked to the gardeners, and we are designing a special vegetable patch—all organic and grown in the Santallia sunshine.'

'Puréed Santallian carrot—' Taking a mouthful of chicken, Holly almost choked as she noticed Casper standing in the doorway.

Sunlight glinted off his dark hair, and he looked so outrageously handsome that her heart dropped.

Why did she have to feel like this?

It was no wonder she struggled to keep a degree of emotional distance when he had such a powerful effect on her.

Right from that very first day at the rugby, she'd failed to hold herself back.

Even now, when she knew he had the ability to hurt her and her child, she was willing to risk it all.

She swallowed the lump of food in her mouth and put down her fork. 'I—I didn't know you were joining me for lunch. Here—' she pushed her plate towards him '—Pietro always cooks for the five thousand—we can share.'

'No, madam!' Appalled, Pietro clasped his hands in front of him and then remembered himself and bowed stiffly. 'I can bring more from the kitchen.'

'*Grazie.*' Casper gave Pietro a rare smile and sat down opposite Holly, his eyes on the pile of envelopes. 'You've been busy.'

'I'm replying to all these children who are sending me pictures and letters. There are hundreds. And look, Cas.' Relieved for an excuse to focus on something other than the way he made her feel, Holly put down her fork and reached for a pink envelope. 'A little girl sent me this soft toy she made. Isn't it sweet?'

Casper's brows rose as he stared at the object. 'What is it supposed to be?'

'Well, it's…' Holly studied the pink fluffy wedge closely and then frowned. 'I thought it might be a pig, or possibly a sheep. I'm not absolutely sure,' she conceded, 'But I love it. She's only six. Don't you think it's brilliant?'

'So you are writing to thank her for sending you a something?' Casper stretched his legs out, his eyes amused. 'That is one letter I would like to read.'

'I'll think of something to say.' Holly put the fluffy object away carefully. 'People are so kind. And talking of kind…' She bit her lip and looked up at him. 'Thank you for arranging for Pietro to come here. And for flying Nicky out for a week. That was so thoughtful.'

'I thought you needed someone to talk to. And she was very loyal to you when you were in trouble.'

'Is that why you gave her that beautiful bracelet? She loved it. And we had such a good time at the beach. Thank you.'

He seemed about to say something in response, but at that moment several staff appeared with lunch.

Pietro served the prince with a flourish. 'If there is anything else, please call,' he murmured and then retreated, leaving them alone.

Casper glanced at Holly. 'Eat,' he drawled, 'Or Pietro will resign.'

Holly smiled, very conscious of his eyes on her. 'I'd be the size of a small tower block if I ate everything Pietro gave me.'

'Does that explain why the palace cats are putting on weight?'

Holly picked up her fork again. 'I *am* eating.'

'I know. The doctor is very happy with your health, including your weight gain.'

Her heart fluttered. 'You asked him?'

Their eyes clashed. 'I care, Holly.'

She believed him. He'd demonstrated that over and over again. But it was impossible to forget the words he'd spoken in Rome. And she couldn't stop asking herself whether caring was going to be enough. 'The nursery is finished.' Pushing the thought away, she gave a bright smile. 'The designer you suggested is brilliant. It looks gorgeous.'

'Good. I bought you a present.' He handed her a box. 'I hope you like it.'

Holly's hand shook as she took it from him. 'I don't need anything.'

'A present shouldn't be something you need. It should be wantonly extravagant.'

Holly flipped open the box and gasped. 'Well, it's certainly that!' Carefully she lifted the diamond bracelet from its velvet nest. 'It matches my necklace.'

He was trying to compensate for the fact that he didn't love her.

The thought almost choked her.

'*Now* what's wrong?' His voice rough, he laid his fork down.

'Nothing.' She fastened the bracelet around her

wrist and gave him a brilliant smile. 'What could possibly be wrong?'

'You're holding back. For once there is plenty going on in your head that isn't coming out of your mouth, and that makes me uneasy.' After a moment's hesitation, he reached across the table to take her hand. 'You're still not yourself, Holly. I feel as though I can never quite reach you.'

'We're together every night.'

'Physically, yes. We have incredible sex and then you turn your back on me and say good night.'

Colour flaming in her cheeks, Holly studied the remains of the chicken on her plate.

She could feel the hot sunshine on the back of her neck, the whisper of a breeze playing with her hair and the blaze of heat in his eyes as he watched her.

'I'm trying to—we're different.' Staring miserably at the glittering diamonds, she wondered absently whether the extravagance of the gift was inversely related to his feelings for her. *The emptier his heart, the bigger the diamonds?* 'I'm very demonstrative by nature, and you're—not. All the worst moments in our relationship have been when I've shown my feelings. You back off. You shut down like a nuclear reactor detecting a leak. Nothing must escape.'

Casper frowned and his grip tightened on her hand. 'So you're protecting me?'

'No.' Finally she lifted her eyes and looked at him. 'I'm protecting myself.'

Chapter 9

Determined to keep busy, Holly threw herself into her public engagements and wrote as many personal replies as she could to the many letters and cards she received. She discovered that if she kept herself busy she didn't think so much and that was a good thing because her thoughts frightened her.

She didn't want to think what might happen if Casper didn't love their baby.

And, since that couldn't immediately be resolved, she pushed the thought away.

When the baby was born, she'd worry. Until then, she'd hope.

And in the meantime she fussed in the nursery, as if being born into perfect surroundings might somehow compensate for deficiencies in other areas of the baby's life.

She was sitting in the hand-carved rocking chair, reading a book about childbirth one morning, when one of the palace staff told her she had a personal visitor.

Not expecting anyone, Holly put the book down and walked through to the beautiful living-room with the windows overlooking the sparkling Mediterranean.

Eddie stood there, looking awkward and out of place.

'Eddie?' Shocked to see him, Holly walked quickly across the room. 'What are you doing here?'

'What sort of a question is that? We were friends once.' He gave a twisted smile. 'Or can't you have friends now you're a royal?'

'Of course I can have friends.' Holly blushed, feeling really awkward and uncomfortable and not sure why. 'But obviously I wasn't expecting to see you and—how are you?'

'OK. Doing well, actually. The job's turning out well.'

'Good. I'm pleased for you.' And she was, she realised, picking over her feelings carefully. She wasn't angry with him. If anything, she was grateful. If he hadn't broken their engagement, she might well have married him, and that would have been the biggest mistake of her life—because she knew now that she didn't love him and she never had.

Loving Casper had taught her what love was, and it wasn't what she'd felt for Eddie.

'I was owed some holiday.' Thrusting his hands into his pockets, he walked over to the windows. 'I'm spending a week in the Italian lakes, but I thought I'd call in here on the way. Booked myself a room at the posh hotel on the beach. Stunning view. Can't imagine Lake Como being any prettier than this.' He took a deep breath, rubbed a hand over the back of his neck and turned to face her. 'I came here to apologise, actually. For going to the press. I— It was a rotten thing to do.'

'It's OK. You were upset.' Touched that he'd bothered to apologise, Holly smiled. 'People do funny things when they're upset.'

'I didn't mean to make things difficult for you.' Eddie shrugged sheepishly. 'Well, I suppose I did. I was angry and jealous and—' he cleared his throat '—I wasn't sure if you'd want to see me to be honest. But I needed to say sorry. I've been feeling guilty.'

'Please don't give it another thought.'

Eddie seemed relieved. 'It was jolly hard getting in to see you. Layers and layers of security. It was that big fellow who fixed it for me.'

'Emilio?'

'That's him. The prince's henchman. Not that the prince needs him. From what I can gather, he can fire his own gun if the need arises. Is he treating you well?'

Holly thought about the diamonds and the long

nights spent in sexual ecstasy. And she thought about the fact he didn't love her.

'He's treating me well.'

'Just thought I'd check.' Eddie gave a lopsided smile. 'In case you'd changed you mind and wanted to escape.' He waved a hand around their luxurious surroundings. 'I might not be able to offer you a palace, but—'

'I never wanted a palace, Eddie,' Holly said softly, resting a hand protectively over the baby. 'Family, being loved—those are the things that are important to me.'

'I was going to say I think I was a bit too ambitious for you, but then I realised how bloody stupid that sounds now that you're living with a prince in a palace!' He pulled a face. 'We weren't absolutely right together, were we?'

'No, we weren't,' Holly said honestly. 'And ambition has nothing to do with the reason I'm living here. Cas is my baby's father, Eddie. That's why I'm here.'

'To begin with I was so angry with you. I thought you'd tried to make a fool out of me—'

Holly frowned. 'I'm not like that.'

'I know you're not,' Eddie said, a bit too hastily. 'I hope the prince knows how lucky he is. Anyway, I ought to be going.'

'Already? Don't you want coffee or something?' Holly walked across to him and held out a hand in a gesture of conciliation. 'It was sweet of you to come and see me. I appreciate it. And sweet of you to apologise.'

He hesitated and then took her hand. 'I just wanted to check you're OK. If you ever need anything…'

'She has everything she needs.' A harsh voice came from behind them, and Holly turned to see Casper standing in the doorway, his eyes glittering like shards of ice.

Visibly nervous, Eddie gave a slight bow. 'Your Highness. I— Well, I just wanted to see Holly—say hello—you know how it is. I was just leaving.'

Casper's threatening gaze didn't shift from his face. 'I'll show you out.'

Shocked and more than a little embarrassed by Casper's rudeness, Holly gave Eddie a hug to make up for it. 'Thank you for looking me up.'

Eddie hugged her back awkwardly, one eye on the prince. 'Good to see you looking so well. Bye, Holly.' He left the living room, and moments later Casper strode back into the room, his eyes simmering black with anger.

'I allow you a great deal of freedom,' he said savagely, 'But I do not expect you to entertain your lover in our living room.'

'That's ridiculous.' Holly watched him unravel with appalled disbelief. 'He is *not* my lover. And I don't understand why you're being possessive.'

He didn't care about her, did he?

He didn't want her love.

'But he *was* your lover!' A thunderous expression on his face, Casper prowled across the living room, tension emanating from every bit of his powerful frame. 'And yes, I'm possessive! When I find the father of your baby in my living room, holding your hand, I'm possessive!'

Something snapped inside Holly.

'I never had sex with Eddie! I have never slept with anyone except you!' Consumed by an anger she didn't know she could feel, Holly threw the words at him. 'All you ever say is *your* baby, but it's *our* baby, Casper. *This is your baby, too*. And I'm sick of tiptoeing round the issue.'

His voice strangely thickened, Casper faced her down. 'Don't ever, *ever* touch another man!'

'Why? I *like* hugging, and you don't want me hugging you!' Flinging the words at him like bricks, Holly took a step backwards, a hand over her stomach. 'I can't live like this any more. I can't live in this—this—emotional desert! I'm afraid to touch you in case you back away, and I'm afraid to speak in case I say the wrong thing. I've tried *so hard* to do everything right. I know this marriage wasn't what you wanted, but I've done my best. I've worked and worked, and I've been *loyal*. I haven't once talked about you to anyone, not even when you pushed me away and I was so lonely I wanted to die! But not once, in all that time, have I ever given you reason not to trust me.'

A muscle flickered in his jaw. 'It isn't a question of trust.'

'Of course it is!' Her voice was high-pitched and unlike her usual tone. 'I forgave you for what you thought about me at the beginning of our relationship because I was honest enough to admit that I didn't exactly behave like a virgin, even though that's what I was. I've made allowances for the fact that Antonia hurt you so badly, and I've made allowances for the fact that your position as ruling prince meant you weren't allowed to grieve. But when have you *ever* made allowances for me? Never. Not once have you given me the benefit of the doubt. *Not once.*' Her heart was racing and she felt suddenly light-headed.

Casper inhaled sharply. 'Holly—'

'*Don't look at me as if I've lost it!* I am *not* hysterical. In fact, this is probably the sanest moment I've had since I've met you. I've always assumed that you act the way you do because of Antonia, but I'm starting to think it has more to do with your bloody ego!'

'I've never heard you swear before.'

'Yes, well, our relationship has been full of firsts. First sex, first swearing, first slap around the face—' Feeling the baby kick, Holly placed a hand on her bump and rubbed gently. 'You know what I think, Cas? I don't think this has anything to do with Antonia. I think it's more to do with your macho, alpha, king of the world, dominant—' she waved a hand, searching for more adjectives '—*man* thing. You couldn't bear the thought that I'd slept with another man, and the really ridiculous, crazy thing is *I haven't*!'

'You were engaged to him.'

'But I didn't have sex with him! That's the main reason he dumped me, because I was too shy to take my clothes off!' She glared at him, silencing his next remark with a warning glance. 'And *don't* ask me what happened when I met you, because I still haven't worked that one out. You have a way of undressing a woman that James Bond would envy.'

'You were devastated when you broke up with him.'

'Obviously not *that* devastated or I wouldn't have been having crazy, abandoned sex on a table with you the next day.' A hysterical laugh escaped from her throat. 'Just because you're incapable of indulging in a relationship that doesn't include sex, it doesn't mean I'm the same. Now get out, and stay away from me until you've learned how to be human.'

In the grip of a savage rage, Casper strode through his private rooms and slammed the door of his study.

He'd lost his temper with a pregnant woman.

What had he been thinking?

But he knew the answer to that. He hadn't been thinking at all.

From the moment he'd walked into the living room and seen Eddie standing there holding Holly's hand, his brain had been engulfed in a fiery fog of red-hot jealousy.

Never before had he felt the overwhelming urge to wipe another person from the face of the earth, but he had today.

The thought that Eddie had been near her.

He felt physically sick, his forehead damp and his palms sweating.

He needed to apologise to Holly, but first he

needed to make sure that Eddie didn't set foot in her life again.

Not pausing to question the sense of his actions, he ordered his driver to take him to the hotel where Eddie was staying. Ignoring the amazed looks of the hotel reception-staff as they gave him the room number he wanted, Casper dismissed his security guards and then took the stairs two at a time.

Outside the room, he took a deep breath.

He was *not* going to kill him.

Having forced that thought into his head, he hammered on the door.

Eddie pulled it open and the colour drained from his face. 'Your Highness—this is—'

'Why did you break the engagement?' Casper slammed the door shut behind him, guaranteeing their privacy.

Eddie's mouth worked like a fish, and then he gave a slight smile and a shrug, his ego reasserting itself. 'Man to man? Actually I met a stunning blonde. She had amazing—you know.' He gestured with his hands and Casper gritted his teeth and forced himself to ask the question he'd come to ask.

'Did you sleep with Holly?' His voice was thickened, and Eddie gave a confident smile and a knowing wink.

'God, yes—she was bloody insatiable.'

Forgetting his promise to himself, Casper punched the other man hard in the jaw and Eddie staggered backwards, clutching his face.

'God, you've broken my jaw—I'll have you for this!'

'Go ahead.' Casper hauled the man to his feet by the front of his shirt, ignoring the tearing sound as the fabric gave way. 'So you had sex with Holly, and then you dumped her. Is that what you expect me to believe?'

Eddie touched his jaw gingerly. 'Some girls you have sex with, some girls you marry, you know what I mean?' Fear flickered in his eyes as he registered Casper's expression. 'Still, money changes a person. I'm sure she's changed since she's married you, Your Highness.'

'Are you? I think Holly is the same girl she's always been.' His tone flat, Casper released the other man, shaking him off like a bug from a leaf.

Eddie spluttered with relief and backed away, his hand on his jaw, and then his chest. 'You ripped my shirt.'

'You're lucky I stopped at your shirt.'

'Do you know how much I'm going to get for this story?' Eddie's face was scarlet with rage and Casper shot him a contemptuous glance.

'So it *was* you who sold the story to the paper the first time.'

'Is that what Holly told you?'

'*Don't* call her Holly. To you, it's Her Royal Highness.' Casper flexed his long fingers and had the satisfaction of seeing Eddie take another step backwards. 'And if you *ever* mention the princess's name again, the next thing I rip will be your throat.'

'I thought princes were supposed to be civilised,' Eddie squeaked from his position of safety, and Casper gave a slow, dangerous smile as he strode towards the door.

'I never did believe in fairy stories.'

'I'll be fine, Emilio, honestly. I just feel like some sea air, and The Dowager Cottage is so pretty, right on the sand. It reminds me of the night before my wedding.' *When she'd still been full of hope.*

Holly's face ached from the effort of smiling, and she stuffed a few items into a large canvas bag, as if a day on the beach was just what she wanted, but Emilio didn't look convinced.

'I will call His Highness and—'

'No, don't do that.' Holly interrupted him quickly, wincing as the baby kicked her hard. 'I just want to be on my own for a bit.'

And she didn't want to be in the palace when Casper eventually returned from wherever it was he'd stalked off to.

She just couldn't stand yet another confrontation.

And she had no idea what they were going to do about their marriage. Could they really limp along like this with just her love and hot sex to hold them together?

Was it enough?

Her head started to throb again and she made a conscious effort to switch off her thoughts for the baby's sake, wondering whether the tension was the reason he was kicking so violently.

For the baby's sake, she needed to try and relax.

Without further question, Emilio summoned her driver, and once she arrived at The Dowager Cottage Holly kicked off her shoes and made a conscious effort to unwind. 'I'm just going to sit on the beach for a bit.' She smiled at the man who had become a friend. 'Thanks, Emilio.'

'Pietro made you this, madam.' He handed her a small bag. 'Just a few of your favourite snacks.'

'He is such a sweetie.' Choked by the warmth that they'd showed her, she suddenly rose on tiptoe to kiss Emilio. 'And so are you,' she said huskily, her lips brushing his cheek. 'You've been *so* kind to me all the way through this. Thank you.'

Emilio cleared his throat. 'You are a very special person, madam.'

'I'm a waitress,' Holly reminded him with a dry tone, but Emilio shook his head.

'No.' His voice was soft. 'You're a princess. In every sense that matters.'

Holly blinked several times and suddenly found that she had a lump in her throat. She was so touched by his words that for a moment she couldn't reply.

She *could* be happy with her life, she told herself. She had friends.

'Well, let's hope that's one kiss that the paparazzi didn't manage to catch on camera.' Lightening the atmosphere with a cheeky wink, she walked onto the sand.

'I'll be right here, madam,' Emilio called after

her, adjusting the tiny radio he wore in his ear. 'You know how to call me.'

'Thanks. But no one has access to this beach. I'll be fine. Go inside and relax. It's too hot to stand out here.'

Her pale-blue sun dress swinging around her bare calves, Holly walked to the furthest end of the beautiful curving beach and plopped herself down on the sand.

For a while she just stared out to sea. Then she opened the bag Pietro had sent, but discovered she wasn't hungry.

Finally she opened her book.

'You're holding that book upside down. And you should be wearing a hat.' Casper stood there, tall and powerful, the width of his shoulders shading her from the sun. 'You'll burn.'

Holly dropped the book onto the sand. 'Please go away. I want to be alone.' *What she didn't want was to feel this immediate rush of pleasure that always filled her whenever he was near.*

'You *hate* being on your own,' he responded instantly. 'You are the most sociable person I have ever met.'

Holly brushed the sand from the book, her fingers shaking. 'That depends on the company.'

His arrogant, dark head jerked back as though she'd hit him again, but instead of retaliating he settled himself on the sand next to her, the unusual tension in his shoulders suggesting that he was less than sure of his welcome.

'You're *extremely* angry with me, and I can't blame you for that.' He studied her for a moment and then reached gently for her hand and curled her slender fingers into a fist. 'You can hit me again if you like.'

'It didn't make me feel any better.' She pulled her hand away from his, hating herself for feeling a thrill of excitement instead of indifference. 'And I'd be grateful if you'd stop looking at me like that.'

'How am I looking at you?'

'You're sizing up the situation so that you can decide which of your slick diplomatic skills are required to talk me round.'

'I wish it were that easy.' Casper lifted one broad shoulder in a resigned gesture. 'Unfortunately for me, I have no previous experience of handling a situation like this.'

'Which is?'

'Grovelling.' A gleam of self-mockery glinting in his sexy eyes, he reached for her hand again, this time locking it firmly in his. 'I was wrong about you. The baby is mine. I know that now.'

Holly closed her eyes tightly, swamped by a rush of emotions so powerful that she couldn't breathe.

He believed her. He trusted her.

Finally, he trusted her.

And then she realised that something wasn't quite right about his sudden confession and her eyes flew open. 'Wait a minute.' She snatched her hand away from his because she couldn't keep her mind focused when he was touching her. 'The last time I saw you, you were accusing me of having an affair with Eddie—when did you suddenly become rational?'

Dark streaks of colour highlighted his aristocratic bone structure, and Casper spread his hands in a gesture of conciliation. 'I believe you, Holly. That's all that matters.'

'No.' Holly scrambled to her feet, knowing that she only stood a chance of thinking clearly if he wasn't within touching distance. 'No, it isn't. You went to the doctor, didn't you?'

A muscle flickered in his bronzed cheek. 'Yes.'

Holly wrapped her arms around her waist and gave a painful laugh. 'So you placed your trust in medical science, not me.'

'Holly…'

'So they've told you that you're capable of fathering a child. That's good. But it still doesn't tell you that this child is yours, does it?'

His stunning dark eyes narrowed warily, as if he sensed a trick question. 'I have no doubt that the baby is mine.' He drew in a long breath, his shimmering gaze fixed on her face, assessing her reaction. 'I have no doubt that you have been telling me the truth all along.'

'Really? What makes you so confident that I didn't have sex with the whole rugby team once I'd finished with you?' Her voice rising, Holly winced as the baby planted another kick against her ribs, and glared as Casper lifted a hand in what was obviously intended to be a conciliatory gesture.

'You're overreacting because you're pregnant. You're very hormonal and—'

'Hormonal? Don't patronise me! And anyway, if I'm hormonal, what's *your* excuse? You overreact all the time! You accuse me of having sex with just about everyone, even though it should have been perfectly obvious to you that I'd never been with a man before. You thought I was some scheming hussy doing some sort of—of—' she searched for an analogy '—paternity lottery. Trying to win first prize of a prince in the "most eligible daddy" contest.'

Casper rose to his feet, a tall, powerful figure, as imposing in casual clothes as he was in a dinner jacket. His mouth tightened and his lean, strong face was suddenly watchful. 'You have to agree I had reason to feel like that.'

'To begin with, maybe. But *not* once you knew me.' Dragging her eyes away from the hint of bronzed male skin at the neck of his shirt, Holly stooped and stuffed her few items back into her bag. She wasn't going to look at him. So, he was devastatingly handsome. So what? 'I loved you, Casper, and you threw it back at me because you're afraid.'

He inhaled sharply. 'I am not afraid. And you're stuffing sand in your bag along with the books.'

'I don't care about the sand! And you *are* afraid— you're so afraid you've shut yourself down so that you can't ever be hurt again.' Frustrated and upset, she emptied her bag and started again, this time shaking the sand onto the beach.

Casper stepped towards her, dark eyes glittering. 'I came here to apologise.'

Holly stared at him, wishing he wasn't so indecently handsome. *Wishing that she didn't still ache for him to touch her.* 'Then you definitely need more practice, because where I come from apologies usually contain the word sorry at least once.' With a violent movement, she hooked the bag onto her shoulder and reached for her hat, but he caught her arm and held her firmly.

'You are *not* walking away from me.'

'Watch me.' With her free hand, she jammed the hat onto her head and then gasped as he swung her into his arms. 'Put me down *right now.*'

'No.' Ignoring her protest and her wriggling, Casper walked purposefully to the end of the beach, took a narrow path without breaking stride and then lowered her onto soft white sand.

'You've probably put your back out,' Holly muttered, her fingers curling over his warm, bronzed shoulders to steady herself. 'And it serves you right.'

'You don't weigh anything.'

Noticing their surroundings for the first time, Holly gave a soft gasp of shock, because she'd never seen anywhere quite as beautiful.

'I had no idea there was another beach here. It's stunning.'

'When we were children, my brother and I called it the secret beach.' His tone gruff, Casper spread the rug on the sand and gently eased the bag from her shoulders. 'We used to play here, knowing that no one could see us. It was probably the only real privacy we had in our childhood. We made camps, dens, we were pirates and smugglers, and—'

'All right—enough.' Emotion welling up inside her, Holly held up a hand, and Casper looked at her with exasperation.

'I thought talking was good.'

'*Not* when I'm angry with you.' Holly flopped onto the rug and shot him a despairing look. 'I'm so, *so* angry with you, and when you start talking like that I find it really hard to stay angry.'

Evidently clocking that up as a point in his favour, Casper joined her on the rug, his usual confidence apparently fully restored by her reluctant confession. 'You find it hard to be angry with me?' Gently, he pushed her onto her back and supported himself on one elbow as he looked down at her. 'You have forgiven me?'

'No.' She closed her eyes tightly so that she couldn't see his thick dark lashes and impossibly sexy eyes. But she could feel him looking at her. 'You've hurt me *really* badly.'

'*Sì*, I have. But now I am saying sorry. Open your eyes.'

'No. I don't want to look at you.'

'Open your eyes, *tesoro*.' His voice was so gentle that her eyes fluttered open, and she tumbled instantly into the depths of his dark eyes.

'Nothing you say is going to make any difference,' she muttered, and he gave a slow smile.

'I know that isn't true. You're always telling me

that I should know who you are by now, and I think I do.' He lifted his hand and stroked her cheek gently. 'I know you are a very forgiving person.'

'Not that forgiving.' Her heart was pounding against her chest, but she refused to make it easy for him.

Lowering his head, Casper brought his mouth down on hers in a devastatingly gentle kiss that blew her mind. 'I am sorry, *angelo mio*. I am sorry for not believing that the baby was mine—for implying that you targeted me.'

Holly lay still, waiting, hoping, praying, *dying a little*—knowing that he was never going to say what she wanted to hear.

His eyes quizzical, Casper gently turned her face towards him. 'I'm apologising.'

'I know.'

He frowned. 'I'm saying sorry.'

'Yes.' His apparent conviction that he'd done what needed to be done made her want to hit him again and he gave an impatient sigh.

'Clearly I'm saying the wrong things, because you're lying there like a martyr burning at the stake. *Dio*, what is it that you want from me?' Without waiting for her answer, he lowered his mouth to hers and kissed her with devastating expertise.

Holly was immediately plunged into an erotic, sensual world that sucked her downwards. Struggling back to the surface, she gasped, 'I don't want to do this, Casper—'

'Yes, you do—this side of our relationship has always been good.' He eased his lean, powerful frame over hers, careful to support most of his weight on his elbows. 'Am I hurting the baby?'

'No, but I don't want you to—' She broke off as she saw his expression change. 'What? What's the matter?'

'The baby kicked me.' There was a strange note to his voice, and Holly felt her heart flip because she'd never seen Casper less than fully in control of every situation. He pulled away slightly and slid a bold but curious hand over the smooth curve of her abdomen. 'He kicked me really hard.'

'Good. Because quite frankly, if you weren't pinning me to the sand at this precise moment, I'd kick you myself for being so arrogant!' Holly glared at him but his face broke into a slow, sure smile of masculine superiority as he transferred his hand to the top of her thigh.

'No, you wouldn't. You're non-violent.'

'Funnily enough, *not* since I met you,' Holly gritted, and he gave a possessive smile.

'I bring out your passionate side, I know. And I love the way you're prepared to fight for my baby.'

'*Your* baby? So now you think you produced it all by yourself? Just because you've finally decided to acknowledge the truth—' Holly gasped as Casper shifted purposefully above her, amusement shimmering in his gorgeous dark eyes as his mouth hovered tantalisingly close to hers.

Tiny sparks of fire heated her pelvis, and her

whole body was consumed by an overpowering hunger for this man.

Her mouth was dry, her heart was thundering in her chest, and she couldn't drag her eyes away from his beautiful mouth and the dangerous glitter in his eyes. 'Cas—you're squashing the baby!'

'I'm putting no weight on you at all,' he breathed, one sure, confident hand sliding under her summer dress and easing her thighs apart.

And then, with a slow smile that said everything about his intentions, he lowered his head. His mouth captured hers in a raw, demanding kiss just as his skilled fingers gently explored the moist warmth of their target, and Holly exploded with a hot, electrifying excitement that eradicated everything from her brain except pure wicked pleasure.

She ached, she throbbed, she was *desperate*, and when he slid a hand beneath her hips and lifted her she wound her legs around him in instinctive invitation, urging him on.

She'd become accustomed to the wild, uninhibited nature of their love-making. Right from the start the sexual chemistry had been so explosive that there had been times when it was hard to know which of them was the most out of control.

But this time felt different.

Casper surged into her quivering, receptive body and then paused, his breathing ragged as he scanned her flushed cheeks. 'Am I hurting you?'

'No.' Not in the way he meant.

Holly closed her eyes tightly, moaning as he eased

himself deeper, every thought driven from her head by the silken strength of him inside her.

She'd never known him so careful, and yet there was something about the slow, deliberate thrusts that were shockingly erotic.

She was no longer aware of the warmth of the sun or the sounds of the sea, because everything she felt was controlled by this man.

Her body spun higher and higher, her excitement out of control, until she gave a sharp cry and tumbled off the edge into a climax so intense that her mind blanked. She dug her nails hard into the hard muscle of his sleek, bronzed shoulders as her world shattered around her and her body tightened around his.

'I can feel that,' he groaned, and then he surged into her for a final time, his climax driving her straight back into another orgasm.

When the stars finally stopped exploding in her head, she opened her eyes and pressed her lips against his satin-smooth skin, desperately conscious that she'd succumbed to him yet again.

'That,' Casper murmured huskily, 'was amazing.' Clearly in no hurry to move, he stroked her hair away from her face and stared into her eyes with a warmth that she hadn't seen before. 'Now, where were we in our conversation? I've lost track.'

Appalled at her own weakness, Holly closed her eyes. 'I was about to kick you but the baby did it for me.'

'You were about to forgive me,' Casper said confidently, and she opened her eyes and looked up at him.

'So is that what it was all about this time? Apology sex?'

Casper didn't answer for a moment, his hand unsteady as he stroked her hair away from her face. 'It was love sex, *tesoro*,' he said huskily, and Holly stilled.

It was like seeing a shimmer of water in the desert.

Real or a mirage?

'Love sex?' She was almost afraid to say the words. 'What do you mean, "love sex"?'

'I mean that I love you.'

Her heart was thudding. 'You told me that you weren't capable of love.'

'I was wrong. And I was trying to show you I was wrong. I think I express myself better physically than verbally.' His eyes gleamed with self-mockery. 'I was always better at maths than English. I'm the cold, analytical type, remember?'

A warm feeling spread through Holly's limbs and she started to tremble. 'Actually, that isn't true,' she said gently. 'You're very good with words.'

'But hopeless at matching them to the right emotion, if my lack of success at an apology is anything to go by.' Gently, he stroked a hand over her cheek. 'I love you, Holly. I think I loved you from the first moment I saw you. You were warm, gorgeous, sexy.' His eyes flickered to her mouth. 'You were *so* sexy I couldn't keep my hands off you.'

'And the moment we'd had sex, you wanted me to leave. Stop dressing it up, Casper. I'm not stupid.'

'I am the one who has been stupid,' he confessed in a raw tone. 'Stupid for not seeing what was under my nose. When we had sex the day of the rugby, I didn't know what had happened. I was living this crazy, cold, empty existence, and suddenly there you were. I was shocked by how I felt about you. I actually did think that you were different—and then you kissed me in the window.'

'You thought I'd done it for a photo opportunity.'

'Yes.' He didn't shrink from the truth. 'That is what I thought. And everything that happened after that seemed to back up my suspicions. You hid from the world and then announced that you were pregnant. It seemed to me that you were trying to make maximum impact from the story.'

'From your description, I should obviously be considering a career in public relations.'

'You have to understand that, when you're in the public eye, these things happen. You grow to expect them.' Casper drew away from her and sat up, his gaze thoughtful. 'Women have always wanted me for what I can give them. Even Antonia, who I thought loved me.'

Holly pulled a face. 'Yes, well, I can see why your experience with her made you very suspicious of women. I'm not stupid.'

'No, you're certainly not. And I'm not blaming Antonia. The blame lies entirely with myself.' Casper's admission was delivered with uncharacteristic self-deprecation. 'I allowed myself to see only bad in women, I expected only bad from women.

And the chances of you having become pregnant on that one single occasion when I'd been told I was infertile—to have believed your story would have required a better man than me.'

'You're obviously super-fertile.'

He gave an aggressively masculine smile. 'So it would seem. And now I need to ask you something.' The smile faded and there was an unusual vulnerability in his dark eyes. 'Do you still love me? *Can* you still love me? You haven't said those words for a long time.'

Holly swallowed, her heart thudding hard. 'You didn't want to hear them,' she whispered. 'When I said them, or when I showed affection, you backed off. I didn't want to scare you away.'

'I taught myself to block out emotion because it was the only way I could survive,' Casper said roughly, leaning forwards and cupping her face in his hands. 'And I'm still waiting for you to answer my question.'

'I'm scared even to say the words,' she admitted with a strangled laugh. 'In case the whole bubble pops.'

'Say you can still love me, Holly. I need to hear you say it.'

'I never stopped loving you,' she said softly. 'I just stopped saying it because it upset you. That's another thing that "I love you" means to me. It means for ever. True love isn't something you can switch on and off, Casper. It's always there, sometimes when you'd rather it wasn't.'

Casper's breathing fractured, and he hauled her into his arms and held her tightly. 'Don't say that, because it reminds me how much I hurt you, and you have no idea how guilty I feel. You must have felt so alone, but I swear to you that you will never feel alone again.'

'I don't want you to feel guilty. I love you so much.'

'I don't deserve you.'

'You might well be saying that to yourself when I'm singing in the shower,' Holly joked feebly, and his grip tightened.

'After the way I behaved, most women would have walked away. I was so afraid you would do the same.'

'I would never do that.'

'No.' He withdrew slightly and stroked her cheek gently. 'You have an exceptionally loving nature. You are kind, tolerant and forgiving. You have tremendous strength, and I truly admire your single-minded determination to do the very best for our baby. And our baby is so lucky to have you as a mother,' he murmured, pulling her against him again with firm, possessive hands.

Holly buried her face in his shoulder. 'I was terrified that you wouldn't love the baby.'

'And I was terrified to open up enough to love anything, because I saw love as a source of pain.'

'I know.' Holly touched his face. 'You were so wounded. I always knew that, and when we got together I told myself that, as long as I was patient, you would heal. I was so sure that everything would turn out all right, but I couldn't get through to you. I couldn't find the answer.'

'You were the answer.' Casper lifted her chin and silenced her fears with a possessive kiss. 'There will be no more problems between us. Ever.'

'Are you kidding?' Half laughing, half crying, Holly shook her head. 'You are stubborn, arrogant and used to getting your own way. How can we not have problems?'

'Because you are kind, tolerant and you adore me.' Casper, looking too gorgeous for his own good with roughened dark hair and the beginnings of stubble grazing his jaw, snuggled her against him again. 'And you have reminded me what true love really is.' His hand rested protectively on her rounded abdomen and his voice was suddenly husky. 'I never thought I believed in fairy tales, but this baby has changed my mind. I have great wealth and privilege, but the one thing I never thought I'd have is a family. You've given me that.'

Holly glanced up at him and then towards the fairy tale turrets of Santallia Palace in the distance. 'A family.' She savoured the word, and then smiled up at him, everything she felt shining in her eyes. 'That sounds like a very happy ending to me.'

* * * * *

POWERFUL GREEK,
UNWORLDLY WIFE

Chapter 1

Leandro Demetrios, billionaire banker and the subject of a million hopeful female fantasies, dragged the 'A' list Hollywood actress through the doorway of his exclusive London townhouse and slammed the door shut on the rain and the bank of waiting photographers.

The woman was laughing, her eyes wide with feminine appreciation. 'Did you see their faces? You scared them half to death! I feel safer with you than I do with my bodyguards. *And* you have bigger muscles.' She slid her hand up his arm, her manicured fingernails lingering on the solid curve of his biceps. 'Why didn't we just use the back entrance?'

'Because I refuse to creep around my own house. And because you like to be seen.'

'Well, we've certainly been seen.' The fact evidently pleased her. 'You'll be all over the papers tomorrow for terrorising the paparazzi.'

Leandro frowned. 'I only read the financial pages.'

'And that's the bit I *don't* read,' she sighed. 'The only thing I know about money is how to spend it. You, on the other hand, know how to make it by the bucketload, and that makes you my type of guy. Now, *stop* looking all moody and dangerous and smile! I'm only in town for twenty-four hours and we need to make the most of the time.' Her lashes lowered provocatively. 'So, Leandro Demetrios, my very own sexy Greek billionaire. *Finally* we're alone. What are we going to do with our evening?'

Leandro removed his jacket and threw it carelessly over the back of a chair. 'If that's a serious question, you can leave right now.' His remark drew a gurgle of delighted laughter from the woman clinging to his arm.

'No one else dares to speak to me the way you do. It's one of the things I love most about you. You're not starstruck and that's so refreshing for someone like me.' The tip of her tongue traced the curve of her glossy lips. 'If I told you I was going to kiss you goodnight and go back to my hotel, what would you do?'

'Dump you.' Leandro's bow-tie landed on top of the jacket. 'But we both know that isn't going to happen. You want what I want, so stop playing games and get up those stairs. My bedroom is on the first floor. Last door on the left.'

'*So-o* macho.' Laughing, she smouldered in his direction. 'According to a poll just last week, you're now officially the world's sexiest man.'

Bored by the conversation, Leandro's only response was to close his fingers around her tiny wrist and pull her towards the staircase.

She gave a gasp of shocked delight. 'You honestly don't care what anyone thinks about you, do you? Indifference is *such* a turn-on. And when it comes to indifference, you wrote the manual.' She walked with a slow, swaying motion that she'd perfected for the cameras. 'There's a special chemistry between us. I can feel it.'

'It's called lust,' Leandro drawled, and she shot him a challenging look.

'Haven't you ever had a serious relationship with a woman? I heard you were married for a short time.'

Leandro stilled. *A very short time.* 'These days I prefer variety.'

'Honey, I can give you variety.' She used the soft, smoky voice that earned her millions of dollars per movie. 'And I'm just dying to know whether everything they say about you is true. I know you're superbright and that you drive your fancy cars *way* too fast, but what I want to know is just how much of a bad boy you really are when it comes to women.'

'As bad as they come,' Leandro said smoothly, his hand locked around her slender wrist as he led her up the stairs. 'Which makes this your lucky night.'

'Then lead on, handsome.' She kept pace with him, a smile on her full, glossy mouth. 'You have a lot of art on your walls. Great investment. Are they original? I hate anything fake.'

'Of course you do.' Leandro focused on her surgically enhanced breasts with wry amusement. At a rough estimate he guessed that ninety per cent of her was fake. The short time he'd spent with her had been enough to prove to him that she was so used to playing other people, she'd forgotten how to be herself.

And that was fine by him.

As far as he was concerned, the shallower the better. At least you knew what you were dealing with and you adjusted your expectations accordingly.

'Oh, my! Only you would have a picture of a naked woman at the head of your staircase.' Stopping dead, she gazed up at the huge canvas and wrinkled her nose with disapproval. 'Strange choice for a man who surrounds himself with beauty. Isn't she rather fat for your tastes?'

Leandro's gaze lingered on the celebrated Renaissance masterpiece that had only recently returned from being on loan to a major gallery. 'When she was alive, it was fashionable to be curvy.'

The girl stared blankly at the exquisite brush strokes. 'I guess they didn't know about low carbs.'

'Curves were a sign of wealth,' Leandro murmured. 'It meant you had enough to eat.'

Throwing him a look of blank incomprehension, the actress stepped closer to the painting and Leandro's fingers tightened like a vice around her wrist.

'Touch it and we'll have half the Metropolitan police force keeping us company tonight.'

'It's that valuable?' Her knowing gaze turned to his and she licked her lips. 'You are one rich, powerful guy. Now, why is that such a turn-on, I wonder? It isn't as if I care about your money.'

'Of course you don't,' Leandro said, his tone dry because he knew full well that her lovers were expected to pay handsomely for the privilege of escorting her. 'We both know you're interested in me because I'm kind to old ladies and animals.'

'You like animals?'

Looking down into those famous blue eyes, Leandro's own eyes gleamed. 'I've always had a soft spot for dumb creatures.'

'That's so attractive. I love a tough man with a gentle side.' She slid her arms round his neck like bindweed around a plant. 'Do you realise we've had dinner three times and you haven't told me a single thing about yourself?'

'Do you realise that we've had dinner three times and you haven't eaten a single thing?' Skilfully steering the conversation away from the personal, Leandro smoothly released the zip on her dress and she sucked in a breath.

'You don't mess around, do you?'

'Let's just say I've had enough of verbal foreplay,' Leandro purred, sliding the dress over her shoulders in a practised movement. He frowned slightly as his fingers brushed hard bones rather than soft flesh.

'People pay good money to see this body of mine

up on the screen.' She scraped her nails gently down his arm. 'And you, Leandro Demetrios, are getting it for free.'

Hardly, he thought, looking at the earrings she was wearing. *Earrings he'd given her at the beginning of the evening.* 'Shame you're not sold by the kilogram,' he said idly, 'because then you wouldn't cost me anything.'

'Thank you.' Assuming his remark was a compliment, she smiled. 'You, on the other hand, would cost a woman a fortune because muscle is heavier than fat and you have to be the most impressively built man I've ever met. And you're so damned confident. Is that because you're Greek?'

'No. It's because I'm me. I take what I want.' He took her chin in his fingers, his eyes steely. 'And when I've finished with it, I drop it.'

She shuddered deliciously. 'With no apology to anyone. Cold, ruthless, single-minded...'

'Are we talking about me or you?' Leandro removed the diamond clip securing her hair. 'I'm confused.'

'I'm willing to bet you've never been confused about a single thing in your life, you wicked boy.' Smiling, she dragged her finger over his lower lip. 'Tell me something personal about yourself. Just one thing. This latest story about you being the father of that baby—is it true? The papers are full of it.'

Not by the flicker of an eyelid did Leandro reveal his sudden tension. 'Are those the same papers that accused you of being a lesbian?'

'The difference is that my people issued a stern denial—you've said nothing.'

'I've never felt the need to explain my life to anyone.'

'So does that mean it isn't your child?' She lowered her lashes. 'Or are you such a stud you don't even *know*? You're not giving anything away, are you? Tell me something about *you*.'

'You want to know something about me?' Leandro eased her dress down her painfully thin body and lowered his mouth to the base of her throat. 'If you give me your heart, I'll break it. Remember that, *agape mou*. And I won't do it gently.' The warmth of his tongue brought a soft gasp to her lips and she tipped her head back with a shiver.

'If you're trying to scare me, you're not succeeding.' Her eyes were dark with arousal. 'I love a man who knows how to be a man. Especially when that man has a sensitive side.'

'I don't have a sensitive side.' Leandro's voice was hard as he lowered his forehead to hers. For a moment he stared into her wild, excited eyes, his breath mingling with hers. 'I don't care about anyone or anything. Lie down in my bed and I'll guarantee you fantastic sex, but nothing else. So if you're looking for happy ever after, you've taken a wrong turning.'

'Happy ever after is for movies. It's my day job. At night, I prefer to live for the moment.' Squirming against him, she lifted her hand and stroked his rough jaw. 'I should make you shave before you touch me, but I like the way it makes you look. You are so

damn handsome, Leandro, it shouldn't be allowed,'
she breathed, lifting her mouth to his. 'My last leading man needed satellite navigation to find his way
round a woman's body. I have a feeling you won't
suffer from the same problem.'

'I've always had a very good sense of direction.'
Leandro backed her against the door and the actress
gasped her approval.

'Oh, yes…' Panting, she wrenched at his shirt,
sending buttons flying. With a low moan of desire
she pushed the shirt off his shoulders and let it fall
to the floor. 'Your body is incredible. I'm *definitely*
going to get you a part in my next movie. I want
you *now.*'

Having reached the part of the evening that interested him, Leandro scooped her up, strode purposefully towards the bed and then froze because his bed
was already occupied.

The woman sat glaring at him, her eyes a fierce
blue in a face as pale as his dress shirt. She'd obviously been caught in the rain because her thin cardigan clung to her body and her long hair curled
damply past her shoulders like tongues of red fire.

Given the state she was in, she should have looked
pathetic, but she didn't. She looked angry—the blaze
of her eyes and the angle of her chin warning him
that this wasn't going to be a gentle reunion.

It was as if a small, unexploded firework had
landed in his bedroom and Leandro felt a dart of
surprise because he'd never seen her angry before—
hadn't known she was capable of anger.

He'd been on the receiving end of her injured dignity, her silent reproach and her agonised pain. He'd witnessed her disappointment and contempt. But a good healthy dose of old-fashioned anger had been missing from their relationship.

She hadn't thought that what they had was worth fighting for.

His own anger bubbled up from nowhere, threatening his usual control, and the emotion caught him by surprise because he'd thought he had himself well in hand.

Unfinished business, he thought grimly, and was about to speak when the actress gave a shocked squeak and tightened her grip on his neck.

'Who's *she*? You bastard! When you said you were going to hurt me, I didn't expect it to be that quick,' she snarled. 'How *dare* you see someone else while you're with me? I expect my relationships to be exclusive.'

Surprised to realise that he'd forgotten he had the actress in his arms, Leandro lowered her unceremoniously to the floor. 'I don't do relationships.' *Not any more.*

'What about her?' Balancing on her vertiginous heels, the actress shot him a poisonous look. 'Does *she* know that?'

'Oh, yes.' Leandro was watching the girl on the bed and his humourless smile was entirely at his own expense. 'She wouldn't trust me as far as she could throw me, isn't that right, Millie?'

Her eyes were two hot pools of blame and he

ground his teeth. *Fight me,* he urged silently. *If that's really what you think of me, stand up and scratch my eyes out. Don't just sit there. And don't walk out like you did the first time.*

But she didn't move. She sat in frozen silence, her eyes telling him that nothing had changed.

The actress made an outraged noise. 'So you *do* know her! Surprising. She doesn't look your type,' she said spitefully. 'She needs to fire her stylist. That natural look is *so* yesterday. This season is all about grooming.' She snatched her dress from the floor and held it against her. 'How did she get in here, anyway? Your security is really tight. I suppose no one noticed her.'

Nothing killed sexual arousal faster than female bitchiness, Leandro thought idly, regretting the impulse that had driven him to invite the actress home. The woman's tongue was as sharp as the bones poking out through her almost transparent flesh.

'Well? Are you going to throw her out?' The actress's voice turned from sultry to shrill and Leandro studied the girl sitting on his bed, noting the flush on her cheeks and the accusation in her eyes.

He met that gaze full on, with accusation of his own.

Silent communication raged between them and the atmosphere was so thick with tension that both of them forgot about the third person in the room until she stamped her foot.

'Leandro?'

'No,' he said harshly. 'I'm not going to throw her

out.' The timing wasn't what he would have chosen but now she was here, he had no intention of letting her go. *Not until they'd had the conversation she'd walked away from a year earlier.*

The actress gave a gasp of disbelief. 'You're choosing that plain, bedraggled, badly dressed nobody over me?'

Leandro sent his date a cold, assessing glance that would have triggered shivers of trepidation through any one of the people who worked for him or knew him well. 'Yes. At least that way I'm guaranteed a soft landing when we tumble onto that mattress. No bones. No claws.'

The actress gasped. 'I won't be treated like this!' Delivering a performance worthy of an Oscar, she wriggled back into her dress and tossed her head in anger. 'You told me you weren't involved with anyone and I believed you! I'm obviously more of a fool than I look.'

Deciding that it was wisest not to respond to that particular statement, Leandro stayed silent, his gaze returning to the girl sitting on his bed. In that single, hotly charged moment he felt the blaze of raw sexual chemistry erupt between them. It was elemental, basic and primitive—the connection so powerful that it was beyond control or understanding. Recognising that fact, she gave a murmur of denial, her expression one of sick contempt as she dragged her gaze from his.

Vibrating with desperation, the actress sent a look of longing towards Leandro's bare, bronzed torso.

'I know you didn't expect to see her here. I know women throw themselves at you. Just get rid of her and we can start again. I forgive you.'

Propelled by a need to ensure that forgiveness would never be forthcoming, Leandro urged her towards the door. 'You need to learn to play nicely with the other girls. I don't mind knives in my boardroom but I do find them shockingly uncomfortable in my bedroom.'

Her face scarlet, the actress snatched her phone out of her tiny jewelled handbag. 'All the rumours about you are true, Leandro Demetrios. You *are* cold and heartless and just missed your chance to have the one thing every man in the world wants.'

'And that would be?' Leandro raised an eyebrow, deliberately provocative. 'Peace and quiet?'

The actress simmered like milk coming to the boil. 'Me! And next time you're in L.A., don't bother calling. And you.' She glared at the girl on the bed. 'If you think he'll ever be faithful to you, you're crazy.' Checking that the diamond earrings were still in place, she stormed from the room and several moments later Leandro heard a distant thud as the front door slammed closed.

Silence closed in on them.

'If you're going to cry, you can leave now,' Leandro drawled softly. 'If you choose to wait in my bedroom, you deserve to get hurt.'

'I'm not going to cry over you. And I'm not hurt,' she said stiffly. 'I'm past being hurt.'

Then she'd done better than him, Leandro reflected grimly. 'Why are you here?'

'You know why I'm here. I— I've come to take the baby.'

Of course, the baby. He'd been a fool to think anything else, and yet for a moment...

Leandro curled one hand into a fist, surprised to discover that his thick protective layer of cynicism could still be breached.

'I was asking what you're doing in my bedroom at midnight.' Strolling across to the bedroom door, he pushed it shut. He trusted his staff, but he was also sharp enough to know that this story was the juiciest morsel the media had savoured for a long time. They were slavering outside his house, waiting for something to feast on.

And everyone had their price.

He'd learned that unpalatable truth in the harshest way possible, and at an age when most children were still playing with toys.

'I'm intrigued as to how you got past my security.'

'I'm still your wife, Leandro. Even if you've forgotten that fact.'

'I haven't forgotten.' Keeping his gaze neutral, he looked at her. 'You really pick your moments. Thanks to you, my night of hot sex just walked through that door.'

Her slender shoulders stiffened, her back rigid. 'I'm sure you'll find a replacement fast enough. You always do.' Her chest rose and fell as she breathed rapidly and then her eyes flew to his, bright with accusation and pain. 'You *are* a complete and utter bastard, she's right about that.'

'I've never heard you use bad language before. It doesn't suit you.' Leandro strolled across the bedroom and lifted a bottle of whisky from a small table. *Funny,* he thought, *that his hand was so steady.* 'And I don't understand why you're angry. You walked out on our marriage, not me. I was in it for the long haul.'

'Only you could make it sound like an endurance test. It's nice to know you had such a positive view of our relationship. No wonder it didn't last five minutes. You're even more unfeeling than I thought you were—' She broke off, as if she was trying to control herself. 'You're horribly, *horribly* insensitive.'

'I'm living my life. What's insensitive about that?' Leandro's hand remained steady as he poured. 'There was a vacancy in my bed and I filled it. In the circumstances, you can hardly blame me for that. Drink?'

'No, thank you.'

'Such perfect English manners.' Leandro gave a humourless laugh as he lifted the glass. 'Don't tell me—alcohol is fattening and you're watching your weight.'

'No. I'm watching my tongue. If I drink, I'll tell you exactly what I think of you and right now that might not be a good idea because what I think of you isn't very flattering.'

His hand stilled on the glass. 'Don't hold back on my account. It's interesting to know you're capable of expressing what you're feeling providing you're sufficiently provoked. Just for the record, I actually prefer confrontation to retreat.'

She closed her eyes, misery visible in every angle of her pretty face. 'I *hate* confrontation. I didn't come here to argue with you.'

'I'm sure you didn't.' Leandro examined the golden liquid in his glass. 'You don't talk about problems, do you, Millie? And you were certainly never interested in fixing the problems in our relationship. It's so much easier to just walk away when things become awkward.'

'How *dare* you say that to me when *you're* the one who—?' She broke off as if she couldn't even bear to say it, and his mouth tightened.

'I'm the one who what?' His silky soft voice was in direct contrast to the passion in hers. 'Spell it out, Millie. Come on—let's hear what I'm guilty of.'

'You *know* what! And I didn't come here to talk about that. 'You're a—a…' She appeared to struggle with her breath and he gave her a long look.

'You really must learn to finish your sentences, *agape mou.*' His tone bored, he offered no sympathy. As far as he was concerned, she deserved none. He'd given her a chance. He'd given her something he'd never offered a woman before. And she'd thrown it back in his face. 'I'm cold and heartless, isn't that right, Millie? Wasn't that what you were going to say?'

'I wish I'd never met you.'

'Now, that's just childish.' Leandro suppressed a yawn and she looked away.

'Our relationship was a disaster.'

'I wouldn't say that. For a short time you were a revelation in bed, and I was reasonably entertained by your gift for saying the wrong thing at the wrong time.'

'It's called telling the truth.' She glared at him through lashes spiked with rain. 'Where I come from, that's what people do. They tell it like it is and that way there's no confusion. When someone says, "Lovely to see you," they mean it. In *your* world when someone says, "Lovely to see you," they certainly *don't* mean it. They kiss you even though they hate you.'

Leandro added ice to his glass. 'It's a standard social greeting.'

'It's superficial—everything about your world is!' She sprang off the bed and walked towards him, her eyes flashing fire. 'And that included our relationship.'

'I'm not the one who called time on our marriage.'

'Yes, you did!' Angry and hurt, she faced him. 'You blame me for walking out, but what did you think I'd do, Leandro? Did you think I'd say, "Don't worry, that's fine by me"?' Her voice rose, trembling and thickened by pain. 'Did you think I'd turn a blind eye? Maybe that's what women do in your world, but that isn't the sort of marriage I want. You slept with another woman and not just any woman.' Her breathing was jagged. 'My sister. *My own sister.*' Her distress was so obvious that Leandro gave a frown.

'You're working yourself up into a state.'

'Please don't pretend you care about my feelings because you've already amply demonstrated that you don't.' Holding herself together by a thread, she wrapped her arms around her body and met his gaze.

Brave, he thought absently, part of him intrigued by the sudden strength he saw in her. Yes, she was upset. But she wasn't caving in, was she? He hadn't known that she possessed a layer of steel. By the end of their relationship he'd come to the conclusion that she was so lightweight that the only thing preventing her from being blown away was the weight of his money in her handbag.

Leandro's hand tightened on his glass and then he lifted it to his lips and drained it. Then he placed the glass carefully on the table in front of him.

'Given the circumstances of your departure, I'm surprised you chose to come back.'

Sinking back onto the side of the bed, the fight seemed to go out of her and she suddenly looked incredibly tired. Tired, wet, beaten. 'If you thought I wouldn't then you know even less about me than I thought you did.'

'I never knew you.' It had been a fantasy. An illusion. *Or maybe a delusion?*

'And whose fault is that? You didn't *want* to know me, did you? You weren't interested in *me*—just in sex, and when that—' She broke off and took a breath, clearly searching for the words she wanted. 'I wasn't right for you. To start with you liked the fact that I was "different". I was just an ordinary girl, living in the country, working on her parents' farm.

Unsophisticated. But the novelty wore off, didn't it, Leandro? You wanted me to fit into your life. Your world. And I didn't.'

Watching her so closely, he was able to detect the exact moment when anger turned to awareness.

Her eyes slid to his bare, bronzed shoulders and then back to his. It was like putting a match to kerosene. The chemistry that had been simmering exploded to dangerous levels and she turned away with a murmur of frustration, although whether it was with herself or him, he wasn't sure. 'Don't you dare, Leandro! Don't you *dare* look at me like that—as if everything hasn't changed between us.'

'You were looking at me.'

'Because you're standing there half-naked!'

'Does that bother you?'

'No, it doesn't.' She rubbed her hands up and down her arms, trying to warm them. 'I don't feel anything for you any more.'

'Oh, you feel plenty for me, Millie,' Leandro said grimly, 'and that's the problem, isn't it? You hate the fact that you can feel that way. A woman like you shouldn't find herself hopelessly attracted to a bad boy like me. It's not quite decent, is it?'

'I'm not here because of you.'

'Of course you're not.' His tone caustic, he watched as she flinched away from his words. 'You wouldn't have made the journey for something as trivial as the survival of our marriage, would you? That was never important to you.' Filled with contempt, Leandro lifted the glass, wondering how much whisky it was going to take to dull what he was feeling.

'Are you drunk?'

'Unfortunately, no, not yet.' He eyed the glass. 'But I'm working on it.'

'You're totally irresponsible.'

'I'm working on that, too.' He was about to lift the glass to his lips when he noticed that the sole of her boot was starting to come away. Remembering how obsessive she'd been about her appearance, he frowned. 'You look awful.'

'Most people would look awful compared with the cream of Hollywood,' she said tartly. She lifted her hand and he thought she was going to smooth her damp hair, but then she let her hand drop as if she'd decided it wasn't worth the effort. 'She's very beautiful.'

He heard the pain in her voice and gritted his teeth. 'Jealousy was the one aspect of our relationship at which you consistently excelled.'

'You're *so* unkind.'

Leandro discovered that his fingers had curled themselves into a fist. 'Unkind?' His mouth tightened. 'Yes, I'm unkind.'

'Do you love her?'

'Now you're getting personal.'

'Of course I'm getting personal! Did my sis—?' Her voice cracked and she cleared her throat. 'Did… Becca know you were seeing the actress?'

The mention of that name made Leandro want to drain the bottle of whisky, as did the unspoken accusation behind her words. 'Are you blaming me for the fact that your sister crashed the car while under the influence of drink and drugs?'

'She drank because you rejected her! She was suffering from depression.'

Thinking about what he knew, Leandro gave a humourless smile. 'I'll just bet she was.'

She sprang to her feet and crossed the room with the grace of a dancer. 'Don't you *dare* speak about the dead like that! If anyone was responsible for my sister's fragile mental state, it's you. You broke her heart.'

And Leandro committed the unpardonable sin. He laughed. And that grim humour cost him.

She slapped him.

Then she put her hand against her throat and stepped backwards, as if she couldn't believe what she'd done. Her skin was so pale she reminded him of something conjured from a child's fairy story.

'I should probably apologise but I'm not going to,' she whispered, her fingers pressed against her slender neck. 'Do you know the most hurtful part of all this? You don't even care. You destroyed our marriage for sex. It didn't even *mean* anything. If you'd loved her maybe, just maybe, I would have been able to understand all this, but for you it was just physical.'

'As a matter of interest, did you say any of this to her?'

'Yes. Actually, I did. I went to see her just after she was admitted to that clinic in Arizona. I...' She rubbed her fingers across her forehead. 'I needed to try and understand. She confessed that she was so madly in love with you that she wasn't thinking clearly.'

'She knew exactly what she was doing,' Leandro said flatly. 'The only person your sister ever loved was herself. That was probably the only thing we ever had in common.'

'That's a very cynical attitude.'

'I'm a cynical guy.'

'So you wrecked our marriage for a woman you don't even care about.'

'I didn't wreck our marriage, *agape mou*,' Leandro spoke softly, his eyes fixing on her white face, as he hammered home his barb. 'You did that. All by yourself.'

If he'd hit her, she couldn't have looked more shocked. 'How can you say that? What did you expect? I'm not the sort of woman who can turn a blind eye while her husband has an affair. Especially when the woman involved was his wife's sister. You made her pregnant, Leandro! How was I supposed to overlook that?' Visibly distressed, she turned away. 'What I don't understand is why, if you wanted my sister, did you bother with me at all?'

Leandro let that question hover in the air. 'And does the fact that you don't understand help you draw any conclusions?'

His question drew a confused frown and he realised that she was too upset to focus on the facts.

She'd seen. She'd believed. She hadn't questioned.

Hadn't cared enough to question and the knowledge that she hadn't cared left the bitter taste of failure in his mouth.

In a life gilded by success, she'd been his only failure.

Leandro flexed his shoulders to relieve the tension and the movement caught her attention, her eyes drifting to the swell of hard muscle. Her gaze was feather light and yet he felt the responding sizzle of sexual heat and almost laughed at his own weakness.

It seemed his body was nowhere near as choosy as his mind.

Millie stared at him for a long moment and then sank her teeth into her lower lip. 'Leandro, do me a favour.' Her voice was strained. 'Put your shirt on. We can't have a proper conversation with you standing there half-naked.'

'This may surprise you, but I've been known to conduct a conversation even when naked.' His sardonic tone masked his own anger and brought a flush to her cheeks.

'I'm sure. But if it's all the same with you, I'd like you to get dressed.'

'Why? Is the sight of my body bothering you, Millie?' His tone silky smooth, Leandro strolled across the bedroom and retrieved his shirt from the floor. 'Are you finding it hard to concentrate?' He shrugged the shirt back on, discovered that there were no buttons and spread his arms in an exaggerated gesture of apology. 'She was a bit over-eager, I'm afraid. This is the best I can do.'

'It's fine.' She averted her eyes, but not before both of them had shared a memory they would rather have forgotten. 'The media have been running the story for days now, and it's *awful*. Somehow they know about you and my sister, and they know the baby's been brought here.' Her voice wobbled. 'Where…?'

'Asleep on the next floor.' His voice terse, Leandro strolled over to the window that overlooked the garden. 'Someone from the clinic brought the baby to me. Your sister left him alone and uncared for while she went for her little drive. He was found crying and neglected.' The anger in him was like a roaring beast and he was shocked by the strength required to hold it back. Control was a skill he'd mastered at an impossibly young age, but when he thought of the baby his thoughts raced into the dark. 'Evidently she didn't have a maternal bone in her body.' *Another woman, another place.*

'She was sick.'

'Well, that's one thing we agree on.' *Infested with greed.* Aware that the past and the present had become dangerously tangled and the conversation was taking a dangerous turn, Leandro changed direction. 'Why do you think they brought the baby here, Millie?'

'The clinic said she left a note saying that you were the father. She wanted the baby to be with family.'

He made an impatient sound, marvelling at her naivety. 'Or perhaps she just wanted to make sure there was no chance of reconciliation between us. Her last, generous gift to you.' His carefully planted seed of suggestion landed on barren ground.

'There never was any chance of reconciliation.' She didn't look at him. 'Where's the baby? I should be going.'

Leandro stilled. 'Where, exactly, are you planning to go?'

'It's already past midnight. I've booked into a small bed and breakfast near here.'

'A bed and breakfast?' Leandro looked at her with a mixture of disbelief and fascination, realising just how little he knew about this woman. 'Are you suggesting what I think you are?'

'I'm taking the baby, of course. What did you think?'

'So you're planning to take in your sister's baby and care for it—this is the same baby that is supposedly the result of an affair between your own sister and your husband. Whether you think your sister was lying or telling the truth—'

'Telling the truth.'

Leandro's jaw tightened. 'Whichever. Your sister wrecked your marriage. She hurt you. And you're willing to take her baby? What are you, a doormat?'

Her narrow shoulders were rigid. 'No, I'm responsible. And principled. Qualities that you probably don't recognise. Am I angry with my sister? Yes, I'm angry. And that feels really horrible because even while I'm grieving I'm hurt that she could have done that to me.' Her voice shook. 'She behaved terribly.

Some people wouldn't forgive that. If I'm honest I'm not sure that I'll ever forgive that. She betrayed my trust. But at least she was in love with you. And I think at the end she was truly sorry.'

Leandro raised an eyebrow but she ploughed on.

'It was the guilt that pushed her into depression. And whatever had happened, I would never have wanted her to...' Her voice trembled. 'We were sisters. And as for the baby—well, I don't believe that a child should be held responsible for the sins of his parents. My sister is dead. You can't bring up a baby, so I will have him. He will have a loving home with me as long as he needs one.'

'So you're proposing to love and care for your husband's bastard, is that right?'

'Don't *ever* call him that.' Her eyes blazed. 'And, yes, I'm intending to care for him. He's three months old. He's helpless.'

Curiously detached, Leandro looked at her. She wasn't classically beautiful, he mused, but there was something about her face that was captivating. 'So you have forgiven your sister.'

'I'm working on it.' She caught her lip between her teeth. 'I understand the effect you have on a woman. Even that Hollywood actress was willing to humiliate herself to spend a night with you. Tell me one thing—why, when you have a reputation for not committing to a woman, did you marry me?'

'Frankly?' Leandro lifted his eyes from his scrutiny of her soft lips. 'At this moment I have absolutely no idea.'

'You *really* know how to hurt. You treated our marriage lightly.'

'On the contrary, *you're* the one who walked out at the first obstacle.'

Her shoulders sagged, as if she was bearing an enormous weight. 'If you've said everything you wanted to say, I'd like to take the baby.'

'As usual you are being quite breathtakingly naïve. For a start there is a pack of journalists on my doorstep. How do you think they're going to react if you leave here clutching the baby?'

'I think it would reflect very badly on you. But you don't care about that, do you? You never care what people think about you. If you did, you wouldn't behave so badly.'

Leandro pressed the tips of his long fingers to his forehead, his control at breaking point. 'We'll talk about this in a minute,' he snapped. 'For goodness' sake, go and use the bathroom. You're soaking wet. And next time use the front door, like my wife, instead of creeping through the garden like a burglar.'

'Whatever you say, you wouldn't have wanted those headlines any more than I did.'

Leandro sent her a brooding glance, marvelling that the male libido could be such a self-destructive force. 'The headlines will stop when they realise there is no story.'

She didn't appear to register his words. Certainly she didn't question his meaning. 'As soon as I'm dry, I'll take him away. We'll both be out of your life.'

Leandro watched in silence, allowing her to delude herself for a short time.

His wife was back.

And he had no intention of letting her walk out again.

Chapter 2

Numb with misery, Millie stood in front of the mirror in the huge, luxurious bathroom. She didn't reach for a towel. She did nothing to improve her appearance. She simply stared at herself.

No wonder, she thought numbly. *No wonder he'd strayed.*

Leandro Demetrios was six feet two inches of devastatingly handsome, vibrant masculinity and she was—she was, what?

Ordinary.

She was just so *ordinary*.

Staring at her wild, curling hair, she reflected on how long it had taken her each day to straighten it into the tame, sleek sheet that everyone expected. And even with the weight she'd lost during the misery of the last year, her breasts were still large, and her hips curvy.

No wonder he'd chosen her sister.

Trying not to think about that, Millie ran the tap and splashed cold water on her face. One thing about already having lost your husband to another woman, she thought, was that you no longer had to pretend to be someone different. She could just be herself. What did she have to lose?

Nothing.

She'd already lost it all.

But life kept throwing boulders at her, and she had a whole new challenge ahead of her. She had to put aside all her dreams of having her own baby, and instead love and nurture the baby that had been the result of her husband's affair with her sister.

Caught in a sudden rush of panic, Millie covered her mouth with her hand. It was all very well to say she was going to do this, but what if she looked at the baby and hated it? That would make her an awful person, wouldn't it?

She wanted to do the right thing, she really did, but what if doing the right thing proved too hard?

Her encounter with Leandro had been a million times harder than she'd anticipated and she'd always known it was going to be awful.

Even though their marriage was over, nothing had prepared her for the agonising pain of seeing Leandro with another woman. And worse still was the realisation that she hadn't healed at all. She wasn't over him and she never would be.

She'd learned to survive, that was all. But life without him was flat and colourless.

'Millie?' Leandro's harsh tones penetrated the closed door and she stilled, fastened to the spot like a rabbit caught in headlights. Then her eyes slid to the bolt on the door. Even Leandro in a black temper couldn't break his way through a solid bolt, could he?

She didn't understand his anger. Surely he should have been grateful to her for solving a problem for him. The last thing he needed in his life was a baby.

An image of the actress slid into her brain and paralysed her. For a moment she couldn't move or think.

What had she expected? That he was sitting in alone at night, thinking of her?

'Wait a minute!' Hands shaking, she looked at herself in the mirror, hoping that she'd turn out to be the person she hoped she was. She didn't want to be a pathetic, jealous wimp, did she? She wanted to have the strength to walk away from this marriage with her head held high and her dignity intact. She wanted to be mature enough to care for the baby and give him the love he deserved, regardless of how much his parents had hurt her.

That was the person she wanted to be.

Gritting her teeth, Millie turned away from the mirror, walked across the bathroom and opened the door.

Leandro was leaning against the doorframe, dark lights in his eyes warning her of just how short his fuse was. 'What have you been doing for the last half an hour? You look exactly the same as you did when you went in. I assumed you were going to shower and change. Or at least use a towel.'

Up until that point she hadn't realised that she'd forgotten to dry herself. 'I…didn't have anything to change into.'

Leandro reached out a hand and touched her damp hair with a frown of exasperation. 'You didn't bring any clothes.'

'I left my suitcase on the train,' she muttered. 'I was…upset. And I'm only staying in London for one night. It will be fine.' She wished she could feel angry again. The anger had given her energy to cope with the difficult situation. Without it, she felt nothing but exhaustion.

His hand dropped to his side. 'You still have clothes here. Wear them.'

'You kept my clothes?' Shocked, Millie stared up at him and his cold, unemotional appraisal chilled her.

'I hate waste and I find them useful for overnight guests.'

The barb sank deep, the pain resting alongside the earlier wounds he'd inflicted, and she wondered why it was that emotional agony could be so much more traumatic than physical wounds.

He'd dismissed her from his life so easily.

Millie thought about all the bleak, lonely hours she'd spent agonising over whether or not she was right to have walked out—*about the tears she'd shed.*

The times she'd wondered whether he was thinking about her. Whether he cared about their break-up.

Well, she had her answer now.

He was just fine. He'd moved on—apparently with effortless ease. Which just proved that he'd never loved her. He'd married her on impulse. He'd seen her as a novelty. Unfortunately it hadn't taken long for her novelty value to wear off. When they'd been living in their own little world everything had been fine. It had been when they'd returned to *his* world that the problems had started.

Did you really think you'd be able to hold him? Her sister's sympathetic question was embedded in her brain, like a soundtrack that refused to stop playing.

'The baby.' Knowing that the only way she was going to be able to hold it together was if she didn't dwell on how she felt, Millie forced herself to ask the question. 'Who has been looking after him?'

'Two nannies. Change your clothes,' Leandro said roughly. 'The last thing I need is you with pneumonia.'

'I'm not cold.'

'Then why are you shivering?'

Did he honestly not know? She wanted to hit him for not understanding her feelings. He possessed confidence by the barrel-load and that natural self-assurance seemed to prevent him understanding those to whom life didn't come quite so easily. What did a man like Leandro Demetrios know about insecurity? He didn't have a clue.

Neither had he shown any remorse for the way their relationship had ended. In fact, he'd made it obvious that he thought she'd been in the wrong.

Maybe other women would have turned a blind eye, but she wasn't like that.

'I'm shivering because I'm finding this situation…' She struggled to find a suitably neutral word. 'Difficult.'

'Difficult?' His sensual mouth formed a grim, taut line in his handsome face. 'You haven't begun to experience difficult yet, *agape mou*. But you will.'

What did he mean by that?

What could possibly be worse than being forced into the company of the man she adored and hadn't been able to satisfy, and forced to care for the child he'd had with another woman? At the moment that challenge felt like the very essence of difficulty.

Feeling as though she was balancing precariously on the edge of a deep, dark pit, Millie took a deep breath. 'I'd like to see my nephew.' She drew the edges of her damp cardigan around her. She was shivering so hard she might have been in the Arctic, rather than his warm bedroom. 'Where's the baby?'

'Sleeping. What else did you expect at this hour?' His mouth grim, he strode across the bedroom and into the dressing room, emerging moments later with some clothes in his hands. 'Put these on. At least they're dry.'

'They're my old jeans.' She frowned down at them. 'The ones I wore when I first met you.'

'This isn't a trip down memory lane,' he gritted.

'It's an attempt to get you out of wet clothes. Get back in that bathroom. And this time when you come out, make sure you're dry.'

With a sigh, Millie turned back into the bathroom. The lights came on automatically and she stopped, remembering how that had amused her when he'd first brought her to this house. She'd walked in and out of all the rooms, feeling as though she'd walked into a vision of the future. Lights that came on when someone walked into a room, heating sensors, a house that vacuumed itself—Leandro exploited cutting-edge technology in every aspect of his life, and for her it had been like walking into a fantasy.

Trying not to think how the fantasy had ended, Millie stripped off her wet clothes, rubbed her cold skin with a warm towel and pulled on the jeans and silky green jumper he'd handed her.

She glanced in the enormous mirror and decided that the lighting had been designed specifically to highlight her imperfections. She looked nothing like a billionaire's wife.

Emerging from the bathroom, her eyes clashed with his. 'Now can I see the baby? I just…' She swallowed. 'I just want to look at him, that's all.' *To get it over with. Part of her was so afraid she wouldn't be able to do it.*

This was a test, and she wasn't sure whether she was going to pass or fail.

Leandro yanked a towel from the rail and starting rubbing her hair. 'You've been in that bathroom twice and your hair is still soaking.'

'You need to invest in a device that automatically dries someone's hair if it's wet.'

Something flickered in his eyes and she knew he was thinking of the time when he'd first brought her here and she'd played with the technology like a child with a new toy. 'What were you doing all that time?'

Thinking about him. About her life.

Trying to find the strength to do this.

'I was playing hide and seek with the lights. They're a bit bright for me.' Millie winced as his methodical rubbing became a little too brisk and tried not to think about the fact that he was turning her hair into a tangled mess.

What did it matter? What did smooth, perfect hair matter at this point in their relationship? They were way past the point where her appearance was an issue.

Leandro slung the towel over the heated rail. 'That will do.'

'Yes, there's no point in working on something that's never going to come up to scratch,' Millie muttered, and he frowned sharply.

'What's that supposed to mean?'

'Nothing.' Trying to forget her appearance, Millie lifted her chin. 'I want to see the baby.' At least the baby wouldn't care whether her hair was blow-dried or not.

She felt inadequate and out of place in this man's life, but she was here because the baby needed her. It was abandoned. Unloved. *Like her...*

For a whole year she'd locked herself away—*pro-*

tected herself from the outside world. And if it hadn't been for the baby she would have stayed in her hiding place. Not that she'd needed to hide. *Leandro hadn't come to look for her, had he?* She'd left, but he hadn't followed.

Leandro gave her a long, hard look, as if asking himself a question.

Knowing with absolute certainty what that question was, Millie walked towards the bedroom door.

'You can see the baby,' he drawled as they walked out of the room. 'But don't wake him up.'

The comment surprised her. Why would he care whether she woke the baby or not? She'd thought he would have been only too anxious for her to remove the child and get out of his life.

Millie glanced at the paintings, reflecting that most normal people had to go to art galleries to see pieces like this. Leandro could admire them on his way to the bathroom.

Following him up a flight of stairs, she frowned. 'You've put him as far away from you as possible.'

'You think he should sleep in my bedroom, perhaps?' His silken enquiry brought a flush to her cheeks.

'No. I don't think that. I can't think of a less suitable environment for a baby than your bedroom.'

Millie leaned against the wall for support, unable to dispel the image of his hard, muscular body entwined with the sylph-like actress.

Of course he'd had relationships since they'd broken up. What had she expected? Leandro was an intensely virile man with a dark, restless sex appeal that women found irresistible. Just as she had. And her sister.

Millie gave a low moan, wondering how she'd ever found the arrogance to think their marriage could work. How naïve had she been, thinking that they shared something special. When they'd first met he'd been so good at making her feel beautiful that for a while she'd actually believed that she was.

Leandro opened a door and stood there, allowing her to go first.

Her arm brushed against the hard muscle of his abdomen and her stomach reacted instantly.

A uniformed nanny rose quickly to her feet. 'He's been very unsettled, Mr Demetrios,' she said in a low voice. 'Crying, refusing his bottle. He's asleep now, but I don't know how long it will last.'

Leandro dismissed her with a single imperious movement of his head and the girl scurried out of the room.

Had he always been that scary? Millie wondered. *Had he been cold and intimidating when she'd met him?*

The answer was yes, probably, but never with her. With her he'd always been gentle and good humoured. That was one of the things that had made her feel special. The power and influence he wielded made others stutter and stumble around him, but when they'd met, she hadn't known who he was. And that had amused him. And she'd continued to amuse him. With *her,* the tiger had sheathed his claws and played gently, but she'd never been under any illusions. She hadn't tamed the tiger and she doubted any woman ever would.

As the door closed behind the girl, Millie wondered how on earth she'd ever had the courage to talk to this man.

'Your nephew.' He spoke the words in a low tone and Millie forced aside all other feelings and tiptoed towards the cot. Her palms were clammy and she felt ever so slightly sick because she'd pictured this scene in her head so many times, but now it was twisted in a cruel parody of her dream.

Yes, she and Leandro were leaning over a cot. But her dream had never included a baby who wasn't hers, fathered by the man she loved with the woman who was closest to her.

Agony ripped through her, stealing her breath and her strength. She thought she gave a moan of denial, but the baby didn't stir, his perfect features immobile in sleep.

Innocent of the tense atmosphere in the room, he was so still that Millie felt a rush of panic and instinctively reached out a hand to touch him.

Strong fingers closed over hers and drew her away from the cot.

'He's fine.' Leandro's low, masculine voice brushed against her nerve endings. 'He always sleeps like that. *When* he sleeps, which isn't that often.'

'He looks—'

'As though he isn't breathing. I know.' He gave a grim smile. 'I've made that mistake several times myself. Once I even woke him up just to check he was alive. Believe me, I don't advise it. He's very much alive and if you poke him just to check, he'll confirm it in the loudest possible way. He has lungs that an opera singer would envy and, once woken up, he doesn't like going back to sleep. I had to walk him round the house for three hours.'

Leandro worried about the baby so much he'd woken him? And then he'd carried him around the house? It didn't fit with what she knew of him.

'What did you do with your BlackBerry?' She asked the question without thinking and he gave a faint smile.

'You think I spoke into the baby and tucked my mobile phone into the cot?' His eyes were mocking and Millie looked away, flustered.

'I didn't think you'd want anything to do with the baby.' In a way her question was a challenge. Would he care for a baby that wasn't his?

For a moment—*just for a moment*—something shimmered between them and then she dragged her eyes away from his and focused on the baby. Her heart was thumping, her stomach was tumbling over and over. But he'd always had this effect on her, hadn't he? He could turn her legs to jelly with just one glance. Everything else became irrelevant.

Except that it wasn't irrelevant and she had this baby to remind her of that fact.

He lay quietly. Even in sleep Millie could see the dark feathering of his eyelashes against his cheek and the shock of dark hair. And her heart melted.

To her intense relief, the baby softened everything inside her. 'You poor thing,' she whispered, gently touching his head with her hand. 'You must be missing your mummy—wondering what you're doing in this strange place.' Aware that Leandro was looking at her oddly, she flushed. 'Sorry. I suppose it's a bit crazy speaking to a baby who's asleep.'

Her eyes met his and in that single instant she knew he was thinking about the child they could have made together. The image was too painful and she looked away, determined not to torture herself with what she would never have. *If she'd produced a child quickly, perhaps this would never have happened.* But that had been another failure on her part. Another failure to add to the list. 'He's sweet. He has your hair.'

'Then the child is a miracle of conception,' Leandro snapped. 'But I can assure you that your sister was definitely the mother.'

Millie struggled not to react. 'Becca was always confident. I think that's why she was so successful. It just didn't enter her head that she couldn't do something or have something.' *Even her sister's husband.* 'Like you, she never questioned herself or doubted herself. You had that in common.'

'Alpha woman.'

Millie looked at him. 'Yes. She was.' And she'd always felt insecure around her big sister. There had been just no way she could ever measure up. Even as a very young child, she'd been aware that she was walking in her sister's shadow.

And even in death Becca had left that shadow—
a dark cloud that had stolen the light from Millie's
marriage. *From her life.*

'Let's leave the baby to sleep.' Taking control, Leandro put a hand in the centre of her back and urged
her out of the room. 'Have you eaten?'

'No.' Millie wondered how he could be thinking
about food. 'It's past midnight. I was going to go
straight to the bed and breakfast.'

'You're not going to any bed and breakfast. We
need to talk—and I need coffee, so we'll have the
conversation in the kitchen.'

Too drained to argue, Millie followed him down-
stairs. The kitchen was another room that had surprised her when she'd first seen the house. It was a
clever combination of modern and traditional, a large
range cooker giving warmth and comfort, while the
maximal use of glass ensured light poured into every
available space. As a result the lush garden appeared
to be part of the room and the table was positioned
in such a way that, whatever the season, it felt as
though you were sitting outdoors.

'Sit down before you fall down.' Leandro strolled
to the espresso machine and ground some beans.

The sound pounded her throbbing head and Millie
winced. 'You still make it all from scratch, then?' It
had been one of the many things that she'd learned
about him early on. He wanted the best. Whether it
was art, coffee or women—Leandro demanded perfection. *Which made it even more surprising that
he'd picked her.*

He made the coffee—as competent in the kitchen as he was everywhere else. Leandro used staff because his life was so maniacally busy, not because he was deficient in skills. And sometimes, she knew, he just preferred to be on his own.

He'd rolled back his shirtsleeves and the muscles of his forearm flexed as he worked.

Strong, Millie thought as she looked at him. He was strong; physically, emotionally—and that inherent strength was part of his devastating appeal. He was a man who led while others followed. A man women were drawn to.

'Why didn't you tell me that the baby had been brought here?' To distract herself, she asked the question that was on her mind. 'Why did I have to read about it in the newspapers?'

'You walked out on me.' His voice terse, he reached for a cup. 'I had no reason to think you'd be interested.'

Absorbing that blow, Millie curled her fingers over the back of the chair. 'Why are you so angry with me? I would have thought you'd be apologetic or at least a little uncomfortable but you're not. You're…'

'I'm what, Millie?'

'You're…' She hesitated. 'Boiling with rage. And I just don't get it.'

He didn't reply, but she knew he'd heard her because his hand stilled for a moment. And then he lifted an empty cup. 'Do you want one?'

'No, thank you. You make it so strong it will keep

me awake.' Not that she'd sleep anyway. The adrenaline was pumping round her bloodstream like a drug. She wanted to walk. Pace. *Sob?*

Leandro waited while the thick dark brew filled the small cup. Then he walked across to the table. 'Right, let's talk.' He put the cup on the table and sprawled in the nearest chair. The edges of his torn dress shirt slid apart, revealing his flat, bronzed abdomen.

Millie kept her eyes fixed straight ahead. 'What is there to talk about?'

'This is going to be a tiring conversation for you if you stand all the way through it. And you already look ready to drop.'

She sat, too emotionally wrung out to think for herself. 'I'm fine.'

'You look wrecked. You should have told me you were coming. I would have sent my private jet.'

'I wouldn't have felt comfortable.'

'You're still my wife. You're entitled to the perks of the job.'

'I don't want anything from you.' Millie sat very upright. 'Except maybe the stuff you've bought for the baby. It's a waste to buy a second pram and things. Tomorrow I'll remove Costas from your life. You can get back to your BlackBerry and your—' She almost said 'actress' but thought better of it. 'And your undisturbed nights.' From the corner of her eye she saw his fingers close round his coffee cup.

'I don't want to talk about Costas.' He let that

hover in the air while he drank his coffee. 'I want to talk about us.'

Her heart started to thump faster because she could feel him watching her and his scrutiny made her squirm. 'How is that relevant?'

'It's relevant.'

'How? There is no "us". There's nothing to talk about.' Why would he want to go back over old ground? Millie wasn't sure she could stand reliving the whole thing again.

'You made promises, Millie. You stood up in that little village church and made those vows.' Leandro put his cup down slowly. 'And then you just walked away. *For richer for poorer, in sickness and in health*—remember that?'

Her chin lifted. *'Forsaking all others...'*

'I might have known you'd throw that one at me.' He inhaled deeply, his eyes holding hers. 'You asked me how it's relevant—let me tell you. You're my wife, Millie. And to a Greek man, marriage is binding. It isn't something you opt in and out of depending on the mood. It's forever.'

'Leandro—'

'You chose to come back, Millie.' His mouth tightened and his eyes glinted hard and dangerous. 'And now you're going to stay.'

Chapter 3

Millie sat in frozen silence, so stunned by his unexpected declaration that she could barely breathe,
let alone speak. It took several uncomfortable moments for the full implications of his words to sink
into her shocked brain.

Then she sprang to her feet and paced to the far
side of the kitchen, so agitated that it was impossible
to stay still. 'You expect me to come back to you?
You're blaming me for walking away?'

'Yes.' His tone was hard. 'I am.'

Millie stared at the row of shiny saucepans on the
wall. 'The fact that you won't let me take the baby
tells me only one thing.'

Leandro gave a humourless laugh. 'I always insist
that my employees are capable of thinking laterally.

For some reason I didn't apply the same standards to my wife. Take a word of advice from me—when you study a picture, there is almost always more going on than first meets the eye.'

'I can see only one reason why you'd be so protective of this baby.'

'Then remind me not to set you up in business. Tunnel vision is a guaranteed path to failure.' He was a tough adversary—intelligent, articulate and able to counter every word spoken with the effortless ease of a practised negotiator. 'Did you really think I'd let you walk out with him? A baby is a massive responsibility, requiring the ultimate commitment. Given your track record, I'm hardly likely to hand him over.'

'*My* track record?'

'When you met an obstacle in life, you walked away.'

His accusation was so unfair that her breath hitched. 'You were with my sister. What did you expect? My blessing?'

'You are my wife. I expected your trust.' He was on his feet, too. And determined to halt her retreat. 'Answer me a question.' His handsome face taut and grim, he closed his hands over her shoulders. 'After everything we shared—after those vows you made— why were you so quick to believe the worst of me? You stalked out that night and you never contacted me again. You didn't ask me about it.'

Her eyes level with his bare chest, Millie's heart was pounding uncomfortably. 'I saw what I saw.'

'You saw what your sister wanted you to see.'

'I know that some of the blame lay with her, but—'

'Not some of it,' his tone was harsh, 'all of it. She set you up, Millie, and you believed all the lies she fed you. And I was so angry that you believed her, I let you go. And that was a mistake, I admit that. One of many I've made where you're concerned. I should have run after you, pinned you to our bed and made you see the truth.'

'Don't do this!' Millie covered her ears with her hands. 'Why are you doing this now when it's all too late?'

'Because this is a conversation we need to have. What about those feelings you claimed you had for me, Millie? Or was it all a damn lie because you wanted the lifestyle?'

She almost laughed at that. The lifestyle had been the problem, but he'd never understand that, would he? 'I didn't care about the lifestyle.'

'Really? For a woman who didn't care, you certainly spent enough time on your appearance.'

It was such an unexpected interpretation of the facts that for a moment Millie just gaped at him. *He had no idea.* 'What you said just now,' she croaked, 'about a picture sometimes having another meaning—'

'Shopping is shopping.' There was an acid bite to his tone. 'It's hard to find another meaning for that. Unless you convinced yourself that it was an act of charity to prop up the world economy single-handed.'

Millie was so shocked and stung by that all she managed by way of response was a little shake of her head. 'I was trying to be the woman you wanted me to be.'

'What the hell is that supposed to mean?'

Wasn't it obvious? She was standing in front of him in her oldest jeans with bubbling hair and no make-up. The shiny surface of his large American fridge reflected her deficiencies back at her. Even in the kitchen there was no escape. 'I'm not your type. We met and married in less than a month. It was just too quick. We didn't know each other. It was a mistake.'

'Which part, exactly, was the mistake?' He made a rough sound in his throat and stepped towards her, trapping her against the wall with the sheer force of his presence. 'The part when you lay underneath me, sobbing my name?'

She felt the hard muscle of his thighs against her. 'Leandro—'

He slid his hand into her hair, tilting her face so that she was forced to look at him. 'Or the part when you came again and again without any break in between—was that when you thought, This is a mistake?'

'Don't do this—please don't do this.' Millie pushed at his chest and immediately regretted it because her hands encountered sleek muscle and it took every fibre of her being not to slide her greedy fingers over the deliciously masculine contours of his chest.

'When you fell asleep with your head on my shoulder, were you dreaming of mistakes?'

He'd conjured up one of her most precious memories and she closed her eyes against the tears and felt them scald the backs of her eyelids. The sex had always been incredible but also a little bit overwhelming because she could never quite let go of the thought that a man like him couldn't possibly want a girl like her. But in those moments afterwards—*those moments when he'd held her and murmured soft words against her hair*—that had been her favourite time. The time she'd actually let herself believe that the fairy-tale might be happening.

'When you told me that you loved me, Millie...' His voice was hoarse and his fingers tightened in her hair. 'Were you thinking that it was a mistake? Was it all a lie?'

'No.'

Her eyes flew to his and for one desperate moment she thought he might actually kiss her. His mouth hovered, a muscle flickered in his lean, dark jaw and his eyes glittered black and dangerous. He looked like a man on the edge.

And then he stepped back from the edge, displaying that formidable control that raised him apart from other men. 'I don't think you know what you want, Millie. And that's why I'm not letting you take this baby.' With a searing glance in her direction, he closed his hand over her wrist and propelled her back to the table. 'Sit down.'

'Leandro, you can't—'

'I said *sit down*. I haven't finished.' His harsh tone was all the more shocking because she'd never heard it before. Always, with her, he'd been gentle. She'd never been on the receiving end of his biting sarcasm or his brutal frankness.

'If you yell, I won't listen.'

'I'm *not* yelling.' But he drew in a breath to calm himself and Millie sat, wondering again why he was so angry.

'Leandro—'

'You walked out without even giving me a hearing,' he said thickly, 'and at the time I was so angry with you that I let you go. Your lack of trust diminished what we shared to nothing. But I can see how skilfully your sister manipulated you. I can almost understand why you might have believed what you believed. You're right. We didn't know each other well enough or you wouldn't have run so fast. You wouldn't have looked at me with that accusation in your eyes. You wouldn't have been so quick to doubt me. You would have known me better.'

'I saw you,' she whispered, but his gaze didn't waver.

'What did you see, Millie? You saw your sister naked in the pool with me. Isn't that what you saw?'

The reminder was like the sting of a whip. 'You're trying to tell me I was imagining things.'

'No. I'm trying to make you see the rest of the picture. Was *I* naked?' His tone demanded an answer. 'Was I having sex with her?'

'Not then, no, but—'

'Can you think of any other reasons why Becca might have been naked in my pool?'

'Frankly, no.' Millie wished he'd sit down too. Staring up at six feet two of muscle-packed male wasn't an experience designed to induce relaxation.

Her answer drew a frustrated growl from him and he muttered something under his breath in Greek. 'Perhaps your sister wasn't quite the person you thought she was.'

'It isn't fair to talk about her like this when she's not here to defend herself!'

'Fair?' His voice exploded with passion. 'Don't talk to me about fair!'

'You blame my sister, but you're no saint, Leandro.'

He gave a twisted smile. 'I have never laid claim to that title.'

'You have a dangerous reputation. Before me you'd dated all those beautiful women and you hadn't committed to any of them.' Millie bit her lip, wondering how she could have been such a fool.

'And what does that tell you?'

'It tells me that you're not good at sticking with one person.'

Tension vibrating through his powerful frame, Leandro stared up at the ceiling, apparently trying to control his response. When he finally looked at her again, his eyes glinted volcanic black and his body language was forceful and menacing as he loomed over her.

'Given that you can only see one image, I am

going to have to show you the rest of the picture. But I'm only going to say this once,' he said softly, 'so make sure you are listening.'

'*Stop* trying to intimidate me.'

Shock shimmered in his eyes and his head jerked back as if she'd slapped him. 'I am *not* intimidating you.'

'That depends on where you're sitting.' Her voice was strong and steady and Millie had the satisfaction of seeing him take a deep breath.

Inclining his head by way of apology, he modulated the tone of his voice. 'Understand that the only reason I'm prepared to give you this explanation is because you're my wife and that allows you a degree of leeway that I would *never* grant to another person.'

Millie wanted to point out that she didn't inhabit that role any more but she couldn't push the words past her dry throat.

'Millie—look at me.'

She looked.

'I did *not* have sex with your sister.' Leandro spoke the words with deadly emphasis. 'At no time in our short, ill-fated marriage was I ever unfaithful to you. The baby is not mine.'

Millie's heart jumped. *She wanted to believe*— and then she remembered her sister. 'Why would Becca lie?' She breathed in and out. 'That would make her…'

Leandro straightened, his expression cold. 'Yes,' he said flatly, 'it would.'

'I know what I saw.'

'I've given you the facts. You decide. I have never doubted your intelligence, just your ability to use it.'

Millie stared at him in confusion, thinking of what he'd just said. *What she'd seen.* Everything she knew, everything she'd believed was suddenly thrown in the air. It was as if someone had dropped a giant jigsaw puzzle and the picture was no longer visible. 'One of you is—was—lying,' she said hoarsely, and he gave a grim smile.

'And your sister is no longer able to tell you the truth. An interesting dilemma, *agape mou.* Who are you going to believe? Live husband, or dead sister?'

Faced with that choice, her head started to throb. 'Let me tell you about my sister, Leandro. Let me tell you what my sister was to me. It was Becca who held my hand on my first day at school. It was Becca who helped me with my maths homework. It was Becca who taught me how to do my hair and make-up. Every step of my life, she was there, *helping* me. She encouraged me when my parents barely noticed I existed. It's bad enough to think she'd have an affair with my husband, but now you're suggesting she made up this entire thing just to hurt me?'

His silence said more than a thousand words would have done and Millie gave a distressed sigh.

'Obviously that *is* what you're suggesting. That's madness. What could she have possibly gained by that? And why would you expect me to believe you without question? I've known you a fraction of the time I knew my sister.'

'I expect you to believe me,' he said acidly, 'be--

cause you're my wife and that role should bring with it trust and commitment, two qualities that appear to be sadly lacking in your make-up. The truth is that our marriage started to go wrong long before you saw me with your sister.' Leandro straightened. 'I presume that's why you started avoiding sex.'

Her face flamed. 'I wasn't…avoiding sex.'

'Night after night you turned your back on me. You pretended to be asleep. And if I arrived home too early for you to play that trick, then you threw excuse after excuse at me—"headache", "tired", "wrong time of the month"—and I let you hold back because I was only too aware that you'd had absolutely no sexual experience before I came into your life. I was extremely patient with you. I had no idea what was going on in your head and you gave me no clues. You just lay there and hoped it would go away.'

The fact that he'd seen through her pitiful attempts to keep him at a distance increased her humiliation. 'I'm sure you really regretted marrying me.' *In fact, she knew he did. Wasn't that why he'd slept with her sister?*

'Do you want to know what I regret, Millie?' His voice was suddenly weary and he ran his hand over the back of his neck to relieve the tension. 'I regret that I didn't tie you to that damn bed and force you to tell me what was going on in that pretty head of yours. I backed off when I should have pushed you for answers, and I regret that more deeply than you'll ever know.'

'There was nothing in my head,' she lied. 'I was

tired, that was all. When you weren't away on business trips, we were always out—every night there was something you wanted me to go to.' *Another event designed to highlight the differences between them and sap her confidence.*

'Tired?' His gaze was sardonic. 'On our honeymoon you had no sleep at all. We had sex virtually every hour of every day. You were as insatiable as I was. Fatigue wasn't the reason you had your back to me when I came to bed.'

'Leandro—'

'The honeymoon was perfect. The problems started when we arrived home. Suddenly you couldn't bear me to touch you. In fact, you went to the most extraordinary lengths to make sure that I didn't touch you.' His lips tightened. 'I even wondered whether the reason you invited your sister to stay with us was because you wanted something else to keep us apart.'

Appalled by the gulf in their mutual understanding, she dug her fingers into her hair and shook her head. 'You think I *wanted* you to have an affair with my sister?'

'I've said all I'm going to say on that particular subject.'

Millie was shaking so much she was relieved she was sitting down. 'I invited my sister to stay because I trusted her. And because I needed her help—she was always the one I turned to when I was in trouble.'

His brows met in a frown. 'How were you in trouble?'

Millie sat in silence, wishing she'd phrased it differently. Talking to him wasn't easy, was it? They didn't have that depth of understanding in their relationship. They'd shared scalding passion and nothing more. And Leandro was so confident, he wouldn't be able to understand anyone who wasn't. 'This is very hard for me,' she muttered, emotion swamping her. 'I didn't just lose my husband, I lost my sister. She was my best friend. And I lost her long before she died on that dusty, lonely road.'

'I want to know why you were so quick to assume that I'd have an affair. We'd been married three months, Millie! *Three months.* Hardly enough time for disillusionment to set in.'

'I knew your reputation.'

'Which was earned *before* I met you.'

Millie smiled through tears that refused to be contained. 'Oh, sure.' Her voice was choked. 'Beautiful me. So vastly superior in every way to those skinny models and actresses who knew how to dress, how to walk—I can quite see how it would have been impossible to notice them with me in the room. You should have reprogrammed the lights in this house so that they went *off* when I walked into a room. That might have helped our marriage.'

'Sarcasm doesn't suit you. It was your sweet nature and your gentleness that drew me to you.' Leandro's eyes narrowed, his gaze suddenly intent and focused. 'You always put yourself down. Why didn't I notice that before?'

'I don't know. At the beginning we didn't do much

talking and after that you were too busy being exasperated with me for getting everything wrong, I suppose.' Millie thought about all those tense hours she'd spent trying to be who he wanted her to be. What an utter waste of time. Obviously she hadn't even come close. Which just proved that even eight hours in a beauty salon couldn't make a billionaire's wife out of a farm girl. 'You were partly to blame—you just dumped me in that situation and left me.'

'What situation?' He looked genuinely perplexed and she decided that there was no reason not to talk about it now.

It wasn't as if she was trying to impress him. She'd given up on that. 'You dumped me at all those really glitzy parties.'

'I did *not* "dump" you. I was by your side.'

'You were either talking business with someone in a suit—or you were smiling your smile at some beauty who was determined to grab your attention even though you were with me. And they all looked at me as though I'd crawled out from under a rock.'

'You were my wife.'

'Yes. That was the problem.'

Leandro gave her a look of exasperation. 'You are making no sense at all! Being my wife gave you status—'

'It was hugely stressful.'

He rubbed his fingers over his forehead. 'If this is a problem you expect me to discuss rationally, you're going to have to be a little more specific. In what way was being my wife "stressful"?'

Millie rubbed her hands over her legs, staring down at nails that had been bitten to nothing over the past year. 'I didn't have the necessary qualifications. I don't know why you married me, but you made a mistake.'

'Yes, you're right. I did make a mistake.' His fingers drummed a slow, deadly rhythm on the table. 'And I'm putting that mistake right and we're ending this mess.'

His words crushed her. For a horrible moment she thought she might make a fool of herself and slide to the floor and beg, *No, no, no.* The pride was stripped from her, leaving her vulnerable and exposed. She felt like a mortally wounded animal waiting for the final blow.

Oddly enough, the desire to cry suddenly ceased. It was as if her body had shut down.

'You want a divorce.' Somehow she managed to say the words, her eyes fixed on the wooden table, studying the grain of the wood. Anything, rather than look at him and fall apart. It was illogical, she knew, but she'd rather be married to him and never see him than cut the ties forever. 'Of course you do. Just let me take the baby, and I'll give you a divorce.'

'*Theos mou,* haven't you been listening to a word I've said?' His voice was rough and angry. 'I do *not* want a divorce.'

'You said you made a mistake.'

'It seems that whatever one of us says, the other misinterprets it.' Clearly struggling with his own volatile emotions, Leandro paused for a moment, his hand to his forehead. The he looked at her. 'The mistake I made,' he said harshly, 'was letting you walk out that day. I should have dragged you back and made you look at the truth. But I was furious that you doubted me. I was furious that you didn't stand your ground and fight for what we had.'

'If something isn't right, sometimes it's better just to let it go.'

Leandro threw her a fulminating glare and then paced to the far side of the kitchen, his broad shoulders rigid with tension.

Millie watched him—*this man she loved*—wondering what was going through his mind. As if reading her thoughts, he turned. The ever-present chemistry flickered across the room, resurrecting a connection that had never died.

'When I said that I'm ending this mess, I meant that we're ending this ridiculous separation. I want you back by my side where you belong. When the going gets tough, I want you to stay and fight instead of running. Those are the qualities I expect in the woman I've chosen to be my wife and the mother of my children.'

Millie pressed the palm of her hand against her heart to relieve the almost intolerable ache. 'Are you saying that you don't think I'd make a good mother?'

Something dark and dangerous shifted in his eyes. 'Let's just say that at the moment I'm not convinced.'

Appalled that he could possibly think that of her, Millie stared at him, seeing dark shadows in his eyes that she didn't understand. 'You don't know me at all.'

'No,' he said grimly. 'I don't. But I intend to rectify that.' He spoke the word with deadly emphasis. 'Let's see how powerful that commitment is this time around, shall we, Millie? If you want to be a mother to that child, you'll do it by my side, as my wife.'

The shock of his words silenced her and he lifted an eyebrow.

'It's a yes or no answer, Millie.'

She stood up, so agitated that she couldn't stay sitting. The fact that he intended to keep the baby suggested that he must be the father. Did he expect her to just ignore that fact? She wondered why he was so determined to continue the marriage. Was it a matter of pride? 'Why do you want this?' Her chair scraped on the floor, the sound grating against her jagged nerves. 'I don't understand you.'

'I know that. But you will have the whole of our marriage to understand me. And I'm going to understand you.' He strolled across to her and she stepped backwards, but he kept coming, backing her against the wall, planting his hands either side of her head. 'You and me, Millie.' His voice was suddenly dangerously masculine and she caught her breath because he was casting the same spell that had drawn her in right at the beginning.

'Leandro, don't—'

His hand caught her face, his gaze intense. 'I want you to stand by those promises you made to me in the church that day.'

His eyes darkened to a fierce black, as if her silence had somehow given him an answer to a question still unasked.

'Millie?'

Millie closed her eyes. She wanted to ask why he was so determined to keep the baby. Couldn't he see how that looked? Her mind was a mess—her thoughts so tangled and confused that she couldn't follow a single strand through to its conclusion. 'You can't just resurrect our marriage. We were a disaster.'

'Our communication was a disaster, that I agree.' Leandro shrugged. 'I rarely make mistakes and when I do, it's just once, so you can relax.'

She'd never felt less relaxed in her life. 'I can't be what you want me to be.'

Leandro gave a humourless laugh. 'Our communication has been so appalling up until this point, *agape mou,* I seriously doubt that you have any idea what I want from you. But this time around you will *not* be turning your back on me. And you will not be walking out when we hit a problem.'

Millie thought about what she had to offer him. *Even less than last time.* 'You want me to come back as your wife, but things have changed, Leandro. You don't know everything. Things have happened over the past year.'

'I don't want to know,' he said roughly, and she realised that he thought she was referring to another relationship.

'There are things I need to tell you.'

'Don't tell me. At least, not right now. I'm Greek,

remember? I'm trying to be modern, but I have a long way to go.' With a low growl of frustration he lowered his head towards hers, the gesture an erotic reminder of everything they'd shared. For a moment his mouth hovered and he was obviously deciding whether to kiss her or not and then he lifted his head and stepped back. 'No. This time we're *not* going to let the sex do the talking. You look exhausted. Get some sleep. Just for tonight you can sleep in one of the spare bedrooms but after that you'll sleep where my wife is supposed to sleep. By my side.'

Chapter 4

'Don't cry. Don't cry.' Crying herself, Millie held
the baby against her, rocking gently as he gulped
and sobbed.

She'd been lying fully dressed and wide awake
on top of the bed in one of the rooms just down the
corridor from the nursery when she'd heard the baby
howling. Instantly she'd sprung from the bed, driven
by a deep instinct that she hadn't felt before.

To begin with she'd stood back and allowed the
nannies to comfort him, reminding herself that they
were familiar to him, whereas she was a stranger.
But after a few minutes she'd realised that they were
getting nowhere and she'd taken over and dismissed
them.

'Are you hungry? Is that what's wrong?' Wiping

away her own tears on her sleeve, Millie lifted the baby out of the cot, feeling his sturdy body beneath her hands as she held him awkwardly. 'I haven't done this before so you'll have to tell me if I'm getting it wrong. Are you missing your mummy?' Although, from what the clinic had told her, Becca had spent precious little time with her baby.

The baby's yells increased and Millie settled herself in the chair and tentatively offered him the bottle that the nannies had left. 'Is this the right angle? I've never fed a baby before so you're going to have to yell a bit louder if I get it wrong.'

But the baby clamped his little mouth round the teat and sucked fiercely, gulping noisily as he greedily devoured the milk.

Millie gave an astonished laugh. 'You really are starving. You certainly don't take after your mother. She never ate anything.' As the baby fed, she stared down at him, examining his features with an agonising pang.

There was no escaping the fact that he had Leandro's hair. And his beautiful olive skin.

'Is he your daddy?' Speaking softly, she adjusted the angle of the bottle. 'And if he is, how do I live with that? I don't know. This is like one of those hypothetical dilemmas you talk about with your friends over a coffee. What would you do if your husband has an affair? Except maybe he didn't—I don't know. Should I really trust his word—or my sister's? Am I supposed to just overlook it? Is that what he means about being the wife of a Greek man? I'm supposed to be in the kitchen stirring a casserole while he's off having fun with his mistress?' The baby sucked rhythmically, his eyes fixed on her face. 'There's no way we can carry on where we left off, even if I wanted to. Everything has changed. Things happened to me—things he doesn't know about. He's assuming everything is the same as when I left, and it isn't.'

The baby sucked happily and Millie gave a watery smile. 'You're not giving me much help, are you? I don't know what to do. If I wasn't attractive enough to keep him the first time, it's going to be even worse this time. He doesn't know what he's taking on.' She thought about the last year and gave a despairing laugh. 'On the other hand, there's no way I'm leaving you here with him. You'll be corrupted in a month.'

One of the nannies appeared in the doorway. 'You persuaded him to take a bottle! We couldn't get him to feed. I'd really had it with him by the time I went off duty last night.' She yawned. 'I even woke Erica because she's been doing this job for twenty years and knows every trick in the book. But he wouldn't take it for her either. He's the most miserable baby we've ever looked after. Probably knows there's this big row about his parentage. His mum's dead, apparently. And sexy Leandro Demetrios is supposedly his father. Scandal, scandal, scandal.' She gave a conspiratorial giggle, and walked across the room. 'Of course, *he* won't say whether the baby is his or not, but he's taken it in, hasn't he? So that must say a lot.'

'It says that he's a responsible human being,' Millie said stiffly, concentrating on the baby and *hating* the thought that everyone was gossiping. 'Am I giving it to him too fast?'

'No. He's fine. He's not crying, is he? I much prefer toddlers. At least you have the option of sticking them in front of the television when you get fed up with them.' The nanny frowned. 'Thank goodness you've got the touch. I was expecting to get fired this morning.'

'Fired?'

The girl gave a fatalistic shrug. 'Well, Leandro Demetrios isn't exactly known as someone who accepts failure, is he? Erica and I decided in the night that if we hadn't got the baby to take the bottle by morning, both of us would be for the chop. Shame. The pay is good and the boss is gorgeous. We're trying to find excuses to be on his floor of the house in case he sleeps in the nude. So—who are you, exactly? I didn't know he was hiring anyone else.'

'I'm his wife.' The moment she'd said the words, Millie wished they could be unsaid because the girl gaped at her in astonished disbelief.

Then the drive for job security overtook her natural astonishment and she cleared her throat. 'I had no idea.' Her eyes slid from Millie's tumbling hair to her old jeans. 'God—sorry. I mean— And you're looking after his—' Her face turned scarlet but it was obvious from the look in her eyes that she thought Millie was a fool. 'We didn't know he was still married.'

'We've been apart for a while.'

'I see.' The girl's expression said, No wonder, and

Millie wished she didn't mind so much. She *knew* she was an unlikely choice. Why did it still hurt so much to see the surprise in people's eyes? Why did she have to be so sensitive? Annoyed with herself for caring, she wished she were more like Leandro, who was always coolly indifferent to the opinions of everyone around him. Or failing that, she would have chosen to be more like Becca, who had been born assuming that the whole world adored her.

Would she have been more confident if she hadn't had Becca as an older sister? Or if she'd been born with Becca's blonde, perfect looks? Becca had appeared on the covers of all the high-class glossy magazines—her trademark slanting blue eyes and flirtatious expression guaranteeing the publication flew off the shelves.

'So…' The nanny looked at her curiously. 'Are the two of you back together, then?'

Were they?

The question was cheeky, but Millie had been asking herself the same thing all night. Instead of snatching some much-needed sleep, she'd locked herself in one of Leandro's many spare guest suites and lain on the bed, wondering whether she had the courage to face what was ahead of her if she agreed to his suggestion.

He'd reject her again, of course. Once he knew…

If she'd disappointed him then, how much more disappointed was he going to be this time?

But if she refused, she'd lose access to her sister's child. Her nephew.

As confused as ever, Millie carefully removed the teat from the baby's mouth. His stomach pleasantly full, he blinked his eyes and focused on her. And then he smiled. A lopsided, not very confident smile, but a smile nevertheless, and the nanny gave a short laugh.

'He's never done that before. He's never smiled at anyone. Can I have a cuddle?' She scooped the baby from Millie's arms and the baby's eyes flew wide and then his face crumpled. 'Oh, gosh, forget it.' Pulling an exasperated face, the nanny lowered the baby back into Millie's arms.

Costas immediately snuggled close and fell asleep.

The nanny rolled her eyes. 'Well, now you're stuck,' she said dryly. 'If you move, he'll wake up.'

'I don't need to move. I'll just stay here with him.'

'You're just going to sit holding him? That will get him into bad habits.'

'Since when is enjoying a cuddle a bad habit?'

'When it stops him wanting to sleep in his cot. You should put him in there and let him cry,' the nanny advised firmly. 'Let him know who's boss. It's five o'clock in the morning. Don't you want to go back to bed?'

To do what? Lie awake, thinking? Going over and over everything in her mind? She could do that here, cuddling the cause of her dilemma. 'I'm fine here.'

And she thought she *was* fine until the door opened and Leandro strode into the room.

'Oh!' The nanny flushed scarlet and gave an embarrassed laugh, the way women often did when they laid eyes on Leandro Demetrios. Then she tweaked her uniform and smoothed her hair. Millie didn't blame her. Women did that too, didn't they? She'd tweaked her uniform and smoothed her hair every minute of every day they'd been together. The only difference being that her 'uniform' had been the designer clothes he'd bought her. Not that any of them had helped. The truth was that no amount of straightening and smoothing had transformed her into something that had looked good alongside his extraordinary looks.

Last night he'd been very much the dominant husband but this morning he was all billionaire tycoon. Smooth, sleek, expensive and indecently handsome. Everything about him shrieked of success in a realm above the reach of ordinary mortals, and Millie took one glance at the elegant dark grey suit and knew that he was off on one of his business trips.

'I need to talk to you before I leave for my meeting.' He turned and delivered a pointed glance at the nanny, who took the hint and melted away, closing the door behind her.

Millie was willing to bet she was standing outside it with her ear pressed to the wood. 'She has to go.'

In the process of looking at the baby, Leandro frowned. 'Go where?'

'Just go. The nanny. I don't want her looking after the baby.' Millie curved the baby against her and fiddled with the blanket that covered him. 'She's a gossip and her only interest in Costas is that his mother is dead and his father is a billionaire.'

'Whoever I appoint can't fail to be aware of the rumours surrounding this baby.'

'I agree, but she showed no warmth or care towards him. And she doesn't even *like* babies—she said she prefers them older. And even then she just sticks them in front of the television.'

'Fine.' He glanced at his watch. 'You want me to fire her, I'll fire her.'

'No. I'll do it,' Millie said firmly, and he lifted his eyebrows.

'You?'

'Yes.'

Leandro gave a disbelieving laugh. 'I'm seeing a totally different side to you today. I wouldn't have thought you were capable of firing someone.'

'It depends on the provocation. I'm thinking of Costas and what he needs. He doesn't need someone who is going to think about his parentage all the time. He needs someone who *likes* him.' She scanned Leandro's immaculate appearance. 'It's five in the morning. I can't believe you have a meeting at this hour.'

'I have a breakfast meeting at my offices in Paris. My pilot is waiting.'

'Of course he is.' Millie gave a weary smile. Other people queued for a bus. Leandro had a pilot waiting for his instructions. It was a reminder of how different their lives were. His house contained a pool, a spa, a media room and an underground garage complete with car lift, and *everything* was automated.

Millie thought of the tiny flat she'd been renting

since she'd walked out a year earlier. If she wanted light, she had to press a switch, and even then it didn't always work because the electrics were so dodgy.

Leandro was frowning impatiently. 'Why was the baby crying?'

'I don't know. He hasn't had a good night. And neither of the nannies you appointed could get him to take the bottle. And having met one of them, I'm not surprised.'

'They have impressive references.'

'From whom?' Millie put the empty bottle down. 'Not the babies they looked after, I'm sure.'

His eyes narrowed. 'Delivering smart remarks seems to have become a new hobby of yours.'

Realising that for once she hadn't felt too intimidated to say what she thought, Millie gave a little smile. 'It wasn't a smart remark. It was the truth. I'm simply pointing out that what pleases a mother or an agency might not please a baby. This nursery is immaculate—everything in order—but they obviously haven't done anything to build a relationship with Costas.' She curved her nephew closer, lowering her voice. 'He was very upset. But he's settled down now. I think he was hungry.'

'The nannies weren't capable of giving him a bottle?'

'He wouldn't take it from them.'

'He seems to be taking it from you.'

'Perhaps he knows I'm on his side.'

'Perhaps.' He gave her a curious look, watching

her with the baby, and she looked at him question-
ingly.

'Why are you staring? Do you want to hold him
or something?'

'Not at the moment.'

'Of course. Sorry.' Millie flushed. 'I'm sure your
suit cost a fortune. Baby sick on designer menswear
isn't a good look.'

Leandro strolled over to her. 'I have more important things to worry about than the state of my suit.
I do, however, care about disturbing an otherwise
contented baby when I want a conversation. He's
clearly comfortable with you at the moment and I'm
wise enough to leave him where he is: If I take him,
he'll protest, and neither of us will be able to talk.'

As if to signify his agreement, Costas nestled
close to her, practised his smile again and then his
eyes drifted shut. Millie felt a warm feeling pass
through her and a fierce stab of protectiveness.

'There's nothing to talk about. You're not the right
man to look after a baby. You spent the first thirty-
two years of your life avoiding babies. He needs
someone who is going to forget the questions about
his parentage and just love him.'

'And that's you?' Leandro studied her for a moment, incredulity lighting his dark eyes. 'Unless I'm
misreading your extraordinarily expressive face, you
still believe this baby to be the child of your husband
and his lover.'

'That isn't relevant.'

'Most people would consider it relevant, Millie.'

With a sardonic lift of his eyebrow, he studied her and then shrugged. 'Make whatever decisions you like about hiring and firing,' he said smoothly. 'Appoint whoever you want, but I do want him to have a nanny. You can care for him if you're willing to do that, but not at the expense of our relationship.'

Millie licked her lips. 'We still have to talk about that part.'

'Then talk. You had plenty to say for yourself a moment ago so don't expect me to believe you're suddenly short of opinions.' Leandro glanced at the Rolex on his wrist. 'Are you staying or going?'

It was her turn to look incredulous. 'How can you be so emotionally detached about the whole thing? This is our *marriage* you're talking about, not a corporate takeover. But I get the feeling I'm just another task on your ridiculously long "action" list! "Find out if Millie is staying or going."' She mimicked his voice. '"Tick that box."'

He gave a faint smile. 'You've changed.'

'Well, I'm sorry, but—'

'Don't apologise,' he drawled. 'I like it. If you're going to speak your mind, I might have a chance of knowing what's going on inside it. Why didn't you ever do this before?'

'Because you're scary.'

Leandro sucked in a breath and looked at her in genuine amazement. 'Scary? What do you mean, *scary?* I have never threatened you in any way.'

'It's not what you say or what you do, it's just who you are—' She broke off. 'I don't know. It isn't easy to describe. But next time you're being really scary I'll point it out.'

'Thank you.' The irony in his tone wasn't lost on her and she looked up at him, wishing he wasn't so insanely good-looking. Every time she looked at him she lost the thread of the conversation. It made it worse that she knew exactly what was underneath that sleek designer suit.

'All right. Let's get this over with. You want to know my decision, but it isn't that easy.' She glanced down at Costas, now sleeping quietly in her arms. 'I need some time to think about it.'

He leaned against the wall, tall handsome and breathtakingly confident. 'I've given you time.'

'I want *more* time.'

'You're my wife. What is there to think about?'

Millie adjusted the blanket. 'Whether or not it can work.'

'If you come back to this marriage expecting us to fall at the first fence, we'll fall.'

Millie thought about what he didn't know. 'Things have changed, Leandro.'

'Good. They needed to change.' He studied her thoughtfully, his gaze sharp. 'Did you find me scary in bed?'

'Sorry?' Her face burned but he refused to let her look away.

'You said you found me scary,' he said quietly, 'and I'm asking you if I scared you in bed. You weren't experienced, were you? And things grew pretty intense between us, pretty quickly. Was that part of the problem?'

Embarrassed by the images his words created, Millie looked down at the baby. 'We shouldn't be talking about this in front of him!'

'He's three months old,' Leandro said dryly. 'I don't feel the need to censor my conversation just yet. Answer my question. Did I scare you?'

'No.' What was it about him that made her body react like this? Her nipples were hard, pressing against her lace bra as if inviting his attention. 'You didn't scare me.'

'But you were shocked.'

Millie wished there was a drink nearby. Her mouth was suddenly as dry as the desert in a drought. 'I was a bit self-conscious.'

'Why?'

Because she hadn't been able to throw off the feeling that he must be comparing her to the beautiful women he usually dated. 'I don't know—you were just very bold and confident, I suppose. You didn't care if it was the middle of the day. And there was that time in your office—'

'Sex isn't restricted to the bedroom at night time.'

'I know—but in the dark I could have been anyone.'

'Which is why I like daylight.' Leandro let out a long breath, his exasperation obvious. 'This isn't good enough for me, Millie. You're saying that you'll think about it, but you obviously don't believe it's going to last. That doesn't work for me. I want your

total commitment to making our marriage work.'
His eyes were hard and she gave a sigh.

'All right, you told me to tell you when you were
doing it and you're doing it now,' she croaked.
'You're being scary.'

He muttered something in Greek under his breath.
'Are you sure "scary" isn't just a word you apply to
a situation that isn't to your liking?'

'No. It's a word I apply to you. It's what you are
when something doesn't meet with your approval.
You're so used to getting your own way, you don't
know how to compromise.'

Leandro looked startled. 'I am perfectly able to
compromise.'

'What if you're the one who wants a divorce?'

'We weren't talking about divorce,' Leandro said
silkily, 'we were talking about marriage.'

Millie stared down at the baby, finding the thought
of marriage to Leandro quite impossibly daunting.
Marriage meant bed and bed meant he'd find out…

How would he handle it? Would he turn away with
revulsion? Or would he feel sorry for her and try and
pretend he didn't care? Could men pretend? No, it
was a physical thing—there would be no pretending.

'There will be no divorce,' he said firmly. 'Neither
will there be any more turning your back on me. Or
piling up resentment in your head and not telling me
why you're glaring at me. This time, if something
isn't working for you, I want to know why.' He was
hard and uncompromising and she felt her heart lurch

because she knew that he was going to be the one who stumbled this time.

And perhaps she wasn't being fair to him, not telling him the truth about what had happened since they'd last met.

But she just couldn't. Not yet.

He'd find out soon enough. And his reaction would decide the future of their marriage. And Costas's future.

Millie stared down at the baby, wishing she was young enough to have someone make her decisions for her. 'I'll think about it today.'

'I want my wife back, Millie. In every sense of the word.' His gaze was hard and direct. 'No more headaches, no more "too tired".'

'What if I *am* too tired?'

'I'll wake you up.' Leandro's eyes gleamed dark with sexual intent. 'I was very patient and gentle with you last time because I knew how inexperienced you were and I didn't want to rush you. It was a mistake. A woman is never too tired for good sex. There was something else going on and I should have pushed you to tell me what it was.'

Millie's stomach cramped and the rush of heat in her pelvis shocked her. 'What are you saying? That this time you're not going to be patient or gentle?'

'That's right,' he said silkily, 'I'm not. This time we're going to have an adult sexual relationship. I look forward to introducing you to the pleasures of truly uninhibited sex. In full daylight.'

Her face turned scarlet. 'You're trying to shock me.'

'No. But neither am I trying *not* to shock you, as I did before.' His eyes lingered on her mouth. 'You're a very sexual woman but we barely explored the surface the first time round. This time, it's going to be different.'

'It might not be! Perhaps I won't find you attractive any more!' The moment she said the words she realised how ridiculous they sounded and he obviously agreed because an ironic smile played around his mouth.

'Do you want me to explore that statement further?'

'No.' Millie was grateful that she was holding the baby. 'I don't. I don't want to talk about it at all.'

'Well, tough, because from now on no subject is off limits.' His mobile phone buzzed insistently and Leandro retrieved it from his pocket, registered the caller's name and then looked at her face. 'What?'

'If I come back, I want you to switch off your phone when you're with us,' she said stiffly, 'otherwise Costas will grow up feeling second best to a mobile network.'

Leandro gave her a long look and then rejected the call with an exaggerated stab of his finger. 'Satisfied?'

Millie nodded, although she had no expectations that it would last. She really didn't need to worry about saying yes to coming back, Millie thought bleakly, because he'd be working all the time. He always did. She'd barely see him.

'I have one rule for our relationship,' he purred, dropping the phone back into his pocket. 'Just one.'

'Go on.'

'No matter what happens—you don't run off. You don't walk away from this marriage. You stay, no matter what.'

Millie licked her lips. 'What if you're the one who wants to run?'

'That isn't going to happen.'

'It might do.' She thought about everything that had happened to her and felt a lurch of unease. If things had been bad before, how much worse were they going to be this time around?

She was dreading the moment when he discovered the truth about what had happened to her.

Leandro wasn't a man to couch his true feelings under a soft blanket of political correctness or sensitivity, was he? He'd say what he thought.

And she knew what he was going to think.

And it would be like hammering nails into raw flesh.

Millie rocked the baby, afraid that her emotional turbulence might somehow communicate itself to the sleeping child and disturb him.

'I'll allow you the rest of the day to think it over.' Having delivered what he obviously considered to be a considerable compromise, Leandro strolled towards the door. 'I have a meeting in Paris. Feel free to fire the nanny and choose someone else. I will be back by tonight and you will give me the answer I want to hear. And after that I will be switching off

my mobile phone. And if you feel even a flicker of
a headache, I suggest you take a painkiller because
I won't be allowing that as a valid excuse.'

Chapter 5

Why had he allowed her time to think it over?

Surrounded by a room full of lawyers, Leandro drove the meeting at a furious pace, determined to close the deal that had been the main focus of his attention for six months. But he was aware that the timing was bad.

His mind on Millie, he was impatient to return to London.

He didn't trust her not to vanish, taking the child with her.

What evidence did he have that she was committed to their marriage? To the baby?

None.

On edge and impatient, he pushed through the agenda with supersonic speed, issuing orders, obtaining clarification on points he considered important, and ignoring issues that he considered irrelevant.

Having condensed what should have been an all-day meeting into a few intense hours, he rose to his feet and paced over to the window that ran from floor to ceiling along one side of the spectacular board-room that dominated his Paris office. 'We're done here. Finish off. If you have any questions, you can speak to my team in London.'

The lawyer in charge of the deal picked up the thick pile of papers that had formed the focus of the discussion. 'I wish everyone was as decisive as you. Clearly the abysmal state of the markets isn't keep-ing you awake at night.'

'No.' Something else was responsible for that. *His personal life.*

The man snapped his briefcase closed. 'I must congratulate you, Mr Demetrios. You have a quite startling ability to predict and understand human be-haviour. Somehow you have still managed to make quite extraordinary profits even though the markets are collapsing around you. You anticipated the shift in the market before there were any outward signs. Stock in the Demetrios Corporation actually rose yesterday and yet market conditions have never been more challenging.'

'One person's challenge is another person's op-portunity.' Distracted, Leandro kept his eyes fixed on the Paris skyline, his mind on his fragile mar-riage. *Was he mad, trying to save it?* Or was it like rare china dropped onto concrete? Shattered beyond repair.

In the past twenty-four hours he'd learned how little he knew about Millie.

Either that, or she'd changed. She was more…assertive. Or maybe she'd always been like that and he hadn't looked closely enough. Certainly there were plenty of aspects to her personality that he hadn't seen.

Leandro frowned. Had she really found him scary?

'Speculation about the parentage of the baby doesn't seem to have had an adverse effect on the price of your stock.' The voice of the lawyer broke into his thoughts and Leandro stilled.

'Our business is concluded for the day,' he said coldly. 'My assistant will show you out.'

Aware that he'd committed a gross error of judgement in mentioning something so personal, the man turned scarlet and stammered an apology but Leandro didn't turn.

Perhaps he couldn't blame Millie for believing the worst of him, he thought grimly, *when the rest of the world was thinking it alongside her.*

His reputation had always been a matter of supreme indifference to him, but he was starting to realise that it was now coming back to bite him.

The lawyers rose, like a room full of children drilled in classroom etiquette, almost comical in their desperation to absent themselves.

Once the room was empty Leandro rolled his

shoulders, trying to relieve the tension. He prowled the length of the boardroom, gazing through the floor-to-ceiling plate-glass window that allowed him to enjoy a view of the Seine as it snaked through the city.

A sense of foreboding came over him. He really shouldn't have left her.

He ran his hand over the back of his neck and withdrew his phone from his pocket. He'd speak to her—tell her that he'd be home in the next few hours. They'd spend some time together.

Tapping his foot, he waited for someone to answer.

And it was a long wait.

When the housekeeper finally answered the phone and informed him that both his wife and the baby had gone out, his tension levels increased tenfold. When he was told they'd gone out without a driver or a member of his security staff, Leandro abandoned thoughts of work for the rest of the day and ordered his car to be brought round to the front of the building.

She'd left.

She'd run again.

What had he expected?

'An astonishing ability to predict and understand human behaviour'—wasn't that what the lawyer had said?

Leandro gave a humourless laugh. Where had that ability been when it had come to understanding his own wife? If he'd studied her as closely as he studied the stock markets and company portfolios, he would never have left London.

At every turn, she surprised him. He hadn't expected her to show up at the house, he certainly hadn't expected her to offer to care for her sister's baby. And as for their relationship, he'd made a number of assumptions—assumptions he was now beginning to question. Her humble confession that she was 'ordinary' had revealed a depth of insecurity that he'd been unaware of. And the fact that he'd been unaware of it made him realise just how little he knew of her.

But he intended to rectify that.

If he wasn't already too late.

'Do you like this one? Shake it and it plays a tune, touch this bit and it's soft and furry, this bit is rough.' Millie held the toy over the pram. 'And you can chew the rings on the end. The book says you're going to want to start chewing fairly soon.'

Baby Costas gurgled quietly to himself and Millie leaned over and gently tucked the blanket more firmly around him. 'I suppose we'd better be getting back. I need the rest of the afternoon to get ready. Believe me, it takes me that long to look even vaguely presentable. And even then I won't look good enough for Leandro. If I'm going to tell him that I'll stay married to him, I need to look the part. Don't pull that face at me.' She smiled down at him. 'You try being married to someone who looks like him. It's hard work, trust me. Especially when you start off with a face and body like mine. Come on—I'll just pay for these and then we'll wander home.'

She put the toy down on top of the pram. On impulse she added a little outfit that caught her eye. Then she made her way across the shop to pay. Standing in the queue, she stared down at Costas, automatically searching for a resemblance to Leandro.

'Oh, my—just take a look at that.' The girl in front of her in the queue gave a wistful sigh. 'What are the chances of my losing ten kilos in the next five seconds?'

'Forget it. Your best bet is to hope he likes curvy women,' her friend said gloomily, pulling in her rounded tummy.

'His type always go for the skinny sort.'

'With blonde hair.'

'*Straight,* long blonde hair.'

'He is truly spectacular. If I had him in my bed I might actually decide that sex was a more attractive option than sleep.'

'He's coming this way.'

'I'd give a million pounds just to be kissed by him once.'

Sensing the shift in the atmosphere and interested to know what kind of man could induce such enthusiasm among the members of her sex, Millie glanced up idly and saw Leandro striding purposefully across the store. Like a lion wandering into the middle of a herd of gazelle, the women all stared at him, transfixed.

Millie gave a whimper of horror. What was he

doing here? Wasn't he supposed to be in Paris? She hadn't expected him to return to the house until dinnertime at the earliest. When they'd been together before, he'd frequently missed dinner, working late into the evening. But here he was, in the middle of the afternoon, clearly looking for her.

How had he known she was here?

Aware that any moment now he was going to spot her and even more aware that she'd spent absolutely *no* time on herself since he'd last seen her, Millie slid out of the queue, turned her back and walked quickly towards the door.

The thought of him seeing her when she wasn't prepared filled her with horror. Even the 'natural' look took her hours to achieve.

Furtively she glanced over her shoulder, taking a roundabout route via cots and prams so that he'd be less likely to notice her. She didn't want him to see her like this.

She'd planned to spend the rest of the afternoon getting ready to face him. *Ready to give him her answer.* True, her outward appearance wasn't going to make any difference at all to the eventual outcome of their relationship, but she knew she'd have more confidence with him if she was at least looking her best on the outside.

Another glance over her shoulder showed him frowning around the shop and Millie melted quietly out of the door, pondering on the fact that to be so ordinary as to be unnoticeable could be a blessing. In this instance, it had worked to her advantage, but once in a while it would be nice to be so beautiful that every man in the shop was staring at her.

Except that she didn't want every man in the shop, did she? She just wanted Leandro.

A hand closed over her shoulder. 'Excuse me, madam. I have reason to believe you're in possession of goods you haven't paid for.'

Millie froze. Several people passing turned to stare and she felt the hot singe of mortification darken her cheeks as she noticed the items she'd selected still sitting on top of the baby's pram. 'Oh, no.' She turned and looked at the uniformed security guard. 'I'm so sorry. I—I completely forgot that I'd picked them up.'

'Don't waste your time thinking up excuses.' The security guard's expression warned her that he was no soft touch. 'I've been watching you for a few minutes. You were behaving in an extremely suspicious manner. Instead of taking a direct route to the door, you took a roundabout route, ducking down and quite obviously trying not to be seen.'

'I *was* trying not to be seen,' Millie said quickly and saw his expression harden. 'I—I don't mean by you. I was…' Realising how much trouble she was in, she pressed her fingers to her forehead and the security guard's mouth tightened.

'We have a very strict policy about prosecuting shoplifters. I'd like you to come with me.'

'I'm not a shoplifter!' Her tone urgent, Millie put her hand on his arm, affronted that he'd think that of her. 'It was a genuine mistake.'

He withdrew his arm pointedly. 'If you just come back into the store, madam, you can explain it to the police.'

'No!' Millie was aware of the crowd gathering and wanted to disappear into a big hole in the ground. *Why was it,* she wondered desperately, *that people were so fascinated by other people's misfortunes?* What pleasure did they gain from standing around, staring? Not one of them had stepped in to support or defend her. She was on her own. 'You don't understand.' She licked her lips and tried one more time. 'This was an oversight, nothing more. I saw something—someone—'

'She saw me.' The deep masculine voice came from behind her and Millie suppressed a groan. She didn't need to look to know who it was. So much for not drawing attention to herself.

Great. Now her humiliation was complete. Not only was she looking a complete mess but she'd been behaving like a criminal.

'You know this lady?' The security guard squared his shoulders. 'She walked out without paying, sir.'

'And I'm afraid I take the blame for that.' Leandro's tone was a mixture of apology and smooth charm. 'She was up in the night with the baby. I'd given her strict instructions to rest today and not leave the house. Do you have children…' his gaze flickered to the man's identity badge '…Peter?'

'Two,' the man said stiffly. 'Boys.'

Leandro smiled his most charismatic smile. 'And

I'm sure they've given you a few sleepless nights in their time.'

'You could say that.' Under Leandro's warm, encouraging gaze, the man relaxed slightly. 'There were days when the wife walked around in a coma. I remember she left the bath running one morning and flooded the entire house.'

'It's unbelievable that something as apparently small and innocent as a baby can cause so much disruption,' Leandro purred sympathetically. 'And unbelievable what sleep deprivation can do, Peter.' Having personalised the conversation, he put a hand on Millie's shoulder and kissed the top of her head. 'This is *all* my fault. Tonight, *agape mou,* I will take my turn with the baby and you will catch up on some sleep.'

There was a collective sigh among the crowd and the security guard looked undecided.

'I still have to take her back inside and call the police. That's my job.'

Millie opened her mouth to defend herself again but Leandro brought his mouth down on hers in a gentle but determined kiss that effectively silenced her. It only lasted seconds but when he lifted his head she was too flustered to do anything except gape at him.

He gave her a smile and pulled her into the protective circle of his arm, taking control of the situation. 'I understand that it isn't part of your job description to make individual judgements so I'm more than happy to be the one to present the details to the manager of the store and the police. I'm sure they'll understand. And perhaps we could talk to the local paper.' Leandro's voice was smooth as polished marble. 'It's ridiculous that you aren't allowed to exercise judgement on individual cases like this one. You should be allowed to take responsibility for your decisions.'

The man straightened his shoulders. 'In some circumstances I can make my own decisions, of course, it's just that—'

'You can?' Leandro looked impressed. 'Then it's lucky for us that *you* were the one on duty today. Someone as experienced as yourself will be able to tell the difference between a genuine mistake committed in a state of exhaustion and an attempt to steal.'

The security man flushed under the attention and then gave a nod. 'If you'll just take your purchases to the till, sir, I'll report to my superiors that this was all a genuine misunderstanding.'

'You're more than generous,' Leandro murmured, lifting the items from the top of the pram and glancing at Millie. 'This is all that you wanted, *agape mou?*'

Swamped with humiliation, still stunned that the brief kiss had affected her so much, Millie nodded mutely and stood there, clutching the pram for support while Leandro strode back inside the store with the security guard.

'Don't worry, love,' one of the women said to her, 'I was the same when my Kevin was born. Didn't get a wink of sleep for two years. I was so tired that I once found my car keys in the washing machine. At least you've got a gorgeous man willing to chip in. Mine didn't lift a finger for the first seven years of their lives. Now, if I'm lucky, he'll kick a football with them.'

Millie moved her lips to reply but she could still feel Leandro's mouth on hers, the latent sensuality in that brief kiss enough to have reawakened something she'd tried desperately hard to bury.

Nothing had changed, she thought helplessly. He still had the ability to turn her to a quivering wreck. Only this time things were a thousand times worse, her insecurities a thousand times deeper.

Leandro appeared by her side. He shot her a questioning look and then gave a knowing smile that indicated that he knew exactly why she was looking so dazed. Without comment, he handed her a bag and then guided her down the paved street towards the main road.

Desperate to escape from what felt like a hundred pairs of eyes, Millie stared straight ahead and then saw a burly man standing next to a sleek black Mercedes.

He sprang to attention as Leandro strode towards him and opened the rear door with military efficiency. 'If you take the baby, sir, I'll deal with the pram.'

Reluctant to be trapped with Leandro in a confined space, Millie stopped dead on the pavement but the firm pressure of Leandro's hand urged her towards the car. 'Inside, now,' he ordered, 'before you draw any more attention to yourself.'

'Does everyone always do exactly as you tell them?' Arching her back to free herself of his lingering touch, she stumbled into the warm cocoon of leather and luxury, shockingly aware of him. He slid in after her, holding the baby safely in the crook of his arm.

Only then did Millie notice the baby car seat.

With surprising gentleness, Leandro laid the baby in the car seat and strapped him in carefully. Then he sat down next to her, the length of his hard thigh brushing against hers.

The driver slid into the car, locked the doors and then pulled into the stream of traffic.

Millie shifted sideways in her seat. 'I wasn't expecting you back so soon.'

'Is that a complaint?'

'More of an observation. Since when did you work half-days?'

His eyebrow lifted in mockery. 'Since you made the rules.'

'I said it would be nice if you were home at some point before the middle of the night,' Millie muttered, stifled by how near he was, 'not halfway through the afternoon.'

'Is this going to be one of those conversations that a man can't possibly win?'

She flushed, realising that she sounded completely unreasonable. 'You shouldn't have kissed me in front of all those people. Why did you do that?'

'To stop you saying something that would have landed you in even more trouble. Every time you opened that mouth of yours, you dug a deeper hole in which to fall.' Leandro's gaze cool and assessing. '*What* did you think you were doing?'

'I—I wasn't thinking. I'm sorry I embarrassed you. I just forgot to pay.'

'I'm not talking about the shoplifting episode, I'm talking about the fact that you were walking around central London on your own.'

'I was shopping for the baby.'

'You left the house without telling anyone.'

'I didn't know I was *supposed* to tell anyone. You told me I could go shopping.'

His jaw tensed. 'I assumed you would have called your driver.'

Millie blinked. 'I have a driver?'

'Of course.'

'But I didn't want to go in the car. I wanted to walk,' she muttered. 'All the books say that babies like fresh air. And I needed the fresh air too. I wanted to think.'

'You didn't appear to be doing much thinking when you walked out of the shop without paying,' he said caustically, and she flushed.

'I walked out because I saw you. You flustered me.'

'I *flustered* you?' His eyes gleamed with sardonic humour. 'Exactly what made you "flustered"?'

'You did. Flustering everyone around you is what you do best.'

Leandro removed his tie and leaned back in his seat, a faint smile touching his mouth. 'I can see that I have a grossly inflated opinion of myself. So far, in our new spirit of honesty, I've discovered that I'm scary, intimidating and that I fluster you. I'm beginning to understand why you left. Who in their right mind would stay married to such an ogre?'

Remembering the circumstances of her departure, Millie glanced sideways at him only to find him watching her—*reading her with almost embarrassing ease.*

'Our problems started before that day,' he observed softly, and she didn't deny it.

'Our problems started the day I married you.'

'No. Our honeymoon was wonderful. The day we returned from our honeymoon. And I'm still trying to work out why.' A muscle flickered in his jaw. 'Did I change?'

'Yes.' Millie frowned. 'Or perhaps you didn't. Perhaps you were just being you. I just didn't know you that well. Once you were back in working mode, our relationship took a back seat to your business.'

'Just for the record, were there any parts of my behaviour that met with your approval?'

'I like the fact that you're confident.'

'Confidence is acceptable?'

She ignored the irony in his tone. 'As long as you're not so confident you make me feel like a waste of space.' Seeing one of his eyebrows lift, she gave an awkward shrug. 'When I can see you grinding your teeth and thinking, idiot, just because someone isn't as quick or as decisive as you, I *don't* like it.' Millie hesitated, naturally honest. 'But I can see why I annoyed you. I had no idea how to behave in your world.'

'You make it sound as if we are occupying parallel universes.' Leandro's lazy drawl was in direct contrast to his sharp, assessing gaze. 'I was under the impression that my world, as you call it, comes something close to female nirvana. You had access to unlimited funds and a lifestyle most people dream about.'

'Well, that's the thing about dreams, isn't it? They don't always turn out so well in reality. All the money in the world didn't save our marriage, did it?' Millie found it hard to think about that time. She turned to stare out of the window, trying not to think of how ecstatically happy she'd been. 'It wasn't real, was it? Those early days when we first met—it was like living in a bubble. We got married in a hurry without thinking through what we both wanted.'

'I knew what I wanted. I thought you did, too.'

'I suppose I didn't know what it was all going to involve.'

'Did it occur to you to talk to me about how you were feeling?'

'When?' Millie looked at him. 'You were always working. And when you weren't—well, you weren't that approachable. You were stern—'

'And intimidating—yes, I got that message.' Leandro seemed unusually tense. 'Just for the record, I had no idea you found me intimidating,' he said gruffly. 'Is that why you scurried out of the shop like a fugitive when you saw me arrive?'

'Partly. I wasn't expecting to see you.'

'You need notice?'

Millie touched her jeans self-consciously. 'I would have dressed up.'

His gaze slid down her body. 'You have fantastic legs. You look sexy in those jeans.'

Her heart danced. 'I—I thought you'd prefer me in a dress.' *And she didn't wear dresses any more.*

'You look sexy in everything. And nothing.' His velvety remark brought a blush to her cheeks and she felt slightly sick because she knew something that he didn't.

'What were you doing in the shop, anyway?'

'Looking for you.'

'Why not just wait for me in the house?'

Leandro drew in a breath. 'I had no reason to believe you'd be returning to the house.'

'You thought I'd run?'

'Yes.' He was characteristically direct. 'Do you blame me? It's what you did the last time. It's understandable that I'd be concerned that you won't do it again. Maybe it's time I introduced a little gentle bondage into our relationship,' he said softly. 'You were so innocent when I met you, I never did introduce you to the possibilities of velvet handcuffs. They might come in useful.'

A disturbingly erotic vision played across her brain and Millie felt the slow burn of awareness inside her. Everything she knew about sex, she'd learned from him. *And he was a master.* 'I'm not innocent any more. You took care of that.'

'We'd barely begun, *agape mou.*' Leandro relaxed in his seat, a dangerous smile playing around his mouth. 'But things will be different this time. This time we're going to talk.' He studied her, his dark eyes resting on her curling hair and then sliding to her faded jeans and her scuffed trainers. 'Today you look exactly the way you looked when I first met you.'

That bad?

Millie opened her mouth to apologise and then stopped herself. She'd spent a year trying to accept the way she was and she wasn't going to let him undo all that good work. She wasn't going to let being with him hammer holes in her confidence.

Self-conscious, she lifted a hand to her hair and then let it drop because she knew that it was going to take far more than a few tweaks of her fingers to turn her into a svelte groomed version of herself. She didn't need a mirror to know that her hair was curling wildly, falling past her shoulders in ecstatic disarray, as if relieved to have been given a break from her endless attempts to tame it.

It was a good job he worked so hard, she thought, biting back a hysterical laugh. It had taken her almost an entire day to tame her hair into the sleek, groomed look, apply her make-up, choose the right outfit.

'I'm dressed like this because I was shopping with the baby,' she said defensively. 'I wasn't expecting to see you.'

'It's lucky for you I found you…' Leandro stroked his fingers down the back of her neck '…or you'd currently be trying to talk your way out of shoplifting charges.'

'How *did* you find me?'

'My security team have inserted a tracking device into Costas's pram.'

'They *what?*' Millie looked at him in astonishment. 'Are you mad?'

'No, I'm security conscious. Which is more than you are.' Leandro's mouth tightened. '*Maledizione,* do you ever *think,* Millie? You are my wife. And you're walking around the streets pushing this baby in his pram. This baby with whom the whole world appears obsessed.'

'They're waiting for you to admit or deny that you're the father.' Her gaze settled on his but he held that gaze, as if challenging her to doubt him.

'Then they're going to be waiting a long time because I will never feel obliged to explain myself to strangers. I'm surprised you left the house with him. Why weren't you mobbed by journalists?'

'Because I sent the new nanny out earlier with a decoy pram.'

'A *decoy* pram?'

'Yes. After you left I rang the agency and they sent someone round straight away. I really liked her. We talked about the problem and decided that it wasn't fair for Costas to be housebound because of these people. So I suggested she leave the house with a doll in a pram. That's what she did. And she

walked fast and kept her head down, like someone with something to hide. And they all followed
her. Poor girl.' Still feeling guilty about that, Millie
pulled a face. 'But I think she'll be all right. She's
very down-to-earth.'

Leandro leaned his head back and laughed. 'I've
definitely underestimated you. Nevertheless, it has
to stop. There are people out there who would use
you and the baby to get to me.'

Millie felt as though her stomach had been
dropped off the side of a cliff. 'They'd kidnap the
baby?'

'I don't want to frighten you. I receive threats occasionally—it comes with the territory,' he said carefully, 'and it's the job of my security team to work
with the police to assess the risk. From now on I want
you to take basic precautions.'

Instinctively, Millie put a hand on Costas's car
seat and looked nervously out of the window.

'He will be fine.' Leandro leaned his head against
the seat and closed his eyes, apparently undisturbed
by the serious topic of the discussion. 'The car is
bulletproof and my chauffeur is an expert in defensive driving.'

'*What?* You think someone's going to shoot at
us? This gets worse and worse.' Millie was rigid on
the edge of her seat, wondering how he could relax
there with his eyes shut. 'And you think we live in
the same world? Where I come from I don't need an
armed guard to go to the supermarket.'

He didn't open his eyes. 'If going to the supermarket forms a high point in your day, I will arrange for them to open early for you. That way you can shop without a security hassle.'

Millie gave a choked laugh. 'You mean I can have first pick of the food.'

'If that's what you want. I would have thought scouring the shelves of the supermarket is an over-rated pastime,' he murmured, 'but I've never claimed to understand women. From now on I want you to discuss your itinerary with Angelo and he will do whatever needs to be done to ensure your safety.'

'Who is Angelo?'

'The security guard that my team has selected for you. He's ex-special forces.'

'So he's going to abseil down the side of the house every morning in a black ski mask and bring me breakfast in bed?' Her caustic remark drew a wolfish smile from him and his eyes finally opened, like a predator who has discovered that there is something worth waking up for.

'No, *agape mou*. If he goes anywhere near your bedroom, he's fired. When you're naked between the sheets, I'll do the protecting.'

Trapped by the molten sexuality in his dark eyes, Millie felt her heart pound and her stomach tumble. Breathless, she dragged her eyes from his, only to find her gaze trapped by the hint of dark body hair visible at the base of his bronzed throat. Looking away from that had her noticing the width of his shoulders and in the end she just closed her eyes because the only way not to want him was not to look. And even then the delicious curl of awareness that warmed her belly didn't fade. *Help,* she thought desperately. Leandro possessed monumental sex appeal, and he knew it.

'Leandro.' Her voice was a croak of denial. 'It's been a year...'

'I know exactly how long it's been,' he purred softly, and Millie glanced at him and then immediately looked away, shaken by the look of sexual intent in his eyes.

'I don't know why you want me back,' she muttered, and he gave a soft laugh.

'You're my wife, Millie. And I expect my wife to stand by my side, no matter what.'

No matter what.

What was that supposed to mean? That she was supposed to overlook his affairs? *Was that what he was saying?*

Her stomach churned and the sick feeling rushed towards her, the same feeling she'd had when she'd seen him with her sister.

He was expecting her to spend a lifetime overlooking the fact that he had other women. Looking the other way while he took another woman to his bed. And she knew that every time she thought he was with someone else, a little piece of her would die.

Millie stared straight ahead, her expression blank.

What self-respecting woman would say yes to those terms?

Chapter 6

'I'm just not like that. He might be my husband, but that doesn't give him the right to walk all over me. I'm not going to let him hurt me a second time.' Millie stuffed baby clothes into a holdall. 'That would make me stupid, wouldn't it?'

The baby cooed and kicked his legs.

'We're just *wrong* for each other. Why can't he see that? There's no point in me trying to talk to him about this because he's good with words and I'm not. With any luck he won't follow me. He didn't follow me the first time and I can't believe he wants a baby cramping his lifestyle.' Millie thought about the actress and then wished she hadn't. 'It isn't easy being married to a man every woman in the world wants. Unless you're the woman every man in the world wants. And I'm not.' Dwelling on that dismal thought, she closed the bag.

'*"I expect my wife to stand by my side no matter what."* Obviously I'm expected to watch while he smiles at models and actresses.' She stowed the bag under the cot out of sight. 'Well, I can't do that. I've spent a year trying to get over him. I'm not putting myself through that again.'

'What are you not putting yourself through again?' Leandro stood in the doorway and Millie jumped.

'B-being chased by j-journalists,' she stammered. Her heart thumping, smothered with guilt, she scooped Costas up in her arms and then faced Leandro.

He was dressed in black jeans and a casual shirt and he looked every bit as sexy as he did in a suit.

No wonder she hadn't been able to hold him, she thought miserably. He was stunning.

She'd be doing him a favour by leaving.

He didn't want her and he didn't want a baby.

He wanted a life.

Clearly undisturbed by her emotional turbulence, Costas fell asleep on her shoulder and Leandro gave a faint smile.

'Someone is tired. Put him to bed and come and eat. We need to make plans.'

It obviously hadn't occurred to him that she might refuse.

Faced with no alternative, Millie followed him to the dining room, but she was too nervous to eat and too nervous to talk. Pushing the food around her plate, her mind explored the safest route and means of transport.

Leandro lounged across from her, relaxed and watchful, as if he was trying to get inside her head.

Millie was frantically searching for reasons not to share his bed when a member of staff approached him and delivered a message.

His mouth tightening, Leandro stood up and dropped his napkin on the table. 'I apologise. This is one call I have to take. After this there will be no more, I promise.'

'Don't worry about it. I'll go and check on Costas.' Almost weak with relief, Millie seized on the excuse to go and hide away with the baby. Maybe she should leave now, except that it was too late in the day and the trains would soon stop running.

No, it had to be tomorrow. But early.

Exhausted after the events of the past few days, she lay down on the bed in Costas's room and immediately fell asleep.

Leandro opened the door of the baby's room, his mouth tightening as he saw Millie asleep on the bed. Her hair was loose and tangled, her cheeks prettily flushed and her body curled up, very much like the baby who slept in the cot next to her.

She was avoiding sex again, he thought grimly. The obvious reason was that she hadn't forgiven him for his 'affair' with her sister, but Leandro knew that their problems went much deeper than that. She'd been avoiding sex long before the 'pool incident' as he now called it.

But whatever the reason, in the end she'd walked out. To him, that was an unpardonable sin that nothing could excuse.

Cold fingers of the past slid over his shoulder and he shrugged them away, refusing to dwell anywhere other than the present. That was what he did, wasn't it? He moved forwards. Always, he moved forwards.

Was that why he was so angry with Millie? *Because her actions had forced him to remember a time that he'd tried to forget?*

His disappointment in her was as fresh today as it had been a year ago.

Disappointment in her, or himself?

Was it his pride that was damaged? Because he'd got her wrong? He'd seen something in her that hadn't been there. On the day of their wedding she'd told him how much she wanted babies and he'd congratulated himself on finding the perfect wife and mother.

He'd thought she was a woman who would stand and fight. Instead, she'd walked out at the first opportunity.

Acknowledging that failure in his judgement hadn't grown any easier over the past year, Leandro mused as he left the nursery and walked towards his own suite of rooms.

So why had he insisted that she stay? Was he a masochist?

No. But his expectations of his wife had been seriously modified.

He'd give the child a home, he'd promised himself that he'd do that.

And as for his wife—well, he'd long ago learned how to lust without love, so that shouldn't be a problem.

Swearing in Greek, he yanked his shirt off and strode into the bathroom. Given that Millie had chosen to sleep with the baby, a cold shower was the only solution.

'Life won't be as fancy with me,' Millie told Costas as she strapped him in the car seat inside the taxi. 'None of this mood-altering lighting system, comfort cooling and underfloor heating. If your feet are cold, you wear socks, OK? It's a simple life, but I *can* promise I won't ever leave you. I know I left him, but that was different. I'll explain it to you when you're older.' It was still dark outside and she'd slipped out through the garden, careful to avoid any journalists who might still be camped at the front of the house. 'I've been renting a little flat in a village near the coast. I think you'll like it.'

She saw the taxi driver glance in his mirror and coloured. He probably thought she was mad, talking to a baby.

Or maybe he'd recognised her.

That horrifying possibility had had her sliding down in her seat, but then she told herself that she was being paranoid.

Who was going to look twice at her?

She'd pushed the pram and carried her bag and the car seat to the next street so that no one would see her emerging from Leandro's house and make the connection.

The driver pulled up outside the train station. He helped her with the pram and the car seat and Millie gave him a generous tip, trying not to think what that money would have bought her.

'There's another half an hour until our train leaves, so we'll find a coffee shop and see if they'll warm your bottle.'

Even this early in the morning, the station was busy, and Millie weaved her way through suited men and women, all of whom appeared to be in a hurry.

She found a quiet corner in a coffee shop, bought herself a cappuccino and lifted Costas out of his pram to give him his bottle.

She was so engrossed in the business of feeding him that she didn't notice anyone else in the coffee shop until a light almost blinded her.

With a murmur of shock, Millie glanced up and what felt like a million cameras flashed.

Horrified, Millie snatched Costas's blanket and threw it around him, concealing him from the cameras. 'Go away!' She recoiled from the intrusive lenses, all pointed in her direction. 'What are you doing here?'

'The whole world wants to know about the Demetrios baby.'

'Well, the whole world should just mind its own

business,' Millie snapped, her eyes searching for an escape route. There was none. The row of journalists between her and the door was now three deep and she could see other people in the station glancing across in curiosity, wondering what was happening.

How could she not have noticed?

Because she hadn't been looking for it. She wasn't used to living her life looking over her shoulder.

'Are you happy to look after the kid? Can't be easy for you.' The rough male voice came from right next to her and Millie turned her head and saw a man in shabby clothes sitting at the table next to her, a tape recorder in his hand.

Had he been there when she'd arrived? No, he'd arrived soon afterwards—which meant he must have followed her.

Hands shaking, Millie started to put Costas back in the pram but the photographers pressed closer, determined to get a shot of his face.

As one particularly persistent journalist stretched out a hand to move the blanket, Millie shifted Costas safely to one side. Her protective instincts going into overdrive, she gave her coffee a small nudge.

The hot liquid spilled over his arm and he cursed fluently, hopping backwards and glaring at her.

'Don't you dare use bad language in front of my child,' Millie snarled, but she was shaking so badly she could hardly speak. And she had no idea what to do. The crowd was building by the minute and she was trapped.

Seeing the determination in their eyes, she did the only thing she could do.

Still holding Costas protectively, she dragged her phone out of her pocket and called Leandro.

She'd expected him to be furiously angry with her for leaving, but instead their interchange was brief and to the point as he demanded to know her exact location and then ordered her to stay where she was and not move.

Looking at the pack of journalists pressing in on her, Millie gave a strangled laugh. Move? How?

Leandro arrived shortly after, the fact that he was unshaven simply adding to the aura of menace that shimmered around his muscular frame as he strode into the small coffee shop.

Radiating power and authority, Leandro said something to the journalists that she didn't catch, but it clearly had an effect because they fell back and a few of them melted away into the station. Millie thought she even heard one of them mutter an apology, but she couldn't be sure.

Wishing she had a morsel of Leandro's presence, she stood up shakily and lowered Costas into the pram, still shielding him from the cameras with her body.

'Is this all you brought?' Leandro picked up her bag, his handsome face taut and unsmiling as he gathered her things.

'Bag, pram, car seat,' Millie muttered, wondering whether she should have just taken her chances with the journalists. 'I'm *not* coming home with you.'

'We're not discussing this here.' He scooped up the car seat in his other hand and stood aside to let her pass. 'Let's move, before we attract any more attention.'

'Is it possible to attract any more attention than this?'

Her remark drew a faint smile from him. 'Believe it or not, yes.'

'I didn't think they had much of a story,' she murmured, and Leandro looked at her with naked exasperation.

'You just gave them a story, Millie. Don't you know *anything* about the media?'

'No. Just as I don't know anything else about your life. Now do you see why our marriage won't work?' Angry with herself for doing something so stupid, humiliated and close to despair, she stalked towards the entrance. Only then did she see the four bulky men from Leandro's security team positioned there.

Wondering why he'd tackled the journalists himself instead of using the heavyweights he'd brought with him, Millie walked through them with as much dignity as she could muster. Which wasn't much.

For a woman who didn't want any attention, she wasn't doing very well, she thought miserably, her face flaming with embarrassment as, protected by a circle of male testosterone, she moved through the now crowded station.

People stopped walking and stared and she could almost hear them wondering why a woman who looked like her required an entourage to keep her safe.

As she walked through the front of the station she would have paused but Leandro's palm was in her back, urging her towards the sleek dark car parked in the no parking zone.

As she slipped inside, the doors locked and the driver pulled away, the security team following in a different vehicle.

Millie braced herself for confrontation, but Leandro said nothing. Instead he drew his phone out of his pocket and made a single call, speaking in rapid Greek.

Moments later the car sped through the gates of his drive, through the private courtyard and straight into the garage. From there they were able to walk into the house without being seen while Leandro's driver used the car lift to take the car down to the basement garage.

Millie stood in the stunning double-height entrance atrium, lit by the skylight far above. She felt small and insignificant and wondered how Costas could possibly still be asleep after so much drama.

Leandro put her bag down in the hallway, left his staff to deal with the pram and gave instructions for the nanny to take charge of the baby. Then he propelled Millie into the beautiful conservatory that wrapped itself around the back of his enormous house.

The room was full of exotic plants, but Millie

was too despondent to derive any comfort from the beauty of her surroundings.

'You left again.' His tone was raw and she flinched, wondering why he even cared.

'I didn't leave the baby,' she muttered. 'I left *you*. You want me to overlook the fact that you're going to have affairs, but I won't do that, Leandro. I won't grow old and grey watching while you play around with other women. Maybe that's what other Greek wives do, but I couldn't live like that.'

'Play around with other women? When did I say I wanted to play around with other women?' He looked stunned by the suggestion and she lifted her chin defensively.

'You said I was supposed to stand by your side, no matter what,' she reminded him. 'I assume "no matter what" means "no matter who I go to bed with". I can't turn a blind eye. It's asking too much.'

'"No matter what" means you and I standing together, facing whatever life throws at us.' His tone rang with incredulity. 'I said nothing about affairs. I have no intention of having affairs. I want you in my bed. No one else.'

Her assumptions having exploded into the atmosphere, Millie stood uncertainly, knowing that he'd change his mind once she was undressed. 'What if you discover the chemistry isn't there any more?'

Leandro moved so quickly she didn't see it coming. One moment he was facing her, legs apart in a confrontational stance; the next he was right in front of her, his hand on the back of her neck and his mouth on hers. And he knew exactly how to kiss to ensure maximum response. With the erotic exploration of his mouth and tongue, Leandro turned a kiss into something indescribably good and as Millie felt her grip on reality sliding away, her last coherent thought was that if she died now, she'd die happy.

Only after several minutes during which she lost track of time and place did he finally lift his head. 'I don't foresee a problem.' He stepped back with all the easy confidence of a man who has proved his point and Millie ran shaking hands over her jeans, not sure whether to slap him or slide her arms round his neck and beg him to kiss her again.

'You shouldn't have done that.'

'People have been saying that to me all my life. If I'd listened to them, I'd still be playing in the dust on a remote Greek island.' Maddeningly relaxed, he glanced at his watch. 'Make up your mind, Millie. I'm only going to ask this *once*. Are you staying or going?'

Knowing that he'd dump her soon enough when he found out what had happened to her, Millie nodded. 'Staying.' At least then she could spend time with Costas.

'Good. I'll instruct my people to put out a statement saying that we are adopting the baby. Hopefully that will kill the story.'

'If I come back to you, I'll be surrounded by media.'

'As my wife you'll have more protection than if you go it alone. This morning has proved that.'

'But Costas and I can't leave the house without a bodyguard and a driver! What sort of life is that?'

'A privileged one,' Leandro drawled, ignoring the buzz of his phone. 'But while they're hovering like hyenas, we'll stay elsewhere.'

'We're leaving London?'

'This media circus presents a risk to the baby. I don't want to have to go through the courts to keep his picture out of the papers.'

Millie bit her lip. 'Where are we going?' It was touching that he was so protective, but at the same time it was upsetting because she could only see one reason why he would care so much for the baby's welfare.

'We're flying to Spiraxos later this morning. I just have some important calls to make.'

'We're going to Greece?' Her heart dropped. He'd taken her to his island on their honeymoon and they'd had three weeks of sun, sea and sex. Three indulgent weeks during which she'd been so happy. At that point in their relationship none of their problems had surfaced. She'd been ecstatically happy and so wildly in love that she'd woken up every morning with a smile on her face. The thought of returning there now made her feel sick. It would be like a cruel taunt, reminding her of that magical time before her life had fallen apart. 'Why Greece?'

'Because the island will give us privacy. And because our relationship was perfect when we were in Greece.' His gaze was bold and direct. 'We had an incredible time there. And if we're going to put the pieces of our marriage together, I'd rather the details of our reconciliation weren't documented in the pages of sleazy celebrity magazines. We will be able to relax, away from the eyes of the world.'

Relax? How could she possibly relax, trapped with him on Spiraxos, where she'd once spent the happiest time of her life? How could she relax, knowing what was coming? 'I— I'm not ready to fly to Greece. I need some time.'

'My staff will make any necessary preparations. All you have to do is walk onto my plane. And if you're worried about clothes, I can tell you now that you're not going to need any. Last night you slept alone, but tonight, *agape mou*...' Leandro flashed her a dangerous smile '...well, let's just say you won't be dressing for dinner.'

Tonight?

It was tonight.

No more excuses.

Millie's stomach churned horribly.

He was going to fly her all that way, only to discover that he didn't want to be with her any more.

It was going to be the shortest reconciliation on record.

Millie checked Costas again, grateful for any excuse to delay joining Leandro on the sun-baked terrace that overlooked the sparkling blue Aegean sea.

The journey to Greece had been smooth. Costas had slept most of the way and Leandro had spent his time reading and deleting endless emails, which meant she'd had far too much time to brood on the evening ahead of her.

Now that it had arrived, she couldn't bring herself to walk down to the terrace.

She was dreading the inevitable rejection.

'Are you planning to eat dinner with the baby? You have a hidden passion for baby milk perhaps?' Leandro's smooth, masculine tones came from behind her and she jumped because she hadn't expected him to come looking for her.

'I was just making sure he's all right.'

'Of course he's all right. He slept for the entire journey and now he's asleep again, which means, *agape mou,* that you have no excuse for not joining me.'

'Why?' Millie heard the ring of desperation in her own voice. 'Why would you want my company?'

'Because that's what married couples do. They eat dinner together.'

'Perhaps I'd better stay with the baby, just for tonight,' she hedged, 'in case he's unsettled after the journey.'

'He's asleep.'

'He might wake up and realise he's in a new environment.'

'In which case he'll yell. One of Costas's qualities is that he isn't shy about letting you know he's unhappy,' Leandro said dryly, staring down at the baby with a faint smile on his handsome face. 'All the bedrooms open onto the terrace, you know that. If he cries, we'll hear him.'

'I don't like leaving him.'

'We have a team of eight staff here, including the nanny that you appointed yourself.'

'He doesn't know them yet!'

'Neither is he likely to, if you don't allow them near him. Enough, Millie. The baby is going to be asleep!' His tone held a note of exasperation. 'Why is it that you're afraid to spend an evening with me? I've made a particular effort to be approachable and thoughtful. Am I such an ogre?'

She shook her head. 'No.'

Leandro gave an impatient sigh and slid his fingers under her chin. 'I am *trying* to understand what is going on here,' he breathed, 'and you're not giving me any clues. I thought you loved Spiraxos. I thought you'd be pleased to be here.'

'It's very quiet.' She meant that she found the intimacy difficult, but he misinterpreted her words.

'I'll arrange a few shopping trips it that's what's bothering you.'

Preoccupied by what was to come, Millie barely heard him. 'Why would that help? I'm not interested in shopping.'

'Millie.' His tone was dry. 'You used to spend hours deciding what to wear, so don't tell me you're not interested in clothes. I've never known a woman spend so long staring into her wardrobe.'

Because she'd had no idea what to wear. She'd been desperately insecure and those insecurities had grown and grown, fed by his gradual withdrawal. The harder she'd tried, the more he'd backed off until

it had become obvious to her that he'd deeply regretted the romantic impulse that had driven him to
marry her. And how much more insecure was she
now? If she'd found it hard being his wife a year ago,
now it seemed a thousand times harder.

This was the perfect opportunity to tell him everything that had happened to her after she'd walked
out that day, but Millie just couldn't get the words
past her lips.

'Given that you're so dedicated to the baby's welfare,' Leandro drawled, 'I will watch him while you
take a shower and change for dinner. Remembering
how long it used to take you, I'll prepare myself for
a long wait.'

Millie cast a last reluctant look into the cot, willing Costas to wake up and yell. *Willing him to give
her an excuse to miss dinner.* But for once he lay
quietly, sleeping with a contented smile on his tiny
mouth, oblivious to her silent signals and growing
distress.

Which meant that she'd run out of excuses.

Leandro glanced at his watch and sprawled in
the nearest chair with a sigh of resignation. Previous experience told him that he was going to be in
for a serious wait. The length of time Millie took to
get ready had been one of the things that had driven
him crazy about her.

Not at first, of course. When they'd first met he'd
been startled and charmed by how unselfconscious
and natural she was. She couldn't bear to be away

from him, even for a moment. Any time spent in the bathroom had been together. Making love. Touching.

She'd been addicted to him, and so affectionate that it had astonished him. Accustomed to women who guarded their behaviour and protected themselves, he'd never met anyone as free and honest with their emotions as Millie. She'd been as straightforward and honest as the fruit that grew on her parents' farm.

Or so he'd thought.

It had all changed on the day they'd arrived in London after their honeymoon.

Suddenly she'd morphed into one of those women he'd spent his adult life mixing with. She'd become obsessed with her appearance. It was as if she'd become a different person. Leandro had given up surprising her at home for a few stolen hours of daytime passion because she'd never been there. She'd spent her days in beauty salons and her nights out partying with him. And she'd spent hours scouring the celebrity gossip, looking for pictures of herself.

Leandro, up to his ears in work as usual, had been unable to work out what had happened to the girl he'd married. Had it all been an act designed to trap him and then she'd shown her true self? Or had it been marriage to a billionaire that had changed her? After all, up until her marriage with him she hadn't had the funds to allow her to indulge her apparent obsession with clothes and beauty products.

And yet over the past two days she'd seemed almost oblivious to her appearance.

Whoever said that women were a mystery hadn't been exaggerating, Leandro mused, stretching out his legs and making himself comfortable.

He looked at the sleeping baby and felt a rush of emotion that shook his self-control.

Alone, abandoned, a mother who had used him as a pawn...

Determined not to continue down that path of thought, he dug his BlackBerry out of his pocket, intending to distract himself with work. Then he heard a noise and glanced up to find Millie standing in the door of the dressing room, which connected directly to both bathroom and bedroom.

Leandro slipped his phone back into his pocket. 'That was quick.' He scanned her appearance, noticing with surprise that she'd left her hair curling and loose in its natural state and that the only make-up she was wearing was a shimmer of clear gloss on the curve of her lips. She was wearing a simple green top over a pair of trousers. 'I was expecting to wait at least an hour while you picked your outfit.'

Colour touched her cheeks and she gave a wan smile. 'There didn't seem much point in that. I'm no longer trying to impress you.'

Leandro frowned. 'Is that what you used to do?'

'Obviously I wanted to look my best.' She stooped, sliding her slender feet into the pair of shoes she was carrying.

Still pondering on her comment, he noticed that the only concession to her old look was a pair of killer heels. 'You never used to wear trousers.'

There was something in her expression that he couldn't read. 'I find trousers comfortable. Is it a problem?'

'Not at all.' They had problems far deeper than her choice of wardrobe, he mused, watching as she walked across to the cot and checked the baby again. Something was very wrong with her, and he had no idea what. 'Are you ready? Alyssa has laid dinner on the terrace.'

Millie stared down at the baby as if willing him to wake up and save her, and Leandro stared at her frozen profile in mounting frustration, searching for clues.

Was she looking at the baby, wondering if it was his? Or was there something more going on here?

Reaching into the cot, she tucked the sheet tenderly around the sleeping baby and then withdrew her hand slowly. 'I'm ready.'

She spoke the words like someone preparing to walk to their doom and her whole demeanour was such a dramatic contrast from the last time they'd stood in this villa that Leandro wanted to close his hands around her shoulders and demand answers.

But his years in business had taught him when to speak and when to stay silent and he chose to stay silent, his expression neutral as he urged her towards the terrace.

The evening was only just beginning, he reminded himself. *They had plenty of time.*

Chapter 7

Millie felt sicker and sicker. Wishing the baby would wake up and rescue her, she pushed the food from one side of her plate to the other, unable to face the thought of challenging her churning stomach by eating.

Candles flickered on the centre of the table and the silence of the warm evening was disturbed only by the insistent chirping of the cicadas and the occasional splash as birds skimmed the beautiful infinity pool, stealing water.

Across from her, Leandro said nothing. He lounged with masculine grace, his relaxed stance in direct contrast to her own mounting agitation. He wore a casual polo shirt, the simplicity of his clothing somehow accentuating his raw masculinity. *What-*

ever he wore, he looked spectacular, she thought helplessly, putting her fork down and giving up the pretence of eating. The beauty was in the man himself, not in the way he presented himself. It didn't matter whether his powerful shoulders were showcased by an elegantly cut dinner jacket or a piece of simple cotton fabric, Leandro was all man. And that fact simply increased the churning in her stomach.

Or perhaps it was just because she was now more conscious than ever of the differences between her and the women he usually mixed with.

Had he had an affair?

The question played on her mind over and over again, a relentless torment fed by her own massive insecurities.

It was typical that he didn't try and put her at her ease, she thought desperately. He was so confident himself, he never thought that someone else might not be so comfortable in a situation.

'Alyssa must have been slaving all day,' she said, making polite conversation. 'The food is fantastic.'

'Then why aren't you eating any of it?'

'I'm not that hungry.'

Leandro leaned across and spooned some creamy *tzatsiki* onto her plate. 'When I first met you, you were always hungry. When I took you out to dinner, you ate three courses.'

'I had a very physical job,' Millie said defensively. 'I worked on a farm. If I didn't eat properly, I would have passed out.'

Leandro sat back in his chair, watching her

across the table. 'Now I've upset you and I have no idea why.'

'You were criticising me.'

He tilted his head and she could see him rerunning the conversation through his brain. 'Exactly how and when did I criticise you?'

'You complained that I ate three courses, and—'

'It wasn't a complaint. It was a comment.'

'Same thing.'

'No, Millie,' he said gently, an ironic gleam in his eyes. 'It is *not* the same thing.'

'You mix with women who don't eat.' She ignored the food he'd put on her plate. 'In the circles you move in, eating is a bigger sin than adultery or wearing the wrong shade of pink. *All* the women are thin. A visible rib cage is as much a status symbol as a pair of Jimmy Choos. So when you point out I ate three courses, what am I supposed to think?'

His gaze was thoughtful. 'You could think that the fact that you enjoy food and eating is one of the things I like about you.'

'Actually, I couldn't,' Millie said hotly, the defensive movement of her head sending her hair spilling around her face. 'Because I'm seeing no evidence to back it up. Apart from your momentary lapse with me, all the women you mix with clearly share DNA with stick insects. Take that actress—she's enough to give any normal woman a complex and a major eating disorder.'

He inhaled slowly. 'Your weight is clearly an issue.'

Millie played with her fork. 'You noticed that? I'm

a woman,' she said sweetly. 'Of course my weight is an issue.'

'You have a fabulous body.'

'By fabulous, you mean fat.'

'I mean fabulous.' His eyes gleamed with lazy amusement and a trace of exasperation. 'Clearly I need a man-woman dictionary. Man says "fabulous", woman translates that into meaning "fat". Are there any other words in this unfathomable language I'm likely to need help with?'

'I'll let you know as we go along.'

'Thank you.' His tone dry, he leaned forward, and spooned some spicy sausage onto her plate next to the *tzatsiki*. 'Eat. Alyssa has spent all day in the kitchen in honour of your arrival. She remembered that you loved all Greek food, especially this. It was your favourite.'

'That was until someone told me how many calories were in each spoonful.'

'*Who* told you?'

'Oh, someone.' Millie felt the colour flood into her cheeks as she recalled that particular encounter. 'I expect she thought she was doing me a favour. Helping me fit into the strange world you live in.'

'I live in the same world as you, Millie.'

She glanced around her, looking at their privileged surroundings. 'If you think that, you're deluded. You move in a whole different world to most people, Leandro. It's no wonder I didn't fit.'

He was very still. 'Is that what you think?' His tone was soft. 'That you didn't fit?'

'It doesn't take a genius to see I wouldn't have had too much in common with some those waif-like celebrities you called your friends. My idea of a facial was splashing cold water to wake myself up at five in the morning during the harvest.'

He didn't answer immediately but she sensed a new tension about him and bit her lip, feeling suddenly guilty.

'Sorry,' she muttered. 'I didn't mean to criticise your friends. I'm sure they're lovely people. It wasn't their fault. If you drop a baby elephant into the middle of a flock of elegant swans, you've got to expect to startle them.'

Leandro's eyes glittered dark in the candlelight. 'And are you supposed to be the baby elephant in that analogy?' He sounded stunned. 'That's how you felt?'

Unsettled by his prolonged scrutiny, Millie shifted in her chair. 'How did you think I felt?'

A muscle flickered in his jaw and he toyed with the stem of his elegant wineglass. 'Honestly? I didn't think about it. Unlike you, I don't look for hidden meanings. Clearly I should have done.'

'Not all communication is verbal, Leandro.'

'Evidently not. But given your talent for reading me incorrectly, I think we'd better stick to the verbal sort for the time being. Tell me why you're not eating tonight.'

'My stomach is churning. I feel…sick.'

His dark brows met in a concerned frown. 'You're ill?'

'No. Just nervous.'

'Of what?'

'You, of course.'

His eyes held hers. 'I make you feel sick?' The incredulity in his tone made her wish she'd kept her mouth shut.

'Just a little bit.' Her cheeks turned pink. 'Well, quite a lot, actually.'

Leandro put the glass down on the table. 'Why?'

'I don't know. I'm not a psychologist. Maybe I'm seriously screwed up about you. But I think it's probably just the effect you have on me. Billionaire marries farm girl. It's pretty obvious that farm girl is going to have some major insecurities.'

'Billionaire marries farm girl,' he countered, 'and her insecurities vanish.'

'They double.'

'The way you think is a mystery to me.'

'Obviously.'

He rose to his feet and dropped his napkin onto the table. His mouth was set and determined, his eyes never once leaving her face as he stood next to her. 'Come.'

Millie looked at his outstretched hand. 'Why? Where are we going?'

'To put your insecurities to rest once and for all,' he purred, drawing her to her feet in a firm, decisive movement that brought her into contact with his hard, athletic frame. 'I intend to closely examine every curve of your fabulous body—and I mean fabulous, *not* fat,' he breathed, covering her lips with his fingers so that she couldn't interrupt, 'and by the time I've finished with you, your insecurities will be in a puddle on the floor along with your clothes.'

But that wasn't what was going to happen, was it? Millie's heart pounded. She thought of her body. *Thought of what he didn't know.* 'I really wanted an early night.'

'For once we agree on something.' His eyes gleamed with sexual promise. 'An early night followed by a lie-in. And another early night. The two might actually run together.'

Millie swallowed, her nerves almost snapping as she thought about the inevitable fallout of him taking her to bed. 'I can't— I just can't— I need some time.'

'I gave you time, Millie.' His voice was steady. 'I gave you space. And it was a mistake. All it did was widen the gulf between us. This time around we're doing things a different way. My way.'

'So I don't have a choice.'

His eyes shimmered with amusement. 'No, *agape mou,*' he murmured. 'There is no need to take on that martyred expression. I'm going to get to know you. Inside and out. In the past two days you have revealed more about yourself than you did in the entire time we were together. I am starting to realise that I didn't know you at all, but that is going to change from this moment onwards.' He trailed a finger over her flushed cheek. 'From now on I want to know everything in your head. And I won't let you shut me out.'

Standing in the bathroom, Millie pulled the robe tightly around her.

What was the best way to play this? Did she undress and walk into the bedroom naked? Or did she let him undress her?

Either way, it was going to be a disaster.

This was the moment she'd been dreading.

What was the point in putting it off any longer? Better to get it over with because the anticipation of what was to come was making her sick.

How would he react?

Forcing herself to move, she pushed open the door and stood for a moment, looking at him.

Leandro was sprawled on his back on the bed, eyes shut. His chest was bare and the light by the bed sent golden shadows across his sleek, bronzed shoulders.

In the year they'd been apart, he hadn't changed. Millie's gaze rested on the tangle of dark hair across the centre of his chest and then moved lower. He was naked, but he'd always been comfortable with his body, hadn't he? And no wonder. He was astonishingly fit, his physique strong and masculine.

His astonishing good looks had attracted the attention of the most beautiful women in the world.

Why did he want her? Was it just that he didn't believe in divorce? Was that the fragile bond that held them together?

Unable to see another possibility, she lost her confidence and would have slid back into the bathroom if his voice hadn't stopped her.

'If you run again, I'll come after you. And if you lock the door, I'll break it down. Your choice.'

Millie froze, her heart pounding frantically against her chest. But she moved forward, her legs stiff, as if they were trying to plead with her to take a different course of action. 'It isn't a choice, is it? You're not giving me a choice.'

'You made your choice when you decided to come back to me.' His eyes were open now, and he was watching her with that shimmering masculine gaze that always turned her stomach upside down. 'Come into the light where I can see you.'

Millie gripped the clasp of her robe tightly, wondering whether she was actually going to have the courage to go through with this.

She stood there shivering and he frowned and sprang from the bed, prowling across to her with surprising grace for such a powerfully built man.

Leandro closed his fingers over her shoulders and forced her to look at him. 'I want to know what you're thinking.'

'Trust me, you don't.' Millie shook her head, the tears sitting in her throat like a brimming cup just waiting to overflow. She couldn't cry now. Later. *There'd be plenty of time for that later.*

With a growl of frustration, he scooped her face into his hands and lowered his head to kiss her. 'I don't understand why you are so insecure. You are a very beautiful woman.'

Her courage failed.

Maybe, just maybe, if he hadn't said those exact words she would have gone through with it.

'I'm not beautiful,' she croaked, dragging herself out of his arms. 'I'm *not* beautiful. And I can't do this. I just can't.'

'Why? Is this about what you think happened with your sister?'

'No, no, it isn't. It's about what happened to *me*. It's hopeless. I'm sorry, Leandro. I'm sorry.' Before he could stop her, Millie stumbled out of the room. Blinded by tears, she banged against the doorframe in her haste to get away from him, but the sudden pain in her arm was eclipsed by the far greater pain in her heart. She took refuge in one of the guest suites at the far end of the villa. Stumbling into the bathroom, she locked the door securely behind her and slid to the floor without bothering to switch on the lights.

It was impossible. The whole situation was impossible.

She should never have allowed him to blackmail her into giving their marriage another try. She just should have stood there, told him what had happened and walked out while she still had some shred of dignity left. And she should have found another way of being close to her nephew. Visits. Letters. Photos. Anything other than this.

Why had she agreed to stay?

Had some small, stupid part of her hoped that this horrible situation could still have a happy ending?

In the pit of despair, she let the tears fall.

The door crashed open and she gave a jerk of shock.

Leandro stood there, a powerful figure silhouetted against the light of the bedroom. 'Every time you lock a door between us I'll break it down,' he vowed thickly, 'and every time you run I *will* find you.' With a soft curse, he flipped on the light and then sucked in a breath as it illuminated her ravaged features. His eyes fixed on her blotched, tear-stained face and his jaw tightened.

'Millie? What the *hell* is going on?' His voice was hoarse and he spread his hands in a gesture of helplessness. 'Why are you crying? *Maledizione,* I *never* wanted to upset you like this. Stop it, *agape mou.* Nothing is this bad.'

'Just leave me alone,' she choked, hugging her knees against her chest and burying her face in her arms. 'Please, leave me alone. Go and ring your actress.' She heard him swear under his breath.

'There is blood on your arm. You must have scraped it when you bumped into the doorframe. Let me look at it—'

'Go away!'

For a moment she thought he'd acceded to her request but then she heard the solid tread of his footsteps and he squatted down beside her, strong and calm, a man able to cope with any problem that came his way.

'You're going to make yourself ill. Enough.' Leandro slid his hands under her arms and lifted her to her feet and she looked up at him through eyes swollen with crying.

'Yes, it is enough.' Somehow she managed to get the words out. 'Enough pretending that our relationship can ever work. Enough pretending we can have any sort of marriage. It's over, Leandro. It's over.'

'You are *extremely* upset,' he breathed, holding her firmly so that she couldn't slide to the floor again, 'and it is never a good idea to make decisions when you're upset.'

'My decision is going to be the same whenever I make it. I mean it, it's over.' Her voice rose and he cupped her face in his hands, forcing her to look at him.

'Millie, I want you to take a deep breath.' His masculine voice was surprisingly gentle. 'Deep. That's right, and again. And now you are going to listen to me, yes? And you are going to trust me. Whatever is wrong—whatever has upset you this much—you will tell me and I will fix it. But for now I just want you to try and calm down.'

His unexpected kindness somehow made everything worse. 'Why won't you just leave me?'

'Because that option doesn't work for me,' he said grimly. 'I already told you, this time you are not walking away from our problems.' He drew her into his arms, but she shook him off and took a step backwards.

'Don't touch me. I can't bear you to touch me.'

She heard the sharp intake of his breath and knew that her apparent rejection had hurt him.

'So you don't trust me.'

'This isn't about trust. This isn't about what happened with my sister. And it can't be fixed. Just—just—wait—and you'll see.' Her hands were shaking so much she couldn't untie the knot of silk holding together the edges of her robe and she almost screamed with frustration. Eventually the fabric loosened in her fingers and she bit her lip, trying to find the courage to do what she had to do. 'I don't know why you wanted me the first time, Leandro. You say I'm beautiful and—well, I never was. And even less so now.'

'I'm the best judge of that.'

'All right. Then judge.' Without giving herself any more time to think about it and change her mind, she allowed the dressing-gown to slip from her shoulders.

Naked, she faced him. Unprotected, she let him see. Vulnerable, she stayed silent and let him judge— *and saw his handsome face reflect everything she herself had felt over the past year.*

Shock, disbelief, distaste.

The emotions were all there.

'Now do you understand why I said this would never work? I wasn't beautiful enough for you before. How could I possibly be beautiful enough now?' Somehow the reality of exposing her damaged flesh was less traumatic than the thought of it had been. Now that she'd done it, she felt nothing but relief.

No more pretending.

He'd divorce her and she'd get on with her life. And it may not have been the life she'd dreamed off, but it would be all right. She'd make sure it was all right. She'd get over him, wouldn't she? It had only ever been a stupid dream.

Quietly sliding the robe back onto her shoulders, Millie cast one final look at his shocked face, reflecting on the fact she'd never actually seen him lost for words before.

'I'm sorry,' she muttered wearily. 'I'm sorry to do that to you—in that way. Perhaps it was cruel of me, but I honestly didn't…' Her pause was met with silence. 'I—just didn't know any other way.' Impulsively she lifted her hand to touch his arm and then realised that the best thing she could do for him was to just get out of his life.

Letting her hand drop, she walked past him towards the door feeling tired and completely drained of energy.

'God damn it, Millie, if you walk out on me one more time I won't be responsible for my actions.' His voice rasped across her sensitised nerve endings. 'You stay right there. I just need to—' He broke off and ran a hand over his face, clearly struggling with his emotions. 'Just give me a minute.'

She stopped walking. 'It doesn't matter. You don't need to work out what you're supposed to say or do. Nothing you say is going to make any difference.'

'Just *wait*.' Leandro pressed his fingers against the

bridge of his nose and exhaled slowly. '*Maledezione,* you have no idea…'

'Yes, I do. I know what you're thinking. And I understand.'

'Do you?' His voice was harsh. 'Then you'll know that I'm asking myself what exactly I did to you that made you think you couldn't talk to me about this. Is this why you turned your back on me night after night?' He frowned and then shook his head, clearly angry with himself. 'No, of course. This…' He glanced towards her now concealed body. 'This didn't happen when we were together, did it? It couldn't have done. I would have known.'

Millie looked at him. 'It happened the day I left you.'

'*What* happened the day that you left me?' His hoarsely worded demand increased her tension.

'Can we talk about this tomorrow?' Seeing his face had been bad enough. She wasn't up to a conversation. She just wanted to hide.

Leandro gave a hollow laugh and his fingers closed around her wrist as he drew her firmly into the guest bedroom. 'No, *agape mou*. We're going to talk. Or perhaps I should say that *you're* going to talk. And you're going to do it now.'

Chapter 8

Keeping her hand in his, Leandro led her across the terrace to the pool. The evening was still stiflingly warm and the stylish curve of the swimming pool was illuminated by the tiny lights that gleamed under the water.

'I always loved sitting out here at night,' she said softly, sinking onto the edge of a sun lounger. 'It's so peaceful.'

'We made love out here. Do you remember?'

Millie didn't answer his question because she knew that the only way she was going to be able to deal with the present was if she didn't think about the past. 'So—what do you want to know?'

He sat down right next to her, the length of his powerful thigh brushing the length of hers. 'I want to know what happened to you. I want to know how you got those scars.' For once there was no mockery in his voice and she stared down at their linked hands with almost curious detachment.

'When I drove away that day I was…' She hesitated. 'Very upset. I didn't really think about where I was going. I drove south and found myself in a very rough part of London. I stopped at a set of lights—and three men took a fancy to the car I was driving.'

His fingers tightened their grip on hers. 'Tell me.'

'Are you sure you want to hear it?'

'Yes.' But the word sounded as though it had been dragged from him and she looked up at his hard, set profile dubiously.

'If you're just going to rant and rave and turn all macho, this is going to be hard.'

'I won't rant and rave.'

'You promise not to go and extract revenge?'

Leandro made a sound that was close to a snarl. 'No,' he said thickly, placing her hand on his thigh and holding it there, 'no, *agape mou,* I don't make that promise.'

'Then—'

'What caused the scars?' he asked harshly. 'Was it a knife?'

'Broken bottle.' Millie felt the horror of it burst into her brain. 'Carjacking. I stopped at a set of lights—they had the doors open before I even saw them coming.'

'They dragged you out of the car?'

'I refused to undo the seat belt—big mistake. I

think I was in a state of shock. But that resistance got me the scar on my stomach.'

The breath hissed through his teeth. 'Why didn't you just give them the keys?'

'You gave me the car as a wedding present,' she mumbled. 'I liked it.'

'Cars are replaceable.'

'Spoken like a billionaire.'

'I would say the same thing if I was living on benefits and someone had just stolen your bicycle.' He spoke in a low, urgent tone. '*Nothing* is worth that sort of risk.'

'Well, I suppose you don't really think clearly when it happens. You just react by instinct.'

'And you were upset and that was my fault.'

She stilled. 'You told me that you didn't have an affair with my sister.'

'I didn't. I'm blaming myself because I was so blisteringly angry that you didn't trust me, I let you walk out instead of dragging you back and proving my innocence to you. If I'd done that, this wouldn't have happened.' The breath hissed through his teeth again. 'Normally I'm not a believer in wasting time on regret but believe me, *agape mou,* when I say that with you, my regrets are piling up. But we'll deal with that in a minute. Finish the story. You were very badly injured?'

'Yes. They dragged me out of the car, attacked me with the bottle a few more times just to make sure I'd got the message and then took the car and my bag. I was unconscious, lying on the road—so I had no identity with me. I woke up days later in hospital with everyone wondering who I was. Initially they thought I was the victim of a hit and run.'

'Did you have amnesia?'

'No.' Millie shook her head. 'I remembered everything. They told me they'd found the car ten miles away, burned out and abandoned. Because no one had reported it missing, they hadn't been able to identify the owner. I was so angry with myself.' She frowned. 'I should have noticed them waiting at the lights.'

'You're not exactly streetwise.' Leandro toyed with her fingers. 'You hadn't even lived in a city until you married me. And on top of that, you were upset. Because of me.'

'You're not responsible for the carjacking. That was my own stupid fault for not locking my doors. But I wasn't used to London. Where I come from we wind the windows down and offer people lifts. People leave their front doors open.' Her frank confession drew a groan of disbelief from him.

'You are ridiculously trusting. And I'm angry with myself for not teaching you to be more careful.'

'*Not* your fault,' Millie said gruffly. 'Just another example of how I'm the wrong woman for you.'

'How can you reach that conclusion? It's becoming increasingly obvious to me that I had absolutely no idea what was going on in your head at any point during our short marriage. But we'll come back to that later. First I want you to finish telling me what happened.'

'I've told you everything.' Millie shrugged. 'I was in hospital for a while, obviously.'

'Why didn't the hospital contact me?'

'At first because I had no identity. And later...' She paused. 'Because I asked them not to.'

Leandro greeted that confession with a hiss of disbelief. 'Why would you do that? No, don't answer that.' His tone was weary. 'You thought I was having an affair with your sister. You thought she was pregnant with my child.'

'I thought our marriage was over.'

'Millie, we'd been together for less than three months and I couldn't get enough of you! Until you started turning your back on me, we were constantly together and it was good, wasn't it?'

'It was incredible. At first.'

'At first?'

'You worked very long hours. You were always jetting off to New York or Tokyo and you didn't want me with you.'

'Because I had trouble concentrating when you were around,' he bit out, and Millie looked at him in surprise because that explanation hadn't ever occurred to her.

'Oh.'

'Oh? What did you think the reason was?'

'I...wondered if you had other women.'

His jaw tightened. 'When, before that incident with your sister, did I *ever* give you cause to doubt me?' Leandro released his grip on her hand and rose to his feet in a fluid movement. *'When?'*

'I suppose I looked at the facts. When I met you, you were thirty-two, rich, good-looking and single. You'd never been committed to a woman, but you'd been involved with plenty.'

'*Before* I met you.'

'And they were all different to me.'

Leandro spread his hands wide, his expression expectant. 'And does that tell you anything?'

'Yes. It tells me that you made a mistake when you married me.'

He sank his fingers into his hair and said something in Greek. 'Always if there are two ways to interpret something, you choose the wrong one.' His usually fluent English suddenly showed traces of his Mediterranean heritage. 'Did no other reason come to mind?'

Millie gave a tiny shrug. 'You're Greek.' At the moment there was no mistaking that fact. 'I was a virgin and you're old-fashioned enough to like that.'

His laugh lacked humour. 'Yes. All right. I concede that point. But I took your virginity within hours of meeting you so that wasn't a reason to marry you.'

'Well. Everyone makes mistakes,' she said simply. 'Even you.'

'Why didn't you contact me after the accident?'

'What for? If I couldn't hold you before I was injured, I knew there was no chance afterwards.' Millie stared at the still surface of the pool. 'And I knew I could never be the sort of wife you needed.

Lying there in hospital gave me the time to think about that.'

'*The sort of wife I needed?* What is that supposed to mean?' His tone raw, Leandro sat back down next to her. His hand slid under her chin and he forced her to look at him. '*You* were the woman I married. *You* were the wife I needed.'

'No.' Millie shook her head, tears swimming in her eyes. 'I wasn't, Leandro. I was *never* the wife you needed. I learned that pretty soon after we were married. We came back from our honeymoon and I was plunged into the life you lead—and nothing about the time we'd spent together had prepared me for what was expected of me.'

'Nothing was expected of you.'

'Oh, yes, people expected a lot.' The tears still glistening in her eyes, Millie moved her head away from the comfort of his fingers. 'You're Leandro Demetrios—declared the sexiest man in the world. Everyone wanted to know who you'd married. And everyone wanted to comment.'

'Who is everyone? Are you talking about the media?'

'Them, too. But mostly your friends. The people you mixed with in your daily life. They used to give me these little sideways glances that showed what they thought of your choice.'

'You were *my* wife,' he gritted. 'I didn't care what anyone thought of you.'

'But I did,' she said simply. 'I'm not like you. When they said I was fat and that my hair was curly,

I cared. When they said I didn't dress like any of your previous girlfriends, I worried. They made me realise that I was totally wrong for you.'

Leandro growled low in his throat. 'And you didn't think I might have been the best judge of that?'

'I met one of your previous girlfriends.' She gave a twisted smile. 'She took great pleasure in drawing comparisons between herself and me. And she made the very apt comment that if she hadn't been able to hold you, how could I?'

'*When* did you meet her?'

'At a charity ball, the first week we spent in London. We were standing in front of the mirror together.' Millie nibbled her lip. 'I looked at what I was wearing and I looked at what she was wearing—well, let's just say I could see what she was talking about. I thought to myself, OK, so I need to dress differently. I treated it like a project. When I joined you at our table, I started studying everyone. And I got home and bought magazines, went shopping…'

'And so began your obsession with clothes. I had no idea.' His tone flat, Leandro gently rubbed her fingers with his. 'Those hours you spent in your dressing room every evening, trying on this dress and that dress—I thought you'd suddenly discovered the joys of shopping.'

'Joys?' Millie gave a hollow laugh. 'I hated it. Not that it isn't fun to have nice clothes, don't misunderstand me, but when you know that everything you wear is going to be criticised… Have you any idea how many clothes there are out there? How was

I supposed to know what to wear? All I knew was that every time I went out, people stared at me. I just never seemed to get it right.'

'Why didn't you say something to me?'

'I presumed you could see for yourself,' she said wearily. 'And the fact that you were getting so impatient with me seemed to confirm that I was getting it all wrong.'

Leandro muttered something in Greek and rubbed his forehead with his fingers. 'We were at cross-purposes,' he said gruffly. 'I didn't think you were getting it wrong. I had no idea you were feeling like this.'

'I didn't know what looked good. Every time I thought I liked myself in something, I'd remember how many times I'd been wrong before. Then my sister rang and told me she needed somewhere to crash in London. You were away all the time—I thought she'd be company and I thought she'd be a good person to give me advice. She'd always helped me before. By then I was a mess,' she confessed. 'My confidence was on the floor. Everything I put on I found myself thinking, What are they going to say about this?'

'Why didn't you ask me if I liked what you were wearing?'

'Why didn't you just tell me?' Millie defended herself. 'On our honeymoon you seemed crazy about me—everything I wore, you stripped it off and made love to me. And then we arrived home and…you changed. And it took me a while to understand what was going on.'

'And what did you think was going on?'

'It was obvious. Our relationship was fine when we were here.' She waved a hand. 'Sort of like a holiday romance. But when it came to living your life, well, that's when the cracks appeared. And I panicked. I tried every outfit, every style—but I could see I was different to every other woman you'd ever been with. Every time we went out was torture. Everyone looked at me, judged me.'

Leandro swore under his breath. 'They didn't.'

'They did. People do it all the time. You don't notice because you don't care what people think of you.' Millie sneaked a glance at him. 'And you're not very tolerant of weakness in others. I remember one evening I begged you not to leave me with that group of women and you just frowned and told me I'd be fine. There was some government dignitary you had to speak to so you just threw me to the wolves and let them devour me.'

He winced. 'Millie—'

'It's all right, you don't have to say anything. The truth is you shouldn't have *had* to hold my hand at events like that. I was pathetic, I realise that, but every time we went out I was hit with another ten reasons why you shouldn't have married me and I was shocked by how nasty people were.'

'Why didn't you talk to me?'

'You were too absorbed in your work to notice what was going on. And you were already starting to get irritated with me. Your favourite trick was to glance at your watch and narrow your eyes when I was fumbling about, getting dressed. So I started getting ready earlier and earlier until in the end it took me most of the day. And then I'd appear and you'd be pacing the room like a caged tiger plotting his way out of captivity.'

'Waiting isn't my forte.'

'I noticed that. But from my point of view the fact that you were so irritated made the whole thing even more stressful. I would have spent most of the day getting ready and you'd look at me in disbelief as if you couldn't quite believe that was what I'd chosen to wear and then you'd usher me out to the car.'

'That is *not* what I would have been thinking,' Leandro muttered. 'I was probably thinking how much you'd changed. When first I met you, you didn't do any of those things. You were straightforward and lacking in vanity.'

'I'm sorry! That's because I had never been to a charity ball in my life! The highlight of my social calendar was the village fete.'

He raked his hands through his hair and gave a groan of frustration. '*That was a compliment, Millie!* Don't you ever hear a compliment?'

Stunned by the force of his tone, she looked at him in confusion. 'But you said— I thought— I thought lacking in vanity meant that I didn't spend hours on myself.'

'Yes, but you didn't *need* to spend hours on yourself. I liked you the way you were. I liked you the way you were that day I first met you.'

'I was working on the farm! You arrived, designer dressed from head to toe, to talk business and I was wearing a pair of torn, ancient shorts and a T-shirt that had belonged to my dad but had shrunk in the wash.'

'I don't remember the shorts,' Leandro growled, 'but I do remember your legs. And your smile. And how sweet you were crawling over that haystack, risking life and limb to rescue those kittens that were trapped. I remember thinking, *I want her in my bed. I want her looking after our babies.* And I remember deciding at that moment that I wanted to wake up every morning looking at that smile. Why do you think I stayed two days? It was supposed to be a two-hour meeting.'

'You invested in my dad's business.'

Leandro gave a wry smile. 'I'm going to be honest here, *agape mou,* and confess that your dad's business is the only investment I've ever made that has lost me money.'

Millie gave an astonished laugh. 'You made a mistake?'

'No. I knew it was going to be a disaster the minute he showed me the numbers. I wasn't investing in the business. I was investing in you.'

She thought of the changes her dad had made to the farm. How excited he'd been by his new venture.

'Oh. It was kind of you to do that for Dad.' For a moment she was too flustered to respond, then she frowned slightly. 'But it doesn't change the fact that you didn't stop to think how I'd cope with it all, did you?'

Leandro took her hand again. 'I assumed you'd love the lifestyle. I knew your parents were struggling with the farm and you were working inhuman hours for a pittance.'

'But I didn't marry you for your money or the lifestyle,' she said in a small voice. 'I married you for *you.* And you were always away being the big tycoon. And when we went out, there were always millions of people around us and I couldn't relax because there were cameras stuck in my face and everyone wanted to criticise me. Yes, I was lacking in vanity, but someone like that can't survive in your world. I hadn't realised just how much was involved in being a billionaire's wife. And those awful celebrity magazines tore me to pieces. At the beginning they said I was fat—or "full figured" was the exact phrase— And then I was in this column about fashion mistakes. Don't even *start* me on that one.'

'Why did you read them?'

'I thought it might help me work out what was expected of me. I wanted to look like the perfect wife.' She bit her lip. 'I wanted you to be proud of me. I didn't want you to sit there at a charity event thinking, Why did I marry her?

'I *never* thought that.'

'Didn't you?' Her smile was wan. 'I don't know. I just know that it got worse and worse. Until I no longer had the confidence to undress in front of you—

until I couldn't bear the thought of having sex with you because I imagined that you must be thinking, Yuck, all the time. I just felt so self-conscious.'

'Theos mou.' His tone raw with emotion, Leandro rose to his feet and stood facing the pool, the muscles of his powerful shoulders flexing as he struggled for control. 'And I didn't see any of this. Never before have I considered myself to be stupid and yet obviously I am.'

'No. You just move in different circles to me. You take it all for granted. The women you dated before know how to do their hair, what to wear, how to talk, what to eat, how much they're supposed to weigh.'

'Who makes these rules?'

'Society.'

'And do you never break rules?'

'Sometimes.' Millie looked at him cautiously. 'But I was desperate not to embarrass you or make you ashamed.'

'Suddenly everything is falling into place.' Leandro spun to face her, his voice harsh. 'Why didn't you tell me you felt this way? Why not just have a conversation?'

'Telling your husband that you feel out of place and unattractive isn't the easiest conversation to have. I suppose part of me thought that if I said it aloud, I'd draw attention to it.' *As if he hadn't already noticed.* 'We had fundamental problems that no amount of words could fix. And after the accident, well, I knew I was going to have bad scars. The break in my leg meant that I was in hospital for ages. There was no way you would want to be with someone like me.'

'You reached that conclusion by yourself?' His tone was tight and angry and she felt her own tension increase.

'Yes. You're a man who demands perfection in every part of his life,' she said quietly, 'and I was so far from perfect. I was already insecure about how I was—the accident just made it all worse. Can't you see that?'

'What I see is that we left too many things unsaid. I also finally understand why you were so quick to condemn me when you saw me with your sister.' His voice was low and rough in the semi-darkness. 'Your own confidence was at such a low point that it didn't occur to you that I could be faithful to you. It seems as though you were resigned to the fact that I'd have an affair. You seemed to regard it as inevitable. You assumed that I would prefer your sister.'

Had she been wrong about that? For the first time ever a significant rush of doubt seeped into her brain. 'You and my sister—that was a much more obvious relationship than you and me.' *But she was starting to wonder.* 'Even if that hadn't happened then—with her—it would have happened eventually. Sooner or later some woman would have come along and caught your attention. Maybe you *did* find me attractive—but the novelty would have worn off. We weren't meant to be together, Leandro.' Millie pulled her robe more tightly around her. 'My accident just brought that home to me.'

'You've just made a great number of assumptions.'

'Did you come after me, Leandro?' Gently withdrawing her hand from his, she stood up. The soft lap of water against the side of the pool mingled with the sounds of the Mediterranean. In the distance she could hear the hiss of the sea on the sand, the chirping of the cicadas as they sang their nighttime chorus. 'If you'd wanted me, you would have tracked me down. You're that sort of man. You go after what you want. And you didn't go after me.' *Whatever doubts might be in her head, that, at least, she was sure about.* 'Not even when my sister sent the baby to you.' She managed to keep the emotion out of her voice. 'I'm going to go to bed now. We can talk about what you want to do in the morning. Can I ask you one favour?'

His jaw tightened. 'Ask.'

'Whatever happened before is irrelevant. What matters is how things are now. Who I am now. You'll want to divorce me, and I understand that.' She stumbled over the words. 'But will you let me have custody of Costas? Whatever the will said, you have good lawyers and I'm his blood relative. I can't afford to fight for him.' She glanced at his face and saw the tension etched there. 'Just think about it.' And then she turned and walked back into the villa.

Chapter 9

Leandro stood in the doorway of the guest bedroom, staring at the slight figure under the silk sheet.

She reminded him of an animal that had crawled away to die. And he knew she wasn't asleep.

She was hurt.

Because of him.

His tension mounted. Wasn't he the one who had told her that there was always more going on in a picture than first appeared? And had he taken his own advice? No. He'd seen and he'd judged.

And he knew why. No matter how distasteful it was to admit it, his own past had coloured the present. When she'd walked out…

Guilt, an unfamiliar emotion, clawed at his body

but he thrust it away, knowing that regret would do nothing to fix the current situation.

So many words unspoken, he thought grimly, closing the door quietly and walking towards her. His bare feet made no sound on the cool tiles but he knew she'd heard him because he saw the defensive movement of her shoulders.

'I have lost count of the number of times you've turned your back on me in our short marriage, Millie,' he said softly, 'and I allowed you to do it. But I'm not allowing it any more. Those days are over.'

'Go away, Leandro.' Her voice was muffled by the pillow and he saw her curl up just a little bit tighter, as if trying to make herself as small as possible.

This less than flattering response to his presence sent new tension through his already rigid frame. 'I'm not good at apologies,' he confessed, and then frowned as she curled up smaller still. 'But I know I owe you a big one.'

'You honestly don't have anything to apologise for. No man in their right mind would find me attractive.'

She thought he was apologising because he didn't find her attractive?

Stunned by her interpretation of his remark, Leandro struggled to find a suitable response and decided that, whatever he said, she wasn't going to believe him.

Abandoning words, he lay down on the bed next to her. He felt her shrink and saw her try and shift away from him but he placed his hand firmly on her hip, halting her slide to freedom. Used to negotiating himself out of difficult situations, it was a struggle to stay silent, but he knew that the time for slick verbal patter was long past. She'd made up her mind about herself and the way he saw her. Words weren't going to make a difference.

Applying a different tactic, Leandro slid his arm round her, drawing her rigid, defensive body against his. Through the thin silk robe he could feel her shivering and he frowned because the evening was hot and the air-conditioning in the unoccupied guest bedroom had been switched off. She wasn't cold. She was afraid.

Of him? *Of rejection?*

Taking unfair advantage of the differences in their physical strength, Leandro rolled her onto her back and shifted himself on top of her, his body trapping hers against the silk sheets.

'Why won't you leave me alone, Leandro?' Her voice was a broken plea and he stroked her damp, tangled hair away from her face with a gentle hand.

'I tried that,' he said softly. 'It was my biggest mistake.' Although there was just enough light shining in from the pool area for him to be able to make out the outline of her body, what was going on in her eyes was a mystery to him. He contemplated turning on the bedside light and then decided that it wouldn't be a good move. Maybe, this time, the dark would be helpful.

She tried to wriggle away from him but he was too heavy for her. 'Leandro, please. Don't do this.'

Leandro curved his hand around her cheek and drew her face back to his. He wanted desperately to see her expression. He also knew that if he turned that light on, her distress would stop him in his tracks.

'Don't do this, Leandro,' she whispered, trying to move her head.

Leandro silenced her plea with the warmth of his mouth. And what had begun as an attempt to silence her objections quickly turned into a sensual feast. With a groan, he deepened the kiss, wondering how he could have forgotten how good she tasted. She was strawberries and summer sunshine, honey and green English pastures. But, most of all, she was innocence. And he took ruthless advantage of her lack of sophistication, pushing aside the niggling thought that perhaps it wasn't entirely fair of him to use every erotic skill at his disposal when she was this emotionally vulnerable. They were past being fair, he reasoned, feeling a rush of satisfaction as her mouth moved under his, allowing him the access he was demanding.

Without breaking the kiss, he eased the sheet down her body and untied her robe one handed, careful to keep his movements slow and subtle. But slow and subtle could only take him so far, and he identified the exact moment she realised that he'd undone the robe because she suddenly stiffened under him.

Her arm lifted, but he anticipated her urge to cover herself and closed his fingers around her wrist. Drawing her arm above her head, he restrained her

gently, feeling her tug against his grip as she tried
to free herself. She writhed under him, the uncon-
sciously sensual movement sending his blood pressure soaring. Just to be on the safe side, he drew her
other arm above her head, holding both with one
hand, leaving the other free to explore her quivering frame.

Leandro dropped his mouth to her throat, feeling her pulse pumping against the hot probe of his
tongue. Her soft groan was half encouragement, half
denial, and he gently moved her robe aside, exposing the soft curve of her breast.

She tugged at her wrists and he tightened his hold,
feeling her instant response as he closed his mouth
over the jutting pink tip of one swollen breast. Millie arched in an involuntary movement that brought
her into direct contact with the hard thrust of his
erection. Denying her feminine invitation, Leandro
pressed her down against the bed with the power
of his body, suppressing her attempts to relieve the
sexual ache he'd created.

Soon, he promised himself. *Soon, he'd give her
what she wanted. And himself, too. But first...*

Dragging his tongue over the rigid peak of her
nipple, he stroked his free hand over the flat, trembling planes of her stomach, feeling the ridge of the
scars under his seeking fingers. He lingered for a
moment, infinitely gentle—*did it hurt?*—and then
moved his hand lower still, this time to the tops of
her thighs. *Another scar here,* and he explored it with

the tips of his fingers and then shifted his weight to give himself the access he wanted.

His fingers rested at the top of her thigh and he felt the tiny movements of her pelvis as her body begged. Taking her mouth again, he moved his hand, encountering soft curls, damp now with the response he'd created. Stroking her gently, he felt her gasp against his mouth and then the gasp turned to a moan as he explored her intimately with sure, confident fingers. She was warm and slick, and he took his time, using all his skill and expertise to arouse her body past the point of inhibition. Her moan of desperation connected straight to his libido and suddenly it wasn't enough to touch. He wanted to taste—all of her.

Easing his mouth from hers, Leandro looked down at her, but he couldn't make out her features. Responding to her soft moans, he released her hands, and this time she didn't move them. She just kept them stretched above her head, like some pagan goddess preparing herself for sacrifice.

Leandro slid down her quivering, sensitised body and gently spread her thighs. He'd expected resistance, but her eyes were still closed, her body compliant as he arranged her as he wanted her and then lowered his head. The touch of his mouth drew a soft gasp from her and he closed his hands around her thighs, holding her still while he subjected her to the most extreme sexual torture, his touch so gentle and impossibly skilled that he turned her from doubtful to desperate within seconds. The air was filled with her cries and he continued his determined assault on her senses, sliding one finger deep inside her, the feel of her slick femininity challenging his own control. His libido bit and fought but he continued to touch, stroke, taste until the excitement was a screaming force inside him and she was mindless and compliant under him.

Like a man clinging to a ledge with the tips of his fingers, Leandro refused to allow himself to fall, and then he felt her hands in his hair and on his shoulders.

'Now—Leandro, please...' Her broken plea was all he needed and he shifted over her, sliding his hand under the deliciously rounded curve of her bottom and lifting her.

He wanted to speak—*he wanted to tell her what he was feeling*—but he was afraid of anything that might disturb this fragile connection he'd created between them, so he stayed silent, rejecting the words that flowed into his brain, reminding himself that there would be time enough for talking later.

Her damp core was slick against the tip of his erection and he gritted his teeth in an effort to hold back and do this gently.

'*Leandro...*' Her hips thrust against him, the movement sheathing him sufficiently to rack up the sexual torture a few more notches. Keeping his weight on his elbows, he eased into her slowly, the sweat beading on his brow as he forced himself to take it slowly. Her body gripped his like a hot, tight fist and his reacted by swelling still further, drawing a gasp from her parted lips.

'Leandro...'

'It's all right,' he breathed, 'just relax—your body knows how to do this. Relax, *agape mou,* and trust me.' He licked at her lips, nibbling gently, coaxing and teasing until he felt her respond. But he didn't move, holding himself still until she moved her hips in a tentative invitation.

By a supreme effort of will, Leandro held onto control, keeping his own ravenous libido in check as he waited for her to reach the same point of desperation.

Millie groaned his name, arched and shifted, but still he didn't move, the muscles in his shoulders pumping up and hard under the effort of holding back. Only when she sobbed out a plea and rubbed her thigh along the length of his did he allow himself to move again, and this time her body drew him in deep, her slick delicate tissues welcoming the hard thrust of his manhood.

Trying to think clearly through the red mist that clouded his brain, Leandro slid one hand down her thigh, urging her to wind her legs around him, and then adjusted his own position in a decisive movement that drew a soft gasp from her.

Her soft moans increased with each rhythmic thrust and he was so aware of every movement she made that he felt the exact moment when her body tumbled out of control. The ecstatic tightening of her body stroked the length of his erection and he finally lost his own grip on control and fell with her, joining her in that scorching, exhilarating, terrifying rush to the very edges of extreme pleasure.

His mind blanked. In those few moments of exquisite perfection he forgot everything except the amazing chemistry that he created with this woman.

And as the sizzling, vicious response of his body finally calmed, he became aware of two things. One, that she was no longer fighting him and, two, that he was still hard.

Which gave him a choice.

He could either withdraw and allow her to sleep, or he could do what his body was urging him to do.

Allowing himself a half-smile in the safety of the darkness, Leandro made his choice.

Millie stared at herself in the bathroom mirror, seeing wild hair and flushed cheeks. And that was hardly surprising, was it? He'd made love to her until dawn.

Until dawn...

Trying to ignore the hurt that bloomed inside her, she pulled on a pair of loose trousers and a simple T-shirt and walked out onto the terrace.

A lizard lay basking in the heat of the sun and, nearby, one of the cats was stretched out, slowly licking his fur.

And as relaxed as any of them was Leandro, lounging at the breakfast table with his legs stretched out, his gaze focused on the financial pages of a newspaper. A coffee cup lay empty next to his lean, bronzed hand, his dark hair still damp from the shower.

Millie cleared her throat and he glanced up. His slow, sure smile made her want to hit him.

Leandro the conqueror, she thought miserably. *Man enough to bed a woman even when he didn't find her attractive.*

'*Kalimera.*' He greeted her in Greek. '*Te kanis?* How are you?'

'I'm fine, thank you.'

His eyes narrowed instantly and Millie quivered with suppressed emotion, so utterly humiliated that if she'd been able to leave the island without speaking to him, she would have.

She didn't want to have this conversation, but she knew that Leandro was far too quick not to pick up on her distress.

He folded the newspaper carefully and put it to one side. 'Obviously you're not feeling so good this morning.'

'I'm fine.'

'Fine?' His eyes rested on hers and then he said something in Greek to the staff who were hovering. They melted away, leaving the two of them alone on the terrace. 'All right.' His tone was even. 'We no longer have company. You can tell me what you think of me.'

'You don't want to know.'

'Yes,' he said softly, 'I do. No more secrets, remember?'

'All right.' Millie curved her hand over the back of the chair, too wound up and upset to contemplate joining him at the table. 'If you really want to know what I think—I think you are the most ruthless, in-sensitive man I've ever met.'

Stunned dark eyes met hers. 'Run that past me again?'

'You heard me.'

'I presume this interesting sentiment has hit you in the cold light of day. It certainly wasn't what was going through your mind last night when you were naked and sobbing in my bed.'

'Don't speak like that! I find it *really* embarrassing. It's bad enough that you do all those things to me and make me—you know…' Hot colour flooded her cheeks and she looked away from his hot gaze, unable to look him in the eye and maintain the conversation. 'It's as if you're sitting there smugly congratulating yourself on your amazing ability to turn any woman to jelly no matter what. What were you trying to prove?'

Leandro was unusually still, his gaze partially concealed by thick, black lashes. 'What makes you think I was trying to prove something?'

'Because why else would you have devoted your night to that whole…' Millie waved her hand wildly '…seduction routine. What? *What was it all about?*'

'They say actions speak louder than words—didn't last night say anything to you?'

'Yes. It said that you didn't know how to apologise, but you do know how to have sex.'

'You think that was apology sex?'

'I'd rather think that than the alternative.'

'Which is?'

'Pity sex. That's far worse than apology sex.'

'You think I made love to you because I felt sorry for you? I'm not sure the male anatomy would allow "pity sex", whatever that is.' His apparent lack of emotion somehow made everything worse.

'I'm sure yours would—you don't exactly have a problem with your sex drive, do you? Although I did notice that even you had to do it in the dark.'

'"Do it"?' He repeated her words with careful emphasis, the subtle lift of one eyebrow reminding her of just how unsophisticated she was compared to him.

Millie rubbed her damp palms on her loose trousers, wishing she hadn't started this conversation. 'It wasn't making love. Making your point would be closer to the mark. Why did you do it? Was it a challenge to your reputation as the ultimate lover? Or was it supposed to be a going-away present? You don't want me to feel bad about myself so you decided to give me a good night before you sent me packing, is that right?' Her emotions were in such a heightened state of turbulence that his calm, watchful gaze was even more infuriating. 'Aren't you going to say something?'

Leandro stirred and drew in a breath. 'I only realised yesterday how insecure you are, and clearly I've underestimated the depths of that insecurity.' Putting his napkin carefully down on the table, he stood up.

Something in the set of his powerful shoulders and the glint in his eye made her step backwards but he was too quick for her. His hand closed around her wrist and when she twisted it in an attempt to free herself he simply drew her closer.

Memories of the way he'd held her hands in the moonlight deepened the flush on her cheeks. Hope warred with her feelings of inadequacy.

'Let me go. You're always grabbing me! What do you think you're doing?'

'You think last night was all about pity sex— you think I'm only capable of only "doing it" in the dark.' He swung her into his arms, strode a few paces across the terrace. 'Well, it's not dark now, *agape mou,* so let's test that theory, shall we?'

'Put me down, Leandro!'

He lowered her onto the nearest sun lounger. 'I've put you down.' His voice was a soft dangerous purr and he undid the clasp of her trousers with a practised flick of his fingers.

With a gasp of shock she clutched at her trousers but she was too late. They were already discarded on the floor and his hands were stripping off her T-shirt with the same decisive force. 'Stop it. Leandro, what are you *thinking?*'

'That you're incredibly sexy,' he growled, releasing the catch on her bra and stripping off her panties without pause or hesitation. It was easy for him, with his vastly superior strength, to keep her where he wanted her. 'And I'm thinking that being thoughtful wasn't the right approach. Apparently what a man sees as sensitive, a woman can see as insensitive.'

Horribly conscious of the sun blazing a spotlight

onto her naked body, Millie tried to slither away from him but Leandro held her firmly, a dangerous gleam in his eyes. 'No more hiding, *agape mou*. No more robes, long trousers or dark rooms. We will do this in daylight and then you will know the truth, *hmm?* You will see how sorry I feel for you—how this injury of yours has affected me. You want to know if I'm aroused? If you still turn me on? Let's see, shall we?'

'Don't do this.' Millie drew her knees up, trying to cover herself but he pushed her legs down with one hand and deftly dealt with the zip of his trousers with the other.

'Do I look as though I'm having a problem becoming aroused, *agape mou?* Do I look like a man doing you a favour?' His eyes glittered as he dispensed with his trousers, boldly unselfconscious as he stripped himself naked, exposing his lean, bronzed body. Lean, bronzed, *aroused* body.

With the flat of his hand Leandro pushed her gently back against the sun lounger and came over her in a fluid movement that was all dominant male.

His muscles were pumped up and hard and she felt the brush of his chest hair against the sensitised tips of her breasts.

When the blunt tip of his erection brushed against her exposed thigh she gave a gasp of shock that turned to a moan as he buried his face in her neck.

'Does that feel like pity?' He moved against her boldly and Millie groaned and turned her head away because the sudden explosion of excitement that consumed her was just too humiliating.

'Don't do this, Leandro…'

'Why? Because you're afraid I'm doing it because I feel sorry for you? I never do things for other people, *agape mou,* you should know that by now. I'm selfish. I do things for myself. Because it's what I want.' His tone rough, he took her hand and drew it down to that part of himself, and her mouth dried because he was velvety hard and she could barely circle him with her shaking fingers. 'I know you had no experience before I met you,' he purred, 'so let me spell out the facts, *pethi mou.* This isn't called pity. It's called chemistry. Hot, sexual chemistry. It isn't me "making my point", as you so eloquently put it, it's me making love.' He caught her face in his hands and lowered his mouth to hers. 'Making love,' he said against her lips. 'Have you got that?'

'Leandro—'

'I want you. I've always wanted you and that isn't going to change. Are you listening?' He slid his hand behind her neck and forced her to hold his gaze. 'Are you listening to me?'

Her hand was still holding him and she stared into the fierce heat of his eyes and forgot everything except the burning need in her pelvis.

His hand slid under her bottom, shifting her position. 'You have scars on your body, yes,' he said thickly, 'but it's still your body. One day, when you have my babies, you might have stretch marks or maybe other scars, but this will still be your body. And it's *your* body that I want. No other woman's.'

Babies?

Her head was spinning, her pulse racing out of control as she struggled to hold onto her thoughts before they slipped away. He'd said— Had he said…?

While she was struggling with his words, he entered her with a determined thrust, sliding deep, and Millie gave up on any thought of responding because the feel of him inside her drove every coherent thought from her brain. Unprepared for his invasion, she tried to make a sound but his mouth closed over hers and he held her hips as he drove deeper still, his virile thrust taking him straight to the heart of her. This time there was no gentle foreplay, no slow, clever strokes of his long fingers. Just an unapologetic demonstration of raw sexuality and male dominance.

His hand locked in her hair, Leandro lifted his head just enough to allow him to speak. 'Can you feel me, Millie?' He growled the words against her lips and ground deeper inside her. 'Can you feel me inside you?' He was big, hard and shockingly male, and she sobbed his name and dug her nails into his back, her body so sensitised by his invasion that she could hardly breathe. In that moment she'd never felt so wanted, truly desired.

His breathing unsteady, he gently bit her lower lip and then soothed it with his tongue. 'You feel incredible,' he murmured huskily, and he withdrew slightly and her eyes flew wide.

'No…'

'No what?' He gave a slow, wicked smile, withdrawing still further. 'No, don't stop—or, no, don't do this?'

'Leandro…'

He kept her on the edge for several agonising seconds and then slid deep again, the movement sending shock waves of excitement through her trembling frame.

'This isn't pity sex,' he breathed, lifting her hips to allow him even, 'it's hot sex, *agape mou*. It's what you and I share. Can you feel it?'

Millie was incapable of speech, her body rushing forward to meet the pleasure that he was creating with each skilled, fluid stroke. For a delicious moment her eyes met his. He held that look, the connection between them impossibly intimate. And then everything inside her splintered apart and she arched her back as her body was convulsed by an erotic explosion so intense that she couldn't catch her breath. The sensations devoured her, tearing through her body like a ravenous beast on the rampage, and she felt the sudden tension in his body and the increase in masculine thrust that brought him to the same dizzying peak of hot liquid pleasure.

Millie lay in dazed, breathless silence for a moment, her mind incapable of functioning. She was dimly aware of the hot sun burning her leg and the roughness of his thigh against her more sensitive flesh. And then she heard the distant buzz of a motorboat somewhere in the distance and was suddenly hideously conscious of the fact they were naked.

'Leandro…' She pushed against his bare shoulder, suddenly panicking that someone was going to see them. 'We have to move.'

'Why?' Typically relaxed, he raised himself onto his elbow and surveyed her from under thick, dark lashes. 'What's the hurry?'

'Your staff—'

'Don't venture near my private terrace,' he said smoothly, dropping a lingering kiss to her parted lips.

'But what if one of them comes to clear up the breakfast things?'

'I'll fire them.' He kissed her cheek. 'Relax.'

But she couldn't relax. 'I should check Costas.'

'He has a nanny, remember? And if he was awake you would have heard him through the baby alarm.'

'What if it isn't working? I need to get dressed, Leandro.'

'No. You don't. You just want to hide your body and I'm not going to let you.'

'You may be comfortable with nudity, but that's only because you look great.'

'Thank you.' Laughing, he caught her face in his hands. 'You have a great body, too. I thought I'd just proved that. You're *not* running away.'

Millie bit her lip and then gave a faltering smile. 'I really do want to see the baby. It's been such an upheaval for him, being passed around as if he's some sort of trophy. He needs stability and security. I want him to know I'm here. I need to take a shower and dress.'

He sighed and lowered his mouth to hers. 'You

are quite extraordinary,' he murmured softly, stroking her hair back from her face. 'Go on, then. I'll see
you in a minute.'

Her senses and emotions churning from what had
happened between them, she drew away from him
and walked awkwardly across the terrace and back
into the bedroom.

Locking herself in the bathroom, she turned on
the shower, wondering what exactly had it all meant
to him. What had he been proving? Convinced that
he'd made love to her in the night out of some mis-
placed sense of guilt, she was no longer sure of anything. Not even herself. Her body still ached and
tingled from their lovemaking and she stepped under
the shower and then changed into a long cotton skirt
and a strap top.

She contemplated blow-drying her hair and decided against it, anxious in case Costas had woken
and was upset.

Hurrying along to his room, she heard happy gur-
gles and cooing and walked in to find him lying in
Leandro's arms.

Millie watched for a moment, her insides turning
to mush as she saw how gentle he was with the baby.
He was speaking in soft, lyrical Greek and then he
looked up and saw her.

'And here is beautiful Millie.' He placed a kiss
on top of the baby's head and handed him over. 'He
seems quite happy.'

Millie took the baby, feeling his solid warmth in
her arms. 'He needs his nappy changed.'

'Now, *that*,' Leandro drawled, 'is definitely out-side my area of expertise. Do you want me to call the nanny?'

'Believe it or not, I'm capable of changing a nappy.' Millie laid Costas on a changing mat on the floor. Relieved to have a reason to avoid Leandro's disturbing gaze, she cooed at the baby who kicked his legs in delight. 'He thinks I can't change a nappy.'

'Why don't you put him on the bed?'

'Because he might roll off.' Millie deftly changed the nappy and scooped the baby against her. 'Time for breakfast.'

'Give him his bottle on the terrace,' Leandro in-structed. 'There are things I want to say to you.'

She looked at him warily. 'Things that can be said in front of a baby?'

He looked amused. 'Absolutely. In the unlikely event that he files our conversation for future ref-erence, it will do him good to know that adults can sort out their problems rather than giving up on their marriage. That is the example I would want to set for the younger generation. And you?'

Millie's heartbeat faltered. 'I— We— It isn't that simple, Leandro—you're unrealistic.'

He guided her towards the door that led to the vine covered terrace. 'The difference in our approach may be rooted in our cultures. Your divorce rate is higher than ours.'

Still holding Costas, Millie sighed as she walked towards the table that had been set for breakfast. 'I think cultural differences are the least of our problems at this point in our relationship.'

His response to that was to turn and deliver a slow, confident smile. 'Problems are merely there to test resolve. If you really want something, you can overcome the problems.' He stepped towards her, closing the gap until she drew in a breath. 'How much do you want our marriage to work, Millie?'

How much? Her heart was thudding and she was trapped by the unshakable confidence in his eyes. 'I—I want it, of course, but you don't—'

'Don't I?' He didn't even wait for her to finish the sentence. 'What do you think this morning was all about?'

'I have no idea. I'm assuming your caveman tendencies ran a little out of control.'

The look in his eyes sent her pulse racing again and she stepped backwards, grateful that she was holding the baby.

'I need to feed Costas.'

'If you think that's going to get you off the hook, you don't know me. We're going to talk about this, *agape mou*. I'm going to explore every last corner of…' His voice tailed off and her breathing quickened because the look in his eyes was unmistakably sexual.

'Of?'

His smile widened. 'Of our relationship,' he purred, and she knew he was perfectly aware that she'd been waiting for him to say 'your body.'

Millie gritted her teeth and was about to stalk

towards the table when he closed his hand over her shoulder and bent his head so that his mouth was by her ear.

'That, too,' he murmured silkily, and the colour flooded into her cheeks.

'You've done enough exploring for one day.'

'I haven't even started.' Leandro pulled the chair out for her and made sure she had what she needed for the baby. Then he took the seat opposite her and poured her some coffee.

'What was it you wanted to say to me?' The anticipation of the conversation to come scraped at her insides like sandpaper, putting her off her food. Trying to distract herself, she slid the teat into the baby's mouth, her expression softening as he clamped his jaws and started to suck.

'Eat some food. This honey comes from a friend's bees. It's delicious.'

'I'm not hungry.'

'Eat, or I will feed you,' he said pleasantly, but his eyes glinted warningly across the table. 'I overlooked the fact that you didn't eat last night. You'd worked yourself up into a state about telling me what had happened to you, and you'd braced yourself for rejection. But that didn't happen, did it, Millie? You are still sitting at my table, having just climbed out of my bed—metaphorically at least—so there is no longer a reason for you to have lost your appetite.'

'Nothing's changed, Leandro.' She watched as he drizzled the thick, golden honey over the creamy yoghurt. 'The issues between us are still there.'

'All right—so let's address those issues because the worry is affecting you badly. First, can I get you anything? This sweet pastry is delicious.'

Millie shook her head, envying his calm. 'You're not stressed, are you?'

'What is there to be stressed about?' He drank his coffee and replaced the cup carefully in the saucer. 'I am relaxing on a beautiful island with a beautiful woman. If I found that stressful, I would be a fool, no?'

She closed her eyes briefly. 'So you're just going to pretend that sex solves everything.'

'No. I'm not going to pretend that. I want to make a few things clear to you. I made love to you in the dark last night because you were clearly very upset and I thought it was the sensitive thing to do, but...' he gave a self deprecating smile '...as I now know, a man's idea of what is sensitive isn't always the same as a woman's. As you keep pointing out, I'm not that good at the whole sensitive side of things, so I need to work on that.'

Millie gave a strangled laugh. 'What? You're suddenly going to turn into a modern man?'

'I wouldn't go that far.' There was humour in his tone and in the glance he sent in her direction. 'Tell me why you think I made love to you in the dark?'

'Isn't it obvious?' *Was he going to make her spell it out?*

Apparently he was, because he showed no inclination to let her off the hook. 'I think we've both accepted that what is obvious to me isn't obvious to you and vice versa. Guessing games haven't done much for the success of our relationship to date.'

Unable to argue with that, Millie grimaced. 'All right.' She adjusted the bottle in the baby's mouth. 'You made love to me in the dark because you didn't want to see my body. I thought being in the dark was the only way you could be sure you'd be able to—' She broke off and his eyes gleamed with sardonic humour as he challenged her unspoken assumption.

'Well, you were wrong about that, weren't you?'

Remembering just *how* wrong, her mouth dried. 'I suppose I was.'

His mind clearly lingering on the same memories, he gave a slow, masculine smile. 'It was fantastic, no?'

Millie looked away from him. 'It didn't solve anything.'

'Yes, it did.' His voice soft, Leandro leaned across the table and took her hand. 'It told me a great deal about you.'

'That I'm easy?'

'Easy?' He gave a hollow laugh. 'You're the most difficult woman I know. In every sense. You're complicated, contrary, you don't say what you think— and you put thoughts in other people's heads.' He paused. 'And that brings us to the most important part of this conversation.'

'Which is what?'

'Your insecurities. We married quickly, as you constantly remind me.' He pulled a face. 'And I didn't take the time to get to know you properly. That was my first mistake. The sex overwhelmed us both, I think.'

'Yes, it did. You can't build a marriage on…' she cast a worried look at the baby and lowered her voice '…sex. Sex isn't communication.'

'Actually, I disagree.' His gaze was direct. 'I think sex is often a very honest form of communication. On our honeymoon you were insatiable—affectionate, uninhibited and spontaneous. When you turned your back on me, I should have made you talk. Instead, I gave you space.' Leandro leaned back in his chair. 'You assumed that I'd prefer your sister to you, isn't that right?'

'Yes.' Millie didn't lie. 'Becca was beautiful, elegant and witty. She wouldn't have had any difficulties knowing what to wear and what to say.'

'So you saw us together and instead of thinking, *He wouldn't,* you thought *I understand why he would.*'

'Sort of.'

'So would you agree that the whole incident said more about you than it did about me?'

Her heart was thumping. *Had she been unfair?* The doubt was slowly growing in her mind. 'Maybe. I don't know. She was my sister.' She bit her lip. 'I just want to put the whole thing behind us.'

His mouth tightened for a moment and then he lifted a padded envelope from the table and handed it to her. 'This is for you.'

'What is it?' Millie slid her hand into the packet and withdrew some discs. 'What are these?'

'It's the CCTV footage of what happened in the pool that day. Take it.' He leaned forward. 'It proves that I'm telling the truth.'

'You had proof?'

'I have a very sophisticated security system in the house.'

'But you didn't show me before?'

Leandro hesitated. 'Two reasons,' he said softly. 'Firstly, because I had this idealistic wish for my wife to have unquestioning faith and trust in me. Secondly, I didn't want to be the one who exposed your sister for what she was. I'm doing it now because I realise how insecure you are and I don't want you to feel that way.'

Her heart lifted and sank and Millie looked at him helplessly. 'So this proves my husband is innocent and my sister is guilty.'

'Yes.'

Struggling with the truth, she fingered the CDs. 'When Becca came to stay, I thought she was helping me. But she was targeting you, wasn't she?'

'I think we have to assume that.'

Reflecting on that, Millie bit her lip and then put the CDs back in the envelope. 'Thanks,' she said gruffly, 'for giving me the chance to see them. Now I'm the one who owes you an apology.'

'Aren't you going to look at them?'

'No.' Millie rubbed her fingers over the envelope. 'I believe you. I think perhaps a small part of me always believed you, but believing you meant ac-

cepting that Becca—' She broke off and Leandro
breathed out heavily.

'I know. I'm sorry.'

'She was my family. Someone I trusted.' Millie
lifted her eyes to his and saw dark shadows there.
'What? You think I was stupid to trust her?'

'No.' His voice was rough. 'You should be able to
trust family. It's just that sometimes…' He muttered
something under his breath and stood up abruptly.
'Enough of this, Millie. It's in the past now.'

Millie looked at him, wondering what was going
on in his mind. 'Leandro—'

'I want you to forget it,' he ordered. 'I want to put
it behind us.'

'But it doesn't really change the facts! You need
a wife who's able to stand by your side at glittering
functions, someone who can hold her own with the
elite of Hollywood, politicians, businessmen—'

'And I have a wife capable of all those things. The
only thing she apparently isn't capable of is believing in herself.' Leandro reached for her hand across
the table. 'But that is going to change.'

'I appreciate what you're trying to do, but you
have to be realistic. That actress was right—I'm not
your type.'

'She was trying to destroy your confidence.' His
fingers tightened on hers. 'Are you going to let her?'

'Very possibly.' Millie gave a weak smile. 'You
think I should look in the mirror and say I'm more
beautiful than her? I'd have to be treated for hallu-
cinations.'

Leandro gestured to a staff member who was hovering discreetly, and she hurried up and carefully lifted Costas from Millie's arms.

'I don't want him corrupted,' Leandro said silkily, 'so I didn't think he should be here for the next part.' He stood up and drew her against him intimately, a smile playing around his firm mouth. 'Are you aware of your own power yet?'

Feeling the hard thrust of his arousal, she looked at him in amused disbelief. 'You're insatiable.'

'With you, yes. You turn me on,' he breathed, lowering his mouth to hers, 'and on, and on. All the time. And I want you, all the time. So next time you don't feel beautiful, remind yourself of that.'

'So what happens now?'

'You learn to be yourself. No more dressing as you think you are expected to dress—no more behaving as you are expected to behave. Just be you. Is that so hard?'

'And when I embarrass you?'

Leandro smiled. 'That won't happen. I find you beautiful, generous and kind and I intend to devote the next few weeks to making you believe in yourself.'

If they could have stayed in Greece forever, maybe their relationship would work, Millie thought. But his life was so much bigger than this one, idyllic island.

And what was going to happen then?

Chapter 10

The idyll lasted two more weeks.

'He loves his afternoon nap. He's sleeping really well now.' Millie tucked Costas into the cot and tiptoed towards Leandro, who was waiting in the doorway. He was dressed casually in shorts and a polo shirt and his dark hair gleamed in the sunshine.

'You are very good with him.' His eyes lingered on her face. 'And extremely generous to give so much of yourself to a child who isn't yours.'

Millie was horribly conscious of his scrutiny. 'He's part of my sister.'

Leandro took her hand and led her across the terrace and towards the narrow path that led down through a garden of tumbling Mediterranean plants to the beach. 'You are nothing like her.'

'I'm well aware of that. My parents were constantly reminding me of that.'

Leandro frowned down at her. 'Really?'

'I don't blame them. I never gave my parents anything to boast about. I was never top in maths, I was only ever picked for the netball team if everyone else was struck down by some vile virus or other, I didn't play a musical instrument, I have a voice like a crow with a sore throat and I don't have the face and body of a model.'

'And is all that important?'

'Among you alpha high achievers, it is. My mum's face glowed with pride when she introduced Becca to anyone— "This is my daughter who works as a top model but she also has a maths degree from Cambridge, you know." And then she'd turn to me and say, "And this is our other daughter—Millie isn't academic, are you dear?" And I'd feel the same way I felt when I got my spelling wrong at school. The teachers would sigh and say, "You're nothing like your sister, are you?" as if that was a major disadvantage in life.'

'No wonder you have no confidence. But all that is going to change.' As they reached the bottom of the path, Leandro tightened his grip on her hand. 'You can't possibly still be feeling insecure,' he murmured, taking her face in his hands and kissing her. 'For the past two weeks we've done nothing but talk and make love.'

'Maybe I'm having problems believing that anyone can be this lucky,' Millie replied humbly, wrapping her arms around his neck. 'And I still can't believe you don't want someone who you can discuss the money markets with over breakfast.'

'I can't think of anything more guaranteed to put me off my food.' He dragged his thumb across her mouth in an unmistakably sensual gesture. 'I work in a very high-pressured, conflict-ridden environment—when I come home I don't want to discuss work. And I don't want conflict. I want a soft, warm woman who can challenge me in other ways. Which you do. So the answer to your unspoken question, *agape mou,* is no. I didn't ever want your sister. But I have told you that before.' He released her and took her hand, leading her towards the jetty.

Millie looked at the sleek motorboat. 'We're going out on that?'

'I feel in need of an adrenaline rush,' he drawled. 'In the absence of anyone to fire, bully or intimidate, I need to find alternative forms of excitement.'

Her eyes slid to his and he gave a slow grin. 'Yes, we'll be doing that, too,' he purred, helping her into the boat and loosening the rope. Lithe and agile, he followed her into the boat, taking the control with his usual cool confidence. 'Do you get seasick?'

'I don't know, but I'm probably about to find out.' Her nerve endings sizzling from the chemistry that constantly flared between them, she tried to concentrate. 'How fast are you going to go?'

His smile widened. 'Fast.'

And he did.

Having eased the boat skilfully out of the shallow bay, he pushed the throttle forwards and sent the boat flying across the waves at a speed that took her breath away.

Millie held tight to the seat, meeting his brief, questioning glance with an exaggerated smile of delight.

Men, she thought, relieved that she hadn't bothered with a hat. Her hair flew around her face and the spray from the waves stung her cheeks.

Leandro kept up the pace until they reached a neighbouring island, and then he cut the engine and dropped the anchor.

'Presumably you could have gone at half the pace.'

'And that would have taken twice the time.' Unapologetic, he leaned forward and kissed her hard. 'I don't like hanging around.'

'I'd noticed.' Millie looked towards the beach. 'Is that where we're going?'

'Later. If you want to. First I want to show you something. Put this on.' He handed her a slim, expensive-looking box with a discreet logo in the corner, which she recognised as that of a top fashion designer.

'If this is another swimming costume, you can forget it. In the last ten days all you've done is make me take my clothes off all the time.'

'That isn't quite all I've done, *agape mou.*'

She blushed. 'OK, so I wore a swimming costume on your island, but presumably this isn't private. Anyone could see me.'

"You have nothing to hide.'

'I still can't believe you got me into a swimming costume.'

'You looked fabulous.'

'From the back.'

'Yes, from the back. And from the front. And the side. From every angle,' Leandro said, sliding his shorts off to reveal the strong, flat stomach and hard thighs. 'You seem a little overdressed for a Greek beach. Open the box.'

'Where did this come from, anyway? You haven't been anywhere to buy me anything.'

He spread his hands in masculine apology. 'All right—I confess I didn't actually choose it. I made a call, gave someone a brief and it was delivered.'

'You made a call.' She mimicked him as she opened the box. Wrapped carefully inside layers of luxurious silken tissue paper was the sexiest bikini she'd ever seen. It was a shimmering gold and she could see that it was brief enough to be virtually non-existent. Her heart thudded uncomfortably. 'No *way,* Leandro!'

'Put it on.'

'I can't possibly wear this.'

'Trust me, you will look sensational in it.' Calm and unconcerned, he stripped off his T-shirt, revealing bronzed shoulders hard with muscle. 'I will enjoy watching you change into it.'

'Leandro.' Her tone was urgent and her fingers tightened on the slippery fabric. 'A swimming costume—well, I managed that. But I can't wear a bikini. I just can't. I have—'

'Scars—yes, I know.' He was as relaxed as she was agitated, and her fingers tightened on the silky fabric.

'You don't understand how self-conscious I feel.'

'I understand *exactly* how self-conscious you feel and I am trying to show you that I find you incredibly sexy in whatever you're wearing.' His voice was husky. 'Or *not* wearing. Get changed.'

Millie held the bikini in her hands. Looked at it. Then she saw the determination in his eyes. 'I can't wear a bikini.'

'You have ten seconds to change,' he warned in a silky tone, 'or I will put it on you myself.'

'You're not very sympathetic, are you?'

'Do you want my sympathy?'

'No. I just want to hide and you won't let me. For the past two weeks you've done nothing but expose me! You make love in daylight, you make me parade around in a swimming costume and now this.'

Leandro glanced pointedly at his watch. 'You're down to one second. Are you going to do it yourself or do I do it for you?'

Sending him a furious glare, Millie snatched up one of the neatly folded towels and retreated to the far side of the boat. Was he being intentionally cruel? Angry and upset, she wriggled into the minuscule bikini, snatched her clothes up from the baking leather of the seat and stalked back to him.

'Satisfied?'

'Not yet.' His smile was wickedly sexy as his eyes trailed down her body. 'But I will be. Remind me to thank the person who chose that. She followed my brief exactly. The emphasis being on the word "brief".'

Flustered by his lazy, masculine scrutiny, Millie stared down at the clear water. Shoals of tiny silvery fish darted beneath the surface and she watched them for a moment. 'I don't understand you.'

'Evidently not. But we're working to change that. You look fantastic in that bikini.'

She opened her mouth to argue with him but he walked across to her, wrapped his arms around her and kissed her. The heat he created with his mouth eclipsed anything produced by the sun, and Millie felt her body melt and her mind shut down. She forgot that she wanted to cover herself. She forgot to feel self-conscious. Instead, she felt beautiful and seductive.

When he finally lifted his head, she felt dizzy. 'How is your confidence now?'

Basking in the sexual appreciation, she gave a reluctant smile. 'Recovering.'

'Good. Because we are flying back to London tomorrow.'

Millie felt as though she'd been punched in the stomach. 'Why?'

'Because my business demands it,' he said dryly, stroking her hair away from her face. 'I have been absent for a long time—there are things that need my attention. And tomorrow night we have a gala evening to attend.'

'Tomorrow?' Millie tensed. 'You haven't given me any warning!'

'I didn't want you turning yourself into a nervous wreck.'

'Who will be there?'

'I will be there.' Leandro released his hold on her and stepped onto the side of the boat. 'And I am the only person that matters in your life.' With that arrogant statement, he executed a perfect dive, his lean, bronzed body slicing into the water with powerful grace.

Millie stared after him in frustration, realising that the only way she was going to be able to finish the conversation was if she followed him.

Knowing that a dive would definitely part her from the tiny bikini, she opted instead to use the ladder that hung from the back of the boat.

Sliding into the cooling water, she swam over to him.

Her confidence had increased a thousand times over the past few weeks, but was she really ready to go back to their old life?

She glanced up at the sky and, instead of being a perfect blue, it was grey and overcast.

And during the night the rain came.

Twenty-four hours later, Millie was back in London, reflecting on how much life could change in a few short weeks.

She looked in the mirror and for the first time ever she didn't wish that she could turn the lights down.

After two weeks alone with a flatteringly attentive Leandro, it was impossible not to feel beautiful.

Which was just as well because tonight they were going to be walking up the red carpet together. And there would be cameras.

To test her new confidence, Millie wore a dress of her own choosing, shoes that made her feel like a princess, and chose to leave her hair loose and curly.

Nestling against her throat was the heart-shaped diamond that Leandro had given her on their wedding day.

As she slipped her feet into her shoes, Leandro strolled into the dressing room.

He looked spectacular in a tailored dinner jacket and Millie felt a little pang as she realised that every woman in the room was going to be looking at him. For sheer visual impact there wasn't a man who came close to him, she thought weakly, and he caught her soft sigh and frowned.

'What are you thinking?'

'I'm wishing you weren't quite so attractive,' Millie said dryly. 'Then maybe women wouldn't all gape at you and I wouldn't feel so insecure.'

'After the past ten days I have no energy left,' he assured her in a silky tone, 'so you have no cause for concern.' He urged her out of the bedroom and down the stairs to the hallway. 'You look beautiful. You *know* you look beautiful.'

'I like hearing you say it.' Oblivious to the staff hovering, Millie wound her arms around his neck and he smiled and lowered his mouth to hers.

'Then I'll say it again,' Leandro murmured against her lips. 'You look beautiful.'

And she didn't argue because she saw it in his eyes when he looked at her.

'I didn't straighten my hair.'

'Good. I love your curls.'

'I've worn this dress before.'

'I know. I remember how good you looked in it the first time.'

'Do you think it makes my bottom look big?'

Leandro backed away from her, his hands spread in a defensive groan. '*Never* ask a man that question.' He laughed, but he turned her sideways and dutifully studied her rear view. 'It makes your bottom look like something out of a man's fantasy. And now I want to—'

'Don't you *dare* rumple me!' Wriggling away from the possessive slide of his hands, Millie couldn't help laughing. 'You're insatiable.'

'Yes. But unfortunately for me I am the guest of honour.' With a regretful sigh, he reached for his BlackBerry and made a quick call. 'Otherwise…' he returned the phone to his pocket '…I would feel the need to devote the rest of my evening examining the size of your bottom at close quarters. My driver is waiting outside for us.'

Millie walked towards the front door, but he stopped her.

'Wait—I have something for you.' His voice husky, Leandro reached into his pocket and retrieved a long black box. Opening it, he lifted out a slim, diamond bracelet.

Millie gasped and covered her mouth with her hands. 'Leandro, you can't—'

'I can.' He fastened it around her wrist and then stood back and narrowed his eyes. 'It suits you.'

'It matches my necklace.'

'Of course.' His hands firm on her shoulders, he turned her so that she could see her reflection in the hall mirror.

The diamonds sparkled against her creamy skin and she lifted a hand and touched them reverentially. 'I might get mugged.'

His jaw tightened and he drew her close. 'Never again,' he said gruffly. 'You're with me. And that's where you're staying. And I will protect you.'

As they stepped into the back of the luxurious car, Leandro spoke quietly to the driver and then turned to her. 'There will be media,' he warned her as they drew up outside the venue. 'Just smile.'

And she did.

Millie smiled her way up the red carpet, smiled at the cameras, smiled at the guests who gaped and jostled each other for an introduction, and she smiled at Leandro, who was as sexy as sin in his role of powerful tycoon. He slipped easily from one environment to another, she thought as she chatted casually to the man seated to her left.

She felt more confident, more at ease than she ever had before, and turned to Leandro with a grateful smile. 'I'm having a nice time.'

'Good.' His searing gaze rested on her cleavage. 'I'm not. All I want to do is take you home.'

Millie reached for her wineglass, enjoying the feeling of power that she had over him. The tension gradually mounted between them and by the time Leandro announced that they could leave, both of them were desperate.

They kissed in the car

As they approached the gates of his house, Millie noticed the hordes of press and her heart sank.

'What are they doing here? I thought they'd lost interest in us.'

'Ignore them.' A frown on his face, Leandro spoke to the driver in Greek and they were driven at speed through a network of roads which eventually brought them to the back of the house.

'I love this secret entrance.' Millie giggled, lifting the hem of her dress so that it didn't drag on the grass. 'It's so romantic. And I love the fact that the press haven't discovered it.'

'It's useful,' Leandro replied, but she sensed he was distracted by something. 'Come on. Let's go inside.'

They were greeted by the housekeeper, who was clearly agitated.

'I'm glad you're home—something terrible…' Nervously she rubbed her hands together and Millie felt her legs turn to jelly.

'Costas? Is he ill?' She stepped forward, panic making her legs shake. 'I shouldn't have gone out. Is something wrong with him?'

'The baby is fine, madam,' the housekeeper assured her, but the pity and embarrassment in her eyes made Millie drop back a few steps.

'Then what's wrong?'

'How anyone can write such stuff—do they have no shame?' Clearly distressed, the housekeeper blinked furiously. 'We've had all the papers put in the conservatory, Mr Demetrios, and I've instructed the staff that they're not to speak to anyone. The press have been knocking and calling, but we haven't answered. It's shameful, if you ask me, a man not being able to have peace in his own home.'

Without uttering a word, Leandro turned and strode towards the living room.

Feeling as though her shoes were lead weights, Millie followed him into the room and closed the door behind her. Even though she didn't know what was wrong, her heart was thudding and she felt sick with dread.

Even without looking, she knew that the newspapers would have done another hatchet job on her. But how? They'd only taken her photograph a few hours earlier.

Leandro picked up the first of the newspapers and scanned it briefly. The expression on his handsome face didn't alter as he threw it aside and picked up the next.

Almost afraid to look, Millie stooped and picked up one of the discarded copies. The Hollywood actress smiled seductively from the front page, and the caption read, 'Loving Leandro—my Unforgettable Night with my Greek Tycoon'.

Millie dropped the paper.

Her mouth was dry and her hands were shaking, but something made her pick up the next paper that he'd dropped. This time she read the copy.

'She's described your night together in minute detail.'

'She has a vivid imagination,' Leandro said flatly, picking up the last of the newspapers. 'They all say the same thing. Leave them. It's filth.' But as he scanned the final newspaper his expression did alter, as if something printed there was the final straw.

His mouth a flat, angry line, he quickly folded the paper but Millie reached forward and tugged it away from him, some masochistic part of her wanting to see what had upset him so much.

'Millie, no!' Leandro stepped forward to take it from her but not before she'd seen the pictures of herself in a bikini.

'Oh, my God.' Appalled and mortified, she felt like hiding under a rock. 'How did they—? We—'

'They must have had photographers near my island.' Leandro jabbed his fingers into his hair and cast her a shimmering glance of apology. 'This is *my* fault. I took you on that boat and I made you wear the bikini.'

'You didn't know there'd be a photographer nearby.' Millie gave a hysterical laugh. 'Where was he? On the back of a dolphin?'

Leandro undid his bow-tie and released his top

button. 'I'm truly sorry.' He broke off and muttered
something in Greek. 'I'll speak to my lawyers immediately. There may be something they can do.'

'It's already been done.' Her mouth dry, Millie
stared at the photos and the close-up of her scars.
Then she looked at the photographs of the actress
taken from her latest film. The cruel positioning of
the two photographs took her breath away. 'You can't
undo this, Leandro. It's out there now. It will always
be out there. And you can't blame them for making comparisons between me and the Hollywood
actress—it's too good a story to miss, isn't it? The
entire British public will now be asking themselves
the same questions I asked myself—why would you
choose me? And that's just going to keep on happening.' Her lips felt stiff and her brain numb as
she stumbled towards the door. 'Excuse me. I need
to check on Costas.'

'Millie—'

'I can't talk about this right now, I'm sorry. I need
to be on my own. I need some time to get my head
round it.' Without giving him time to intercept her,
Millie shot from the room and took refuge in the
nursery. She felt as though she'd been stripped naked
and the sense of violation was worse than the vicious
attack that had caused the scars in the first place.

Everyone across the country would be staring at
those intimate photos and everyone would be making judgements.

As if in sympathy with her distress, Costas was
screaming uncontrollably and Millie dismissed the

nanny and lifted him out of his cot, holding him close, deriving comfort from his familiar warmth.

'There, angel. It's all right,' she whispered, 'I'm here now. It's all right. You're fine.'

'I'm so sorry,' the nanny apologised. 'I can't do anything with him. I think he's going down with something. He's been hot all evening and fretting.'

'It's OK, I'll sit with him,' Millie muttered, feeling the baby's forehead burning. 'You go to bed. There's no sense in everyone being awake.'

'Shall I stay while you get changed? I'd hate for him to ruin your dress.' The nanny looked at her pityingly and Millie realised that she knew about the papers.

Her face turned scarlet because she *hated* the thought of people pitying her. 'I don't care about the dress. You go to bed. Thanks.'

The girl hesitated and then quietly left the nursery.

Millie sat down in the chair, Costas in her lap, happy to hide away with the baby for a while. The alternative was facing Leandro, and she wasn't up to that at the moment.

She needed to get her thoughts straight.

'What a mess,' she murmured. 'You have no idea what a mess this is. Why can't people just mind their own business? Why do they love reading about trouble in other people's lives? I'm never buying a newspaper again on principle. I'm going to read gardening magazines. They don't hurt anyone.'

Exhausted by the demands of the conversation,

Costas hiccoughed a few times and eventually drifted off to sleep on her shoulder.

As she laid him carefully in the cot, Millie stared down at him. She looked àt the dark lashes and the dark hair and felt her stomach flip uncomfortably.

The gossip and speculation was endless.

It was always going to happen, wasn't it?

Maybe he wouldn't have affairs, but while she was with Leandro there was always going to be someone willing to sell him out for money, or point out her imperfections for an audience of millions to laugh at.

There would always be women willing to talk about their experiences in bed with him.

Millie dragged the chair next to the cot and flopped down into it, miserable, vulnerable and worried.

For half an hour she watched the baby sleep, checked his temperature and listened to his breathing.

Leandro stood in his study, his tension levels soaring into the stratosphere as he finished talking to his lawyers. The newspapers were strewn in front of him. Ordinarily he wouldn't have given any of them a first read, let alone a second, but this wasn't about him. It was about Millie. And he knew that today it was newspapers, but next week the celebrity magazines would pick up the story and it would run and run.

Thinking about Millie's fragile confidence, he wanted to punch something.

Being exposed to this wasn't fair on her, was it? She was too sensitive.

He had no idea where she was now but, knowing Millie, he suspected she'd be curled up in an insecure heap somewhere, convinced that their relationship was never going to work.

His jaw tightened.

Perhaps she was right. Perhaps it never was going to work. Who on earth wanted to live with this?

Needing to do something to relieve his frustration, Leandro took the stairs to the top floor and pushed his way through the door that led to the secluded roof terrace.

Here, there were no cameras. No one watching.

Just the soothing rush of water from the fountain in the centre, the scent of plants, darkness and his thoughts.

He strolled to the balcony, from where he was able to see over the rooftops of London.

Up until this point in his life he'd been indifferent to the media intrusion. It hadn't bothered him. But now...

Millie was a living, breathing human being with feelings.

And those feelings had been badly hurt.

Leandro thought about those few seconds before they'd known what was wrong. Her thoughts had immediately been with the baby.

And when she'd seen those pictures of herself...

Guilt ripped through him, intense and unfamiliar

as he dealt with the knowledge that he'd put her in a position that had allowed those pictures to be taken.

But the truth was that the media interest in his life was such that there would always be a photographer lurking, waiting to snap their picture. Even if he'd protected her from that one, he wouldn't necessarily have been able to protect her from the next.

And every time the press printed something nasty about her, another layer of her confidence would be shredded.

To be able to withstand the media you needed the hide of a rhinoceros, and Millie's flesh was as delicate as a rose petal.

She'd be torn, he thought grimly. *Ripped apart.*

And the decent thing would be to let her go— set her up somewhere new, where no one was interested in her.

From below in his courtyard he heard the roar of a car engine, but Leandro was too preoccupied to give it any thought.

Remembering that the last time he'd let Millie go had proved to be a mistake of gigantic proportions, Leandro strode back into the house and down the stairs, only to bump into the housekeeper, who was looking anxious and stressed.

'Don't tell me—more journalists?' Leandro spoke in a rough voice, a sinking feeling in the pit of his stomach. 'What's happened this time?'

'Millie has gone,' the woman told him. 'I heard her running through the house and then she said something like "No, don't do this to me" and then she took your car and drove like a maniac out of the drive. Gone. Just like that. She almost ran over the journalists waiting outside the gates.'

Gone. Crying.

Don't do this to me?

Remembering the roar of the car engine, Leandro's jaw tensed. 'Did any of the security staff follow her?' But he didn't need to see the appalled look on the housekeeper's face to know the answer to that one.

'It all happened so fast—'

Remembering what had happened the last time Millie had driven away from him upset, it took Leandro a moment to wrestle his emotions under control and think clearly.

He'd known she was upset but he'd given her the space she'd requested. And now he regretted it. He shouldn't have left her alone.

Leandro ran his fingers through his hair, his tension mounting as he thought of all the dangers she could now be facing. She was in London, alone and unprotected with a pack of press as hungry as hyenas. She was alone in his high-performance sports car in a cosmopolitan city where driving could be a life-threatening experience.

His expression grim, he strode into the house and walked straight to his study. Once there he contacted his head of security, gave him a brief and then proceeded to get slowly and methodically drunk.

After his third glass he discovered that there

were some pains that alcohol couldn't numb, and he stopped drinking and closed his eyes.

How, he wondered, could he have made such a success of his life in every other area, and yet have made such a mess of his entire dealings with Millie?

Exhausted and anxious, Millie pushed the door open to Leandro's study.

Leandro lay sprawled in the chair, his dark hair rumpled, his shirt creased and his jaw shaded by stubble.

'Leandro?' Her voice was soft and tentative and he opened his eyes and looked at her.

Then he gave a hollow laugh. 'What did you forget?'

Thinking that it was a strange question, Millie gave him a rueful smile. 'Just about everything.' Not wanting to wake everyone else in the house, she closed the door quietly behind her. 'I was in such a state, I ran out of the house with nothing.'

'I know. The housekeeper heard you go.'

'You must have been a bit surprised.'

'Not really. Why would I be surprised? I know you were upset by everything. I understand that. What I don't understand is why you're back.'

Millie noticed the bottle and the empty glass by his hand. 'What are you talking about?' Confused, she took in his rumpled state and the lines of tiredness on his face. She'd never seen him anything other than immaculate before, neither had she seen him tired. He had endless energy and stamina. Only now he seemed spent. 'Why wouldn't I have come back?'

'I would have thought that was obvious.' Leandro growled. He lifted his glass to his lips and then realised that it was empty and put it down again.

Millie looked at him in exasperation. 'You're not making sense. And I don't know why you're getting drunk. I expect you're worried, but it's all going to be fine.'

'It is *not* going to be fine,' he said in a raw tone. 'This is going to keep happening.'

'No, they think it was just a one-off. It happens sometimes.'

'You're deluding yourself.'

Millie frowned, thinking that his comment was a little harsh. 'The doctor seemed to know what he was talking about.'

'Doctor?'

'That's where I took him. To the hospital.' She looked at him defensively. 'Maybe I was overreacting, but I thought it might be life-threatening. I was so worried about him. What if I'd stayed here and he'd got worse? I looked for you and you'd disappeared. And after the stress and worry I've had this evening, I would have thought even you could be a little more sympathetic.' Hurt and not understanding his reaction, Millie turned away. 'I'm going to bed. I'm sleeping in Costas's nursery in case he needs me.'

'Wait a moment.' Leandro snapped out the words, his body still, his beautiful eyes narrowed to dark slits. 'What are you talking about? Why did you see a doctor? And why would Costas need you?'

'Because…' Millie was so tired that she couldn't even think straight and it took her a moment to absorb the implication of his question. 'Do you *honestly* not know what's been going on here? Where do you think I've been? Why do you think I dashed off?' She broke off and her breathing quickened as understanding dawned. 'Oh, my God, you thought I'd—'

'Yes,' he said softly. 'I did.'

Millie's heart started to pound. 'Why would you think that?'

'Do you really need to ask that question? The papers are full of my affair with that actress and extremely revealing pictures of you. Last time I saw you, you were upset.'

Millie walked across to him and stuck out her hand. 'Give me your phone.'

'I don't have it.' His voice was faintly mocking and a sardonic smile touched his mouth. 'Since you laid down your ground rules for our relationship I frequently lose track of where I've put it.'

'Well, isn't that typical of a man. The one time I need you to have your phone on you, you don't have it.' Bending over his desk, Millie shifted files and papers with scant regard for order and retrieved it from under a stack of papers. 'Here.' She thrust it towards him. 'I'm hopeless at technology. Switch it on.'

He switched it on.

Millie folded her arms. 'Now play back your messages. On speaker.'

Sending her a curious glance, Leandro played his messages.

Millie heard her own voice coming from the loud-speaker. *'Leandro, where are you? Costas is ill—I need to get him to a hospital. I'm taking your car. Call me when you get this message or meet me at the hospital.'*

Raising her eyebrows, Millie removed the phone from his hand. *'Now* I know why you didn't call. Really, you are going to have to be a bit more supportive when our own baby is born. If I'm going to have night-time panics, I want you with me. You're the one who is always calm in a crisis. I'm a mess. I'm never doing that again without you there to tell me that everything will be fine. What's the matter with you? I've never known you silent before. *Say* something.'

There was a long, tense silence during which Millie was sure she could hear her own heart beating.

When Leandro finally spoke, his voice was hoarse. *'Our* baby?'

'Yes. Our baby. I'm pregnant.' She gave a faint smile. 'Hardly surprising after all the sex we've had over the past few weeks.'

He inhaled sharply. 'Is that why you came back?'

'I never left,' Millie said softly, and Leandro held her gaze.

'Our baby.' He sounded stunned. 'All that stuff in the paper...'

Millie's heart missed a beat because everything she needed to know was in his voice and in his eyes.

'Well, I'm not pretending it wasn't upsetting. But I had plenty of time to think about it while I was watching over Costas in his cot. For a start, that actress is too thin for you. You hate women whose bones stick out. And you're forgetting, I was there that night. I could see that she was angry that you rejected her. The talk is that her latest film is rubbish. I expect she wanted to attract some different publicity—kick-start her career. And she wanted to hurt you.'

'It only hurts me if it hurts you,' Leandro said hoarsely, and then shook his head. 'I don't know why you're smiling. You like seeing me miserable?'

'No,' Millie said softly. 'I like seeing you in love.'

His eyes met hers. 'You're very confident all of a sudden.'

Millie shrugged and slid onto his lap. 'That happens when you're loved. And when you love back.' She leaned her head against his shoulder, feeling his strength. 'You should have known I wouldn't have left you.'

'Alexa said she saw you drive off, very upset.'

'I *was* very upset.' She sat up so that she could explain. 'I was sitting with Costas, just watching him, because I was worried about his temperature. And I was thinking about Becca—and us—and those awful pictures of me. Everything. And then Costas sort of went all floppy. I was terrified. I don't know. I'm not that experienced with children. He seemed so hot, and I was worried—'

'Why didn't you come and find me?'

'I did! You weren't here!' Millie was indignant. 'I ran around the house yelling your name but this house is so stupidly big and I couldn't find you. Neither could I find any of the staff.'

'I was up on the roof terrace. I needed fresh air.'

'Well, it's a shame you chose that particular moment because I was in desperate need of a serious dose of your decisive-macho-Viking-invader approach to life. Leandro?' She curled her hand into the front of his shirt. 'What is the *matter* with you? I've never seen you like this before. You look as though you have no idea what to do next, and you always know what to do.'

Leandro slid his hand into her hair. 'Not always. Tonight I thought I'd lost you forever and I had no idea what to do about it. My first instinct was to find you and haul you back, but I love you too much to involve you in the media circus that is my life. It's always like this, Millie. There's always someone wanting to sell me out to the media for money. And I blame myself for those photos of you,' he confessed in a raw tone, letting his hand drop so that she could see the look in his eyes. 'I should have known better than to expose you to that.'

'I don't care what they think,' Millie said softly. 'I only care what *you* think.'

Leandro wrapped his arms around her. 'When you left the first time, I was so angry. I'd thought you were the sort of woman who would stay by my side no matter what. I didn't understand how insecure you were and I didn't understand how much my behaviour had dented your confidence. When you were prepared to take on Costas, even though you still thought he was my child—' He broke off, his eyes bright. 'That was when I realised that I didn't know you at all.'

'I found it impossible to believe that a man like you could possibly want me.' Millie gave a wry smile. 'The media finds it hard to believe, too, so you can't exactly blame me.'

'The media don't know you,' he said roughly. 'And I understand now why you felt that way. I understand why you would have believed your sister.'

'I always just thought she was helping me.' Millie pulled a face, unable to disguise the hurt. 'Stupid me.'

'Not stupid. Generous. You don't see bad in people. And why would you? She was your sister. I see how growing up with her must have made it hard for you to see your own qualities. But those qualities shine from you, *agape mou*. And those qualities are the reason I love you. I love your smile and your values, I love the way you were prepared to care for a child that might have been mine, and I love the way you still treasure the good memories of your sister, despite everything.' He inhaled deeply. 'And you're right when you say that I love you. I do. I loved you the first moment I saw your legs in that haystack.'

'That was lust, not love.'

A sexy smile tugged at his mouth. 'Perhaps, but it was love soon after. That's why I was so upset when you walked out. I thought I'd found a woman who would be by my side always.' His hand tightened on hers. 'I should have come after you.'

'If you'd known me better, maybe you would have done. And if I'd known you better, maybe I wouldn't have left.'

'I understand now why you did.' His hand slid into her hair in a possessive gesture. 'But at the time I thought you were like my mother.'

Millie stilled. 'You've never talked about your mother. You've never talked about your family at all.'

'Because I try to keep that part of my life in the past, where it belongs. I built myself a new life.' His voice was husky. 'She left me. When I was six years old—old enough to understand rejection—she went out one day and left me with a friend of hers. And she never came back.'

'Leandro—'

'She was a single mother and life was tough.' He gave a weary shrug. 'I think she just woke up one day and thought life might be easier without the burden of a young child.'

Millie didn't know what to say so she just leaned forward and hugged him. 'Where did you go?'

'I was taken back to Greece and put into care. But I found it hard to attach myself to anyone after that. If your own mother can leave you, why wouldn't a stranger?'

'Why didn't you tell me this before?'

'I thought I'd put it all behind me, but scars don't always heal, do they?'

'But you can learn to live with scars,' Millie said

softly, tasting her own salty tears as she pressed her mouth to his. 'If you can live with mine, I'll teach you to live with yours.'

His hand slid into her hair and tightened, as if he were holding on. 'You're sure you want this life?'

'I want to spend my life with you. You've given me so many things, Leandro. Diamonds, houses, cars, a lifestyle beyond my wildest dreams, but the most important thing you've given me is self-esteem. You make me feel special.'

'You *are* special.' He cupped her face in his hands. 'You took on your sister's child, despite everything.'

'So did you.' Millie's eyes filled. 'You took him on knowing that he wasn't yours. Knowing that everyone would make assumptions.'

'I didn't want Costas to go through what I went through.' He gave a twisted smile. 'The situation was different, I know, but for me it felt like a healing process. I was able to give this baby a home, a name—an identity. Everything I never had. Millie…' He was hesitant. 'This lifestyle isn't going to change. If you stay with me, there are always going to be people hunting you down, wanting to make you believe bad things about me.'

Millie leaned forward and kissed him. 'Is this a good moment to confess that I might need the services of your lawyer after all?'

'Why?'

She shrank slightly. 'I was in a panic when I put Costas in your car…'

'And…?'

'I think I might have accidentally damaged one of the motorcycles that the journalists had propped against your gate. It was in the way. I was also responsible for the fact that one of the journalists dropped his camera.'

'Sounds like you need driving lessons.' Laughter in his eyes, Leandro raised an eyebrow in mocking contemplation. 'Dare I enquire after the health of my Ferrari?'

Millie squirmed. 'It's nice to know where your priorities lie. It might need a teeny-weeny touch of paint.'

Leandro closed his eyes. 'I don't love you any more.'

Millie giggled and wound her arms round his neck. 'Yes, you do.'

'You're right, I do.' Leandro took her face in his hands and kissed her. 'I love you, *agape mou*. I will always love you, no matter how many Ferraris you get through or how many journalists sue me. You say that you're different to every other woman I've ever been with and that's true—you are. That's why I fell in love with you. I saw instantly that you were different. You weren't interested in my money and you had values that I admired and respected.'

'I can see why you were disappointed when you thought I'd turned into a shopaholic.'

'I didn't look for a reason for the change in your behaviour. I accused you of not trusting me, but I was guilty of that charge, not you. I assumed you'd suddenly discovered how much you enjoyed having the money.'

'Leandro, I *do* like the money,' Millie muttered. 'Anyone would be mad not to, wouldn't they? I love the fact that I don't have to queue for a bus in the rain. I'll never stop being thrilled when the lights turn on by themselves, but most of all I love the fact I'm going to be able to stay at home with Costas and our baby and not work.'

'Bab*ies*,' Leandro purred, his characteristic arrogance once more in evidence. 'I intend to keep you very busy in that department. I'd hate Costas to be lonely.'

Millie grinned. 'This one isn't cooked yet.'

He slid his hand over her flat stomach in a gesture that was both intimate and protective. 'You will be a fantastic mother.'

Millie kissed him, feeling the roughness of his jaw against her sensitive skin. 'What are we going to do about Costas? I can't bear to think of him growing up with this question of his parentage hanging over him.'

'My lawyers have started adoption proceedings,' Leandro told her. 'I can't pretend it's going to be a quick and simple process, but we'll get there, I promise you that. We're his parents.'

'And I think we should have a couple of dogs. Big dogs. Trained to bite journalists.'

Leandro laughed. 'I was so wrong about you. I used to think you were gentle and kind.'

'I am, most of the time. As long as no one upsets me.' Millie grinned. 'It's no good frowning. You don't scare me any more.'

'I'd noticed. In fact, I'm not sure I like the new, confident you,' he drawled. 'I'm not sure you know your place.'

Millie wound her arms round his neck. 'I know my place, Leandro Demetrios,' she said softly, and he lifted an eyebrow in question.

'So where is your place, *agape mou?*'

'By your side, bearing your children, loving you for the rest of my life. That's my place.'

And Leandro smiled his approval just moments before he kissed her.

* * * * *

We hope you enjoyed reading

THE PRINCE'S WAITRESS WIFE

and

POWERFUL GREEK, UNWORLDLY WIFE

by *USA TODAY* bestselling author

SARAH MORGAN

If you liked these stories, then you will love
Harlequin Presents.

You want alpha males, decadent glamour and
jet-set lifestyles. Step into the sensational,
sophisticated world of **Harlequin Presents,**
where sinfully tempting heroes ignite a fierce and
wickedly irresistible passion!

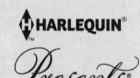

Glamorous international settings…
powerful men…passionate romances.

Look for eight *new* romances every month!

Available wherever books and ebooks are sold.

"I would much rather find a way for you to be useful to me." He slid his thumb along the flat of her blade. "But where I could keep an eye on you, as I would rather this not end up in my back."

"I make no promises, sheikh."

"Again, we must work on your self-preservation."

"Forgive me, I don't quite believe I have a chance at it."

Something in Ferran's face changed, his eyebrows drawing tightly together. "Samarah."

He'd recognized her. At last. She'd hoped he wouldn't. Not when she was supposed to be dead. Not when he hadn't seen her since she was a child of six.

She met his eyes. "Sheikha Samarah Al-Azem, of Jahar. A princess with no palace. And I am here for what is owed me."

"You think that is blood, little Samarah?"

"You will not call me little. I just kicked you in the head."

"Indeed you did, but to me, you are still little."

"Try such insolence when I have my blade back, and I will cut your throat, sheikh."

HPEXP1014-2

"Noted," he said, regarding her closely. "You have changed."

"I ought to have. I'm no longer six."

"I cannot give you blood," he said. "For I am rather attached to having it in my veins, as you can well imagine."

"Self-preservation is something of an instinct."

"For most," he said, drily.

"Different when you have nothing to lose."

"And is that the position you're in?"

"Why else would I invade the palace and attempt an assassination? Obviously I have no great attachments to this life."

His eyes flattened, his jaw tightening. "I cannot give you blood, Samarah. But you feel you were robbed of a legacy. Of a palace. And that, I can perhaps see you given."

"Can you?"

"Yes. I have indeed thought of a use for you. By this time next week, I shall present you to the world as my intended bride."

* * *

Don't miss
TO DEFY A SHEIKH,
available November 2014.

HARLEQUIN®

A *Romance* FOR EVERY MOOD™

Save $1.00

on the purchase of any
Harlequin Series book.

Available wherever books are sold, including most bookstores,
supermarkets, drugstores and discount stores.

Save $1.00

on the purchase of any
Harlequin Series book.

Coupon valid until December 31, 2014. Redeemable at participating retail outlets
in the U.S. and Canada only. Limit one coupon per customer.

52612015

5 65373 00076 2 (8100)0 11987

HIINC0413COUP

Presents®

Rev up for

Miranda Lee's

tantalizing tale of driving desire!

TAKEN OVER BY THE BILLIONAIRE
December 2014

Jess isn't impressed by Benjamin Da Silva's wealth, but each glimpse in the rearview mirror has her aching to climb into the backseat and submit to his *every* command. She knows she should steer clear—so why can't she get off the collision course leading right toward the tempting billionaire?

HP13296

HARLEQUIN®

Presents®

Caitlin Crews

brings you a sensational story of pride and passion!

HIS FOR REVENGE
December 2014

Chase Whitaker is only interested in his dark game
of revenge against Zara Elliot's father. Zara only
marries Chase to safeguard the family business.
What they haven't counted on? A wedding night
that unsettles their rock-hard defenses.

Losing is never an option for Chase, but winning
suddenly takes on a *very* different meaning…

HP13298